THE FAMINE FIELD

Fergus P Egan

THE FAMINE FIELD

Author and Publisher: Fergus P Egan

ISBN: 978-1-9993941-6-5 (Paperback Edition)
ISBN: 978-1-9993941-8-9 (Hardcover Edition)
ISBN: 978-1-9993941-7-2 (Electronic Book Edition)

Email: FergusEganPublishing@gmail.com

Story Development: Aisling Egan
Editor: Andrew Niall Egan
Cover design and back cover photograph: Andrew Niall Egan
Front cover photograph: Fergus Egan

ISBN: 978-1-9993941-6-5

Killbawn, County Mayo, Ireland
Monday 19 August 1946

"Stop!" Everyone freezes. "All right," says Sally Plunkett, the archaeologist. "I'll take over from here."

Sally Plunkett is tasked by the county council to conduct an archaeological study of 'the Famine Field' to determine if it contains any evidence of famine-era artefacts from one hundred years ago. Her current probe has encountered an unexpected interruption. She digs to investigate.

Sally is now the sole occupant of the excavated trench in the sandy moraine of the dolmen. She skillfully employs a pastry brush to the soil surrounding the piece of exposed fabric protruding from the wall of the trench.

Danny the Divil, the annoying and curious bystander, comments in a drunken lisping slur. "Cloth. That can't be more'n a few years there. Sure cloth disintegrates in the ground. What do you make of it, Arsy-ologist?"

Sally blinks in irritation. The drunken Divil is right. This is cloth, likely wool. It cannot date from the famine era. In soil this moist, wool would not remain intact beyond a year, three years at most. She wonders how much more cloth is still hidden from view within the sandy soil of the dolmen. Sally recovers sufficiently to respond to the Divil. "This cloth is a lady's stocking."

"No, it's not."

She turns to look at the Divil. He walks to the edge of the trench, takes a quick swig of whiskey from his miniature bottle of 'Three Swallows', and continues to speak. "A lady's stocking ends here." He slaps his thigh. "That thing yonder goes higher than here." At this, he slaps his pelvic area.

The Divil's comments rile her. Agitated, Sally argues her case to him. "So it isn't a stocking. It's tights."

The Divil ignores her retort. He looks past her and remarks, "That's a leper down there," pointing to the piece of exposed cloth.

"Mother of God!" Sally exclaims. "These ignorant country bumpkins know nothing about lepers or ladies' undergarments – or much about anything." She pauses. They gaze at the length of exposed fabric and reluctantly come to an undeniable conclusion – they have unearthed a dead body.

TABLE OF CONTENTS

LIST OF CHARACTERS

<u>Gardaí:</u>
Detective Inspector John Patrick Murphy (Murf) – Police detective in rural Ireland
Superintendent David Fox – District Officer of Killbawn Garda Station
Garda Seamus O'Reilly – Member of Killbawn police and assistant to Detective Inspector Murphy
Garda Eddie Caldwell – Member of Killbawn police
Phil Divers – Head of the Forensics Unit
Chief Superintendent Ultan O'Neill – Garda Divisional HQ
Garda Jerry Coulter – Member of Castlebar police

<u>Circus Community:</u>
John Edge – Owner of a travelling show
Marvin – A Hungarian displaced person and leader of a troupe of acrobats
Edmund Ludwig – Acrobat and a German U-boat deserter

<u>Mayo County Personnel:</u>
Finbar Dorrian – County Medical Examiner
Sean Macilmyra – County Engineer
Ned Reid – Surveyor for Department of Roads

<u>Archaeological Team:</u>
Gerald (Geraldus Magnus) Folan – Dean of Arts, UCG
Sally Plunkett – Archaeologist
Sandra McCurry – Archaeological student
Brian Tobin (B Tobin) – Archaeological student

<u>Clergy:</u>
Patrick Byrne – Bishop of Killala
Paul Anthony MacMorrow – Canon and parish priest of Killbawn
Barry Glen Dennagher – Vicar Forane in Diocese of Killala

<u>**St Bawn's Parish Members:**</u>
Maggie Friel – Parochial housekeeper
Marie Antoinette McBratt – Killbawn district doctor
Danny (the Divil) Begley – Doctor McBratt's driver and local inebriate
Patrick Joseph Casey – Killbawn merchant and parish benefactor

<u>**Killbawn Community:**</u>
Pat Delahunty – Farmer and owner of 'the Famine Field'
Mick Cannon – Owner of Cannon's pub in Killbawn
Bill Tunnery – 'Big Bill', ganger of a work crew
Liam Tunnery – Bill Tunnery's son, who went missing
Robert Scott – Owner of Scott Manor in Mayo and a plantation in Uganda
Tom Buckley – House steward of Scott Manor
Sarah Fegan – Housekeeper of Scott Manor
Bobby Fegan – Sarah Fegan's son, who went missing

<u>**An Chúilfhionn Private Club:**</u>
Fergal McKenna – Barman and manager of the private club
'J' – Jonathon Kirby – Commercial traveller
'B' – Benedict McCusker – Men's tailor

CHAPTER ONE

U-1211

Tuesday 08 May 1945
North Atlantic 53° 39' 30"N, 18° 51' 55"W

08:00 GMT. Kapitänleutnant Rudolf Bahn requests all crew members to attend to an important announcement. Edmund Ludwig is awakened along with other sleeping seamen. Crew conditions on a Type V11C U-boat are so cramped that seamen are obliged to sleep in three shifts throughout a 24-hour period. Bunks are always warm due to 'hot-bunking'. As soon as one seaman leaves a bunk, another drops into the vacated spot.

It was much more cramped at the start of their tour of duty. They had fresh food when they left Wilhelmshaven. They also had two extra torpedoes. The fresh food was stored in every nook and cranny, even taking up an entire lavatory. That left just one operational lavatory for the entire crew. Sadly, and as expected, the fresh food spoiled rapidly in the damp conditions of the U-boat – the fruit rotted and the bread grew beards of fungus faster than a man could grow whiskers. The extra torpedoes were stored in passageways until they replaced the expelled torpedoes in the torpedo room. Many of the crew were forced to sleep in the busy walkway, sleeping while their mates stepped over them in the execution of their tasks.

Today, living conditions are better in some ways, yet far worse in other ways: The replacement of two torpedoes has freed up sufficient space to accommodate four more bunks. Both lavatories are now available and are in working order. On the other hand, underwear and socks have been reduced to shreds. Some crewmen are wearing both pairs of socks as a single pair, held together by insulation tape. To get more life out of their allotted two pairs of underpants, seamen wear both pairs simultaneously; one pair is worn back-to-front and inside-out.

The total crew is 36 – all bearded and unwashed for over 50 days now. Kapitänleutnant Rudolf Bahn is very strict regarding the performance of duties. Apart from that, he is lax about dress and is quite casual and friendly in his relationship with the men who serve under him. He eats the same cold tinned food and endures the same harsh conditions as the seamen, only he works longer shifts. To alleviate boredom between enemy engagements, he organises games and competitions to keep morale high – singing competitions and draughts competitions. For some, like Edmund Ludwig, this is too much trouble. He spends his idle time alone, playing solitaire or perfecting his skills in marine knots. He sleeps in the midst of the radio equipment in the funkraum where he is assigned to funkmaat duties – thus he sleeps and works in the same place.

Rudolf Banh looks at the men. He glances from one to the other, straining to see past the row of stooped heads and bent shoulders in the cramped interior of the U-boat. Kapitänleutnant Rudolf Bahn is fifty-two. At 170 cm, he is shorter than some of his crewmen and, in the control room, he manages to stand erect during his duties. Like the crewmen, the captain has no change of clothes. He is dressed in a black leather smock coat. If he is wearing a shirt, it is not apparent. He wears a scarf around his neck, thus concealing whatever, if anything, he wears underneath. He gazes paternally at the men under his command. They are all dressed in a mismatch of clothes – a mixture of civilian clothes and British stock (clothing abandoned at Dunkirk). Much of what they wear is all-weather clothing.

Notwithstanding the apparent lack of 'uniform' in their clothing, there is an unwritten rule of dress code. The captain wears a white peaked cap, and he positions a replica of his cherished Iron Cross at his neck – the actual Iron Cross is locked safely away, to be worn only at formal meetings. The U-boat officers wear grey-brown denim jackets and blue service caps – except for the leitender ingenieur who gets to wear the 'checkered shirt' with civilian trousers and suspender-braces. Seamen on duty, or on deck, are required to wear garrison covers on their heads.

This is his crew of fighting-men. All are silently waiting for the important announcement. The only sound is from the throbbing of the one remaining working engine – a supercharged Germaniawerft, 6-cylinder, 4-stroke M6V 40/46 diesel. The boat is struggling to maintain a surface speed of 6kt, about a third of their normal surface top speed – that is the normal speed if both engines were working efficiently. The boat is designed to operate at a top speed of 17.2kt surface speed, and at 8kt submerged speed. Cruising speed, required to maintain optimum fuel consumption, is 12kt surface speed and 4kt submerged speed. Unfortunately, their current maximum speed is less than half their normal cruising speed.

Rudolf regards the men fondly. They, in turn, look to him with admiration and respect. Focused on the pending important announcement, the men ignore the smells of body odour and diesel fuel that assail the senses unrelentingly in the confined space of the damp boat. He begins to speak, not with his usual exuberant decisiveness, but softly, as one exhausted from fatigue. "The war is over. Yesterday, General Alfred Jodi signed the unconditional surrender of all German forces. We are returning to Wilhelmshaven. I have no information as to our immediate fate. I trust that we will soon be reunited with our families in Germany – if there still is a

Germany. That's all for now. I will keep you informed of any new information as soon as it is received. Return to your duties. Or to your sleeping; or to whatever you were doing."

The men disperse to attend to their activities or, like Edmund Ludwig, they return to their rest. Rudolf Bahn is left to his thoughts. Will there still be a Germany when he returns to Wilhelmshaven? Will the Allies carve up Germany and annex it? Russia will likely expand its Soviet empire and bring part of Germany into the USSR. France will claim disputed areas for sure, and they may extend their national frontier deep into Germany. And what might Britain do? Establish an English shire on the Rhine? The Americans – would the Americans establish a U.S. state or territory in Europe? No, not likely. In any event, an English or American territory is more palatable than a French or Russian one. Germany may cease to exist as a country or as a national entity. But that's not the worst. Will the German people survive the influx of inferior races and undesirables that will henceforth lord over us? The German race will become diluted, and the German language will be suppressed. In another hundred years, the mighty German Empire will exist only in dusty old history books.

Rudolf Bahn feels his shoulders drooping. He makes the effort to stand erect. For another few days, or maybe for a few more hours, they are still German. Thus, they will perform their tasks efficiently and behave honourably – not like inferior undesirables. Undesirables are detrimental to the purity of the race; they diminish the core integrity of the people. Rudolf Bahn mentally enumerates the ruinous people who will govern Germany on the heels of the military occupation – starting with Slavs and down to the insane, to cowards who run in the face of the enemy, and to men and women who capitulate. His shoulders slump. He realises that he and all German servicemen are now undesirables. What a humiliating defeat.

10:44 GMT. Kapitänleutnant Rudolf Bahn assembles the seamen once more and he provides an update on the surrender. "We are not going to Germany after all. We have been instructed to proceed to England, to Harwich. There, we will be interred as POWs. It looks like we will not be repatriated to Germany immediately. Under the conditions of the Geneva Convention, the Allied powers could hold us in prison camps for three years. Only neutral countries are likely to repatriate us immediately. Alas, we are commanded to make for the port of Harwich in the south-east of England."

Rudolf turns to address the funkmaat petty officer. "Send a radio message confirming our position, and inform Kriegsmarine that we are sailing to Harwich as ordered."

The men remain assembled while the message is sent. What other alternative is there? The news of their surrender and their inevitable detention has filled them with apprehension and dejection. Their U-boat tasks and duties, which were hitherto of primary importance, are relegated to secondary status, even the requirement to repair the malfunctioning engine. Almost immediately they receive a radio response. Because of their location, they are directed to proceed to the closest Allied port that can accommodate U-boats. North Atlantic boats are instructed to sail to Scotland or to Northern Ireland. U-1211 is instructed to proceed to Lisahally – coordinates 55° 2' 30"N, 7° 15' 38"W.

The men are unfamiliar with this location. To clarify, the oberstreuermann chief petty officer speaks to them, "Londonderry. It's the port of Londonderry in the northernmost part of Ireland, the part that's in the United Kingdom. To get there from here, we will sail around Malin in neutral Ireland, and we should arrive in Lisahally in two days' time."

"Not with this engine, we won't." It is the leitender ingenieur who speaks. "It will take four days at best. To avoid strain on the engine, we need to reduce our speed to 4kt. To maintain a speed of 6kt, there is the risk that the second engine will also fail. If this occurs, it would necessitate conducting extensive repairs at sea. At 4kt, expect to be in port on Saturday 12 May."

"And on Sunday 13 May, expect to be in a POW camp," adds the kapitänleutnant. He instructs the obersteuermann to control the drinking-water rations to last another four days.

Wednesday 09 May. For the next day, they continue on course at a modest speed of 4kt with the turret hatch open. Kapitänleutnant Rudolf Bahn makes a point of spending some time with each of the seamen on a one-to-one basis. They are despondent and need comforting. He instructs the oberbootsmann to assign duties to keep them occupied. The North Atlantic is uncharacteristically calm today – well, less rough than usual. Swells, which typically wash over the boat, splash against the hull sending plumbs of spray into the air to splash upon the deck. Men are directed to go up top and engage in hygiene activities. Some of the men strip naked and lean into the frigid sea spray to shower. They link arms to guard against being washed overboard. The sea breeze is bitingly cold, but their bare bodies experience a stinging warmth from the salty spray beating against them. Rudolf Bahn observes the patches of inflamed skin on the otherwise pale bodies – mostly around the feet and crotch areas. Others use a pail on a rope to scoop up seawater and attempt to shave. Scissors and blades are employed as barbering tools, somewhat unsuccessfully, to trim hair. Rudolf is pleased with the action taken by the oberbootsman to keep the men occupied and disciplined.

In mid-afternoon, Rudolf Bahn is standing in the turret surveying the horizon and watching the men bathe. His attention to duties is more demanding since the surrender. Now he is required to refrain from engaging the enemy – no more hit-and-hide engagements. He is anxious. His U-boat is struggling to remain operational long enough to reach port. Rudolf hears a distant plane. He recognises the sound – Spitfire. He estimates that the U-boat is currently located at the extreme edge of the Spitfire's range of 680km. Lifting his binoculars, he scans the sky. He locates it. It is an RAF Supermarine Spitfire. He tries to determine the purpose of the plane. Is it an unarmed photo-reconnaissance aircraft, or a fighter plane? The Spitfire is high up. It makes a long wide circle around the U-boat and disappears. This would indicate that it has spotted the U-boat and that the Spitfire is purely on reconnaissance. Rudolf lowers his binoculars. He is not surprised at the presence of reconnaissance aircraft. After all, he gave his location and intent to proceed to Lisahally. Of course, the Allies need to confirm his position and that he is proceeding as directed.

Just then, Rudolf Bahn hears the Spitfire again. This time it is lower and it is in a tighter circle. On this occasion, the men up top hear the plane too and brace for the expected order to man the guns. They look at the 88mm 'acht-acht' cannon and at the 20mm flak. Both guns are currently unmanned. Alternatively, they could be ordered back below and the U-boat would execute a dive. "Hold your positions!" Rudolf Bahn shouts. "Do not move!" He continues to hold the Spitfire in his binocular sights. The aircraft is fitted with four guns, not the usual eight. A modified Spitfire – it could operate as a reconnaissance plane, but with fighter capabilities nevertheless. The flight circle is not a suitable attack approach, but if the Spitfire alters course, there is no time to have the U-boat execute an evasive defensive dive. The Spitfire manoeuvres out of the circular flight path and away from the U-boat. Then it turns and descends to 20 meters, and heads straight for the U-boat. Rudolf Bahn continues to direct the men to remain still. "Hold your positions! Do not move!" He lowers his binoculars and looks at the approaching plane. It is so close now that he is able to read the details on the plane without the aid of binoculars. He clearly sees the lone pilot tilt his head towards him and wave. Rudolf waves back. The Spitfire climbs rapidly and disappears from view. The men up top, exhale in relief in one unified gasp. Someone mutters in a stage-whisper, "The war must be over."

Wednesday late afternoon, 09 May. "Edmund Ludwig!"

Edmund Ludwig awakens to the sound of his name. As usual, he had been sleeping in the funkraum. He recognises the voice of the kapitänleutnant. He jumps up to attention and salutes. "Ja, Kapitän!"

Rudolf Bahn chuckles, "Relax, Seaman. I didn't mean to startle you. You must be looking forward to sleeping in a real bed in three days' time. You may speak freely, Edmund."

"No, Captain. I'm not looking forward to it. Not under the present conditions."

"So what would you prefer?"

"To be put ashore in neutral Ireland, sir."

"What? So that you can avail of speedier repatriation? That consideration applies only to servicemen who entered a neutral country accidentally – like airmen who bailed out, or to seamen who survived a sinking, or to non-combatant civilians. An armed naval vessel is not permitted to enter neutral waters."

"No, sir. That's not the reason. I prefer not to return to Germany at all."

"Well if you jump ship, it's desertion. And you know the consequences of desertion?"

"I'd be shot."

"Unquestionably and without hesitation. So tell me, why would you decline repatriation to Germany anyways?" Rudolf considers his own opinion that there may not be a Germany anymore – at least not the Germany he wants to live in. He cannot fault Edmund for feeling the same way.

"My family. They are all dead. And I'm regarded as…" Rather than finish the sentence, Edmund glances down at his preferred sleeping spot.

"How old are you now, son?"

"Seventeen."

Rudolf looks keenly at the youth. Edmund Ludwig is 170 cm tall, from the soles of his fleece-lined boots to the top of his sandy-blonde head – the same height as the captain himself. He could serve as a poster boy for the perfect Arian Nation – slim athletic build and with intense slate-blue eyes. Only now, his sandy-coloured beard is unkempt and uneven. The captain is suddenly aware of his own unkempt brown beard, recently grey-streaked from stress and anxiety. He self-consciously rubs his chin. "Edmund, you are still young enough to have a fulfilling life. You'll find a way to get through this. I, on the other hand, am too set in my ways. I may not be able to adjust." Rudolf looks down at the spot where Edmund sleeps. He knows that the men whisper that Edmund is an 'undesirable', not suited to Hitler's Germany. However, Hitler's German Third Reich is gone now; and who is 'desirable' or 'undesirable' anymore? Captain Rudolf sighs. He has always demanded dedication to duty from those who serve under him, and Seaman Edmund Ludwig has never fallen short.

They are interrupted by the leitender ingenieur. "Captain, we are currently proceeding at 2kts."

"Why is that? Is the second engine failing?"

"It's not the engine; it's the propeller. The propeller is slipping. It is not fully engaging and it is likely to cease functioning at any moment."

"Can the propeller be fixed?"

"That is an easy task in dry-dock, but not out here in the Atlantic swells. However, fixing the propeller is not what I recommend."

"How so?"

"It is an easier task to take apart the working engine and use the parts to repair the broken engine."

"Let me understand. The working propeller is currently attached to the broken engine; the faulty propeller is attached to the working engine. You propose to interchange the two engines. You replace the broken engine with the operating engine and thus re-engage the working propeller. I see. How difficult is it to make the repairs? And how long would that take?"

"Not difficult. Give me four hours. Four and a half hours at the most."

"And then we are good to go again? But at half-speed?"

"Not quite. We need to ensure that the second propeller has not seized from being idle. That is easy to check, and if it is stuck, it is fairly easy to free. On the other hand, if we start the repaired engine and suddenly engage a seized propeller, the propeller could snap off."

"It is easy to fix, you say? But…"

"But we need calm waters in which to conduct the exterior examination and make any required external repairs. The external repairs would take just a few minutes and maybe the application of some grease."

"You want calm waters?"

"To avoid the risk of damage. Yes."

"Is submarine depth calm enough for you to execute the task?"

"At submarine depth, we could certainly dismantle the faulty engine. In fact, we could execute all the work except for the external tasks."

"And you need the current good engine with the slipping propeller to get to calmer waters? Is that so?"

"I need one hour in calm surface waters."

"Come with me. We are going to the obersteuermann. "Oberleutnant zur See! Leutnant zur See!" Rudolf Bahn summons his two other officers.

Rudolf Bahn and his three officers consult the navigator. Once he establishes their current position on the charts, Rudolf orders the U-boat to a location – 54° 32' 0"N, 8° 30' 0"W.

"Captain, that's Ireland's territorial waters. Do you intend to encroach on neutral waters in an armed U-boat?"

He instructs his second in command, the first watch officer, "Release all torpedoes to the bottom of the ocean." And he orders the second watch officer, "Dismantle the deck gun and the flak gun, and throw both overboard." He turns to the engineer. "Now we are unarmed. Can you get us to this location?" He taps the chart.

"Aye, Captain. It's very close. We should be able to make it in an hour or so – if the propeller holds out that long."

A short time later, the U-boat, travelling at 2kts, reaches the location. The U-boat stops the engine and the captain permits it to drift. The Atlantic swells are still present. This cannot be the location to conduct the repairs. His officers are still with him.

"What now, Captain?"

Rudolf Bahn is studying a coastal chart. "We submerge and commence work on the engines. Then we surface and wait for nightfall and for favourable tides."

Three hours later, the engineer reports that the faulty engine has been dismantled. The problem piece has been identified. It will take another hour to remove the matching part from the working engine and install it in the broken engine, and then conclude with the external inspection and test. Regrettably, this final part of the repair procedure cannot be executed until the U-boat is in calm surface water.

During the three-hour period below the surface, the U-boat had operated on battery power. At 20:00 hours, the captain orders the U-boat to the surface. Whereupon he orders the diesel engine to start and to proceed slowly to 54° 37' 43"N, 8° 9' 23"W. From the turret, the officers perceive that the U-boat is entering a river estuary. On its own, the boat has insufficient power to sail against the river current, but the captain's calculations are sound and, as he expected, they ride on the force of the moving tide. The tidal surge pushes the U-boat into the estuary. A little thrust here and there is required to give the rudder sufficient effect to navigate between islands and headlands and to maintain a course in the navigable water of the river. Once past the islands and headlands, they enter placid still waters. "Maintain position at location 54° 38' 24"W, 8° 8' 17"N." They stop within sight of a brightly-lit coastal town, and within earshot of traffic and music. The U-boat floats in the dark water outside the range of the town's lights, and it nudges gently against a silt bar coming to a stop.

"Now, Ingenieur, you have one hour and fifty minutes to conclude all repairs. That's when the tide turns. If we miss the tide, we will be stranded on a silt bar for ten hours."

The leitender ingenieur knows how to proceed with the work in silence, and how to cloak and conceal the lights used in the exterior work. Forty-eight minutes later, the engineer reports that the engine is refitted and is working. The bootsmanner provides a black dinghy for a motorman to inspect the propeller. The motorman is required to duck beneath the surface numerous times to conduct the inspection. Carrying heavy tools is out of the question. The propeller checks out and he dabs it with grease. Within ten minutes he has completed his work and he returns. Now to engage the propeller and, if the repairs are successful, they proceed back out to sea.

Rudolf Bahn, the Kapitänleutnant, orders Edmund Ludwig on top. "Edmund Ludwig, as we cast off, I need you to ensure that the propeller does not snag on any branches or debris. It is very shallow here and there is an accumulation of waste and rubbish. We need to manoeuvre delicately so as to disengage safely from the silt-bar." Edmund understands. He realises that to float free from the debris-laden silt, the manoeuvre requires the assistance of the still-rising tide. A retreating tide would work against them and could render the U-boat beached until the next high tide. Rudolf Bahn has accounted for this in his calculations. A final cautionary task is required at this stage to guard against a snagged propeller which could render a disastrous delay.

It is fifty minutes until the tide turns. Edmund Ludwig enters the dinghy and proceeds to the task as ordered. He is puzzled as to why a radioman is asked to perform a motorman's duty. The U-boat's propeller engages successfully and the U-boat inches out into the estuary without encountering any mishap. Once clear of the silt, it turns to face the sea. Edmund paddles the dingy to catch up. The side of the U-boat is only a meter away from him. But the U-boat increases speed and departs, leaving Edmund

Ludwig in its wake. Captain Rudolf Bahn, the sole occupant of the turret, looks back at Edmund Ludwig barely visible in the faint light of the deepening night. He just stands expressionless in the turret, not waving, not speaking, as he drifts farther away. The anthracite-grey U-boat becomes indistinguishable from the surrounding dark waters. Edmund holds the departing submarine in his sights by focusing on the white lettering on the conning tower – U-1211. Nothing else is visible, except for the captain's white cap bobbing with the motion of the boat. Moments later, the captain raises his white peaked cap and waves it slowly in a wide circle. Then he departs from the turret and goes below. The U-boat disappears into the night and continues to its destination.

At first, Edmund paddles after the U-boat in an attempt to reach it. This proves futile. Exhausted and bewildered, he lies down and shuts his eyes. Helpless, he permits the dinghy to float aimlessly. He fears that the dinghy will drift out to sea and will capsize in the swirling eddies and currents of the islands and headlands. A few minutes later he hears a thump. The dinghy has hit an object. He looks back to investigate. The tide has not yet turned and the dinghy has drifted back inland. It has bumped against the slipway beside the pier. He grabs onto the slipway wall and makes his way up to the pier. Looking back, he sees the dinghy drift out to the current of the river and, as the tide turns, it follows the course of the river out to sea. He checks his watch in the dim light of the pier's one solitary electric lamp; the tide turned at 21:50 just as the captain had calculated.

Edmund Ludwig is standing on the pier of a coastal town in a neutral country. It becomes clear to him, upon reflection, that the captain, who is judicious in his calculations, has landed him in a neutral country in an intended manoeuvre. Yes, this is what Edmund Ludwig wanted. So what now?

CHAPTER TWO

THE CIRCUS

Wednesday 09 May 1945
Inver Eske, County Donegal, Ireland

21:55 GMT. Five minutes to 11:00pm local time. The pier is poorly illuminated by a single light. Edmund Ludwig stands on the pier, well outside the arc of the light. He looks upstream in the direction of the town. He observes a second smaller pier there, adequately illumined by the adjacent street-lighting. There are small boats moored there, and fishing nets are hanging to dry on racks in the centre of the pier. Edmund walks to the landward side of the main pier and encounters a stone wall. There is an opening in the wall with an access gate. Could it be an entrance to a property, perhaps? He is unable to tell; the area behind the wall is in darkness. Running away from him, to his left, is the access road, the road that connects the main pier to the town. There is a low stone wall on the seaward side of the access road; the other side is lined with mature trees. Should he choose to take this route, he will walk about 50 meters to the smaller pier and thence enter the town. The town is brightly lit. There is vehicular traffic on the quay-side street facing the small pier, and distant pedestrians are visible walking along the flanking sidewalk.

Edmund Ludwig shrugs and turns around to his right. He walks a few meters to where the road ends at the slipway. The slipway runs at a right angle from the road and slopes down to the channel parallel to the pier. Although the roadway proper ends at the slipway, there is a narrow concrete path, clearly visible in the near-darkness, running straight onwards past the slipway. The path appears to be a deliberate projection of the road. Edmund decides to take the concrete pathway. Curiously, the pathway is the only geometrically exact feature here. Everything else curves, or widens, or narrows or slopes. Rather than follow the course of the channel, or even follow the curve of the coast, the concrete pathway maintains an exact level path, straight as a die, to an abrupt termination at a silt bar.

The 'pathway' is actually the top surface of a culvert – a watercourse conduit for the town's drainage. Although the termination of the culvert is a dead-end, it affords Edmund a view of the shoreline and outskirts of the town. From this vantage point, he puts his surroundings into perspective. The estuary is surrounded by hills. Not round circular hills, but long elongated low hills clustered in rows like a family of giant reclining pigs. The 'pigs' range in size from one to two kilometres in length, some of which lie with their snouts in the water – the headlands, peninsulas and islands of the bay. The darkened area on the landward side of the pier, the area that is separated from the pier by a stone wall, is actually a gently sloping hillside. The town, to judge by the lights, extends farther inland to the left of, and to the back of, the dark area. There is a brightly-lit field to the right of this dark area, the side more distant from the town. Music is emanating from this field. This is the music he heard earlier from the U-boat. Clearly, this is the site of a circus. He recognises the big top; and he observes lorries, trailers, vans and caravans encircling the perimeter of the field. Just then, as Edmund places his surroundings in perspective, the music stops. The circus lights extinguish one at a time until just a few lights remain. The circus performance is concluded for the day.

Now that he has a sense of the geography of his surroundings, Edmund walks back to the main pier. This time, when he confronts the stone wall, he enters through the gateway in the wall and proceeds into the darkened property.

Once through the gateway, he ascends stone steps until he is level with the elevated ground of the hillside. The pathway here is surfaced with light-coloured pebbles and is discernible in the faint light of the night sky. There are gravestones on both sides of the pathway. He realises that he is in a graveyard. Ancient ruined walls stand erect among the gravestones, yet the pathway is well-maintained. This is an old graveyard still in use, he deduces.

He continues to walk up the gentle incline on the pebbled pathway to where the graveyard narrows. Here, the pathway is thickly tree-lined and is in complete darkness. Coming to the end of the pathway he encounters another gate. This gate gives him access to a street – a street with street-lighting, traffic, and a sidewalk with lots of people. These people, he assumes, are the stragglers returning home to the town having attended the circus. He stands back, out of sight, in the dark shadows of the pathway and listens to the cheery voices of the people. It is a long time since Edmund heard cheery voices like this. But more importantly, Edmund needs to get a sense of the political and social climate of this town.

He tries but fails to understand a word of what is being said. Edmund slaps himself on the head. He realises that no one here speaks German. This is something he hadn't accounted for. What else did he fail to consider, he wonders? He realises that his decision to enter a neutral country may have been rash and ill-conceived. He is totally unprepared for this – no familiarity with the geography of Ireland and unable to speak English. Or is it English? He struggles to identify some words.

"Stop!"

He heard the word 'stop'. A young woman runs to catch up with her boyfriend. She said 'stop!' That's an English word, surely. Her boyfriend shouts back some words. He recognises 'eleven o'clock'. But he must have misunderstood.

Surely, the time is ten o'clock. He consults his watch, tilting it outwards to catch the light from the street. It is 22:07, seven minutes past ten o'clock according to his accurate Kriegsmarine timepiece. Irish summer time is one more thing Edmund Ludwig has failed to account for.

Edmund Ludwig backs away from the gate. He is not yet prepared to expose himself to the Irish populace. Instead, he decides to investigate the circus. He speculates on the possibility of hiding among the circus animals. Then, when the circus moves to another location, he may be afforded a better opportunity to find a favourable place of sanctuary.

Edmund steps off the pathway and makes his way past the rows of gravestones. At the graveyard's ivy-covered stone wall, he levers his foot on a gravestone for a toe-up and climbs to the top of the wall. From here he surveys the circus field. There are a few 40-watt bulbs burning at the caravans and trailers close by. In the centre of the field, the big tent is clearly visible, but its interior is in darkness. There is a line of leafy trees growing alongside the wall and, immediately past them, there is a hedgerow running down to the inlet shore. Edmund drops from the wall and stands hidden behind the trees. He leans his back against the wall and tries to come up with a plan of action. He hesitates. He is unsure what his next move should be.

"Ein Deutscher Seemann, der überfällt. Ja?"

Startled, Edmund turns in the direction of the voice. There is a still figure standing next to a tree. The figure is in profile to Edmund and, being so close to the tree, he mistook it for part of the tree trunk. The person is facing out to sea, at right angles to where Edmund is facing.

The figure continues, speaking in German, "Relax, Seaman." It is a man's voice speaking in German in an unfamiliar accent. The man flashes his cigarette lighter and applies the flame to the cigarette in his mouth. This action reveals the nature of the man. In the light of the flame, Edmund identifies the man's garb – a royal-blue cloak that parts with the man's movement, thus revealing a powder-blue bodysuit underneath. This is a circus performer.

Edmund recovers sufficiently to find his voice, and tentatively asks, "Why do you say I am a seaman; and why do you say I am deserting?"

The man turns to face Edmund. He walks closer. "Stealth is not your forte, Seaman. For the past few minutes, I have been listening to your walking on the pebble pathway in the old abbey. You went as far as the gate by the roadside; you stopped and changed your mind and walked back, and then you hopped the wall here. You are unable to decide where to go? Yes?" The man drags on the cigarette while taking the measure of Edmund. "Look at you," he continues. "Your hair is too long; your beard is unkempt, and you smell of diesel and you stink like last year's rotten cheese. You are a U-boat seaman." The man draws on his cigarette again and looks at Edmund more closely. "And you are dressed in a standard-issue U-boat seaman's all-weather coat and garrison cover."

Edmund feels limp. How many things has he overlooked in undertaking this venture? Clearly, it is ill-planned. How can he expect to succeed? In another day, perhaps, he may be handed over to the Allies, or interred in Ireland for repatriation to Germany.

The man continues to speak. "How do I know you are a deserter? Well, it takes one to know one."

"You? You are a German soldier? A deserter? Here in Ireland?"

"I am Hungarian – from a Hungarian division in the German army. That was five years ago. Now I prefer the term 'displaced person'. But you – who are you and why are you here? And where do you expect to go?"

"Who am I?"

"Not your name, rank and serial number. What name do I call you?"

"Edmund Ludwig."

"That's your real name? You know you should change your name if you are deserting. But are you sure that this is what you want to do? Why desert now? The war is over."

"I don't want to return to Germany. I got off my U-boat while on its way to surrender at Lisahally, somewhere in the British part of Ireland. We stopped for repairs in the inlet and I think the captain of the U-boat let me leave."

"You think the captain actually let you get off the boat?"

"He said that he would shoot me if I tried to desert. And then he leaves me behind after sending me outside to check the propeller."

"I see. But don't you want to reunite with your family?"

"I have no family in Germany now. They are all dead. And I fear that should I return I will be treated as an undesirable."

"An undesirable? But not a coward. Perhaps we have something in common." With that, the man throws his cigarette on the ground and stubs it out with his heel. He extends his hand to Edmund. "Welcome to 'The John Edge Travelling Show'. My name is Marvin – my new name since coming here."

Edmund is much relieved at his good fortune just when he thought his luck had run out. He could weep with joyous emotion but controls himself.

"Come, Edmund. First of all, we need to clean you up. You stink. Then we'll decide what to do with you. Perhaps we may find a use for you."

They walk towards the trailers and caravans. Edmund asks, "So you are a circus acrobat?"

"It's not a circus; it's a travelling show. There are no performing animals here. We are singers and dancers, comics and clowns, acrobats and magicians. But yes, I am an acrobat."

"What? No horses? No lions? No bears? Or dogs?"

"No. There are no animals here – except for a dog. There is one dog. But his only trick is to find his feeding bowl at mealtime."

"Marvin, you say that you are a 'displaced person'. Are there any others in the circus, I mean, in the show?"

"Are there other displaced persons in the show? All the entertainers and performers here are displaced persons."

"All of them? How so?"

"John Edge is from Somerset…"

"He is English?"

"…and is a committed pacifist. He is a Quaker. He does not approve of smoking or drinking. He doesn't actually prohibit it but, out of courtesy, we do not drink or smoke in his presence."

"That's why you were smoking back there by the wall."

"He believes that it is his calling to assist those who have been displaced by the war. And so, he put together this travelling show – 'The John Edge Travelling Show'."

Marvin leads Edmund to the back of a caravan, to a stand with a basin and a bucket. "Here you go, Edmund. Off with your clothes and wash yourself thoroughly. I'll find something for you to wear."

Sometime later, Edmund is clean and shaved and is wearing grey flannel trousers with a white shirt and a dark-blue pullover. He retains his seaman's shoes, but with clean socks on his feet.

Marvin invites him inside the caravan. It is cramped inside, but much roomier than the U-boat. There is a poster on one wall depicting a human pyramid. It features nine acrobats – 'Marvin and the Marvellous Magyars'. Marvin introduces Edmund to the other occupant of the caravan. "This is my daughter, Annie. She is the top part of the human pyramid." He points to the poster.

Annie accepts Edmund's handshake in silence. Edmund determines that Annie could only be twelve years old. She is wearing white ballet slippers and is dressed in either a primrose-coloured leotard-and-tights combination or in a unitard. Edmund cannot tell. Over these, she is wearing a light periwinkle-coloured wraparound skirt. Edmund accepts the peculiar theatrical attire of these circus acrobats. Their performance clothes must influence their choice of daywear. Annie returns to her task of moving cups and plates onto a small fold-up table. He notices that she walks with a limp. Marvin whispers to Edmund, "Annie doesn't talk much. She does not understand German. She understands Hungarian, of course, but now she prefers English."

"You are teaching her English?"

"I speak English with her, but I wouldn't say 'teaching'. Father Ambrose, the chaplain who travels with us, has undertaken her education here."

This is something that Edmund had not previously considered – a circus is a community with its travelling families so it would have a chaplain and school. "Annie is very young to be a displaced person working in a circus. How old is she?"

"I don't know exactly."

"You don't know how old your own daughter is?"

"I am not Annie's biological or legal father. I found her five years ago. She has no recollection of her life prior to that time – not even her name. I took her with me when I fled the

Nazis. She could only have been six or seven at the time. I have been her protector and provider ever since."

Marvin gestures to Edmund inviting him to come to the table. There is one chair, which he offers to Edmund. The edge of the bunk serves as a seat for Marvin and Annie. Annie ladles stew onto plates and Marvin obtains bread from a metal bin at his side. This is the first food Edmund has seen in seven weeks that is not cold and is not from a tin. "Eat, Edmund. Tomorrow you will meet John Edge. If you desire to travel with us, you will need to impress him with whatever skills you have. You do have skills, don't you, being a seaman?"

Edmund responds with a puzzled expression. This situation is unexpected. At no time did he consider, or expect, to join a circus.

Marvin reads Edmund's confused expression. "Ah, you hadn't planned on this either, had you? So tell me, what skills have you mastered? As a seaman, you ought to be skilled at ropes and sail-making. Yes?"

"Yes. I know all about ropes and knots, and I am adept at repairing sail-cloth."

"That makes you valuable in working with the big tent. It's a pity that you are not acrobatically skilled…"

"Oh yes, I am. Der Führer shook my hand last year."

"Shaking Hitler's hand does not make you an acrobat, no matter what acts of contortion you executed to achieve that honour."

Edmund is offended by Marvin's remark. He quickly reacts with an explanation. "It was a demonstration of gymnastics by the Kriegsmarine. We, the class of summer 1944, impressed Der Führer with our performance. As the leader of the gymnastic group, I was selected to meet Der Führer for his personal expression of praise. So there. Is this a suitable skill for a circus?"

Marvin smiles at Edmund's terse argument of defence. "Edmund, maybe we can make a tumbler out of you. Oh, and this is not a circus."

After supper, Marvin unfolds a camp cot and places it on the floor near the door of the caravan. He gestures to Edmund indicating his sleeping accommodation for the night. He apologises for the Spartan conditions of the travelling show. Edmund smiles. A canvas camp cot is a luxury compared to the sleeping conditions he endured inside the U-boat.

It is customary, and prudent, to relieve oneself before retiring for the night. Edmund exits the caravan and walks to the line of trees, to the same spot where he first encountered Marvin. On a whim, he turns and walks down to the shore. Locating a boulder, he sits on it and stares out at the ebbing tide in the estuary. The starlight reflects in the water. He sees the path of the river more clearly now, from when he first saw it at high tide. It wends its lazy way like a silver ribbon through the glar, stretching to catch up with the retreating tide. Even then, its path is discernible against the darkness of the surrounding seawater as it continues onwards past the islands and out to the ocean.

Edmund considers his current situation. Is this his good fortune, or is it his ill-fortune? Had he remained on board the U-boat, he would be interred as a POW and eventually repatriated to Germany. Regardless of which path he chooses, there is no going back to the routine and discipline of U-boat duties. For a time, the U-boat gave Edmund a sense of belonging in a protective environment. Edmund laughs audibly at this realisation. The harsh and dangerous conditions of the U-boat were protective? Or was it the captain?

Edmund shifts his weight on the boulder. He speculates on what life might be like in an internment camp. He knows that enlisted men are separated from officers in POW internment. Remaining under the protective wing of Kapitänleutnant Rudolf Bahn was never an option. Furthermore, Edmund has no surviving family in Germany. He grunts in acknowledgement of his irreversible decision and is resolved to accept the consequences. Whatever the future brings to him in Ireland, even though the unknown fills him with a sense of trepidation, nothing could be as bad as what he would likely undergo in an internment camp and ultimately upon repatriation to Germany.

Edmund's reverie is interrupted by the arrival of the travelling show's dog. It is a friendly dog of indeterminable breed. The dog is curious to see what Edmund is looking at. He too peers out to the estuary. He sees nothing of interest so he turns and walks back to the circle of caravans. Edmund slides off the boulder and follows the dog. He considers the dog to be an omen of good luck. What possible catastrophe could befall him here in Ireland?

CHAPTER THREE

THE TWO-MILE STONE

Killbawn, County Mayo, Ireland
Wednesday 31 July 1946

It is a quiet day in Killbawn. Every day is a quiet day in Killbawn. Usually, the quietest places are St Bawn's Church and the graveyard in the ruined Killbawn Abbey. Today, the garda station is just as silent. District Officer Superintendent David Fox is in his office on the first floor of the garda station. He stands at the window overlooking the town. He idly peers out at the drizzling rain. He watches a raindrop trickle slowly down the windowpane. This is a Killbawn summer's day. Fox is not displeased with the rain. His mood is usually in tune with the weather. A soft day is in harmony with an unhurried day.

For something to do, Fox wanders out of his office and descends the stairs to the ground floor to the front desk. He has not seen Inspector Murphy all day. It is 14:00 hours, which is Fox's way of referring to 2:00pm. He wonders if Inspector Murphy – Murf – is actually working at all today, or if he has gone off fishing.

"O'Reilly! Caldwell!" Fox shouts to get the attention of the two junior gardaí. Garda O'Reilly and Garda Caldwell jump up from their desks and run up to Superintendent Fox.

"Sir?" they chime in unison.

"The notice board! I want it cleaned up and arranged according to date and priority. Look at this. Here is a lost racehorse in England placed on top of sheep dipping in Ireland. And O'Reilly, did you decalcify the kettle yet? I don't like little bits of chalk in my tea."

O'Reilly and Caldwell set about their mundane tasks. How they wish for a robbery or brawl or something – anything that would require the attention of a police officer.

They get their wish sooner than expected. The quiet of the station is disturbed by the blustering entrance of Danny the Divil. The three police officers cease what they are doing and look at Danny the Divil in amazement. It is two in the afternoon and Danny the Divil is still sober? Something is truly wrong. By now he would have exhausted his maintenance dose of whiskey and is apt to be cantankerous until he imbibes his afternoon requirements – but not until he is first relieved of his driving duties for Doctor McBratt. Something serious has disrupted Danny the Divil's routine and, hence, the peacefulness of the day. They deduce from the look of concern on Danny the Divil's face that this might even be a police matter.

"I've just come from the two-mile stone. There's a car stuck in the ditch out there again. This is the third time this month. Why don't you guards do something about that dangerous bend in the road out there, instead of sitting here on your arses all day long?"

"Danny, is the doctor's car stuck in the ditch?"

"No, not the doctor's car. Sure am I not after driving here in the doctor's car? It's Mick Sweeney what's stuck there. Doctor McBratt is still back there with him. I think he bumped his head."

Fox dispatches O'Reilly and Caldwell to the scene of the accident – much to the relief of both officers. Fox instructs them to take measurements and statements, render proper police assistance and compile the pertinent information for an accident report. Danny the Divil hurries off too. The quicker the doctor is excused from attending to the accident, the sooner Danny can attend to his daily routine perched on a barstool in Cannon's pub in the Market Square.

The garda station returns to its previous state of calm. Danny the Divil's remarks are still ringing in Superintendent Fox's ears. In truth, Fox agrees with Danny's opinion that something ought to be done about the dangerous bend at the two-mile stone.

The two-mile stone is 2.8 miles from Killbawn. The milestone was installed back before statute miles were the standard measurement. It is located on the Blackwater Road to indicate the distance to Killbawn in Irish miles.

The Blackwater Road runs out of the town in a northerly direction. It doesn't really go anywhere important – not to Castlebar, not to Ballina, not to Belmullet. Maybe that's why it is overlooked when the county allocates its scarce funds for road improvements. Limited funds are prioritised and directed elsewhere. The Blackwater Road follows the Blackwater River four miles to the sea. It serves the local farming area. It swings up and around and eventually joins the R314 to Killala and Ballina. It is a picturesque road that gives access to the sea – to cliffs and beaches. The two-mile stone is located at a point in the road that is one mile from the mouth of the river. But this is a tidal estuary, and during spring tides the seawater reaches the road at this point.

Narrow tidal inlets pierce the coast here. Against that, the coastland is comprised of dolmens that protrude out into the estuary to compete with the inlets for superiority. At the two-mile stone, the dolmen and the inlet struggle against each other for dominance. The road follows the path of where the dolmen and the inlet collide – an S-bend protruding out to sea and retreating back into the land again.

In the quiet town of Killbawn, Detective Inspector John Patrick Murphy (Murf) is leaning on the Blackwater Bridge staring at the swirling water underneath. The movement of the water is mesmerising and holds his attention. He is dressed in 'plainclothes' – or, to be more accurate, dressed in Murf's understanding of plainclothes for north Mayo. His jacket is blue worsted, the kind favoured by the local farming community. His trousers are a light-grey flannel with no crease – actually his trousers have multiple creases from crushing the ends into his socks and thence into his rubber-soled boots. Is there any other policeman in Ireland who wears his trouser ends tucked into his socks? His socks are the thick woollen multi-dotted socks worn by county council work crews. His shirt is pinstriped with a detachable collar – which is missing – and the buttons on the shirt probably don't line up. He looks more like a farmer on a visit to market than a policeman. His choice of dress is tolerated by District Officer Superintendent David Fox. Fox does not approve, but there is no denying that Murf's rapport with the public is of great advantage to the police. Murf knows everyone, and everyone trusts Murf. Murf knows about every potential crime in the district hours before it is committed. Hence, he is a jump ahead of whatever illicit business is being considered. The parish of Killbawn experiences a low rate of crime and, of the few offences that actually occur, the perpetrators are quickly apprehended. Murf is regarded as the best detective in the county. So why is he stationed in rural north Mayo? Murf has a downside – he argues with his superiors, and with court judges and with most authority-figures. For everyone's sake, Murf's service is best suited to a remote rural district. Murf is quite content with this arrangement.

It is past 2:00pm. Murf ought to be in his office. He decides to proceed to the garda station, partly out of a sense of duty, and partly because he can only take so much of Killbawn's fine drizzle. He turns around from the bridge wall to face the street. He sees Garda O'Reilly cycling with haste across the bridge and on to the Blackwater Road. Judging from the rain-cape and the cycle-clips he is wearing, Murf presumes that O'Reilly must be on a serious mission. Garda Caldwell is following close behind, but he is cycling with less energy and less determination. Caldwell is not wearing a rain cape or cycle-clips. In place of clips, he has tucked the bottom of his trousers into his socks. Murf smiles at this. This is something Murf himself would do, even though it fails to meet the standard of dress required by Superintendent Fox. Notwithstanding his lack of proper cycling attire, Caldwell has securely fastened the chin strap of his cap beneath his chin. Murf scrutinises the two guards as they proceed out of town on the Blackwater Road. He wonders what urgent police work requires the attention of two gardaí. Murf is curious. He hurries in the direction of the garda station to inquire. Just as he is clearing the bridge, Murf sees Doctor McBratt's car approach. It pulls up alongside and Danny the Divil leans over to the passenger side and rolls down the window.

"Guard Murphy! There's been an accident out by the two-mile stone."

So that is the serious matter that has demanded the attention of O'Reilly and Caldwell. "So, Danny, where's the doctor? Are you going for her?"

"The doctor is there already. I left her there when she told me to report to the guards."

"The doctor is at the accident scene?"

"Yes. I'm going back to fetch her now. Do you want to come along?"

Murf opens the car door and hops inside, and Danny the Divil drives off along the Blackwater Road to the two-mile stone.

The caution signs on the road are in Irish.

'GO MALL'

This is the sign to slow down for the bend ahead at the two-mile stone. There is a second sign ten feet beyond that.

'NÍOS MOILLE'

This is a prudent warning to motorists to reduce speed to slower than slow.

The Divil navigates the bend at a cautious speed. They stop at the accident scene. O'Reilly and Caldwell have just arrived at the scene ahead of Murf. The two guards take charge of managing the situation. Pat Delahunty from the neighbouring farm has his tractor at the scene. Garda O'Reilly directs him to tug the car out of the sheugh and back onto the roadway.

Murf steps out of the doctor's car and walks over to Mick Sweeney. Mick is standing at the roadside observing the tractor's effort at moving his car. "Hello, Mick! Are you all right?"

"Oh, Guard Murphy! I'm fine all right. Just a bit of a bump. The car is all right too if we can just haul it back onto the road."

"So, Mick, how did you manage to drive into the ditch? Sure you know this road like the back of your hand."

"Oh, Guard Murphy, I feel so stupid. I thought I saw a woman standing in the middle of the road right here at the bend."

"A woman? So where is she now?"

"Well when I swerved to avoid her, she just disappeared – whoosh. There was no one there at all. I feel so stupid, swerving to avoid nobody on the road."

"Mick, can you describe the woman?" Murf is concerned that there may be a pedestrian injured by the accident – perhaps fallen off the roadway or absent from the scene and in need of assistance.

"Well, it was a white woman. I didn't see her face."

"What do you mean by a 'white woman'?"

"White. Like a statue in St Bawn's. Or like a nun in a white habit. But listen to me, Guard Murphy, there was nothing there at all. For an instant, I saw a white woman, and then – whoosh – nothing."

Danny the Divil approaches. He picks up on what Mick is describing. "Lord, Murf, what Mick saw was one of the ghosts from the Famine Field over there." He points to the other side of the road, to beyond the low wire fence and scrawny hedge. "I see them ghosts all the time…"

Murf smiles inwardly. When the Divil is recovering from a previous night's drinking, he sees rats and spiders and all sorts of vermin too.

"…and I pay them no heed. I just drive on through them. It doesn't do them no harm. They just disappear or fly off and come back again." He turns to speak to Mick. "The next time you see one of them famine ghosts, Mick, just drive through them."

Mick's car is back on the road. Murf inspects it. There is no damage to it, no bumps or scratches – just some mud around the wheel well. Murf determines that an investigating detective is not required at the scene. He stands back and watches. Clearly, there is no damage done. Mick Sweeney has suffered just a minor bump to his forehead and is eager to resume his journey. Pat Delahunty needs to get back to spreading manure. Danny the Divil is impatient to complete his daily duties for Doctor McBratt and get to his barstool in Cannon's pub. Mrs Cannon, if she is in a kind mood, may invite him into the kitchen for food scraps to share between the Divil and the dog. Doctor McBratt, dressed in a fashionable navy-blue gabardine raincoat with matching hat, has outpatients arriving at the dispensary at 3:00pm. She is anxious to attend to her patients. O'Reilly and Caldwell would rather be out of the drizzle. No traffic violation occurred and no damage was caused, so a police accident report is not required. Everyone has a reason to be on their way. The Divil shouts at Murf from out the car window as he drives off. "Guard Murphy, do you want a lift back to town?" Murf waves at him to continue on without him. Within minutes, everyone has left the bend at the two-mile stone.

Murf looks up at the sky. The clouds are clearing. The drizzle ceases. Murf decides to walk back to Killbawn via the farms. This is not any faster or shorter, but it affords him the opportunity to speak with the locals and catch up on the goings-on. He steps past the sparse roadside hedge and enters the adjacent field through the wire fence that borders the road. This field is on the northern face of a drumlin and is reserved exclusively for grazing. No plough pierces the ground here; no spade or pick disturbs the soil. This is the revered 'Famine Field'.

Murf walks to the brow of the hill. From here he surveys his surroundings. The drumlin is shaped like a half-buried egg and is smaller than average – it is 5 furlongs long by 325 yards wide. The highest point, where Murf is standing, is 120 feet above the base. The Famine Field, measuring 100 yards by 50 yards, is the smallest of six fields on the drumlin. There are a number of drumlins here at the coast. They form peninsulas and islands which are sliced through by narrow inlets cutting deeply into the land. The dolmens here are not as numerous or as spectacular as those at Clew Bay, but they were formed by the same retreating ice sheet of the last glacial period some 12,000 years ago. The drumlin typography, interesting as it may be, is not the overriding feature of this field. This place is the revered resting-place of untold numbers of undocumented burials from 1847 and 1848.

Murf casts his eyes back inland to Pat Delahunty's farm. About a half-mile away is Pat's big stone building for storing his tractor and farm implements. Previously, this was the workhouse for famine relief. Thousands, on the point of death, came to the workhouse seeking relief. This was after the Act of Union when Ireland was administered by Britain and, according to the political policy of the time, charity was not permitted. The needy were required to work in order to obtain food and shelter. Those weakened by the famine were killed by the physical labour that was forced upon them. No one survived the workhouse. Those who were considered healthy did not qualify for relief and were turned away; only those who were already near death were accepted – and then killed by unnecessary arduous labour. The tragedy of the famine was not in the shortage of food, it was in the shortage of **available** food for the poor. They died in the midst of plenty. There was an abundance of food throughout the 'black 47'. Food – mutton, beef and grain – was produced for the English market and exported for profit at record levels. The poor, however, were unable to pay the market prices so they died of hunger, disease and mistreatment. In north Mayo, the population plummeted by over 30% in the famine years; whole communities were wiped out never to be revived. Here in the Famine Field, the workhouse dumped the bodies of their deceased malnourished inmates in unmarked graves and covered over the evidence. No records were kept. No one knows how many are truly buried here, or where exactly in the field they are interred. For 98 years the field has lain undisturbed, and a deep enduring hatred of the English persists.

Murf surveys the area from the old workhouse to the Famine Field. He pictures the area as it might have been in 1848. The road is now tarred; it would have been surfaced with loose stone chips and gravel in 1848. Otherwise, the area here is unchanged. There is no evidence of internment in the field below – at least there is no visible sign. The only sure way to confirm the existence of mass burial in the Famine Field would be to excavate the site. This is unlikely. The presence of ghosts, a strongly-held conviction, is the accepted evidence of internment to the locals. The popular belief is held so strongly that any attempt to disturb the revered resting place of the famine victims would raise the ire of the people. And the Diocese of Killala would surely object.

Murf points to the old workhouse and slowly swings his arm horizontally in a circle. There is one suitable place for a mass burial, and only one suitable place, within easy access to the workhouse – the north face of the drumlin. The east, south and west faces are used for crop cultivation. The north face, the cooler darker side, is reserved for grazing. Hence, there would be little or no disruption of the land's usage from burials in the north face. Secondly, where else but in a hill of moraine could a large pit be dug with ease? In any other location, the bedrock is too close to the surface. As to burial in a strand, an option frequently adopted in other communities, the closest suitable beach is four miles away. The estuary here at the two-mile stone is unsuitable for burial. It is much too rocky at the shoreline, and the inlet is unworkable further out in the black sticky glar. No, the Famine Field is the only likely site for the workhouse burials.

Some fifteen minutes have elapsed since Murf stepped into the Famine Field. In that time, ground-fog from the sea-marsh has wafted along the shore. It lazily encroaches on the roadway below. Murf watches a car slowly navigate the bend with care. In the wake of the car, the fog swirls and spirals into a conical shape, and then it gradually dissipates. For just a brief moment, Murf discerns a shape in the twirling wisp of fog that could easily be mistaken for a 'white woman'. Murf determines that the sightings of ghosts from the Famine Field likely pertain to sightings of spinning spirals of sea-fog suspended over the surface of the road. This fog is just one more hazard to contend with at the bend of the two-mile stone.

It is a little after 4:00pm when Murf returns to his office. There is a message waiting for him. He is to go to Doctor McBratt at the dispensary at five o'clock closing time. Murf has time for a cup of tea. In pouring the boiling water he notices flakes of calcium at the spout. He smiles at this. O'Reilly, it appears, has dodged the kettle-cleaning task once again.

5:00pm. Murf enters the Killbawn Dispensary. The stone building predates the workhouse and predates the Great Famine. It was constructed soon after the 1805 act that established dispensaries in Ireland. The dispensary is defined by the act as 'an institution where medicine and advice are given gratis to the poor'. It is different from a county infirmary or a voluntary hospital in that it has no wards or inpatient beds. Agnes, Doctor McBratt's medical assistant, recognises Murf as he enters the waiting room. She shouts into the surgery room, "Inspector Murphy is here, Doctor!"

Doctor Marie Antoinette McBratt enters the waiting room from surgery. She is twenty-eight – or 'twenty-one' – and is undoing her white medical coat. "Thanks, Agnes. You may as well leave now if you are finished. I'll lock up." And turning to Murf, "Hello, Murf. Let's go into my office."

"Hello, Ant." Murf shrugs at the brisk greeting and follows her into her office, puzzled as to why the doctor would need to consult with him in her private office. Doctor McBratt hangs her medical coat on a coat rack and goes behind her desk where she sits down heavily on her chair. "Sit, Murf. I want to put something to you."

Murf sits in the chair indicated and tries to read from her body language where this is leading. McBratt slides open a desk drawer and extracts a bottle of French brandy and two glasses. These she puts on the table.

"Murf, be a gentleman and pour the drinks."

A consultation over drinks? Murf considers the import of this. Doctor McBratt picks up a cigarette case from within the same drawer. She flips it open and selects a cork-tipped cigarette. She places a lighter on the desk without glancing at it. Her eyes are on a non-object on the far wall. Murf lifts the lighter, clicks it, and applies the flame to her cigarette. Antoinette McBratt draws on the flame. She smokes Bette-Davis-style but avoids inhaling. Murf realises that Doctor McBratt is not really a smoker. This is the current fashionable trend among modern forward-thinking women. She takes a sip of brandy. Not a smoker, but whereas her smoking is a fashion-statement, Murf deduces that the drinking is for real.

Having gathered her thoughts, Doctor McBratt brings her eyes into focus and looks at Murf with purpose. "The Divil," she says, "seldom speaks, especially when driving. Today he went on and on about the dangerous bend at the two-mile stone." She blows a puff of smoke towards the ceiling. "The Divil has never driven off the road into the ditch. Would you believe that? He must be the only driver on the Blackwater Road who has NOT hit the ditch there."

"Is that a fact?" Murf sees where this is going.

"The Divil is right. We must do something to get that bend fixed before there is a serious injury."

It is true. A car and a lorry travelling in the opposite direction are unable to manoeuvre around the bend simultaneously. One is required to stop and reverse until the other vehicle clears the bend before proceeding. And, since the view ahead is obstructed, a lot of horn-blowing is required to warn oncoming traffic. "Surely, Ant, we are not in a position to lobby the Mayo County Council. Should we not be speaking with the local county councillor, Patrick Gildea?"

"Ah, that's where you are wrong, Murf."

"How so?"

"Sean Macilmyra."

"The county engineer?"

"The **new** county engineer – he assumed the position seven months ago. Wait until six o'clock. Then I will make a phone call."

"What? Phone the county engineer at home? Are you sure this is wise?"

"My sister Bernadette has tea at six. I will phone her."

"And what will that achieve?"

"She is married to Sean Macilmyra."

Murf understands Doctor McBratt's scheme. "Sean Macilmyra sits down to tea with her at six o'clock. Ah." Brazen and smart.

At 6:00pm, Doctor McBratt lifts the telephone receiver and spins the handle. She requests the operator to place the call to Castlebar 104. Murf listens while Antoinette and Bernadette discuss the merits of 'The Bells of St Mary's' and Bing Crosby's performance. Eventually, Doctor McBratt broaches the subject of the dangerous bend at the two-mile stone outside Killbawn on the Blackwater Road. Unexpectedly, Doctor McBratt passes the receiver to Murf.

"Here, Murf. Sean is coming on the line. Talk to him."

"Me?"

"Of course. That's why I asked you here."

Murf takes the receiver. "Hello. Mr Macilmyra? I apologise for disturbing you at home.

"This is Inspector Murphy of Killbawn.

"It's about the dangerous bend outside Killbawn – the one on the Blackwater Road. I was hoping to…

"Of course. I understand.

"Goodbye."

Murf returns the receiver to Doctor McBratt who recommences her chatter with her sister. After a minute she hangs up.

"So, Murf, how did it go? It was a very short conversation."

"I think he just blew me off."

"Why do you say that?"

"First he told me that he does not discuss county business at home. Secondly, he told me that should I wish to inquire into work projects – proposed, pending or approved – I should come to the county council office on Wednesday at 7:00pm."

"That doesn't sound like a dismissal. It sounds like an invitation to me. Tell you what. Let's finish our drinks and I will phone back."

"I don't think Sean Macilmyra will take kindly to a second phone call at home."

"I'll talk to Bernadette and get her take on it."

Doctor McBratt smokes another cigarette. Murf pours another brandy. At 6:30pm, Doctor McBratt places another call to Castlebar 104.

"Bernadette, was Sean upset to receive the call about the dangerous bend?

"Ah, I see. Okay. Cheers." And she hangs up.

She places her elbows on the desk and leans over towards Murf. "Murf, Sean Macilmyra is fully aware of the dangerous bend at the two-mile stone. He proposed reconstruction of that section of the roadway some months ago and failed to get approval from the council. It is a matter of prioritising the allocation of funds. It is currently on his short-list for another submission – with some amendments – to the council next week. He appreciates any support to push this through for approval. Our local county councillor will be at the presentation of course. Patrick Gildea should be on our side in this. And a representative of the bishop of Killala will be there. I don't know which way the Diocese of Killala leans on this – pro or con. And then there is you, a representative of

An Garda Síochána. And myself, Killbawn's dispensary doctor."

"Ant, I can't present myself as a representative of An Garda Síochána…"

"Well then, as a representative of Killbawn's Parish Council, or something-or-other important. Does it matter? We are going to the Mayo County Council meeting next week to help Sean Macilmyra get this project approved. So there!"

CHAPTER FOUR

Mayo County Council

Castlebar, County Mayo, Ireland
Wednesday 07 August 1946
Áras an Chontae, The Mall, Castlebar

To get from Killbawn to the Mayo County Council building in Castlebar is quite easy. The R310 runs right to the doorstep of Áras an Chontae. The Divil is driving. Doctor McBratt is in her usual place in the back seat. Murf is in the front passenger seat. As is her habit, Doctor McBratt maintains a commentary throughout the journey.

"We're in Castlebar now, Danny. Look out for sudden turns. Take a left here. And from Linenhall Street, take a right onto Market Street."

Danny the Divil grunts is agreement, but he is not listening. He knows the R310 and is not likely to get lost notwithstanding the unexpected turns upon entering the county town of Castlebar. Inside the town, the route is known by the names of the streets it passes through. Market Street becomes Ellison Street.

"This is Ellison Street, Danny. You need to swing left onto The Mall. If you go straight on here you'll take us to the Westport Road."

Danny turns left with the curve of The Mall. He sees the destination ahead on the right – Áras an Chontae.

"Look out for parking here, Danny. Oh, you missed a spot. You missed another spot. No, don't park there. Maybe we should ask a guard."

The Divil turns to Murf. "Guard Murphy, should we park here?"

Murf smiles at the Divil's humour. Doctor McBratt is oblivious to it. Murf is particularly familiar with the route. He drives here to the Garda Divisional HQ every month. Murf responds to the Divil's humorous invitation to help find a parking spot. "Take the next right."

Doctor McBratt is still issuing driving instructions from the back seat. "Danny. You have driven past the county council building. And why are you turning onto John Moore Road?"

Murf continues to guide the Divil. "Bear left onto Pavillion Road and turn sharp left into the first driveway."

Doctor McBratt continues to berate the Divil. "Pavillion Road? Lord, Danny, you are going way off course. Now where are you taking us? What building is this?"

Murf directs the Divil into a parking lot at the rear of a building. "Park up there by the door." The spot is marked 'Reserved for Garda'. "That's Sergeant Matthews' spot. He's most likely gone for the day. Let's go inside and check."

Doctor McBratt slaps Murf on the shoulder. "Lord, Murf. Why did you have us park here? We are nowhere near the county council building."

"We came in the back way to the garda station. It fronts onto The Mall, and it is right next door to Áras an Chontae. You won't find a safer place to leave your car than here in Sergeant Matthews' parking spot."

Doctor McBratt calms down. "Well, I suppose you're right. So how far do we walk from here?"

"Come with me into the station. I need to sign in if I'm parking here."

Inside the building, Murf leads them to the front desk. Garda Jerry Coulter is on duty. "Inspector Murphy? I wasn't expecting you here tonight. Who are you meeting?"

"Hello, Jerry. My meeting is next door, at the county council. Is it all right to park in Sergeant Matthews' spot for an hour or two?"

"No problem. Leave the keys. I'll move the car if needs be." He opens a register on the counter and writes on a line while speaking aloud to Murf. "Inspector Murphy, Killbawn Garda, licence no. IZ4912."

Murf interrupts, "IZ5104."

"That's not your car, Murf; nor is it any of the patrol cars. Is it a new car you have, Murf?"

"No. It's Doctor McBratt's car."

Garda Coulter glances at the two people who came in with Murf – a well-dressed lady in a stylish tan trench coat with exaggerated shoulders; and beside her, a blood-shot-eyed man in an oil-stained suit. Coulter sees that the Divil's suit is an expensive suit that is ill-fitting and looks like it had been dragged through mire by a farm tractor. Doubtless, it is a gentleman's cast-off suit – actually donated to the Divil by Casey of the general store. Coulter tenders his help to the trio. "Ah yes. The meeting with the county council. You realise that the council is not meeting tonight? The only meeting scheduled there is a subcommittee of the Roads Department. You are not going to a meeting on road repairs, surely?"

"And that's where we are headed, Jerry."

Garda Coulter has Murf sign the register. He takes the car keys from him and labels them, and hangs them on a small corkboard at his desk. He shakes his head as he watches the misfit trio depart from the station. "Killbawn must be the strangest place," he mutters under his breath.

Outside the garda station, they turn left and cross John Moore Road. Doctor McBratt resumes her tirade of disapproval. "Murf, you said that the county council building is next to the garda station. Well, it's not. We are crossing John Moore Road, and that is not the council building ahead."

"I lied. There is one building – a row of five shops – between the garda station and Áras an Chontae. See. We are here already."

Doctor McBratt and the Divil walk up to the entrance door of the county council building. Murf walks past it and peers around the corner. Annoyed, Doctor McBratt scolds Murf. "Murf, what on earth are you doing now? We are going to be late for the meeting."

Murf rejoins them and they enter the building. He comments, "There are two EI-Sligo cars in the car park."

Doctor McBratt is irritated at Murf. "So, what is strange about that?"

"Why would a Sligo resident be interested in road repairs in Mayo?"

"A Mayo resident could drive a Sligo car. Sean does."

"Sean Macilmyra drives a Sligo-registered car?"

"Of course he does. He came to Mayo from Sligo in January, and he has not changed his car since then. Come on, Murf. And where in the building is this meeting being held? Let's find someone to direct us."

"The Roads Department is on the second floor. That's where the meeting is being held. See. It is posted on the notice-board."

The Divil and Doctor McBratt check the notice-board. The Divil remarks, "Well, why don't yous two go on up to the meeting. I'll meet you all after, like."

"No, you won't, Danny," replies the doctor. "You're coming with us." This is to ensure that the Divil remains under her watchful eye. If he disappears now, he will seek out a pub and it may take days to locate him. The doctor slips him an almost-empty Baby Power. The Divil swigs it and attempts to suck the bottle dry. One ounce of whiskey should keep him functioning for another half hour or so. They ascend the stairs together and all three reach the meeting room.

Tony Kavanagh, Sean Macilmyra's assistant, checks off the attendees' names at the entrance door. "Guard Murphy, and Doctor McBratt. You may sit anywhere in the visitors' section." He gestures to a section of the room where chairs are arranged in theatre-style. "But hold on. Who is the third person?" He eyes Danny the Divil with disapproval. This doesn't look like an invited guest or a concerned citizen.

"It's Danny the Divil." Doctor McBratt says this as if it explains it fully. "He's my driver." Tony Kavanagh blocks the Divil from entering the meeting room. Doctor McBratt, seeing Sean Macilmyra at the head table, gestures to him to intervene.

Sean Macilmyra is sitting calmly. Both elbows are resting on the table. They form an arch with his hands overlapping. His hands are poised level with his mouth and a smouldering Sweet Afton is held by his fingertips. With his hands thus positioned, he is able to drag frequently on the cigarette with more comfort than having it hang unceremoniously from his mouth. He wears a brown herring-boned tweed sports coat. His hair is brushed back flat on his head and he peers out at the assembly through the wafting cigarette smoke. He notes all who are present in the room. Councillor James Quigley, the chairman of the sub-committee sits beside him. Other councillor-members are in attendance, as is Patrick Gildea of Mayo North. Also attending is Pat Delahunty whose land borders the bend at the two-mile stone, and within whose land the Famine Field is located. Father Barry Glen Dennagher is there as the representative of the Diocese of Killala. Sean observes Garda-Inspector Murphy entering the room. Standing beside him at the doorway is Sean's own sister-in-law, Doctor Marie Antoinette McBratt from Killbawn, accompanied by her faithful divil-driver.

Recognising Doctor McBratt's sign-language, Sean catches Tony Kavanagh's eye and gives him the nod to permit the Divil to pass. Reluctantly, Tony steps aside and the Divil enters. On the list of attendees, Tony records their admittance on a single line – 'Doctor McBratt and driver'.

The chairman, James Quigley, calls the meeting to order. He proceeds through the mandatory preamble to establish the purpose and authority of the meeting. He welcomes the councillor-members and other guests present. At the first item on the agenda, he hands the meeting over to the county engineer, Sean Macilmyra, to present his proposal for road reconfiguration at the two-mile stone on the Blackwater Road outside Killbawn.

To assist with the presentation, Tony Kavanagh proceeds to the easel beside the head table. Sean describes the current state of the bend in the road. Tony flips over the top sheet on the display stand to reveal a map of the location under review. He slaps the map loudly with a cane to identify the specific points of interest as they are described and enumerated by Sean. Everyone present is familiar with the road, the bend, the river, the sea inlet-estuary and the dolmen-hill.

Tony flips over to map no. 2. Everyone peers at it. It shows a proposed new roadway cutting across the inlet to rejoin the existing road 440 yards later, bypassing the 'S' of the bend. Construction in the inlet would entail building a causeway and would require special attention to drainage, Sean explains. "This was proposed in April and was rejected due to the cost."

Tony flips to map no. 3. Sean continues. "Since then, we have met with Mr Pat Delahunty, the owner of the land here" – 'slap' from Tony's cane to indicate it on the map – "and we are confident that this new proposal will meet with approval. Rather than cut across the inlet ('slap'), this plan is to cut through the dolmen ('slap') located in Delahunty's land. The dolmen is moraine – mostly sand – and has a solid flat rock base. Excavation would be easy, and there would be no disruption to drainage. And, best of all, a new roadway construction through the dolmen is within our budget."

The chairman invites questions and comments. The first question is presented by Father Barry Glen Dennagher. "Let's look at the dolmen. From what I see on the map, your proposed roadway through the dolmen actually cuts through the Famine Field. Is this correct?" Tony Kavanagh continues to slap the map. Sean opens his mouth to respond, but before he speaks, Father Glen Dennagher approaches the head table and purposefully places a letter thereon. "Here is a letter from his lordship the bishop. He makes it absolutely clear that there will be no digging in the Famine Field. Nothing is to disturb the burial ground of the unfortunate famine victims – may God grant them rest."

More questions and objections are thrown about from the floor. The councillor from Mayo West wants the project shelved in favour of road reconfiguration at Clew Bay. The chairman attempts to restore order. Murf sits quietly observing the lapse in decorum and wonders if this is the usual behaviour at a sub-committee meeting of the county council. Sean sits quietly smoking, patiently waiting for the restoration of order. Legitimate questions and comments need to be addressed, but not in the present free-for-all state of the meeting. Danny the Divil is agitated, not by the argumentative state of the members, but by his craving for a drink. He paces up and down the room and comes to a halt at the display on the easel.

Doctor McBratt shouts to him. "Danny! Get back to your chair. You can't be up there messing with the county's maps."

This draws attention back to the head table. Patrick Gildea exclaims, "Lord, look at Danny the Divil up there examining the engineer's maps." This brings some relief to the hostility that was brewing, and there is laughter. Someone shouts, "Come on, Danny the Divil. Tell us what you think of the engineer's plans."

Danny the Divil mutters, "Aw, don't call me that."

With the shift in the atmosphere, the chairman manages to restore order. Except that Danny the Divil remains peering at the display map. He addresses the map. "This isn't right at all, at all. This makes it more worse than before."

Doctor McBratt whispers to him, "Please, Danny, just came back here and sit quietly."

Sean Macilmyra turns his head slowly, blows smoke out of the side of his mouth, and addresses the Divil in a low calm voice. The softness of his voice brings a hush to the meeting. "Mr Danny, (Sean has no knowledge of Danny's surname) you are a driver for Doctor McBratt. Are you not?"

"Indeed and I am."

"And you are familiar with this stretch of road at the two-mile stone?"

"Like the back of me hand I know it. Sure I drive it every day on the doctor's rounds."

Sean holds up one finger of his arched hands to command silence from the meeting. The members realise that Sean Macilmyra is taking the Divil seriously. "Why do you say that the planned reconfiguration of the road is 'more worse', Danny?"

"Well, it's like this." Danny flips back the maps to the first one, the map showing the current configuration. He points to it. "Here, you travel fifteen miles an hour. And if you're unlucky you drive into the ditch at the two-mile stone." He flips forward to map no. 3. "Now here you have a winding road, and suddenly a new bit that's straight for two furlongs, and then it's windy again. So when you come to the straight bit you speed up. Then, where the straight road ends, if you are unlucky, you'll hit the ditch at forty or fifty miles an hour instead of fifteen. Y'see, that's much worse than before."

"And what do you suggest, Danny?"

"A curve. You need a curve in the road to make people drive straight." There is sniggering at the Divil's contradiction. But Sean holds up his finger again. Danny the Divil continues. "Not a tight curve, but a gentle bend in the road. This way. And that way." The Divil gestures with his hands and body to demonstrate the motion and speed of a car. Unable to communicate comprehensibly, Danny tears the map off the stand and brings it to the head table. He grabs a pencil from Sean's hand – the hand not holding the cigarette – and draws curves on the paper.

Danny points to his markings. "You don't need to go THERE; and there is too much to dig anyways. And you don't want to go THERE; you don't know how deep the glar is. Now, THIS is where you should put the road; it's a solid rock base and all."

Sean stubs out his cigarette. He spins the map around and checks his own markings and calculations in relation to Danny's pencil marks. He stands up and addresses the meeting.

"I agree with Mr Danny here. Considering the numerous bends in the road, a sudden straight section is not prudent. But this is not the best part of Mr Danny's plan." He actually said 'plan'. Sean speaks aside to Tony Kavanagh. "Get Mr Danny a chair to sit up here while I present this ingenious modification." He continues to address the meeting. "Lady and gentlemen, Mr Danny has drawn a modification for the new road. He proposes that we construct a gentle curve. It will encroach into the hillside by no more than twenty feet." He indicates on the map. "The dolmen at this spot here is no more than four feet deep. This is much too shallow to contain a mass grave. The burial site could only be in deeper ground, here, or here. Secondly, this new road, as proposed by Mr Danny here, would skirt the inlet, intruding no more than thirty feet. At this point," indicating on the map, "the rocky shoreline is visible. The deep glar is farther out. The entire road can be constructed on a solid foundation without extensive excavation or causeway construction."

Danny the Divil is now seated at the head table. He pipes in, "And Pat Delahunty doesn't lose any land, neither."

Sean clarifies the Divil's statement. "That is correct. The moraine and topsoil that is removed from here" indicating on the map, "will be re-deposited on the previous section of road – here."

"And tell them about the car park."

"And the existing bend at the two-mile stone will serve as a lay-by, either to accommodate access to the river or to visit the Famine Field."

"And don't forget the sign."

Sean suppresses a smile at the Divil's continuing embellishments to the plan. "In recognition of, and with due respect to the revered burial site, the county council will erect a plaque to commemorate the victims of the famine interred in the Famine Field." There are nods of approval from the members. "As to cost, this will come in much lower than estimates for the two previous plans." The meeting breaks into appreciative applause.

Sean sits down. The chairman rises. "If there are no objections to the revised plan for the Two-Mile Stone Project for roadway construction and reconfiguration, I would ask the voting members to vote in support of the amended proposal for presentation to the county council for final approval – subject, of course, to the usual engineer's report and financial costing."

Danny the Divil raises his hand.

"You have an objection, Mr Danny?"

"I have. You can't call it the 'Two-Mile Stone Project' now that it bypasses the two-mile stone."

Patrick Gildea remarks to the chairman, "He's right. Why not call it 'Danny the Divil's Gentle Curve'."

And from another member, "How about 'Danny the Divil's bend'?"

Danny mutters, "Aw don't call it that."

Tony Kavanagh writes the name of the project on the map, the map containing Danny the Divil's pencil marks and artistic curves. At Danny's objection to 'Danny the Divil's Bend', he alters the wording to 'The Divil's Bend'. Dissatisfied with a non-dictionary word, he changes it to 'The Devil's Bend'. And thus, the proposed project receives its official title.

"Wait!" All eyes turn to Father Barry Glen Dennagher. "You are forgetting the bishop's directive – 'Do not disturb the Famine Field'."

Sean lights another cigarette and looks at the representative from the diocese of Killala. He rests his chin on his arched hands. A cigarette is held in the fingertips of his left hand, his pencil held in his right hand. He addresses the priest. "Father Glen Dennagher, it is unlikely that we will encounter any burial remains in the area of our proposed excavation. However, to satisfy your concerns, we will conduct non-intrusive probes in the area in question. Should we encounter any evidence of interred remains, we will abort the project. Is this agreeable?"

"Read the bishop's letter. His lordship makes it abundantly clear – 'no digging in the Famine Field'."

The meeting is stunned at this. How could the diocese object? The bishop has no authoritative status to direct the Mayo County Council; nevertheless, a command from his lordship cannot be ignored, such is his prestige in the region. Murf observes Sean's calmness. He sits motionless, quietly smoking. Murf notices that the pencil in Sean's hand snaps in two.

Doctor McBratt storms out of the meeting room. She turns to direct a remark at Father Glen Dennagher, loud enough for all to hear. "The damn bishop should think less about the dead and more about the living!" Murf and the Divil take it as their cue to leave also.

For the journey back to Killbawn, Doctor McBratt instructs Murf to drive the car rather than the Divil. The Divil's agitation has become extreme. The doctor gives him her remaining stock of Baby Powers – two four-ounce miniature bottles of Three Swallows. The Divil, sitting in the front passenger seat, opens both bottles and places them to his mouth simultaneously. He slugs the 'six swallows', in two noisy swallows and thence settles to a calm silence. Doctor McBratt sits in her usual back seat. She too sits in silence. But, unlike the Divil, her silence is turbulent. She is fuming at the 'damn bishop' who has quashed Sean Macilmyra's proposal to fix the dangerous corner at the two-mile stone. Murf drives in silence as he contemplates the consequences of the diocese's decision to axe the Two-Mile-Stone project – now the Devil's Bend project.

CHAPTER FIVE

THE CANON INTERVENES

Killbawn, County Mayo, Ireland
Thursday 08 August 1946

It is 8:30pm at St Bawn's parochial house. Canon Paul Anthony MacMorrow is resting on his bed in the parlour. He is not **in** bed. He relaxes after tea with his feet raised and his shoulders propped up with pillows and cushions. Due to his rheumatism, Canon MacMorrow no longer ascends the stairs to his bedroom. Instead, a bed is installed in the parlour. Hence, the parlour doubles as his personal receiving room during the day, and as his bedroom at night. He will not actually retire for the night until he has said his office and night prayers in the church at 9:00pm. He has kicked off his shoes, but his black hat is still on his head. Without his hat, his head gets cold and his nose runs. He is sipping hot cocoa liberally laced with Black Bush whiskey. The room is rich with the comforting smells of burning turf, hot cocoa and whiskey fumes.

Doctor Marie Antoinette McBratt knocks and enters the room. She is expected of course. Doctor McBratt performs the Way of the Cross every evening in St Bawn's before the church is locked for the night at 9:00pm. She always visits the canon on her way to her devotions. She enquires after his health, and she partakes of the canon's port as per their daily custom.

"Good evening, Canon. And how are we all today?"

"Doctor Antoinette, sure I'm grand. But I heard that you and Danny the Divil kicked up a bit of a storm at the county council last night."

"And how do you know about that, Canon?"

"I got the entire news from Patrick Gildea. You know, the councillor."

"Of course I know the local county councillor. But sure what all did he tell you?"

"Everything. Including the part where you bit off Father Barry Glen Dennagher's head."

"Well, that may be so. But I didn't bite nearly hard enough. Do you know what that stupid priest did at the meeting?"

"And you referred to his lordship as the 'damn bishop'."

"And with good reason. The meeting was unanimous in supporting the amended proposal to fix that dangerous bend at the two-mile stone. Everyone, that is, except for the bishop of Killala. At least that's how Father Glen Dennagher presented it. I hope I never have to meet that stupid man ever again."

"Aw now, don't be getting yourself upset. You'll get the chance to meet Father Barry Glen Dennagher again in three days' time. He is saying Mass in St Bawn's on Sunday."

"Really? Well, I don't care. I still think he is a nasty stupid man. And I won't hesitate to tell him that either."

"I wouldn't call Father Barry Glen Dennagher stupid. He speaks Hebrew, Greek and Latin. He is an expert in Canon Law, in Theology and in the rubrics of liturgical rites. He is more knowledgeable than the bishop himself, hence he holds a position of importance in the diocese. He is also an amateur boxer – he **was** an amateur before joining the priesthood. He is an avid supporter of keep-fit programs. Sure you can see him in his boxing shorts every morning running along the strand in Enniscrone punching the air with his fists."

"Why does he go to Enniscrone to keep fit? Sure that's in County Sligo."

"He lives near there, in Kilglass, County Sligo. It's just outside Ballina, and even though it is in County Sligo, it is part of the Diocese of Killala. You realise that our diocese encompasses part of north Mayo and a small part of Sligo?"

"Well, he should stay put in Enniscrone or in the diocesan office in Ballina, and not be out and about upsetting things around the county. And what is he doing coming to St Bawn's?"

"That's to do with the Confirmation. Confirmation will be held on Sunday 18 August…"

"And isn't the bishop himself coming to confirm the children?"

"…and Father Glen Dennagher is coming this Sunday, one week before the Confirmation, to examine the candidates on their catechism after the Mass. Doubtless, he will also remind me of the correct protocols of proper conduct."

"Regardless of all that, what are we to do about the dangerous bend at the two-mile stone? Have you any pull with the bishop to get him to soften his objection to the project?"

"Well now, I have been thinking about that. After Father Glen Dennagher examines the children, I would like a few parishioners to meet him here in the parochial house. I was thinking of yourself and Murf, and our benefactor, Casey of the general store."

"And what will that achieve?"

Canon MacMorrow places the tip of his index finger to his forehead and twinkles. "Ah now, Antoinette, you must have faith in God – and in his humble servants."

Sunday 11 August 1946. Father Barry Glen Dennagher presides at Mass in St Bawn's Church. During the Mass, he gives his favourite sermon – some would say, his only sermon – on a homiletic theme based on Mark 9:43-48 '*If your hand causes you to stumble, cut it off.'* He exhorts the people to follow the example of the founders of Killbawn – the monks of the monastic settlement in the ninth century who lived lives of poverty and humility in this very spot. "Do not be possessed by your possessions," he stresses. "If your wealth controls your life, cast it away; if drink controls your life, shun the pub!" The congregation agrees. This is the ideal to which all of them aspire, but they know equally well that they are unlikely to attain it. Most of the congregants silently resolve to advance a little bit closer to the saintly goal.

J. J. McPhee, the publican, is sitting in the first pew. He bites his lip. He likes to make extra profit by serving drinks under the counter well after closing time. He resolves to close the pub at closing time – unless pressured by his loyal patrons to accommodate them, and then… well, at least it is a goal worth considering.

Casey, the general merchant, sitting midway back, bows his head. He realises that he is guilty of under-the-table transactions to make a sale at every opportunity. He resolves to quietly place two half-crowns in the penny collection today, rather than his usual custom of flamboyantly displaying a silver half-crown aloft and dropping it noisily on top of the copper coins. Such is the effect of Father Barry Glen Dennagher's sermon on the parishioners of St Bawn's Church.

At 12:00 noon, at the conclusion of Mass, Father Barry Glen Dennagher conducts the examination of candidates for Confirmation. Seventeen school children, nine-year-olds and ten-year-olds, sit in the front pews and answer the questions he directs to them – questions relating to the Creed and to the Commandments of the Church. Master McGinnelly and Mistress Connolly sit in the back pew. They smile with pride at their students answering the catechism questions confidently and promptly. Murf, Casey and Doctor McBratt sit alongside.

Doctor McBratt is especially impressed with the ease in which Father Glen Dennagher relates to the children. When they correctly answer the question on fasting regulations – 'must be fasting from midnight and have the right intention' – he defines 'midnight' for their edification. There is 'clock midnight,' he explains, and there is 'true midnight'. He holds their attention as he explains how the position of longitude relative to the prime meridian determines the time. And further, there is the impact of summer time, which also must be taken into account. "Here in Killbawn, in summer, true midnight is actually thirty-two minutes past one o'clock." This is not totally foreign to the children. They understand that 'clock time' is in some way unreal. Those who live on farms operate on 'old time' all year long; the town dwellers operate on 'new time', which alters from winter time to summer time.

At the conclusion of the examination, Father Glen Dennagher instructs the children to stand. At this point, he commences singing. All present expect him to lead the children in a hymn, but he surprises them by rendering "Heads, Shoulders, Knees and Toes..." He demonstrates stretching exercises in tempo to the song. The children gladly participate, amused that such activity is approved in a church.

Father Glen Dennagher holds up three fingers. He makes reference to the Trinity, to the Three Divine Virtues and, surprisingly, to the Three Pillars of Good Health – a healthy body, for a healthy mind, for a healthy soul.

In the back pew, Master McGinnelly and Mistress Connolly look at each other quizzically. This is a novel idea; nonetheless, it meets with their approval. Father Glen Dennagher gives parting advice to the children – to continue religious instruction for their spiritual maturity; to continue their education for their mental development and, lastly, to live clean active lives for a healthy body. "There is a circus coming to Killbawn on Sunday the twenty-fifth – you see the posters already displayed around town. I want you all to go to the circus and study the acrobats, to see what a healthy body can do with discipline and training. I will be there and I hope to see you all there too."

Father Glen Dennagher blesses the children and dismisses them. The five adults in the back pew look at each other and smile with approval. Maybe Father Barry Glen Dennagher isn't so bad after all.

A few minutes later, Father Barry Glen Dennagher is seated in the meeting room of the parochial house. Seated around the table are Canon MacMorrow, Inspector Murphy, Doctor McBratt and Casey (who goes solely by his surname). Casey is the owner of the general store. He is a generous benefactor to St Bawn's Parish and is not above making a sale at every opportunity. Father Glen Dennagher gives no indication that he recognises Murf or the doctor. Surely he must remember them from the county council meeting of four days' ago. He places his briefcase on the table and extracts a leather folder of writing material within which are his instructions on the protocol of Confirmation and the bishop's visit. He starts with the 'Ecce Sacerdos' and proceeds through the entire rite.

Throughout his discourse, the canon nods respectfully and patiently. "Father Barry," he says, "I should make a few notes. Permit me to take a few sheets of paper from you."

"Of course. Help yourself." Father Glen Dennagher slides his folder closer to Canon MacMorrow.

The canon extracts two sheets of paper. Murf notices that the canon chooses two sheets of letterhead rather than two blank sheets. Murf continues to observe the canon. The canon is fully cognisant of the rite of Confirmation and on the protocol pertaining to a bishop's visit. He has no need to make notes. Does the crafty canon have need of diocesan letterhead? What is he up to? Murf glances around the table. No one else appears to have noticed the canon's devious move.

The canon speaks again. "Father Barry, the children answered their catechism questions correctly?"

"They were excellent."

"Perhaps each should be presented with a little cross by the bishop?"

"Excellent idea. I'll note that." Father Glen Dennagher retrieves his folder.

"Blest by the bishop with water from St Bawn's holy well."

"Excellent." Father Glen Dennagher continues to note.

"At the very site of the holy well itself."

Father Glen Dennagher ceases writing. "The site of the holy well? Where's that?"

"Oh, it is just a few miles outside town on the Coast Road at Tubberbawn. It's not far from here."

"I don't think the bishop…"

The remaining three take the canon's cue and interject with supporting comments. "The road to the holy well swings around to connect with the R314, the Killala Road, and thence to Ballina. It will not take the bishop out of his way at all," Murf comments. He sees where this is going. The canon is scheming to have the bishop travel out the Blackwater Road to experience the hazardous bend at the two-mile stone firsthand.

"And won't it look nice with papal flags out at the well?" Casey adds, calculating that he will make some sales on flags.

"Oh, the bishop's visit to St Bawn's holy well has not occurred in ten years. This will surely be an occasion for the people," Doctor McBratt enhances the case in support of the canon.

"An occasion for the Connaught Telegraph to cover the event," concludes the canon.

Father Glen Dennagher resumes writing. "I do believe you are right. This is an occasion for his lordship to honour the patron saint and connect with his flock, and to have coverage of the event in the Connaught Telegraph. Yes, I'll note that in his lordship's schedule." Four pairs of eyes interconnect to register a successful gambit.

Two hours later, the crafty canon meets with the wily Casey. "Casey, I need you to do something for me."

"Is this to do with the bishop's visit to the holy well? You know that he will need to pass by the two-mile stone to get there?"

"Yes. I know that."

"And he drives a big brute of a car and all."

"He doesn't drive, Casey. Father Tommy Martin drives the bishop's car. But you are right about his car. It is a Jaguar Mark VII."

"Well, Father Tommy Martin will have a hell of a time getting that big car around the sharp bend in the road. Is he a good wheelman – this Father Tommy?"

"Father Tommy Martin is not just his wheelman; he is the bishop's personal assistant. He attends to the bishop's needs and carries his bags…"

"His bag-man."

"…and turns the pages in the lectionary for him when he reads, and so on."

"His lackey."

"Casey, next Sunday I want you to proceed ahead of the bishop from St Bawn's to the holy well to ensure that the route is adequately marked with big papal flags."

"You want me to hang yellow-and-white flags for the bishop along the road? And sure what will I hang them big flags on? Do you want posts erected too?"

"Ah, no, Casey. Just use the existing road signs."

Casey gets the picture. With flags draped on the road signs, Father Tommy might miss the warning signs to slow down for the bend at the two-mile stone. The crafty canon is up to something.

Sunday 18 August 1946. At noon, Casey drives from Killbawn to Tubberbawn on the Blackwater Road. Peter Meehan is with him. Peter, his delivery man, is a wee man with long limbs and long arms. Where climbing is required, Peter is as nimble as a monkey. At intervals, along the three-mile processional route to the holy well at Tubberbawn, Casey has Peter climb up a tree or a signpost to hang papal yellow-and-white flags. Peter is happy to help Casey in marking the processional route in this way. Nearing the two-mile stone, Peter asks Casey, "Mr Casey, why didn't you do all this flag-hanging yesterday. Now we have to rush to get it done in a hurry. Sure look, the flags are not hung proper. Y'see they are covering up the road signs. Don't you think that's a dangerous thing to do?"

"Ah, not at all, Peter. Sure it's only for a few hours. What harm can it do in two hours?"

"Well, the guards won't like it."

"We put up the flags fast, just ahead of the procession, and then we take them down fast afterwards. The guards will not know of it. So there. Come on, let's finish the job before the bishop comes along." Thus, they complete the task. Minutes later, when the bishop's car travels the route to the holy well, the signs forewarning traffic of the dangerous bend are no longer visible.

2:00pm. It is a quiet afternoon in the garda station in Killbawn. The tranquillity of the station is disturbed by the blustering entrance of Danny the Divil. The police officers look at Danny the Divil in amazement. It is two in the afternoon and Danny the Divil is still sober? It was only two weeks ago that the Divil burst into the garda station in this same manner.

"I've just come from the two-mile stone. There's a car stuck in the ditch out there again."

District Officer Superintendent David Fox speaks to him. "Danny, is the doctor's car stuck in the ditch?"

"No, not the doctor's car. Sure am I not after driving here in the doctor's car? It's the bishop's car what's stuck there."

The bishop requires special attention, so Fox decides to go to the scene of the accident himself. He takes Garda O'Reilly and Garda Caldwell to accompany him to the two-mile stone. Driving along the Blackwater Road, he notices Casey folding up the large papal flags. Fox is impressed at Casey's diligence in removing the decorative flags so promptly. These flags, if not promptly removed, can become detached and blow about and prove to be a hazard to traffic. He does not suspect that these same flags concealed the warning signs on the road just a few minutes earlier. Casey waves respectfully to Superintendent Fox as he drives by – and smiles inwardly.

Arriving at the accident scene, Fox observes that the front passenger-side wheel of the bishop's car is lodged in the soft earth of the sheugh. A small car could be pushed out by a few stout men. But the bishop's car is too heavy. To make matters worse, it is a Sunday – there are no farm tractors out working today; and there is no break-down service available to assist a stranded car. There is no vehicle on hand to dislodge the car from the ditch until the following morning.

The passenger side of the bishop's car is lodged inside the drainage ditch. The bishop is furious at his driver, Father Tommy Martin, blaming him for the mishap. Eventually, he fatigues from his blustering and decides to make his way out of the car. To accomplish this, the bishop is required to step into stagnant water. From this lowly position, he fumbles clumsily to extricate himself from the water-logged ditch. He claws his way up the muddy embankment of the sheugh and eventually manages to reach level ground. He kneels with one knee in the wet mud of the embankment and reaches out his right hand to Superintendent Fox for assistance in order to stand upright. Fox expresses sympathy for the bishop's plight and inquires if he is hurt. He rushes over to take hold of the bishop's outraised hand. The bishop's feet are wet and his black clerical clothes are noticeably smeared with dirt and he fears that he may slide back into the mire of the sheugh.

While in this undignified pose, the bishop is blinded by the flash of a camera. The reporter from the Connaught Telegraph smiles at him. The indignity of being caught in an unflattering pose is a greater injury to the bishop than the actual car accident itself. The bishop is red-faced with fury knowing that this is how he will be depicted in the local newspaper – kneeling in mud with his hand outstretched appealingly. He orders his driver, Father Tommy Martin, to accost the reporter and prohibit him from lodging the story, with descriptive pictures, for publication. Father Martin hurries off to locate the reporter, relieved to get some distance from the enraged bishop. Alas, he is too late. The astute reporter disappears and the bishop is unable to deal with him. And to add insult to injury, Danny the Divil, smelling of whiskey, drives the enraged bishop back to St Bawn's Church in the doctor's car.

Back in St Bawn's parochial house, the bishop paces up and down ranting. He refuses to have anyone drive him to

Ballina. He will not endure another Killbawn inebriate driving him any farther. He has Father Tommy Martin contact Father Barry Glen Dennagher to come and pick him up. And he instructs Father Tommy to remain in Killbawn until the following morning and to drive the Jaguar Mark VII to Ballina as soon as it is hauled back onto the solid surface of the road.

Canon MacMorrow, Doctor McBratt, Inspector Murphy and Casey attempt to pacify the bishop. They express sympathy for his plight. Of course, the blame lies squarely with the Mayo County Council for failing to improve the road and maintaining it in a safe state. Canon MacMorrow suggests that, since they must wait a half hour or more for Father Glen Dennagher to arrive from Kilglass, they should make good use of the time and draft a complaint letter to the county council. The bishop considers this a brilliant suggestion and instructs Father Tommy to draw up a letter.

"Ah, no, your lordship, don't bother Father Tommy," says the canon. "Sure he would only struggle with my old wreck of a typewriter. I'll type the letter myself right now."

Within a minute the canon has prepared a letter addressed to Mayo County Council. The letter recommends a reconstruction and reconfiguration of the Blackwater Road at the bend at the two-mile stone by cutting through the hill at the place known locally as 'The Famine Field', thus bypassing the dangerous bend. He hands the letter to the bishop. The three co-conspirators hold their collective breath as the bishop reads the letter and signs it. The bishop does not question how the canon was so quick in preparing the letter, or how he was able to type it on Killala diocesan letterhead. The bishop hands the signed letter to the canon, who hands it in turn to Doctor McBratt.

Doctor McBratt waves the letter and says, "I'll have the Divil deliver this first thing in the morning, my Lord."

"The Divil? What divil?"

"I mean, Danny, my driver, my Lord. He will deliver this letter to the county council office at nine o'clock tomorrow morning."

The bishop regards this as some positive outcome from his mishap and inconvenience. He calms down. Mrs Friel, the housekeeper, enters with a tray of tea and cake. Mrs Friel craftily ensures that the tray contains cherry pound cake, reputed to be the bishop's favourite treat. The bishop views the contents of the tray with approval and settles in to partake of the tasty delight. He is settled from his earlier tirade and calmly awaits the arrival of Father Glen Dennagher.

The conspirators take their leave. They are anxious to have the letter delivered before the bishop changes his mind. Thankfully, Father Glen Dennagher has not yet arrived at St Bawn's. They remember that he was the diocesan representative at the county council meeting and was the sole objector to the road-building project. They cross their fingers and hope that Father Glen Dennagher doesn't learn of the bishop's letter, at least not until it is safely delivered to the county council.

On Monday morning, the bishop's letter is successfully delivered to the county engineer at the department of roads in Castlebar. Sean Macilmyra is surprised to receive the letter from the Diocese of Killala. He opens the envelope in expectation of seeing a reiteration of the bishop's objection to road works encroaching on the Famine Field. He is surprised at the unexpected contents of the letter. He is quick to realise the import of it. He immediately calls for an extraordinary meeting of the council to reconsider 'The Devil's Bend Project'. Thus, the project is revived and is fast-tracked for approval.

CHAPTER SIX

FATHER GLEN DENNAGHER VISITS

Killbawn, County Mayo, Ireland
Sunday 18 August 1946

On Sunday evening, 'The Home' resounds with music from the band of The John Edge Travelling Show. 'The Home' is actually 'Home of Fitzpatrick-McHugh' – land donated to the community by two local landowners, Fitzpatrick and McHugh. The Home is the site of the sports field and is a popular venue for outdoor events in Killbawn. The circus is in town today. The large tent, termed 'the big top', is erected. People are streaming in as the band welcomes them with the popular music of the day. The John Edge Travelling Show is at pains to inform patrons that it is NOT a circus – there are no performing animals – it is a travelling show featuring acrobats, magicians and musicians. Out of habit, everyone refers to it familiarly as a circus.

Father Barry Glen Dennagher parks his car near the entrance. It is five minutes to eight. He glances up at the name of the park displayed on the large wooden welcome sign beside the entrance gate alongside rules of behaviour and penalties pertaining to littering offences. He smiles. He has reasons to smile. First, he smiles at the misspelling of the word 'Home'. The flat ground here, situated beside the bank of the Blackwater River, was once in the riverbed. As mud was deposited over time, the course of the river shifted until the accumulated mud became an island. A flood from a burst dam in 1917 dumped a large volume of mud and sand in the main channel and forced the stream of the river to reroute through a secondary channel. With the previous main channel completely blocked, the river island became attached to the adjoining land. Thus the holm was formed – dry land formed from the riverbed is termed 'a holm' – hence, the misspelling of the homophonic word. Regardless, the denizens of Killbawn are quite content with the spelling 'h-o-m-e'.

The second reason why he is smiling is because of his favourite adage – '*If your hand causes you to stumble, cut it off.*' – and in how this adage was successfully employed here at 'the Home'. When the field here was formed from the holm, a dispute arose between the two neighbouring farms. Previously, the river was the agreed-upon boundary line of the adjoining farms, but when the river changed course and the island joined the adjacent land, Fitzpatrick and McHugh failed to agree on a new boundary line. Throughout 1918 and 1919 the dispute escalated to a feud, threatening property and livestock with malicious damage. Fitzpatrick had the stronger argument, claiming that the previous land measurements should remain unchanged notwithstanding the altered course of the river. But Fitzpatrick had few supporters due to his pro-British stance during the Anglo-Irish war from 1919 to 1922. Pro-British landowners were subjected to threats and property damage by republican rebels. Many vacated their homes and sold off their properties in the face of extreme ostracism. Happily, in Killbawn, a truce was achieved when Fitzpatrick agreed to donate his disputed parcel of land to the community, inviting McHugh to do likewise. McHugh, not wishing to be outdone by Fitzpatrick, agreed. The disputed land, the source of their enmity, was 'cut off' from them, thus removing the source of their hostility. Fitzpatrick was warmly accepted back into the community and peace between the feuding farmers was restored. The current generation of Fitzpatricks and McHughs operate their farms in a congenial atmosphere of friendship and cooperation.

There is a third reason for his smile. This is his fourth attendance at the travelling show this year, one more than last year. Marvin the Magyar will be delighted to see him again. In the past week, Father Glen Dennagher attended performances of the show in Killala, in Ballina and in Owenbeg. At each venue, he renewed his acquaintance with Marvin and the Marvellous Magyars. He greatly admires their acrobatic skills and he hopes to include some of their routines into his own exercise regimen. He is looking forward to meeting the Marvellous Magyars once more tonight.

Father Glen Dennagher enters the big top at eight o'clock as the band plays 'A Bicycle Built for Two'.

At twenty minutes past nine, Father Glen Dennagher leaves the travelling show. He is smiling again – this time in contentment. He is feeling good. He decides to drive along the Blackwater Road to the Coast Road and join the Killala Road five miles farther up. He is humming 'Daisy, Daisy…'

He passes by the old workhouse – now a storage building for farm equipment. He drives slowly and calls to mind the short ill-fated history of the workhouse. It was opened and operated to provide famine relief in 1846 when the potato crop failed the second year in a row. It would have been evident in August 1846 that there would be no potato harvest in Mayo that year. The first victims of the workhouse relief labour would have occurred right here in Killbawn, one hundred years ago.

As a historian, Glen Dennagher has a dedicated interest in The Great Famine and he is keenly aware of its disastrous economic consequences. As a relief program, the workhouse was woefully lacking and, for all intents and purposes, was judged a failure. The last inmates were removed from the workhouse in September 1848. Some feeble attempts were made to put the building to some further altruistic use. But the building was deemed unfit for human occupation. It sat derelict for thirty years until the property – the workhouse building and lands – was acquired by the adjacent farm. The current owner is Pat Delahunty, who utilises the land in crop rotation, except for a section of the hill facing north. This section is reserved solely for cattle-grazing. Out of respect, the revered ground of 'the Famine Field' is never broken or ploughed for crop cultivation.

And there it is, 'the Famine Field', situated at the bend at the two-mile stone. Father Glen Dennagher brings his car to a halt. He rolls down the side window and studies the field with interest. He is curious as to why there are little pink ribbons pegged into the ground at intervals along the slope of the dolmen hill. A little mound of sand is present at each ribbon. Had he not peered intently into the field he would not have noticed the little ribbons lodged into the grass-covered ground. He speculates that this must be the result of some local commemoration to mark the one-hundredth anniversary of the first burials (unconfirmed) in the Famine Field. Before he can wonder any further, Father Glen Dennagher hears a car-horn honk behind him and realises that he is blocking the traffic on the narrow road. He puts the car into gear and continues on his way home to County Sligo.

CHAPTER SEVEN

PROBING THE FAMINE FIELD

Killbawn, County Mayo, Ireland
Monday 19 August 1946

At 8:20am, Sean Macilmyra, the county engineer, parks his car in Pat Delahunty's farmyard, with prior permission of course, and steps out. There are two other cars parked in the yard, clearly not farm vehicles, judging from the absence of mud splatter on the sides. His surveyor colleague, Ned Reid, exits through the passenger door and walks back to the boot of the car to retrieve his surveyor equipment. He shoulders his theodolite and tripod and both men walk side by side to the north slope of the dolmen hill and thence to the Famine Field one hundred yards away. Once across the spine of the hill, they spot a party of four at work in the lower portion of the field. This is an archaeological team from the College of Arts, Social Science, and Celtic Studies (University College Galway). The team has been working here since Thursday at the invitation of Sean. Sean and Gerald Folan belong to a tight circle of friends. When Sean told him that Mayo County Council was about to excavate a famine field in north Mayo, subject to preliminary investigative probes, he jumped at the opportunity to engage in an archaeological excavation of the site.

Professor Gerald Folan is the Dean of Arts in the University. He is a large man, still active as a hooker in rugby football, who is given to quoting adages in Latin (hence his nickname – 'Geraldus Magnus'). He is dressed in a three-piece tweed suit, a Panama hat and wellington boots. This is much more clothing than is prudent to wear in the mild August weather. It is clear that Gerald is not intent on any physical activity here in the field. He has just dropped by to check on any possible progress on the dig. The actual workers are his assistant, archaeologist Sally Plunkett, and two archaeological students: B Tobin (actually Brian Tobin, but known exclusively as 'B Tobin') and Sandra McCurry, all of whom Sean met at the commencement of the project.

"Hello, Gerry!" Sean addresses his friend.

"Ave, Sean," he replies.

Sean smiles inwardly. He ought to have addressed him with a 'Hail'.

Ned Reid is already fully prepared and is working on marking the area for the road-building project. Last week, he marked the spots where investigative probes are to be conducted by the archaeological team. Sally and her team are required to employ soil samplers to determine the presence of, or absence of, a historical famine-era burial site in the path of the proposed road. Each spot is plainly identified by a distinctive piece of pink ribbon pegged into the ground. The locations of Ned's markings are in an area of the field where the drumlin depth ranges from two to four feet. This is a suitable depth for an auger.

The archaeological team is prepared to search for artefacts and ecofacts with their instruments of excavation – a soil-sampler auger, a sieve, a folding table, small trowels, nail-brushes, paint-brushes and toothbrushes. At each marking, the archaeological team inserts an auger into the ground, twisting it down to the rock base of the drumlin. The screw of the auger holds the soil sample and, when extracted, the drilled-out materials of each probe are examined methodically from top to bottom. Operating the auger is a simple task. Very little effort is required to bore into the sandy substratum of the dolmen. It is silent except for the rhythmic grunting sounds of the operator. However, some effort is required to withdraw it from the ground, whereupon there is a faint sucking sound followed by a sudden rush of air filling the vacuum of the borehole. Borings are conducted with care. Should they encounter any resistance, or an object other than drumlin sand, the boring would cease. Then, they would conduct a wider delicate hand-probe using a small trowel and toothbrush. So far, they have encountered only sand beneath the thin layer of topsoil.

Gerald surveys the scene before him. "Maybe we'll be lucky today and strike some evidence of a famine-era burial site."

Sean replies, "Maybe we'll be lucky and NOT find any such evidence."

Their objectives are in opposition. The archaeological team hopes to uncover evidence of a famine-era graveyard. In contrast, the Mayo County Council Department of Roads needs to ensure that the proposed road will not disturb a burial site.

Gerald Folan takes his leave, "Vale! Valete!" (Farewell to one and all.) Sean Macilmyra walks down to the hard-working trio. Sally Plunkett is extracting the auger carefully, while B Tobin and Sandra McCurry kneel with eyes fixed on the materials slowing rising up from the bore-hole. Sally extracts the auger fully and lays it flat on a sheet. Seeing Sean approach, they break from their work.

Sean greets them. "Find anything strange or interesting, Sally?"

Sally answers him. "Below ground – no. Above ground – yes." Sean raises one eyebrow quizzically. To clarify, Sally elaborates. "We have not located anything of archaeological interest – not a button or a bead. But on Thursday afternoon, at one o'clock or so, a quiet man stood down there by the road and studied us for over two hours. On Friday, he came back and stood inside the fence. Throughout the afternoon, he made his way progressively closer to us. He remained here until we left. By that time he was no more than five feet from us, studying what we were doing."

"Did he bother you?"

"Oh, no. He was just a little strange. He was dressed in an old suit greatly smeared with oil, and he drank at intervals from a small bottle of whiskey."

"Ah, that sounds like Danny the Divil. And did he say anything to you?"

"Yes. He said that he knows who we are. He looked at me and said, 'You're the arsy-ologist, aren't you?' And he spoke to B Tobin and Sandra and said, 'And you youngsters are the arty-feckers.' That's all he said." Sean turns his face and scratches his chin in an effort to suppress a smile. Sally continues, "So, we just went on working. He continued to look on and take quick swigs of whiskey at intervals."

Sean remarks sympathetically, "Oh, that's Danny the Divil all right. He drinks 'Three Swallows'. He is the doctor's driver. He drives by here every day when the doctor is on her professional rounds. Undoubtedly, he would have seen you here in the Famine Field and is curious. He has a particular interest in the two-mile stone and the Famine Field. Now you may find this hard to believe, Sally, but Danny the Divil is the person most responsible for getting this project off the ground."

"What? This 'divil' person?"

"Don't underestimate him, Sally. Although he is an inebriate and uneducated, had circumstances been different, he might have been here today standing in **my** shoes. That's life, and that's Danny the Divil."

"Oh, you're having us on, Mr Macilmyra. The Divil as county engineer? Oh, sure!" Attracted by the laughter, Ned Reid wanders over to be within earshot. Sally shouts to him as he approaches. "Mr Macilmyra here says that the Divil could make county engineer!" Ned attempts a feeble laugh.

He looks at his boss and stops. Ned is not sure what Sally means by 'the Divil', and he cannot tell when Sean Macilmyra is joking – he may be making a point for serious consideration.

Sensing his discomfort, Sean speaks to him. "Ned, I'll have someone from the county council pick you up at four as I must get back to the office now."

"Hold on, Mr Macilmyra," Sally addresses him. "Sure we can give Ned a lift in our car. There's room for the four of us, and sure aren't we all going to Castlebar anyways?"

"All right, if that's agreeable."

Sally returns her attention to the soil sample in the auger. She inspects it and determines that there is nothing of interest in the sandy material. She clears the sand from the auger, spilling it onto the sheet. The trio slides the sheet and tilts it to the relative bore-hole. The sand trickles down the sloping sheet and into the hole from whence it came, leaving a little sandy mound atop. They turn their attention to the next marked spot two feet away.

At 12:30pm Sally calls a break. She glances over the marked area to judge their progress. At this rate of progress, and provided they fail to encounter anything of archaeological interest, they should conclude their work by 4:00pm tomorrow. She checks with Ned Reid to confirm that all the markings for the required probes are in place. Ned confirms that he had finished placing the markings on Friday. He is currently engaged in marking the route of where the new road will cut through the dolmen hill and skirt the inlet shoreline.

The four workers fetch their lunch-bags and walk to the Delahunty farmhouse where Mrs Delahunty, in keeping with the local custom of hospitality, boils the water for their tea. Thereupon they avail of the shelter of the haybarn and consume their bread-and-butter sandwiches in comfort. Sally has the added luxury of a hard-boiled egg. Ned's sandwich has a thick layer of butter on one slice of bread and no butter at all on the accompanying slice. He is content that the butter content averages out overall.

At 1:30pm, they are refreshed and eager to get back to work. Just then, Danny the Divil drives into the farmyard. He parks the doctor's 10HP Ford Prefect alongside Sally's 8hp car. The Divil goes to the boot of his car and removes a 4' plank of wood. Then, carrying the plank balanced on his shoulder, he walks off in the direction of the Famine Field.

When activity resumes in the Famine Field a few minutes later, the Divil sits on his plank and studies the archaeological team at work. Between swigs of whiskey, he mutters compliments and encouragement. "Ah, sure 'tis great work you're doing. So when will work on the road actually start?"

No one responds. It is unclear whether the Divil is muttering to himself, or if he is addressing a real question to the team. The team is focused on their work. They endure the annoying midges from the marsh, and they ignore the annoying comments from the Divil. Sally concentrates on the auger's progress. She stops when the augur is two-feet-four-inches deep. This is unexpected. B Tobin and Sandra look up at her from their kneeling positions. The rock base is four feet down at this point. Why did Sally stop? In recognition of their questioning look, Sally says to them, "There is something there. I can feel it in the ground, two feet down."

Although she says this softly as in imparting a secret, both the Divil and Ned Reid hear her clearly. The Divil drops his whiskey-bottle; Ned parts from his theodolite. They both approach close to Sally and the auger. Sally grabs a trowel and strikes the top of the auger. She listens to the sound of her tapping. Then she gingerly extracts the auger out of the ground and places it on the sheet.

"All right, you two. I want this examined and brushed and the contents sieved. We are looking for anything foreign to dolmen moraine – seeds, roots, fibres, ANYTHING."

Sandra and B Tobin jump to it with urgency. What is down there, they wonder. Sally kneels down and peers into the bore-hole. Turing to Ned Reid, she says, "Ned, hand me one of your sticks." She refers to Ned's supply of three-foot-long rods which he cuts into six-inch lengths to employ as marker pegs. Sally inserts a rod into the hole and feels around using the rod as an extended finger. She withdraws the rod and holds her hand to her face while considering the next course of action. Before she can pronounce her decision, the Divil unnerves her by beating her to the same conclusion.

"Whatever is down there," he says. "You can't be going and digging straight down. Sure you'll only damage it. Dig over there, where you know there is nothing but sand down to the rock bottom, and work sideways."

"Damn it." She curses inwardly. "The drunken Divil is right and he came to the decision faster than I." Of course, the appropriate excavation in this instance is a horizontal excavation. She removes her hand from her face thus smearing her brow with soil. This annoys her further. She attempts to brush the soil away with her other hand and realises that she is still holding the rod. She drops the rod and rubs this now-freed hand against her head, but smears even more soil on her face. Thus distracted, she fails to speak before the Divil continues imparting his advice.

"Bore two more holes. Here and here, just to be sure."

These are 'cautionary probes' to ensure the safety of the area under consideration. How did the Divil know this? Sally wonders.

"And while you are doing this, run up to the farm and get spades and shovels. It won't take long to dig down through sand."

Sally coughs and finds her voice. "Yes, let's do this. Sandra and B Tobin, have you finished sieving the sample?"

"Yes. And there is just the usual sand and gravel. Nothing else."

"Right-oh. Now here's what we do. B Tobin and Ned, run back to the car and get the spade and shovel from the boot. If Delahunty is in the farmyard, ask him for help. We can do with a few more spades and shovels down here. Meanwhile, Sandra and I will conduct cautionary probes. This will determine the precise spot to commence digging – probably two feet away from the place of our primary interest. Then we will conduct a horizontal excavation, a gentle excavation with brushes and toothbrushes."

By issuing these instructions with authority, Sally considers that her status is restored. She looks at the Divil with renewed curiosity. The Divil returns to his plank, oblivious to the unsettling effect he has had on Sally. He sits down and retrieves his whiskey-bottle from where he dropped it earlier. He drains it, replaces the stopper and places it in his pocket. In the same continuous motion, he extracts a second bottle and settles into a comfortable position – watching the heightened activity while calmly sipping his whiskey. Sally reflects on the import of Sean Macilmyra's earlier comment pertaining to the Divil.

Before Sally can further dwell on the Divil and his intrusion – albeit a positive and constructive contribution – her attention is diverted to the return of B Tobin and Ned who are accompanied by four farmhands, all bearing picks and shovels and snub-nosed spades. Sally directs them where to dig, in what manner, and to what depth. The Divil adds, "Make enough room for two arty-feckers to work down there." The farmhands grin at the Divil's comments but follow his advice nevertheless. They take to the task enthusiastically. They are strong and skilled at this work.

They expertly dig and shovel the earth and quickly hollow out a trench in the drumlin to Sally's exact specifications.

Sally views the resulting pit. The digging stopped short of the bedrock four feet below. The strata are visible as horizontal lines in the wall of the pit. At the top is the humus level comprised of the growing grass and previous grasses not fully decomposed. The farmhands refer to this as 'the sod'. Sandra ensures that the excavated sod is kept separate from the 'A surface' which, in turn, is heaped apart from 'the spoil'. The 'A surface' is a three-inch layer of black organic matter which imparts petrichor, the pleasant earthy scent of bacteria-rich soil. The 'B subsoil' is a mere one inch thick. It is brown and has a weak structure. The 'C substratum' is four inches below the surface, only half a spade-depth, and continues to the bedrock. This stratum is comprised of neutral-smelling sand with some pebbles present. It is mid-brown and crumbles easily when exposed to the air, whereupon it changes to a lighter colour of yellow-brown.

B Tobin and Sandra apply themselves to the task of brushing the wall of the trench deftly and gently. They advance, millimetre by millimetre, through the crumbling sand in the direction of the borehole, to the location of where the auger probe was aborted at a depth of two feet four inches. At intervals, they employ a small hand-shovel to clear the dislodged sand from the pit. Sally lies face down flat on the ground at the edge of the archaeological trench. She peers intently at every grain of sand and gravel that is dislodged. She stretches her arms down into the trench and feels along the side with her fingers, closer and closer to… to what?

"Stop!" Everyone freezes. "All right," says Sally. "I'll take over from here." Eight bodies crowd around the trench – B Tobin and Sandra, Ned and the Divil, and the four farmhands. Their attention is fixed on Sally, who is now the sole occupant of the trench. She skillfully employs a pastry brush as delicately as any pastry chef. Something other than sand or gravel or soil is exposed by the brushing. It appears to be cloth or fabric. Sally avoids invading any farther but works along the edge in an attempt to ascertain the size of the item. Could it be a sack? Or a bag of someone's hidden loot or treasure deposited here to be retrieved later?

The Divil comments, "Cloth. That can't be more'n a few years there. Sure cloth disintegrates in the ground. What do you make of it, Arsy-ologist?"

Sally blinks in irritation. The Divil is right again. This is cloth, likely wool. In soil this moist, wool would not remain intact beyond a year, three years at most. Sally now works horizontally along the edge of the cloth material in an attempt to determine its length. She measures her progress. At thirty-six inches she rests from her effort. She leans back against the bank of the trench and attempts to picture the exposed line of cloth as it once had been. She wonders how much more is still hidden from view in the moraine. The edge is roughly in a straight line – not quite. It bulges and dips slightly along its length. This does not look like a swag bag. It is shaped more like a leg… Sally is unable to finish the thought. She drops her brush and measuring tape and presses hard back against the bank in an attempt to gain more distance from the exposed cloth.

Sandra and B Tobin read her face. It displays a realisation of recognition. "What is it?" they ask. Sally remains still and silent. They press her for an answer. "Do you know what it is, Sally?"

Sally recovers sufficiently to give a response. "This cloth is, is…" She struggles to say what is in her mind. "A lady's stocking."

"No, it's not."

All eyes turn to look at the Divil. He walks to the edge of the trench, takes a quick swig, and continues to speak. "A lady's stocking ends here." He slaps his thigh. "That thing yonder goes higher than here." At this, he slaps his pelvic area. "And no lady wears heavy woollen stuff like that. School-girls do. But school-girls are not as tall as that leg down there."

The Divil's comments rile her. And agitated, Sally argues her case to him. "So it isn't a stocking; it's tights." She knows what tights are, having worn them herself when she was twelve years old. But the Divil is correct about the height. Sally was not tall at twelve-years-old. "Tights on a tall girl. And what do YOU know about stocking and tights, Divil?"

The Divil ignores her retort. He looks past her and comments to the farmhands. "That's a leper down there," pointing to the piece of exposed cloth.

The four farmhands nod in agreement. "Oh, the Divil is right. That's a leper for sure."

"Mother of God!" Sally exclaims. "These ignorant country bumpkins know nothing about lepers or ladies' undergarments – or much about anything."

Ned intervenes. "Regardless, it looks like we have unearthed a dead body. We have to do something other than engaging in a pointless argument."

"Help me out of here, Ned." Ned grabs Sally's wrist and hauls her out of the trench. She sits down on the Divil's plank and composes herself. "First, B Tobin, secure the site. It needs to be examined by experts. We can't be tramping all over it." Ned gives B Tobin his supply of pink ribbon and his marker-stakes. B Tobin proceeds to cordon off the area around the trench.

"Second, Ned, take my car keys and drive into town and contact the county engineer. And we need to inform Geraldus Magnus. Can you look after that?"

Ned runs off across the hill to where Sally has parked her car. Sally remembers something and shouts after him, "And report it to the guards!" But Ned is already out of earshot. In frustration, she slaps her head with her muddy hand.

One of the farmhands informs her, "Sure the Divil went off to fetch the guards. He was off like a shot when he said 'leper'."

"Oh aye," says another one. "The minute he recognised that it was a dead leper down there, he was off like a greyhound after a hare."

Sally sits with her face in her hands. The blasted Divil is one step ahead of her once again. There is no more for her to do until the guards arrive.

Sally has been working this site since Thursday. For the first time since coming here, she feels the dampness. Her clothes are muddy, her face is smeared with soil. Her hair has come loose from her ponytail and falls over her eyes. She peers through muddy fingers at the road below. The malodorous fog from the marsh drifts in from the inlet and settles in the bend in the road. She is annoyed at the Divil. She wonders why. She reflects on what he said. The Divil was right all along. But he didn't have to undermine her position with his off-hand manner. They have definitely unearthed a corpse and the Divil was right to dash off to inform the guards. The exposed leg is undoubtedly human – man, woman or child. The Divil was right that the exposed leg may not be a girl's or a woman's leg. Yet, the stocking material suggests that neither is it a **man's** leg. The Divil appears to have deduced that. But what does he mean by a 'leper'? And how was he so quick to conclude that? It's as if he is sure – or knows.

CHAPTER EIGHT

THE LEPER IN THE FAMINE FIELD

Killbawn, County Mayo, Ireland
Monday afternoon 19 August 1946

At the garda station in Killbawn, the quiet of the day is disturbed by the blustering entrance of Danny the Divil. The police officers cease what they are doing and look at Danny the Divil in amazement. It is two-thirty in the afternoon and Danny the Divil is still sober? Something is truly wrong. By now he would have exhausted his maintenance dose and is apt to be cantankerous until he imbibes his afternoon requirements – but not until he is first relieved of his driving duties for Doctor McBratt. Something serious has disrupted Danny the Divil's routine and hence the peacefulness of the day. And from the serious look on Danny the Divil's face, this might even be a police matter.

"I've just come from the two-mile stone."

Garda O'Reilly asks, "What? Is there a car stuck in the ditch out there again?"

"There's no car stuck in the ditch. I've come to tell you that the arsy-ologist was digging in the Famine Field and came across a body."

"The archaeologist discovered bodily remains in the Famine Field? Sure that's great news, Danny. We always believed that famine victims were buried out there in the 1840s, but we never had any proof – not even any surviving records of interment from the workhouse."

"This is no famine victim, Guard O'Reilly. This is a leper."

"And sure Danny, how can you tell it's a leper? Back then, they all died from hunger or from hard work."

"Lord, Guard O'Reilly. Sure I know a leper when I see one. I can tell from the clothes they wear."

"Let me understand, Danny. The archaeologist uncovered a body…"

"…three foot down,"

"…and you can tell it's a leper from the clothes…" O'Reilly stops talking, his mouth fixed open. He suddenly realises that a body buried three feet below ground, still wearing discernible clothes, can only be a recent burial. "Homicide!" O'Reilly finds his voice. He lifts the desk phone to connect to the station superintendent. But for some reason, the familiar intercom number eludes him. Dropping the receiver, Garda O'Reilly runs up the stairs to the office of District Officer David Fox. Running along the hallway, he shouts 'homicide', even before he enters the DO's office. He enters the office and stops at Fox's desk, panting to regain settled breathing.

Superintendent Fox, the DO, seated at his desk with a copy of the Irish Independent in his hands, looks up at O'Reilly and says calmly, "Garda O'Reilly. You may enter. Now take a deep breath and tell me about 'the homicide'."

"The Divil just came in…"

"Danny Begley, I presume?"

"Yes. Danny the Divil. He says that there is a dead leper out at the Famine Field. The archaeologist found it, or so he says. And that he saw it with his own eyes."

"Danny Begley, 'the Divil', reports that he observed a dead body, a deceased leper, in the Famine Field?"

"Yes, sir. Just now. He is downstairs at the moment."

"And this is the same Danny the Divil who reports that he sees ghosts and spirits out by the Famine Field?"

"Ah, yes, sir."

"And that he drives right through them, whereupon they disappear and reappear later?"

"Yes, sir." O'Reilly feels that he may have jumped to the conclusion of homicide prematurely.

Fox rises from his chair and places the newspaper on his desk. "Come, Garda O'Reilly. If there is a report of a possible homicide we are obliged to investigate – even if the information is rendered by an inebriated Danny the Divil."

"Sir, he is not drunk. The Divil is downstairs, and he isn't drunk."

Fox consults his pocket-watch. "It is past fourteen-thirty hours. And you say that Danny the Divil is sober? Maybe his report is credible after all. Let's find out, shall we? If we have a homicide on our hands, Inspector Murphy will need to investigate."

"Sir. Inspector Murphy is not in his office."

Superintendent Fox proceeds down to the front desk followed by Garda O'Reilly. "Caldwell! Clancy! Where is Inspector Murphy?"

"We don't know where Murf, er, Inspector Murphy is right now."

Fox has interrupted the Divil's lengthy account of the discovery to Garda Caldwell and Garda Clancy. The Divil looks at Fox and says matter-of-factly, "Guard Murphy is at the Blackwater Bridge. I just saw him now as I came into town."

"And what is Inspector Murphy doing at the Blackwater Bridge?" He directs the question at the three police officers. The duty officer should know the location of all officers, or know which cases they are investigating.

Again, the Divil answers. "What is Guard Murphy doing at the Blackwater Bridge, you ask? When I saw him he was pitching pebbles into the river."

"O'Reilly!" Fox bellows. "Get the patrol car and fetch Inspector Murphy and drive him to the Famine Field."

"Ah, Sergeant," (The Divil is unclear as to the ranking within An Garda Síochána, and incorrectly addresses the superintendent as 'Sergeant') "sure I'll drive Guard Murphy out to the Famine Field myself in the doctor's car. I can fill him in on the way. It will be quicker than waiting for Guard O'Reilly and the patrol car."

"Fine." And turning to O'Reilly, Fox says, "Get the patrol car anyways. We'll follow them. If this really is a homicide, we will need all our accessories to secure the crime scene. Furthermore, we will require the car radio at the site in order to have a communication link. Once confirmed, we are required to contact the divisional office in Castlebar."

A few minutes later, Danny the Divil is driving over the Blackwater Bridge. He stops the car at the sidewalk and rolls down the side window. He shouts to Inspector Murphy who is leaning over the bridge wall peering at the swirling black water below. "Guard Murphy! Sergeant Fox says you are to come with me to the two-mile stone!"

Murf turns around and faces the car. "Foxy wants me to go the two-mile stone with you? Why is that, Danny?"

"That arsy-ologist woman dug up a dead leper out there in the Famine Field. Guard O'Reilly says it might be a homicide. And Sergeant Fox wants you to investigate it."

Murf opens the front passenger door and slides into the seat. "All right then, Danny, let's investigate."

At the two-mile stone, Danny brings the car to a halt. "Out you get, Guard Murphy. I'll drive around the bend and park in Delahunty's farmyard."

Murf walks across the narrow road to the fence at the Famine Field. Four of Delahunty's farmhands are standing inside the fence. They are leaning on spades and shovels and are in quiet discussion. The focus of their attention is on an excavation trench situated within a square area marked with pink ribbon. The trench is close by the fence and hence it is close to the roadway. The farmhands look at Murf and then glance over at a figure seated on a plank of wood. In this manner they indicate who is in charge, and thus to whom Murf should address his questions and elicit an explanation. The person seated is a woman – that would be the archaeologist. Two others, younger than she, stand close by – that would be the other members of the archaeological dig team.

The woman is dressed in boy's clothing – a work-shirt, over which she wears dungarees. Her shoes are a girl's city shoes rather than farm boots. They are so heavily mud-encrusted that their colour is totally concealed. Her face is undoubtedly a woman's face, notwithstanding the mud and sand that is widely smeared across her cheeks and head. She is in her mid-thirties. Her long fair hair is pulled back from her face and she has tied it at the back in a ponytail. Well, mostly. Strands of hair are dislodged and are dangling in front of her face. She is resting her hands atop her up-stretched knees, and she is cradling her chin on her clasped hands. Her hands are exceedingly muddy. Clearly, she applies herself to her work in earnest. Aware of Murf's approach, she lifts her gaze to him but remains seated.

Murf introduces himself. In turn, she identifies herself as Sally Plunkett, and her two student-assistants, B Tobin and Sandra McCurry. She adds that Ned Reid, the surveyor, has gone to town to contact the county engineer and the university to inform them of what they have uncovered in the site.

"So tell me, Sally. What have you discovered here in the Famine Field?"

"Nothing like what we were expecting or hoping for. What we found is not in any way related to the famine. It's…" Sally waves a muddy hand in the direction of the excavated trench. This indicates to Murf that whatever is unearthed in the trench can speak for itself.

Murf approaches the excavated pit and peers inside. He clearly sees the outline of a leg protruding from the wall of the trench, extending in length from the ankle to the pelvic bone, still covered in what appears to be a long stocking. Prudently, Murf declines to enter the trench or to probe at the discovery notwithstanding his strong desire to investigate. The state of the evidence would be delicate and needs to be protected. The medical examiner and the police forensic team are essential to the investigation at this point.

"See, Guard Murphy. It's like I said. This is a leper what's buried here." Danny the Divil has returned to the field and stands next to Murf as if he too were an investigating officer.

Murf considers the Divil's comment to be unusual, not so much in the conclusion he expresses, but rather in the matter-of-fact manner in which he renders his comment – he pronounces it with certainty. "Danny, let's step back a bit. We don't want to collapse the wall of the trench. The ground here is soft and sandy."

"Ah, to be sure. That sand crumbles and spills way too easy."

Murf considers how best to communicate with the district garda station to request the required forensic team. He is reluctant to leave the site unattended by a police officer. The site is now a crime scene. The body may have been a murder victim, or maybe not. Regardless, to be buried in this manner is an indignity committed on a deceased body. There is no doubt in Murf's mind that a crime has been committed and this warrants a proper police investigation.

"Danny, I may need your help here. I'll write a quick note for you to deliver to the garda station to the attention of Superintendent Fox…"

"Why bother? Sure isn't he on his way out here coming after us? That's what he said to Guard O'Reilly – 'Get the patrol car. We'll follow them'."

Murf accepts the Divil's retort that the patrol car is on its way. He walks back to the road. From here he looks back at the location of the crime scene and how visible it is from the roadway. Why would someone dispose of a body in this spot? True, the ground is soft and easy to dig. But the location is close to the road. It is a simple task to quickly bury a body here. But it is within view of passing traffic. The burial was probably executed by a local person familiar with the area. And it likely would have been a very brazen or frightened person – someone prepared to risk being observed from the road.

The Divil is still hovering close to him and is making similar observations. The four farmhands shoulder their tools and prepare to walk away. Murf hails them and detains them for questioning. He ascertains that all four are quite familiar with the field. They herd the cattle here. But none of them has any reason to walk down to this part of the field in the course of their duties. "Except that one time last autumn when we slashed and uprooted the briers and scrub that were threatening to encroach on the grazing land. That would have been in October."

"Show me the area where you removed the briars and scrub."

They point to an area running along the roadside between the road and the fence. "You see all them blackberry briers growing all along the roadside? They are on this side and on yon side, and all along the road from here to town."

Murf understands the invasiveness of briers. "So were they thick, those briers last year?"

"They were growing up to the fence and climbing up here, and here."

Murf views the crime scene again from the roadway and allows for the presence of briar brambles. The burial could have occurred before the removal of the briars, depending on how long the body has been in its current location. A person seated in a car would not have had a view of the crime scene if the line of sight had been obstructed by blackberry plants or scrub. A tall person standing on the roadway might have had a partial view of someone digging in the location of the crime scene. This is unlikely if the burial occurred at night. The local people believe that the Famine Field is haunted by active ghosts that wander the roadway between here and the inlet at night. Any perceived night-time activity in the field would surely frighten off a curious person very quickly.

Murf's mental deliberations are interrupted by the arrival of the garda patrol car. Murf steps off the roadway and onto the grass verge at its approach. O'Reilly is driving. He gives Murf a wide berth due to the narrowness of the road. Alas, he miscalculates the sharpness of the bend and he drives the front-left wheel into the ditch where it sinks into the soft soil of the sheugh. He attempts to reverse the car back onto the road, but the front axle is lodged in the ground and the car is immobile. Fox, sitting in the front passenger seat, is unable to exit the car, at least not without stepping into the drainage ditch. Fox dunts O'Reilly with his elbow and orders him out of the car. Whereupon Fox struggles to slide off the front passenger seat and over the gear stick to the other side. With great puffing and panting, he manages to slither into the driver's seat. From there he exits the car. All this affords amusement to the farm labourers standing at the roadside. But not to O'Reilly. O'Reilly is apologetic. Fox waves him to silence eager to get past the embarrassing occurrence.

The Divil and the farmworkers are adept at extricating cars from the ditch at the two-mile stone. The Divil deftly hops into the driver's seat of the patrol car. With familiar ease, the farmhands employ their picks and spades to lever the car sufficiently high enough to clear the front axle off the ground. The Divil engages the gears and, with a tap to the accelerator and a twist of the steering wheel, he reverses the car onto solid ground. He immediately changes gears and drives off around the corner and out of sight.

"Quick, O'Reilly!" Fox shouts. "The Divil has stolen the patrol car. Run after him and retrieve the car. Lord, we'll be a laughing stock if the Divil gets away with it." O'Reilly sprints after the car. He, too, disappears around the bend.

Murf silently observes the whole episode from the grass verge. He quietly reassures Superintendent Fox. "I wouldn't worry about the patrol car. The Divil is just parking it out of the way in Delahunty's farmyard back there behind the hill." Fox relaxes somewhat.

Murf scales the wire fence and returns to the excavated trench. Fox, not wishing to risk any further embarrassment, declines to cross the fence. He is wary of snagging his trousers on the wire. Instead, he cranes his neck and attempts to peer into the trench from the grass verge.

"So, Murf, what's down there? Is Danny Begley correct?" Fox has recovered sufficiently to refer to the Divil by his legitimate name.

"There is definitely a body buried here. By the look of the cloth covering, it could not be in the ground for more than a few months. Yet, it is has been there long enough for the cloth to have integrated with the soil. See, the material is so muddied that its original colour is obliterated and, apart from its texture, it is indiscernible from the moraine sand."

Fox nods in acknowledgement. "I can see that. So it's a homicide?"

"Yes. Or improper disposal of a body – 'Committing an Indignity to a Human Body'."

"For now, let us refer to it as a 'Suspicious Death'."

"Absolutely. Until we are able to establish the cause of death and the circumstances surrounding the death, we have nothing more than an unidentified corpse." Murf speculates on what possible circumstances could lead to burying a body in this location. To bury a body this deep indicates a deliberate attempt at concealment.

Fox continues to address Murf. "Any distinguishing identification marks?"

"Only the outline of a leg is exposed. A badly discoloured stocking is visible. That's all."

"Is there any reason to support Danny's opinion that it is a leper?"

"Foxy, there is no way to tell if the body is male or female, young or old. It is impossible to say what ailment, if any, afflicted the deceased – the Lord only knows where the Divil gets his notions from. I'm done here for now. I don't want to disturb the body or the surrounding area. We need to secure the site to protect it from contamination."

"And we need to inform the medical examiner."

"Yes. We need to contact Finbar Dorrian, the county medical examiner. And notify Phil Divers and the garda forensic unit in Castlebar."

"We can radio from the patrol car – if we ever succeed in retrieving it. Where could O'Reilly be?"

"I hear voices. That must be him coming over the hill now."

Three heads appear over the spine of the hill. Walking towards them is Garda O'Reilly with Danny the Divil and Ned Reid. Ned shouts to Sally Plunkett. "The county engineer is on his way. He should arrive here before four o'clock – in another half hour or so. But I was unable to get in touch with your man Geraldus."

Sally is still seated on the plank. The mud and sand are caked on her hands and on her head. The sand dislodges as it dries. It trickles down her face. She endures it and decides to await the arrival of the county engineer. There is nothing more she can do now that the site is a crime scene. She is weary and her work-day is almost over.

Fox is relieved that O'Reilly and the Divil are side by side, which means that O'Reilly has recovered the patrol car. "Garda O'Reilly!" he shouts. "Fetch the patrol car and come back here. We need to contact Castlebar. I'm going back to the station. You, O'Reilly, are the official garda on duty to safeguard this site here. Secure an area six feet from the trench on all sides."

Shortly thereafter, the field is quiet. All activity has ceased. The Divil has left. He is impatient to return to Doctor McBratt to finish his duties, and thence to his bar-stool in Cannon's pub in the Market Square. The four farmhands have returned to their tasks at the farm. The archaeological team and the surveyor have gathered their tools and are sitting around awaiting the arrival of the county engineer. Murf and O'Reilly stand at the fence near the roadway to discourage curious onlookers.

At 3:50pm, Sean Macilmyra, the county engineer, arrives. Murf shows him the excavated pit with the partially-exposed body. Sean views the scene with a grim face. He requires no further explanation. The situation is clear to him. County council road-building activity will be delayed until the police clear the crime scene. This could take a few days or even weeks. As expected, Macilmyra instructs his surveyor and the archaeological team to gather up their equipment and vacate the field. He informs them that work will resume later when the gardaí have concluded their investigation of the crime scene. Until then, they are to await further instructions. He turns to Murf for affirmation. "Inspector Murphy, is this correct? Are we free to leave now or do you want to question us further?"

"You are correct in what you say, Sean. The site should be cleared by everyone except the police investigation team. You may go now. I have no more questions at this time."

At 4:30pm, Murf sits on the Divil's plank awaiting the arrival of the medical examiner, Finbar Dorrian. He should arrive shortly along with the police forensic team. Meanwhile, O'Reilly diligently stands on duty at the grass verge of the road. He watches the sea-fog drift in lazily from the marsh in the inlet. The malodorous fog settles like gossamer suspended above the road surface. The day is still bright, and there are a number of hours of daylight left. But the north side of the dolmen falls into shadow and draws in the ghostly dank fog. O'Reilly takes a step backwards from the encroaching miasma. He considers the body, the Divil's 'leper', lying in the pit behind. This site is assuredly a seemly abode for the dead.

At 4:35pm the silence at the Famine field is broken by the approach of three cars. O'Reilly recognises them as garda cars from Castlebar. He directs them to the farmyard to park. The driver of the last car stops at the bend. He steps outside and peers over the fence. "So it's a hole, is it?"

Murf responds. "Hello, Divers. We have a trench four feet deep. The body is concealed in the wall of the trench about two-and-a-half feet to three feet deep. There is room for two officers in the trench at any one time, but in your case, Divers, there is room for just one."

"All right then. I'll need my wellingtons and my step-ladder." Phil Divers, the head of the forensics team, returns to his car and drives to the farmyard to park.

Within minutes the quiet of the field is assaulted by a team of six officers. Divers has changed into wellington boots and he is toting a small step-ladder. Finbar Dorrian, the county medical examiner, stands aside while the team begins work on securing the area. They insert sturdy poles into the ground and erect a rudimentary fence around the site. Then they erect additional taller poles and cover the trench area with a tarpaulin canopy. Divers notices Murf's quizzical expression. "It's for the rain, Murf. We will not be able to conduct a thorough examination until tomorrow. It is too late in the day now. This canopy will protect the site from rain damage until tomorrow. You realise that it rains in north Mayo, Murf?"

"Divers, in north Mayo at the seacoast, the rain falls sideways."

Divers glances out to the inlet and then squints to focus his attention on the rough sea waters beyond. From thence, dark clouds scud inland. "Good point there, Murf." He directs the team to erect side-walls to the canopy. When finished, the trench is concealed within a tent.

"Right, lads, roll up the sides for now," Divers instructs. He invites Murf to come closer to observe the work. One forensic officer and the medical examiner enter the trench. First, they take samples from the soil immediately beneath the body. Divers continues to enlighten Murf. "A decaying body leaches fluid into the soil beneath."

Throughout the evening, the work continues while there is sufficient daylight. They remove the grass sod from the surface and commence brushing the soil and sand gingerly. They make their way down to where they encounter the clothing of the body. Only there is no 'body' anymore. It has reached the stage of dry decay and is reduced to a skeletal state, except for a small fringe of stained hair still present at the forehead. The clothing is discernible. The shoes appear to be dancing pumps. The leg covering appears to be woollen stockings. A woman, perhaps? No, a girl, surely. The upper body is covered by a man's jacket. The clothes have become discoloured to a dirty yellow-brown indicative of wool. The fibres are identifiable. The jacket is wool tweed. The jacket appears to be too large relative to the size of the leggings. Could this be a girl buried in a man's jacket? There is no indication from the chest area that it is an adult woman. On the other hand, the body is too tall to be a young girl. Murf tries to read the evidence. Is this a tall girl in winter underwear wearing a man's jacket? Or is it a slight man in long combination underwear wearing girl's shoes and a jacket too large? Could it be a cross-dresser still wearing his man's jacket? Would not a cross-dresser favour more feminine attire? Murf concedes to himself that he does not know what attire a cross-dresser would favour. Before he can speculate any further, the medical examiner calls it quits for the day. He is satisfied that there are no visible signs of violence or injury. He has fulfilled the requirements of the 'preliminary examination' with the 'scenes of crime officer' present. In accordance with procedures, a forensic autopsy is required in order for a comprehensive examination to be conducted. That will be carried out later in a fully-equipped autopsy room in Garda Divisional HQ in Castlebar.

The team packs up and prepares to leave. They will return at first light on the following day. Divers addresses Murf. "There should be a guard on duty here all night."

"Garda O'Reilly is on duty here."

Divers speaks to O'Reilly. "Guard O'Reilly, do you understand your responsibilities here?"

"Is a guard really required here throughout the night?" O'Reilly is not comfortable spending the night in the ghostly Famine Field. "I don't think anyone is likely to come here at night."

"Not someONE. SomeTHING!"

O'Reilly swallows at the mention of 'thing'.

"We don't want a stray dog sniffing around the exposed skeleton. And there are foxes and badgers that could disturb the evidence. Not to mention the grazing cattle on the hill that are in danger of falling into the pit before morning."

10:00pm. Garda O'Reilly is sitting alone in the Famine Field on the Divil's plank of wood. The glar, the sodden mire of the sea marsh, glistens in the starlight. The malodorous fog creeps across the roadway and spills into the trench. It swirls lazily in the pit as if there is something heaving and struggling underneath. Suddenly, a screeching cry fills the air. O'Reilly falls off the plank in alarm. He runs, then dives, unceremoniously into the shelter of a hawthorn bush, oblivious to the thorns scratching his hands and face. The shrieking cry follows at his heels. He shuts his eyes and holds his breath. The frightening sound passes over him and abates over the marsh. O'Reilly recovers. He thumps his head and exclaims, "Curlews. It's just a flock of screeching curlews returning to their marsh nesting grounds at twilight." Relieved, he extricates himself from the shelter of the thorn bush. He has lost his garda cap. He finds it after searching for some minutes in the dark. He resumes his seat on the plank, deliberately putting a distance between himself and the ghostly fog that swirls about the tent of the pit. The drifting fog reaches out thin tentacles of malodorous vapour and draws them back again as if searching for him. O'Reilly is unable to relax. He is aware of constant sounds and movements from things unseen. He moans inwardly, "Whoever said 'quiet as a graveyard'?"

CHAPTER NINE

The Cadaver from the Famine Field

Killbawn, County Mayo, Ireland
Tuesday 20 August 1946

Midnight in the Famine Field is not a pleasant experience for Garda O'Reilly He is dressed in his dark-blue uniform and is practically invisible against the dark hillside of the dolmen. He sits on the Divil's plank and surveys his inhospitable surroundings. He is still shaken by his recent scare when a flock of marsh birds flew close overhead in returning to their nesting ground. It is not entirely dark. Occasionally, a section of the Milky Way appears through a break in the clouds and reflects on the wet surface of the black marsh. The reflected stars unnerve O'Reilly. It is as if the sodden glar conceals a mass of reptiles, each of which protrudes its unblinking eyes through the surface mire to stare at the solitary Garda O'Reilly. The 'eyes' disappear and reappear with the passing of the clouds overhead. The gurgling and hissing sounds from the marsh gases sound as if the preying reptiles are breathing beneath the surface. The marsh emits a miasma of methane, hydrogen sulfide and carbon dioxide. The foul breath of the marsh drifts lazily inland in a visible vapour of fog. O'Reilly shivers. He takes cold comfort in the cadaver, his solitary companion in the field. The marsh assails his every sense – his eyes, his ears, his nose and his mouth. His entire skin shivers in repulsion. If this is the result of decay, surely it must be dead. But here in the Famine Field, the dead are active.

O'Reilly hears a car approach. He sees the beam of headlights on the briars at the roadside. This visitation from the land of the living affords him some comfort. The car passes slowly around the bend and continues onward. O'Reilly listens for the sound to fade into the distance. Instead, he hears it drive into Delahunty's farmyard on the other side of the hill. O'Reilly conjectures that Delahunty is returning home from having had a late night out. He returns his attention to the roadway and to the inlet beyond. It is strange that notwithstanding how unwelcome these marsh discharges are to him, O'Reilly is unable to divert his attention elsewhere. He is fixated on the fog still swirling in the wake of the car. The disturbed fog settles into spiral shapes that morph into forms resembling hunchback hags. These ghostly shapes drift silently towards the Famine Field, whereupon they encounter the grass verge that halts their progress. Here they transform once more into formless shapes with tentacles reaching out to O'Reilly. This time, the fog encroaches deeper into the field. It inches closer, and closer, to O'Reilly. Unsettled, O'Reilly rises from the plank as the misty tentacles reach out to him. He cautiously steps backwards and proceeds slowly up the hill clear of the invasive fog below.

He had forgotten that a herd of cattle occupies the upper level of the field. Now, as he nears them, he hears their steady breathing. The company of living creatures, these docile domestic animals, eases his troubled state. But his presence disturbs their slumber and some cattle rise and plod towards him, curiously observing the human standing amongst them. In the dark, they are large black shapes. Then, one by one, they resume their rest. O'Reilly hears one last plodding step behind him. He turns to view the friendly beast.

"O'Reilly!"

O'Reilly almost jumps out of his standard-issue garda boots. The black shape that addresses him is dressed in a dark-blue garda uniform.

"Aren't you meant to be down there at that tent thing, guarding it?"

O'Reilly recognises Garda Caldwell. It must have been Caldwell's car that he saw rounding the bend and proceeding into Delahunty's farmyard. Caldwell is carrying a deckchair and is wearing a haversack. Caldwell flips the chair into position next to the tent. He throws his haversack on the ground beside it and sits down noisily. He fishes in the sack to obtain a flask, pours hot tea into a mug, and then retrieves an egg sandwich. As he eats, he looks up at O'Reilly.

"This is great, O'Reilly. I get to spend a day at the seaside – a night, actually – and get paid overtime for it."

"Why are you here, Caldwell?"

"Ah, then they haven't told you, have they? Well, I'm relieving you. I'm here from midnight to 8:00am. As of now, O'Reilly, you are relieved." Caldwell is not aware of how relieved O'Reilly actually is.

O'Reilly finally breathes normally and relaxes his shoulders. "Very well, Caldwell, I'm off now." O'Reilly hurries away in the direction of the farmyard, not wishing to remain any longer in the Famine Field. He fails to notice the suppressed mischievous smile on Caldwell. Caldwell settles comfortably into the deckchair and whistles '*The Last Rose of Summer*'. Caldwell likes to play pranks on O'Reilly. If O'Reilly is headed for Killbawn, he is walking in the wrong direction. Within a minute, O'Reilly is back.

"What is it, O'Reilly? You don't want to leave?"

"I forgot that I don't have transportation back to town. I was almost at the farmyard when it struck me."

"So walk. You're an athlete, after all, a full-back for the county team."

"I'm the full-**forward**…"

"Then forward with ye to Killbawn."

"…and it's three miles to town…"

"No, O'Reilly, it's only **two** miles. It's carved on the mile-stone down there at the roadside."

"That's in Irish miles."

"Why are you complaining? You have long Irish legs and you can walk fast. So, for you, that's only two miles."

O'Reilly realises that Caldwell is 'taking the mickey with him'. Except that O'Reilly is not in the mood for frivolity. "Blast you anyways, Caldwell. And how did **you** arrive here? Sure you don't have a car… unless you borrowed one." O'Reilly remembers the car he heard drive into the farmyard moments before Caldwell's arrival.

"I came in the garda car."

"What? Foxy let you have the garda car?"

"Of course. The garda car has a radio. I am to report to the station by radio while on duty here."

O'Reilly raises his eyebrows, unsure of the credibility of Caldwell's statement. "That's not like Foxy to let you have the use of the car."

Caldwell extracts the car keys from his pocket and holds them aloft for O'Reilly to see. "Tell you what, a Sheamus (rendering his name in Irish), here are the car keys. Take the car and drive home. But be cautious lest Foxy finds out. Be sure to be back here by 8:00am when I must radio in a status report to the station."

O'Reilly grabs the keys from Caldwell and runs speedily on his long Irish legs to the farmyard to avail of the garda car. A minute later, Caldwell sees the car rounding the bend and proceeding to Killbawn. He ceases whistling and laughs loudly. What he has told O'Reilly is true, but not entirely so. District Officer Fox instructed Garda Caldwell to radio in a status report at midnight upon arriving at the crime site. Caldwell complied when he parked the car in the farmyard. He was further instructed to radio in a status report at 8:00am when the forensic team and the investigating officer would be present at the site. In addition, he was instructed to make the garda car available to Garda O'Reilly until 8:00am. Only it is much more enjoyable to have O'Reilly believe that he is borrowing the garda car without permission.

Garda Caldwell is unconcerned with the unusual phenomena of the sea marsh and, unlike O'Reilly, he is unperturbed by his surroundings. For him, this is an easy assignment. He laughs again, pours another mug of tea and recommences whistling.

At 7:00am things start to get lively in the Famine Field, and by 8:00am it is a hive of industry. Murf is present to view the activity. O'Reilly arrives to fetch Caldwell as promised. Caldwell appears relaxed and rested from his 'night at the seaside'. He performs the required radio call to the garda station, whereupon he and O'Reilly are instructed to return to the station and recommence normal duties.

In the Famine Field, Murf feels like a spare wheel – he is the officer in charge of the investigation but, oddly, he feels out of place and in the way amid the high activity of the forensic team. The Divil quietly arrives and stands beside Murf. Finbar the medical examiner requests the team to remove the cadaver undisturbed from the ground. By 'undisturbed', he means to remove the remains, together with the soil underneath to a depth of three inches, all in one whole section. It is a delicate operation. Murf compares it to the first slice of a chocolate sponge cake with delicate cream topping. The slice is required to be removed without upsetting any of the layers. Except, this is no simple chocolate cake. Divers, the head of the forensic team, is too robust to fit inside the trench alongside two other men. He is issuing caution and advice from ground level. The Divil, standing close to Murf, joins in. He, too, shouts encouragement and advice to the team. Whereupon Divers turns and sees the civilian in the restricted area and shouts, "Who the divil is that?"

"Aw, don't call me that."

"Get back there to the security fence. This is a restricted police area."

The Divil takes a few steps in the direction of the security fence. However, the grunts and comments from the forensic team pique his curiosity and he cannot help but walk back even closer to the pit and stand alongside Divers. Divers, concentrating intensely on the delicate task on hand, is unaware that the Divil has returned to the excavation trench and is standing closer then hitherto. The cadaver, including the layer of soil below, is successfully hoisted onto a stretcher-like bier. Next, they carry it carefully across the field to their van and thence they depart for Castlebar where Finbar will conduct a forensic autopsy. Divers descends his stepladder and enters the pit. He takes more soil samples and records moisture content and temperature of the soil at various depths.

"We're done here, Murf. That was the easy part. The real work begins now. Come and see me in Castlebar tomorrow for a progress report. We'll see if the dead speaks, and what the cadaver reveals." Divers climbs out of the trench, retrieves his stepladder and walks off with the others.

"So, the county council can resume work here?"

Divers shouts back. "Murf, you may have some investigating to do here. When you are done, the county council can get back to work on the site."

The Divil is still standing at the bank of the trench. Murf joins him. There is nothing of interest in the trench now. It is just a hole containing moraine sand. The site of the crime has been physically removed from the ground and is heading to the crime laboratory in Castlebar. The Divil turns to Murf. "It's a leper, you know. Anyone can tell it's a leper."

At twelve noon, Murf is sitting back in his office. He reflects on the unusual attire of the cadaver. Was this the normal dress of the person when alive? Or was he/she dressed (or undressed) for a special occasion? Could the clothes have been changed post-mortem? If so, to what purpose? He considers the possibility of the cadaver having been a cross-dresser when alive. Murf, who prides himself on knowing everyone and every group in Killbawn, is not aware of any cross-dressers in the area. Of course, a cross-dresser would be unaccepted in Killbawn and would need to practice in secrecy.

Murf leaves his office and visits Doctor McBratt. As a doctor, she uncovers a lot of personal secrets in the exercise of her practice. Seated in the doctor's office in the dispensary a few minutes later, Murf quizzes the doctor.

Doctor McBratt tenders her opinion of the body found in the Famine Field. "Let's see. A person dressed in tights, but with no evidence of women's underwear in the chest area, doesn't sound like a conscientious cross-dresser to me. At least, not in the context of a fetishist or a homosexual. You know, Murf, people cross-dress for a lot of valid reasons – for comfort, or for ease of performing a task."

Murf calls to mind, and pictures, how the archaeologist was dressed. "You are right, Ant. It isn't unusual at all when you look at it in that context." Thus informed, Murf considers that cross-dressing does not in itself imply gender identity. "So, what task would a man perform in tights and singlet?"

"I don't know, Murf. Why don't you ask a wrestler?" Doctor McBratt, having given her opinion, is eager to continue with her work. Murf understands that in referring to a 'wrestler' she is really saying 'I've given my opinion, and if you don't accept it, go elsewhere for one.' Thus dismissed,

Murf leaves the dispensary. He decides to get a second opinion – from someone familiar with effeminate men.

At 12:30pm Murf drives to Castlebar, and thence out the Westport Road to a private club, 'An Chúilfhionn'. This venue purports to be a 'whist club'. But it is known to the police to be a private club for homosexuals. Murf is quite aware that homosexuality is a criminal offence. Sodomy is punishable by life imprisonment – although prosecutions are rare. Gross indecency, a term used where sodomy cannot be proven, is punishable by imprisonment 'for a term not exceeding two years, with or without hard labour'. In practice, the police overlook these offences provided that the acts are committed in private and that no complaints are lodged. Hence, there are a few of these private clubs around, their membership is strictly monitored and they are located far away from the prying eyes of populated communities.

It is past 1:30pm when Murf passes through Castlebar and onto the Westport Road. Once past the cemetery he joins the N5 at the junction and finds himself travelling behind Mulrines delivery lorry. The lorry is travelling slowly and kicks up dust from the road. Murf needs to be attentive to the T-junctions in order to identify his intended turn-off, but the lorry obscures his view of the road ahead. Once past Ballynaboll, he takes advantage of the straight section of roadway at Ballymacrath, and he safely overtakes the slow-moving lorry as it pulls in at a roadside pub. Shortly thereafter, he identifies the small roadway on the right on the outskirts of Cloggernagh West. He slows the car, turns right, and continues to his destination on the narrow road.

It is close to 2:00pm when Murf approaches the clubhouse in a secluded wooded area near Islandeady Lough. There are a number of cars parked in front and around the back. Murf declines to approach the front door. He would be challenged in attempting to gain entry. Upon identifying himself as a garda, the patrons would disappear in fright. Murf has no desire to cause disquiet in the club; he is looking for help in understanding the choice of dress (or undress) of the body found in the Famine Field.

He drives to the rear of the building and remains seated in his car while he considers the appropriate course of action. He sizes up the area. Judging by the crates stacked at the back door, this is where deliveries are made. He glances around. Of the seven cars parked here, one is a Sligo-registered car that he has seen someplace else – EI 4493. Murf notes the licence number. He wonders if it might be the county engineer's car. He walks to the car and reads the tax disk on the windshield. He records the road-tax identity details in his notebook. This will permit him to trace the owner through the Motor Taxation Office, knowing that it could take up to three weeks to get a response. Thereupon he returns to his car to consider his next move.

A few minutes later, Murf hears the sound of another vehicle entering the yard. It is Mulrines delivery lorry, the same lorry he had passed earlier on the main road. The lorry stops at the back door of the clubhouse. The clubhouse door is thrust open and a man exits carrying a crate. He is dressed in a colourful red-and-blue paisley-patterned waistcoat over a white shirt with the sleeves rolled up – barman attire. Murf rolls down his side window in order to observe more clearly from his concealed position. The barman places the crate of empty stout bottles on top of the existing stack of crates. The lorry driver slides open the back of the lorry and proceeds to load the empty crates inside. The barman speaks with the driver. Murf is close enough to hear them speaking in loud impatient voices. They negotiate a delivery, whereupon the driver unloads six crates of ale and beer. The barman returns inside and reappears with money to complete the transaction.

Thus satisfied, the driver secures the rear hatch and drives off to his next customer.

The barman props open the door and carries in the full crates one at a time. While the barman is thus engaged, Murf exits his car and proceeds stealthily to the corner of the building. He continues to watch the barman's activity from behind the rain barrel. The barman lugs in the final crate and nudges the door to swing shut behind him. The door swings slowly and noisily on its protesting hinges. Before the door clicks shut, Murf deftly catches it and pulls it open. He steps inside discreetly.

Murf finds himself in a storeroom. The sour smell of stale porter assails his nose, the smell associated with unwashed empty bottles. The barman is busily arranging his recent consignment onto shelves and is unaware of Murf's presence. Murf speaks matter-of-factly and identifies himself. The barman hears 'Garda' and freezes, too surprised to react. Murf quickly assuages him lest he fears a police raid on the club. The barman recovers, but he is clearly uncomfortable. He darts his eyes left and right and attempts to peer through the solid wall to the patrons on the other side. "I don't mean to sound mysterious, but I am conducting an investigation on a missing person. The missing person may have been a cross-dresser and may have been a patron of your club. Do you have any person absent from your usual clientele in, say, the last year?"

"Sorry. I can't help you there." Now that he has recovered from his initial shock at seeing Murf, the barman is emboldened to speak. "Since when have you guards become interested in helping us or in protecting us? The only member of this club who disappeared was five years ago. And you did nothing about it. And **now** you want to help us? Or is it that you want **us** to help **you** with your case?"

"Both, actually. I would welcome any leads you might have in assisting us in our current investigation. As to the previous disappearance, I am not aware that there was a disappearance of a suspicious nature. What can you tell me about it? I will certainly look into it."

"The disappearance was before my time here."

"When was that?"

"I started here part-time in the autumn of 1940. It would have been a few months before that."

"In the summer of 1940?"

"I suppose so. All I know is what I gathered from the talk in the club and that we should keep to ourselves and not expect help from the guards." The barman grunts cynically and resumes his task of stacking bottles on the shelves. Clearly, he has little faith in the guards, and he chooses to say no more.

"Well, should anything come to mind, contact me at Killbawn Garda Station – Inspector Murphy. The phone number is easy to remember – Killbawn two."

The barman remains silent and concentrates on sorting his bottles. He turns his back to Murf in a strong indication that he is finished with him. Murf has no reason to press him further and it would be pointless. If Murf is to expect any future cooperation, it is best to depart on cordial terms. Murf politely thanks the barman and reiterates his promise to look into past missing person cases.

On the way through Castlebar, Murf pays a visit to the garda station. He greets Garda Jerry Coulter at the front desk. "Jerry, EI 4493. Could that be Macilmyra's car?"

"No. That would be EI 4498. Are you sure you have it right there, Murf? You're not investigating the county engineer, are you?"

"No. Of course not. I just thought I saw his car unexpectedly, and I was hoping to speak with him. But it wasn't him at all."

"Well, he's up in your area at the minute, up at the Famine Field. Sure you must know that. I'll inquire into that car for you – EI 4493. If it's around Castlebar at all, I'll know of it. As to Sligo cars around here, well, they are quite common. One in five; no, one in ten…?" Jerry is calculating in his head from his local knowledge, "…no, more like one in seven cars around here are Sligo-registered cars."

"Is that a fact, Jerry?" Murf brings up the issue of a missing person. "Jerry, the barman at 'An Chúilfhionn' tells me that there was a disappearance six years ago. Is there any record of a case or a complaint to substantiate that claim?"

"Murf, people disappear from the country all the time. In most cases, they simply up and leave to escape poverty. Sure you can't blame them for emigrating to England, or to wherever, unexpectedly and without forewarning. Some are never heard from again. But, no doubt, you are referring to a disappearance of a suspicious nature. Well, let me tell you, in the past seven years, there were none."

"Are you not going to check the files?"

"No need to. I would not forget a disappearance of a suspicious nature. And who would? Sure the whole county would be upset over the likes of that. The closest we ever got to a missing person's case was three years ago when two schoolgirls went off to Dublin for a lark. They had intended to get the last train back to Castlebar. But the two colleens were confused in the big city, not realising that there are a number of train stations in Dublin serving different routes. The station master in Amiens Street station on the GNR line found the two distraught girls and contacted Pearse Street Garda. Well, we quickly sorted it out and got the two lassies home next morning. But, to put you at ease, Murf, I'll inquire of the other garda stations in Mayo and let you know the result."

Murf hurries off. The owner of the Sligo car at 'An Chúilfhionn' is still playing on his mind, even though it is not relevant to his current enquiry. He tries to forget it but it gnaws at him. As soon as he returns to Killbawn, he'll send off an inquiry to the Motor Taxation Office and trace the owner.

Travelling from Castlebar to Killbawn, Murf counts the number of cars he encounters:

Ten Mayo cars, followed by

One Sligo car, then

One Mayo car,

Lorries and vans don't count, then

One more Sligo car,

Five more Mayo cars and then – EI 4498.

Murf sounds his horn and slows down. The approaching car does likewise until they stop alongside.

It is Sean Macilmyra. "Sean, are you coming from Killbawn? Surely you were not working in the Famine Field, in the crime site?"

"No, Murf, not in the Famine field. We were taking measurements and readings on the other side – on the shore along the inlet." Murf sees Ned Reid sitting in the front passenger seat beside him. "The project is much larger than just the Famine Field. It cuts through the Famine Field and on through the edge of the marsh."

"Ah, yes. So it does."

"So, tell me. How long will that police tape be up anyways?"

"We will be finished our examination of the site in another day. I'll be with Divers tomorrow. If we need to do any more investigating in the field, it will be conducted then. You will be able to resume your work on Thursday."

"Thursday? Right, Murf. I'll inform the team."

They both resume their journeys. Murf meets two more Mayo cars before reaching Killbawn. Jerry's calculation was spot-on – one in seven cars is Sligo-registered. Murf admits that Garda Jerry Coulter knows his stuff.

CHAPTER TEN

THE CADAVER IS REVEALED

Castlebar, County Mayo, Ireland
Wednesday 21 August 1946

"What can you tell me about the body you dug out of the Famine Field?" It is nine o'clock and Murf is in the autopsy room at Garda Divisional HQ. Finbar Dorrian, the county medical examiner, stands next to the stainless steel table containing the skeletal remains of the cadaver. He is dressed in a white medical gown with a face-mask and a medical cap on his head. He checks the fit of his gloves in an idiosyncratic habit every few moments. Murf is adjusting to the smell of alcohol that hit him upon first entering the room. His eyes cease watering and the fumes no longer catch his breath.

The alcohol smell that pervades the room is evidence of the sterile environment. The alcohol of choice in the autopsy room is formaldehyde, a derivative of methanol which is the simplest form of alcohol. Not only is formaldehyde effective as a disinfectant, but it also kills most bacteria and fungi, including their spores. And in Murf's case, it brings tears to the eyes. To Finbar Dorrian, however, this is the air he routinely breathes.

Murf peers at the remains. He understands that the items found with the cadaver are not here. The clothing and soil are undergoing examination and analysis under the expert guidance of Phil Divers and his forensic team next door.

Finbar releases the mask from his face in order to speak clearly. He removes his glasses and wipes them on the lapel of his white medical coat. "Male; five feet seven inches; young adult…"

"Definitely male?"

"No doubt." He continues. "No sign of injury; the body was in good health. The cause of death is not apparent from the skeleton remains."

"Are you suggesting that he died of natural causes?"

"No. The corpse shows no **evidence** of a violent death. But that does not rule out suffocation, poisoning, heart attack, exsanguination: any damage suffered by the muscles or organs of the body, which have since decayed, is no longer detectable and is not in evidence."

"Let me understand. He **may** have died of natural causes?"

"Yes."

"Or death could have been induced through outside interference?"

"Yes, if the cause of death did not inflict damage to the skull or bones."

"Any sign of disease or illness?"

"None."

"Not a leper, then?"

"Why on earth would you ask that, Murf? There is no sign of any disease, but that is not to say that he was free from disease at the time of death. He may have had a skin condition. But the fact remains – there is no EVIDENCE of illness or disease. Oh, except for the teeth. There is a filling in one molar, but otherwise, the teeth are in perfect shape."

"So, he went to the dentist. Could he be identified by dental records?"

"Certainly, provided you find the dentist who has his record."

"There is only one dentist in Killbawn…"

"Murf, first speak with Divers before you choose which dentists to contact."

"Are you suggesting that there might be a problem locating the dentist?"

"Murf, that is detective work. Now may I continue?"

Murf nods. Finbar positions his glasses back on his nose and lifts a clipboard from a hook on the wall. He consults the information on the chart clipped to the board. "The body was dead for 365 days, give or take a fortnight."

"365 days? How are you able to be so precise?"

"See the skeleton? There is just a little hair left on the scalp. Otherwise, there is nothing left but bone and nails."

"What does this tell you?"

"At the ground temperature and moisture content of the site where the body was located, total decay would occur between 190 days and 365 days."

"So the body was buried there between six months ago and one year?"

Finbar is not finished. "The body was clothed in wool – woollen body-clothing and a tweed coat. Wool, in the conditions of the site, would not decay until at least a year, and would not fully decay until three years. Furthermore, the shoes were also intact."

"So the rate of body decay coupled with the rate of wool decay…"

Finbar ignores the interruption. He is not finished consulting his notes. "The clothes under the body were completely decayed. The acid from the decaying body rendered the clothes beneath into a syrupy mess that leached into the soil below. Soil samples taken from beneath the body revealed the extent to which the decayed wool interacted with the soil."

"365 days."

"Give or take a fortnight. There was no extreme weather in the past year or two that could have altered the conditions conducive to the rate of decay. Yes, Murf. 365 days."

"Give or take two weeks you say? Could the body have been moved from another location and reburied?"

"Murf, you need to respect the breakdown stages of decomposition. The body undergoes changes in precise stages starting fifteen minutes after death. Pallor mortis, followed by algor mortis and then rigor mortis. That brings us to one to three days after death. And then we take livor mortis into account. That occurs from twenty minutes to twelve hours after death. The initial decay takes place in the period of the first three days. We are certain that this body was placed in its final resting place within three days of death. And it has not been disturbed or moved since then. We are able to establish this from the traces of the succeeding stages of decay. Three days after death, and for the following four to ten days, the body goes through a stage of putrefaction. This, in turn, is followed by black putrefaction and butyric fermentation. All those stages leave identifiable traces in the clothing and in the soil under the body."

"I see. So, this body here has been in the ground, and in the same spot unmoved, since mid to late August last year. And this establishes when death occurred."

"Good, Murf. I believe you have it now. I will send a detailed written report in a day or two."

"Thanks, Finbar. Now I'm off to see Divers."

9:20am. Murf enters the forensic laboratory. He braces for another whiff of alcohol. This time it is different. The alcohol of choice in the forensic laboratory is methylated spirits, which is denatured ethanol with 10% methanol added. Here, it is the alcohol of choice as a disinfectant and antiseptic where various instruments are employed in forensic examinations. Ethanol is also a drinking alcohol, so to render it unpalatable, methylated spirits is deliberately imbued with a foul smell and a sickening taste. Murf is familiar with methylated spirits. It is an inexpensive cleaning agent employed in most farms and in some households. When mixed with raspberry cordial, the foul taste is reduced sufficiently to achieve a cheap drink known as 'Red Biddy'. Red Biddy is the drink of the very poor or the very desperate. Not even Danny the Divil would stoop to consume it but, alas, some unfortunates succumb to it.

Divers is hard at work, running from table to table and interacting with his team. Divers is a mite too stout for running gracefully, or for running in any reasonable manner at all. He is perspiring and his glasses refuse to stay in place on the bridge of his nose. At Murf's entrance, he plops heavily into a chair at his desk and gestures to Murf to be seated beside him. He is thankful for the interruption. It gives him some respite from his unaccustomed expenditure of energy.

Murf addresses him. "Divers, Finbar tells me that the body next door is a young male, five feet seven inches, interred in its resting spot since death for one year."

"Aye. That's right."

"And that you have something to tell me about the teeth, in particular with regard to the filling in the molar."

"Ah yes, the filling. But that's not all. I have a lot to tell you, Murf."

"What's the story on the filling? Surely a filling is a filling?"

"The composition of the alloy is unusual. Unless the patient had a very peculiar need for such an alloy, I don't see a reason for it."

"It follows that the patient, in this case, the cadaver, was an unusual person…"

"…or a foreigner."

"A foreigner?"

"I have contacted the dental college in Dublin to ascertain if the alloy is peculiar to any known dental practice. I'm waiting for them to report back." Divers removes a large paisley handkerchief from his trouser pocket and wipes the sweat from his face. His nose thus attended to, regains its ability to hold his glasses in place. Divers reaches across his desk to his scattered notes. At first, Murf considers Divers' notes to be scattered randomly. As Divers stretches his portly body to grab a file, Murf sees that the papers are positioned strategically in an arc so that Divers may adequately reach them without upsetting their order. He grunts from the strain of stretching, but he maintains a conversation nevertheless. He opens a manila folder and consults his hand-written notes. "Murf," he says. "Here's what I have to tell you."

"About the case – the body found in the Famine Field? I'm listening."

"First, the feet. The shoes are in good condition. He was wearing soft-soled dancing pumps."

"Dancing shoes?"

"And he was clothed entirely in a unitard – a one-piece body garment combining tights with leotards. Woollen. Similar in construction to long combinations, but usually worn body-tight."

"One-piece? Then it cannot be underwear – that would be functionally awkward as underwear. It sounds like a dancer, all right. Any identifying labels?"

"The back of the garments had completely disintegrated. We were unable to recover labels from the clothing."

Murf attempts to picture the body when alive. A dancer? An adult male dancer? Or maybe it is doctor McBratt's wrestler. But not the Divil's leper.

An assistant in a laboratory coat enters the room and hands an envelope to Divers. "Sir, the pictures from the photo lab are developed and printed. Here they are."

Divers takes the envelope. He opens it and peers inside. "Perfect. Thanks, Pat." The assistant leaves.

Divers inspects the contents inside the envelope and resumes his explanatory commentary to Murf. "The garments are over there on the table. As you can see, there is also a tweed jacket. The clothing is so discoloured that the original colours are indiscernible. The portions of material from atop the body are in sound condition. But the clothing from below the body was transformed into stains in the soil."

Murf glances over at the evidence table. The tables in the lab are wooden and are scrubbed white with disinfectant bleach. The odour of bleach competes with the smell of methylated spirits – and they are not in agreement. There is a tray of small instruments placed on the right-hand side of each table. On the table indicated by Divers, Murf sees where small tongs and tweezers are positioned in the centre as though the work here has been interrupted. He recognises the items described by Divers. "I see. There are the unitard and a tweed jacket."

"Yes. The deceased was wearing a tweed jacket. And judging from the size of the unitard, I would say that the jacket was some sizes too large for him."

"Could not the unitard have shrunk?"

"That is a factor. But the dimensions of the skeleton are in keeping with the size of the unitard, but not so with regard to the jacket."

Murf thinks aloud. "A dancer, or an athlete, possibly a foreigner, and wearing someone else's jacket. In Killbawn, such a person could not go unnoticed. Did he drop out of the sky?" Murf rises from the chair and approaches the evidence table. He peers at the objects displayed. He speaks aloud for Divers' attention. "This looks like a tweed jacket all right."

"And not just a tweed jacket, it is a brier-proof tweed jacket – fashionable with the young and sporty. It's not like that rough gabardine stuff you wear. Here, I'll show you." Divers rises from his chair and fetches his own coat from the coat-rack by the door.

"You wear a brier-proof tweed jacket, Divers? You are young and sporty I see."

Divers ignores the humorous jab. "See the fibres? You can touch them. They are the same as the sample on the table. Now, look here at this." With that, Divers opens his jacket and turns the inside breast pocket inside out. This reveals a product imprint in the pocket lining:

Hand-woven and distributed by McHugh of Donegal. Inspected by RA – Batch no. 010545 item 12

"May I inspect the jacket on the table?"

"Go ahead." Divers, in anticipation of Murf's inspection, thrusts a pair of gloves at him. Murf understands that evidence must be kept free of contamination and puts on the gloves without hesitation. Thus suitably outfitted, Murf lifts the frail garment delicately. He carefully inspects the pocket lining of the partial jacket on the evidence table. The pocket lining is heavily stained and faded. However, there is no visible product imprint like the marking in Divers' jacket. "I don't see any identifying marks on the pocket lining. Is this correct, Divers?"

"Ah." Divers steadies his glasses on the bridge of his nose and winks at Murf. "None visible, but there are invisible markings. But first, finish inspecting the items on the table."

"Have you any idea as to the colour of these items prior to burial?"

"None at all. Over time, colours fade and wool returns to its natural colour. And in this case, the materials were additionally subjected to staining from the soil. The original colours have been obliterated."

Murf points to the objects on the table. "What is this here? Bits of tangled string?"

Divers is expecting the query. He switches on the lamp on the table and bends the goose-neck pole to better angle the beam of light. He hands Murf a magnifying glass. "The string was found in one of the pockets of the jacket. Look closely. It is not tangled."

Murf gingerly lifts the bits of string and holds them to the light to conduct a close visual examination. "It is twine knotted in an intricate manner. Four pieces of intricately knotted twine. Why? What purpose could it serve?"

"The string is the standard shop string. You encounter it every day tied to your groceries or hardware purchases. But these are not a grocer's or ironmonger's knots."

Murf evaluates this piece of information. Then he carefully places the string back on the surface of the table. He continues to survey the four items on the table – the string, the shoes, the jacket and the unitard. In addition to these four items, he notes nine glass jars. Each jar is labelled to identify the contents – soil samples from the excavated site. Depth, location and elemental components are noted on the labels of each jar. Murf views the evidence and considers what is missing from the list of items. He observes from the hem of the unitard that, unlike a body stocking, it has no feet. "There are no socks here, Divers. Did you find socks on the body?"

"We did not find any evidence of socks."

"He was wearing dancing shoes but not any socks?"

"Not necessarily, Murf. Not everyone wears woollen socks as you do. It is likely that this dancer-person, or whoever he was, was wearing cotton socks."

"And cotton decays rapidly in the soil."

"Exactly. Within weeks. And certainly long before 365 days. But come. I must show you the most revealing piece of evidence." Divers returns to his desk and lifts the manila envelope that was recently delivered to him. "This, Murf, is the invisible stuff I was telling you about."

Divers extracts photographic sheets from the envelope. They are all either of a reddish hue or of a bluish hue. "Infra-red and ultra-violet photography reveals much of what is hidden in full-spectrum light."

"This is different from what one can distinguish in normal light with the naked eye?"

"Precisely." Divers selects two photographs and hands them to Murf. "This is what I want you to see."

Murf inspects the two photographs. They are pictures of the inside breast pocket of the cadaver's jacket. The pocket is inverted so that the inside is exposed. The product imprint is clearly displayed:

Hand-woven and distributed by McHugh of Donegal. Inspected by RA – Batch no. 210744 item 18

Murf delivers a congratulatory slap-on-the-back to Divers knocking his glasses down his nose. "Divers, this is great! This could very well be a decisive factor in leading us to the owner of the coat, and thence to the person associated with the disposal of the body."

Divers slides his glasses back into position and says, "Yes, you may, Detective."

"What's that, Divers?"

"You were about to ask if you could take these two photographs. I have duplicate copies – those two are for you."

"Lord, Divers, you think of everything."

"Don't I ever. Now be gone. You are taking up valuable time and space here."

Murf has a lead. His next step is to visit McHugh of Donegal in an attempt to track down the purchaser of the jacket. This could lead him to the owner of the jacket, and thence to the last person who may have interacted with the deceased prior to his death. Donegal is a two-hour drive from Castlebar. Murf avails of the phone in the garda station and contacts the garda station in Inver Eske.

After the introductory greetings, Murf requests the assistance of the station sergeant. "Sergeant Gilligan, are you familiar with 'McHugh of Donegal'? I believe they are located in the Diamond in Inver Eske."

"That's correct. What do you require?"

"It's a 'suspicious death' investigation. I am attempting to trace the purchaser of a McHugh tweed coat from the identifying product imprint on the pocket lining."

"Then it's not McHugh in the Diamond you need – that is their office and retail shop. You need McHugh of Donegal Factory and Distribution Warehouse. That's in Milltown, across the river from Inver Eske."

"I'm in Castlebar at the moment. I need to pay them a visit and I am about to leave to go there. I should be in Inver Eske in about two hours."

"Tell you what, Murf. Come to the station here and I'll take you to the tweed factory myself. I know the production manager quite well – Robbie Ashe. Do you know where we are located?"

"Yes. I remember. As I enter the town I go down a hill…"

"…to the bottom of Quay (pronounced 'kay') Brae; swing hard left to the wee pier and park there. The garda station is fornenst the wee pier on the other side of Quay Street."

"Right you be, Sergeant. I'll see you in a couple of hours."

12:30pm. Murf and Sergeant Gilligan enter the tweed factory in Milltown. Murf is carrying a thin briefcase. Gilligan knows his way around the factory. Once through the side door in the factory wall, they stride past the shipping office and proceed up a flight of stairs to the upper-level office. Murf notices the absence of staff. Gilligan explains. "They break from twelve to one – lunchtime, you know. But don't worry, Robbie is expecting me."

There is the distinctive heavy smell of wool in the air. Being familiar with sheep-shearing activities in Killbawn, Murf is no stranger to the expected odour of wool. He also identifies the smell of wood. It is a pleasant fragrance and seemingly out of place in a tweed factory.

Robbie Ashe hears the footsteps ascending the stairs. "Come in, Sergeant Gilligan!" Gilligan and Murf enter Robbie's office. "Hello, Sergeant." Robbie rises from his chair and shakes hands with Gilligan. He turns to Murf. "And this must be…?"

Gilligan informs him. "This is Inspector Murphy."

The office of the production manager is vast, taking up the entire length of the gable side of the building. Clearly, it is not just an office, but also a meeting room, a sample room and R & D. Two walls are decorated with awards and certificates of appreciation. 'London' and 'New York' appear numerous times. Filing cabinets line these same walls occupying the area immediately below the posted tributes. There is one large window on the outside gable-end wall which provides a panoramic view of the Eske River and the estuary. The opposite wall is comprised entirely of glass and affords a complete view of the factory floor below. Murf expects to see looms. But instead, the factory floor is filled with cutting-tables, tailors' workbenches, shelves and pallets – all made from wood, presumably ash. The wood is untreated, free from staining or polishing, except for the polishing applied by the workers in the execution of their tasks. This explains the ever-present fragrance of wood. Bolts of tweed and cuttings of cloth appear to be everywhere – on shelves and pallets, and on tables and workbenches.

Robbie Ashe reads Murf's quizzical expression and tenders a quick explanation. "There are just two looms down there for the one weaver employed here. The only weaving conducted in the factory is to produce samples of new products in different widths of wool and in various colours and patterns. The approved samples are then demonstrated to the actual weavers. Whereupon the weavers are provided with the required pre-dyed wool which they take home to their own cottage-looms. That's where the tweed is woven. 80% of our sales are in complete bolts of tweed. These are shipped from our warehouse to our domestic and overseas customers. What you see down there is for the tailoring and crafting of finished garments for our special-order customers. That accounts for about 10% of sales. The remaining 10% is from our shirt factory in the adjoining building. Finished products are usually accompanied by shirts and blouses in complementary tones and colours. You may recognise our shirts by the trade name *Silveresque*."

Murf nods in understanding. Gilligan continues with his interrupted introduction. "Inspector Murphy from Mayo."

"They call me 'Murf'." Murf shakes hands with Robbie and comes directly to the purpose of his visit. "Mr Ashe, we need your assistance in an investigation."

"Ah, the 'missing person' case that Sergeant Gilligan mentioned. And you can call me 'Robbie'." Robbie returns to his chair behind the desk and invites Murf and Gilligan to sit in the two facing chairs. "So, what can I do to assist you?"

Murf extracts a file from his briefcase and places it on Robbie's desk. He slides two photographs from within the file and shows them to Robbie. "Do you recognize this? And can you tell me what it means?"

Robbie glances at the two pictures. One is of a reddish hue and the second one is a bluish hue. Robbie instantly understands the marking in the photographs:

Hand-woven and distributed by McHugh of Donegal. Inspected by RA – Batch no. 210744 item 18

"That's our batch and item identity mark. What do you want to know?"

'Manufactured here?"

"This tweed was hand-woven in a homestead. The bolt was subsequently delivered to us. The finished garment was manufactured here. This is a unique tweed. It is 'brier-proof'. You could thrust a six-inch nail through the fabric and then pat the material back into shape without causing any damage."

"I see. So it is resistant to tearing and ripping if it gets snagged in thorns or brambles."

"Exactly. Hold on a moment." Robbie rolls his chair to a filing cabinet, one located under pictures of Gregory Peck and David Niven, both sporting *McHugh of Donegal* tweed, and extracts a thick file from the middle drawer. He spins the chair around and plops the file loudly on the desk. "Let me see now…" He is flicking rapidly through the records. He stops and extracts a page. "The garment you are enquiring about is a herring-bone black-and-white man's brier-proof tweed jacket, size 42 inches. It was manufactured on the twenty-first of July 1944. It was delivered to *Cleary's of Sligo,* on Tuesday the twenty-fifth of July 1944, as part of a consignment of men's and women's clothing for their

Christmas market. I see that the consignment contained four tweed jackets from the same bolt – a size 38″, two of size 40″ and one of size 42″. The garment identified from your photograph is one of these four. All four are from Batch no. 210744, and are numbered 'item 15' to 'item 18' inclusive. Here, I'll write down Cleary's address and phone number for you."

Murf is impressed with Robbie Ashe's record-keeping. "One more thing, Robbie. I have no idea what the tweed jacket looks like. Could I have a sample of the cloth?"

"Sure. I could give you a swatch. But why not get a ready-to-wear jacket made from the same bolt? There is one in the shop in the Diamond."

"There is? Well, that would be great. Could I obtain it?"

Robbie lifts his phone. "Murf, I am checking with the shop. Today is a half-day in the shop, but not in the factory. They close at one, and it is five to one now. I'll ensure that the manager stays back for you."

"Thanks, Robbie. We'll go right away." Murf and Gilligan rush off to McHugh's shop in the Diamond.

Thursday 22 August 1946. It is 9:00am. Murf enters Cleary's on Lower O'Connell Street, Sligo. He is carrying his briefcase and he has slung his newly-acquired herring-bone black-and-white brier-proof tweed jacket over his arm. He makes his way to the men's clothing department and introduces himself to the manager. Ernest Corr, the manager, is agreeable to assist Murf. He brings him into his office. Murf quickly learns that Cleary's records are not as meticulous as McHugh's. Most sales are cash sales, in which case the identity of the purchasers is not recorded. The manager attempts to remember what he can, but his memory of sales made two years ago is vague.

Murf coaxes an answer from him. "Who would purchase a jacket like this?" pointing to his recently-acquired jacket.

"Well, it is stylishly cut and is fairly expensive."

"Like a well-to-do young man, perhaps?"

"No. The style is fashionable but the colour is subdued. It is black, but the white flecks render it as grey. It would interest a country gentleman or a city person who enjoys the country. But not a fashionable young man. And it certainly would not be appropriate for working in."

"A stylish non-fashionable gentleman?"

"Yes. Like a teacher or a…" Ernest Corr suddenly raises his eye-lids and his eyes register alertness. "Give me a minute. I know where to look." He goes to a filing cabinet and rifles through files. "I keep files here of all customers who have clothes tailor-made and charged to their account. These are not cash sales. These are repeat customers who are permitted to maintain accounts."

"Like 'gentlemen'?"

"Yes. And clergymen. Clergymen, well some clergymen, like to dress stylishly but in black or grey. Protestant ministers, for example. I have seven such accounts – six from Church of Ireland parishes and one Roman Catholic Diocese. Just give me a moment to thumb through these files."

Murf notices that the contents of the files are topsy-turvy and are askew, but they appear to make sense to Ernest Corr. "A-hah!" He extracts a page. Then he returns to his burrowing. "A-hah!" He extracts a second page. He thumps the files onto the table, changes his mind and retrieves them. "I should look into the Catholic ones also." Moments later he exclaims a third 'a-hah' and produces another sheet of paper. Exhausted, he sits down in his chair and selects the three sheets of paper that caught his attention.

"Inspector, I can account for three of the four jackets."

"Are you sure they pertain to the order you received on 25 July 1944?"

"The order was not repeated until January 1945; these three sales are in November and December 1944. Yes, this accounts for three of the four jackets from that order."

"I see. But there is a missing one. Of the three sales you show, is there one for size 42″? That's the one I am interested in."

"Sure I don't know. The files here do not indicate the size – just the price and a description of the style and material."

"But, surely you know the size of your customers."

"Of course I do. But these sales are to churches. There are multiple clergymen to each account."

"So, any one of these three accounts could have purchased a jacket, like the one I have here, for any of the four garments delivered to you?"

"No. Not quite. Not the size 38″. 38″ is for a very slim build – a youth more likely. None of the clergymen here," waving to the dishevelled files, "would be comfortable in a size 38″. These clergymen are all size 40″ or larger."

Murf acknowledges that this is some progress. The jacket was purchased by one of these three churches. "Mr Corr, I need the names and addresses of the three churches and the dates of purchase."

"Of course." Ernest Corr writes in his desk pad and tears off the page. He hands it to Murf.

Murf glances at it:

C of I, Deanery, Sligo, Dean Simon Jackson, 25/11/44
C of I, Taunagh Riverstown, Rev John Turk, 02/12/44
RC Diocese of Killala, Bishop Patrick Byrne, 05/12/44

Murf sees that this must be handled delicately. He is to question three churches in connection with a sensitive investigation. The jacket in question, the one unearthed from the Famine field and identified as *Batch no. 210744 item 18,* was purchased by one of these three entities. Murf mentally enumerates all the items found with the cadaver – the dental filling (still undergoing identification analysis), the pieces of string, the clothing and shoes. At this point, the tweed jacket is his only tangible lead.

CHAPTER ELEVEN

THE CADAVER IS IDENTIFIED

Town of Sligo, Ireland
Thursday 22 August 1946

The Deanery on Strandhill Road is easy to find. It turns out that this is the residence of Simon Jackson, the dean of the cathedral. Murf knocks at the door at 10:00am. He is admitted by the maid. He identifies himself and requests a meeting with the dean. Mrs Jackson, the dean's wife, meets with him. Mrs Jackson is apologetic for the dean's absence from the house at this time of day. The dean is at St Mary's Cathedral in Elphin, about an hour's journey away. She inquires as to the nature of a police visit and offers to help. Rather than seek out the dean at the cathedral in Elphin, Murf states the purpose of his visit to Mrs Jackson. He shows his sample tweed coat to her and explains that he is attempting to locate the owner of a similar coat that turned up recently in one of his investigations. Mrs Jackson insists on serving him tea and brack while she locates 'Simon's seldom-worn tweed jacket'. She quickly locates it and brings it to Murf.

"See, Inspector. Here is Simon's tweed jacket. I don't know why he ever bought it. He seldom wears it. Actually, I intend to donate it to the poor. He will never miss it. Is this the coat you wish to see?" She hands the tweed jacket to Murf who quickly inspects the label and product imprint – *Hand-woven and distributed by McHugh of Donegal. Inspected by RA – Batch no. 210744 item 16*

"I see that it is size 40"."

"Oh, Simon can be a silly man sometimes. He thinks that he is a size 40", but he really is a 42". He won't admit to putting on weight. Anyways, as you can see, Simon has not lost his tweed jacket."

Minutes later, Murf exits the deanery. Mrs Jackson wishes him luck in his investigation. She is impressed with the police going to such lengths to find the rightful owner of a lost jacket.

Murf is satisfied that the dean is not the owner of the cadaver's jacket. This brings the number of possible owners down to two. Next, he heads to Riverstown and, after that, he intends to return to Killbawn via Ballina.

The Church of Ireland in Riverstown is actually in Fannybrook at the edge of the town. It is a fifteen-minute drive from the deanery in Sligo. At 10:45am Murf knocks at the door of the rectory of the Taunagh Parish Church in Fannybrook. The door is opened by a young minister. He is thirty-something, has a mop of unruly brown hair, and he is smoking a pipe. And most significantly, he is wearing a brier-proof tweed jack identical to the one Murf is carrying. He laughs upon seeing Murf with the tweed jacket. Murf quickly introduces himself and explains his purpose. The Reverend John Turk is eager to assist Murf. He removes his jacket and permits Murf to examine it. He theatrically and jokingly dons Murf's sample jacket.

"You know, Inspector, I don't know why more people don't wear these brier-proof coats. They are perfect for a rural living – smart, yet durable. Do you know that you could pierce it with a six-inch nail and not damage it?" With that, he rushes off and returns moments later brandishing a six-inch wood-nail. Before Murf can stop him, he gathers a fistful of cloth from the arm of the jacket, Murf's sample jacket, and sticks the nail into the gathered material through to the other side. He takes his pipe from his mouth, blows a puff of smoke, and smiles broadly. He places his pipe back into his mouth, gripping it in his still-smiling teeth, and removes the nail with a sharp tug. Then he pats the material where a hole has appeared and strokes the fabric gently with the palm of his hand. The fabric returns to its smooth undamaged state. "See? It is brier-proof and nail-proof."

"So it is." Murf is relieved. He is also alert to any further enthusiastic demonstrations the reverend gentleman may wish to engage in.

"And did you find what you were looking for?"

"Yes. Your jacket is *Batch no. 210744 item 17.* See the imprint here? I'm looking for another jacket from the same batch."

"The jacket you are looking for – it is lost, yes?"

"No. It's not lost. I have it back at the station with case evidence."

"Ah, I see. You are looking for a jacket that is NOT lost. Is that correct?"

Murf laughs at this. "Not quite. I am looking for the OWNER of a jacket we found, one identified by its product number. It is from the same batch as yours."

"And it might be in two places at the same time? Police work must be very interesting," laughs the cheery John Turk.

Having thus eliminated the dean and the minister, Murf's last inquiry is at the Diocese of Killala in Ballina. Murf drives back to the N4 and thence on to the N59. He arrives at the diocesan office in Riverside, Ballina, within an hour. He parks his car close to the diocesan administrative building at 11:50am. As he walks to the entrance, Murf notes the cars parked close by. He stops. There it is again – a Ford Prefect, licence plate EI 4493, the same car he spotted parked at An Chúilfhionn, the private club outside Castlebar. Could it be someone connected to the diocese? He glances in through the side window in the hope of seeing something that might identify the owner. The interior of the car is clean and is free from any identifying objects. He continues into the building carrying his briefcase and the sample tweed jacket.

Inside the building, Murf is addressed by a friendly young cleric in a black cassock. The cleric is standing beside a reception counter and is engaged in sorting papers. "Welcome to the pastoral centre." He places his papers to the side of the counter in order to give full attention to the visitor.

Murf identifies himself and enquires, "Perhaps you could help me in identifying a tweed jacket that was purchased in the name of the Diocese of Killala."

The young cleric looks at the jacket slung over Murf's arm and smiles. "I see that Father Glen Dennagher misplaced his jacket again. So, you are returning it?"

"Father Glen Dennagher lost his jacket? I did not know that."

"I'm sorry, Inspector. I assumed that the jacket you are carrying is his. Is it not?"

"Father Glen Dennagher has a jacket like this? And he has lost it?"

"Yes. He has a jacket just like that. But I don't know if he has lost it. It's just that he misplaced it once or twice before."

"Be that as it may, I need to trace a jacket like this, purchased by the Diocese of Killala in December 1944. Would you have a record of such a purchase?"

"Oh, we keep meticulous records. 1944 files would be in archives by now. The person in charge of archives is Father Glen Dennagher himself. He will know for sure."

"What all does Father Glen Dennagher do? I understand that he is not assigned to a parish."

"You are informed correctly. Father Glen Dennagher is the diocesan archivist. He knows all about the diocese – current records and historical records going back to 1111. Do you know that the diocese was created by the Synod of

Rathbreasail in the year 1111? And that the current boundaries were revised and placed us within the Province of Tuam in 1152?"

"I did not know that."

"Father Glen Dennagher is also the diocesan legal expert – both in civil law and in canon law."

"Yes…"

"And he is also one of our vicars forane. He is a very knowledgeable man, and is quite a busy priest."

"He is? And what does a 'vicar forane' do?"

"A vicar forane is an experienced priest appointed by the bishop and is charged with a special purpose."

"And Father Glen Dennagher's special purpose is law?"

"No. That's not his 'special purpose'. The bishop has put him in charge of a special outreach ministry for estranged and separated Catholics – those members of our church who live outside the fold. Father Glen Dennagher helps to bring them back – to return them to union with Holy Mother Church."

"What kind of 'estranged Catholics' are these?"

"Mostly Catholics in illicit unions or unlawful relationships."

"Such as?"

"Oh, bigamy, or homosexual relationships, or incestuous relationships… Well, that sort of thing."

To Murf, this is quite revealing. He wonders how prevalent these situations are in Killala. Interesting as this might be, it is not the focus of his inquiry. "To get back to the jacket, Father…"

"McGill. My name is Father McGill."

"…Father McGill. Could I have a word with Father Glen Dennagher?"

"Of course. You are investigating the purchase of a jacket. Please have a seat. I'll inform Father Glen Dennagher that you wish to see him."

Moments later, Father Glen Dennagher, dressed in a cassock, enters the reception area and greets Murf. "Inspector Murphy. Yes, I remember you from St Bawn's Parish in Killbawn. And how may I help you? I understand you are inquiring about a jacket?"

"Yes, if you don't mind. On 05 December 1944, the Diocese of Killala purchased a tweed jacket – similar to the one I have here – and I need to know if you have a record of the purchase."

"No problem. Was there a theft at Cleary's that you are looking into? Regardless, come with me to the records room. I can find a copy of the purchase receipt in a jiffy."

In the records room, in one of the many filing cabinets, Father Glen Dennagher opens a drawer marked 'Expense Receipts 1944'. He quickly whips out a folder and places it on top of the filing cabinet. "December should be at the back of this folder. Ah, here it is." He removes a sheet of paper and hands it to Murf. Murf places his sample jacket on top of the filing cabinet and takes the page from him. At a glance, Murf sees that it is a receipt and that it pertains to a tweed jacket of the description and date consistent with the information he obtained from Ernest Corr, the manager of the men's wear department in Cleary's.

"Yes, Father Glen Dennagher, that's the item I am investigating."

"Investigating? And this purchase is relevant to your investigation?"

"Yes, it is an item of interest. Do you know the present whereabouts of this jacket?"

"Yes. It is in the boot of my car. At least, I hope it is there and that I have not misplaced it."

"And may I see it?"

"Sure. Follow me."

They exit the building and Murf, still in possession of the purchase receipt, follows Father Glen Dennagher to his car – right to the car with licence plate EI 4493. Murf considers this piece of information with interest. Could Father Glen Dennagher's outreach ministry have brought him to a private club two days ago – a club reputed to be a meeting place for homosexuals? That would be in keeping with his outreach work. But Castlebar is in the Archdiocese of Tuam. Would he conduct his outreach ministry in a neighbouring diocese? Murf resolves to investigate this further. But first, he must arrange his 'dots' before confronting Father Glen Dennagher, and then only if it is relevant to the case. Murf is aware that Father Glen Dennagher is speaking.

"…in the diocesan office. The bishop insists that we all dress in cassocks. Once I get away from here, I dress for the country." He unlocks the boot and flips open the hatch. "Ah! It's there all right. See, here is the jacket that you are enquiring about."

Murf notes the interior of the boot. It contains a large bulky gym bag and a neatly-folded tweed jacket. The contents of the boot are consistent with a keep-fit clergyman. "If you don't mind, I would like to inspect the jacket."

"Help yourself."

"And this is the jacket that was purchased in Cleary's on 05 December 1944?"

"Yes. I bought it for myself. And here it is – safe and sound."

"That's the jacket? You are sure of that?"

"Absolutely."

"Fine. I have just one or two questions and I will be on my way. Do you mind if we return to the diocesan office? I need to retrieve my briefcase. And I left my sample jacket on top of the filing cabinet there. I would like to compare the two jackets."

"No problem."

They re-enter the diocesan office. This time, Murf has Father Glen Dennagher's jacket slung over his arm. Father McGill is still in the reception area. He is standing in a huddle with two other clerics. As Murf and Father Glen Dennagher stride through the reception area, the three clerics cease speaking. Three pairs of eyes follow their progress from the entrance door through the reception area until they pass through the inner doorway to the corridor. Murf's meeting with Glen Dennagher has aroused the curiosity of the clerics in the pastoral centre.

In the records room, Murf retrieves his jacket. "Father Glen Dennagher, do you mind if we go somewhere where I may show you what is of interest to me? Perhaps your office would be more suitable?"

"And what do you want to show me?"

"There could be something of interest in the two jackets that I would like to point out to you."

"Come this way. My office is close by."

Minutes later, in Glen Dennagher's office, Murf lays the two jackets side by side on the desk there. He then places the purchase receipt from Cleary's to the left of the two jackets. Glen Dennagher invites Murf to sit in the guest chair. Both men are seated. Murf indicates to the items on the desk. "Now, Father, look at…"

The office door bursts open and Bishop Patrick Byrne strides in noisily. "So what's all this then? The police presume to conduct a questioning here in the diocesan office without my permission?" Bishop Byrne is dressed in the requisite ankle-length soutane, similar to the cassocks worn by the priests, except for the amaranth-red piping and the purple cincture hanging down by his left side and ending in silk fringes. The bishop has no need for distinctive clothing in order to be recognized. His bearing and demeanour clearly identify him as the man in charge.

Both Murf and Father Glen Dennagher jump to their feet. Father Glen Dennagher genuflects. He takes the bishop's proffered hand and kisses his ring. "My Lord Bishop," he says in obeisance. The bishop next extends his hand towards Murf. Murf ignores the invitation. He glances at the bishop's black shoes, polished to a high shine, and looks at his own scuffed boots. Then, he snubs the bishop by pointedly directing his attention to the sheet of paper on the desk, more worthy of consideration that the intruding prelate.

The bishop is further enraged at Murf's apparent brush-off. He directs a question to Murf. "And who the hell are you anyways?"

"Detective Inspector John Patrick Murphy. And you must be the bishop…"

"You address me as 'My Lord'…"

"…and I am indeed conducting an inquiry…"

"Not here, you're not. Now get out!"

"Very well, if you insist, I will leave." And turning to Father Glen Dennagher, "Father Glen Dennagher, I must ask you to accompany me to the garda station in Killbawn where I will conclude my questioning…"

"Father Glen Dennagher stays right here," barks the bishop angrily.

Murf approaches the enraged bishop and speaks slowly and quietly to him. "My Lord" – rendering it more like an insult than as a formal address, "do I understand that you intend to obstruct a police inquiry? I must caution you…"

"You, you… how dare you! Who is your superior officer? I am going to report you…"

Murf is already spinning the handle on the phone. He connects to Castlebar and passes the receiver to the bishop.

"Chief Superintendent Ultan O' Neill on the phone, My Lord. You wish to speak to him?"

"Give me that!" The bishop grabs the receiver from Murf and shouts into the phone, "O'Neill is it? And do you know a John Patrick Murphy, one of your detectives?"

"Oh, he IS one of your lads. And what is he doing coming in here asking questions without a by-your-leave?" The bishop listens to O'Neill. He walks to the desk. He sits down in the chair vacated by Father Glen Dennagher. He quietly and slowly places the receiver back on the cradle and whispers, "Detective Inspector Murphy is investigating a suspicious death."

Father Glen Dennagher turns from embarrassed red to a deathly white. "Death?" he says as he inhales sharply. He slumps down in the chair vacated by Murf. "I thought it was an investigation into lost property or theft or..." His voice trails off.

The bishop looks up at Murf. "Inspector, I believe you have some questions of Father Glen Dennagher?"

"Yes, My Lord."

"And I would like to hear them," and turning to Father Glen Dennagher, "and I would like to hear Father Glen Dennagher's responses." The bishop removes a gold fountain pen from his inside pocket and places it on the table. He lifts it and removes the cap, placing the pen back on the table. Immediately, he lifts it once more and replaces the cap. There is no notepad on the desk. The bishop's actions serve no purpose other than to seek attention and to express his rank and importance. For a third time, the bishop places the gold fountain pen on the desk. He positions it at arm's length at precisely 180° and stretches his arms on the table at right angles. With that, he looks up at Murf to indicate that he thus grants him permission to resume questioning.

Murf extracts a small notepad and a stubby little pencil from his breast pocket. He returns the bishop's gaze with an unmistakable message – a stubby pencil with a notepad trumps a gold fountain pen without a writing pad – Murf takes charge of the interview. He resumes speaking. "Father Glen Dennagher, observe the items on the desk – two tweed jackets and a receipt from Cleary's of Sligo." Murf unfolds both jackets and spreads them out on the desk thus compelling the bishop to remove his gold pen and arms from the desktop. He continues to speak while thus engaged. "This receipt is from Cleary's and is dated the fifth of December 1944. It denotes a purchase by 'RC Diocese of Killala, Bishop Patrick Byrne', and it describes the purchase of a tweed jacket, a jacket like this one here." He points to Father Glen Dennagher's jacket. Murf directs a question at Glen Dennagher, "Father Glen Dennagher, did you make this purchase?"

"Yes! Yes! I already told you that."

"A purchase for what exactly?"

"For that jacket there; the one you are holding."

"Are you sure?" Murf hands the jacket to Glen Dennagher. "Check it."

Father Glen Dennagher takes the jacket. He turns it inside out and upside down and every which way. "Yes, I am certain. This jacket here is the one I purchased from Cleary's."

"On the fifth of December 1944 as per the receipt?"

Father Glen Dennagher is irritated at the questions. "You keep asking the same thing and I keep telling you the same thing – this is the jacket I bought from Cleary's on December the fifth in 1944." He hands the jacket back to Murf and drops his arms in frustration.

"Now look at the other jacket. How can you tell which is which?"

"Well, yours is a bit crisper, never worn, and it still has a label attached."

The bishop interjects. "But two coats of the same size and pattern would be indistinguishable from each other if they were both equally worn."

"Observe," says Murf as he places the jackets side-by-side. He opens both jackets and exposes the inside breast pockets. Then he inverts both pockets to display the product identification marks inside. "My jacket displays the product imprint clearly." Both clerics strain to view the marking on Murf's jacket:

Hand-woven and distributed by McHugh of Donegal. Inspected by RA – Batch no. 070646 item 37

"Now observe Father Glen Dennagher's jacket." The marking is clearly discernible:

Hand-woven and distributed by McHugh of Donegal. Inspected by RA – Batch no. 150645 item 09

Murf continues, "The jacket you purchased from Cleary's in December 1944 is identifiable by the mark '*Hand-woven and distributed by McHugh of Donegal. Inspected by RA – Batch no. 210744 item 18'*. However, this jacket here on the desk, the one you claim that you purchased in December 1944, is not that one." To emphasise, Murf states, "This jacket, **your** jacket, Father Glen Dennagher, is not the item you purchased from Cleary's on December the fifth 1944."

Murf waits for this piece of information to sink in. After a moment of silence, the bishop speaks. "All that this tells us is that Cleary's mixed up the jackets from different batches. So they sold a jacket from a different batch. So what? It doesn't mean anything."

"It is true that Cleary's could mix things up. But all the jackets from their stock in December 1944 are accounted for. And no mix-up, no matter how extreme, can explain how a jacket obtained from Cleary's in December 1944 was manufactured in June 1945. The product mark indicates the date of inspection when the item was released from McHugh's factory-warehouse." Murf points to the product mark on Glen Dennagher's jacket.

The bishop stands up erect, scraping the chair on the floor, his ire redirecting from the detective to the priest. His face glows red and saliva appears at the corners of his mouth. "By God, Glen Dennagher, you better have an explanation for this. And it better be a good one, or you'll find yourself in Krilly Island first thing tomorrow morning where you'll spend the rest of your life."

"It's… I mean… I… I…" whimpers Father Glen Dennagher as he slides lower in his chair.

The bishop slaps his hands loudly on the desk. "Explain!"

Murf moves in front of the bishop and faces Glen Dennagher in order to regain control of the questioning. "Father Glen Dennagher, think carefully about your answer. What happened to the jacket you purchased from Cleary's on the fifth of December 1944?"

Glen Dennagher composes himself. He sits erect in the chair and regains his confident manner. He looks Murf in the eye and exclaims, "I lost it."

"You lost it?"

"Yes. It had slipped my mind. I lost it and I obtained an identical replacement the following day."

"Where did you lose it?"

"At the circus. I remember it now. I was sitting at the circus on a wooden seat. I removed my jacket and folded it. I used it as a cushion so that I could sit in comfort. Afterwards,

I left the circus without it and then I went back to retrieve it. I returned to my seat, but the jacket was gone."

"What circus was that?"

"The John Edge Travelling Show."

"And which date and location was that?"

"It was last year in Killbawn. I don't remember the date – sometime in August of last year."

"You don't have the information in your 'meticulous records'?"

The bishop shouts over Murf's shoulder, "Damn it, man! What day was it?"

Glen Dennagher swallows. "It was the Sunday after the fifteenth of August."

Murf calculates. "That would have been Sunday the nineteenth. At what time did you realise you had forgotten your jacket?"

"About nine o'clock, when the show ended."

"At what point after you left the show did you return?"

"A few minutes later. I had reached my car when I realised that I had left my jacket behind on the circus seat."

"Did you notice anyone in particular at the time?"

"There were hundreds of people milling about as they left the circus. I did not notice any one person in particular within the crowd; I certainly did not see anyone with the jacket."

"And then, what did you do?"

"I drove home. And the next morning I went to Cleary's and obtained a replacement jacket."

"This jacket here?"

"Yes. The one there on the desk."

"From the time you realised that the jacket was missing and before you drove home, did you make enquiries at the circus? Maybe someone found it and brought it to lost-and-found."

"I did not think to do that; I just asked the few random people I encountered inside the tent."

"I see." Murf wonders why Glen Dennagher did not engage the circus staff to search for the missing jacket. Is he so affluent that he can afford to lose a jacket and not worry about the cost? Or is he too proud to admit that he lost it through his own negligence? "These are all the questions I have for now. If your explanation checks out, you have nothing to worry about. Be advised that I may need to confirm some facts with you later, so please be available." Murf places his pad and pencil back into his breast pocket. "Thank you for your cooperation, Father."

Murf turns back to face the desk. He gathers up his sample jacket and the purchase receipt from Cleary's. The bishop sits down. Murf asks him, "May I hold on to this receipt for the duration of the investigation?" The bishop nods his consent. Murf places the receipt in his briefcase and prepares to leave. "Good-day, gentlemen."

"Inspector," the bishop addresses him, "what happens if you find the jacket, the one from Father Glen Dennagher's original purchase on December 1944?"

"My Lord Bishop, it is not a question of 'if'. We found the jacket two days ago. We are interested in locating the last person to have possessed it." Both clerics cease breathing for a moment. There is an audible silence as they presume a connection between the new-found jacket and the current case under investigation – the case of the 'suspicious death'. Murf leaves them before either one of them recovers sufficiently to press for an explanation.

As he is about to depart the building, Murf turns to Father McGill. "Father McGill, the bishop mentioned 'Krilly Island' to me a moment ago. Where is it? I thought I knew every island in the country, but I am unable to place it."

"Krilly Island? Well, it's not really anywhere…"

"What? It doesn't exist?"

"Oh, it exists all right, Inspector. But it is a euphemism. It refers to 'sabbatical'."

"I see. Well, thank you, Father McGill." Murf is familiar with 'sabbatical'. It too is frequently employed as a euphemism. Whereas it literally refers to a paid leave of absence, a 'Krilly Island sabbatical' would likely mean an absence that is out-of-sight and out-of-mind. Murf exits the building with his briefcase and sample tweed jacket.

On the drive back to Killbawn, Murf considers the meeting he just had with Father Glen Dennagher. If the priest's account checks out then it is unlikely that he can be considered a suspect in the case. The explanation he tendered is plausible. To confirm the story, however, will be like finding the proverbial needle in the haystack. The jacket, Glen Dennagher's previous jacket, is Murf's only tangible link to the crime. Notwithstanding the daunting odds, Murf realises that he must follow the evidence and pursue the jacket to the circus. He speculates on the number of people that would have been at the circus last year. Perhaps two thousand? First, he must start by questioning the circus staff and performers. Interviewing potential witnesses is the slogging part of police detective investigation. It is onerous and trying but it often gets results.

It is close to 3:00pm when Murf enters the garda station in Killbawn. Garda Eddie Caldwell greets him. "Inspector Murphy, there was a phone call for you from Forensics – Mr Phil Divers. He phoned about an hour ago. He wants you to phone him."

"Eddie, place the call. When you connect, put it through to my office."

Murf ascends the stairs and enters his office. He carefully places his briefcase and sample jacket on the floor in the only clear space amidst his apparent disorder. He sits down at his desk and proceeds to write in his blotter. When the phone connects to Divers he is ready with a pencil and pad. "Divers, you phoned. Tell me some good news."

"Here's something to stick in your pipe. The dental college phoned me. They have an opinion on the filling in your Famine Field cadaver. Now, Murf, the usual filling here in Ireland is an amalgam of tin, silver, mercury and copper. The usual ratios are…"

"Divers, I have that noted from your report. What is significant in the filling in this case? You said that it is in an unusual ratio."

"Ah, and this is what I found out. The mix of the alloy was likely altered due to the scarcity of some of the components during wartime. The body from the Famine Field would have had his tooth filled in war-time Germany."

"In Germany?"

"In WARTIME Germany. This is not certain, but it is more than likely."

"Thanks, Divers. That is indeed significant." He hangs up the phone.

Murf turns his attention to his case file. He amends the information on his evidence wall. He studies his notes and considers what he has learned today – the body from the Famine Field was wearing the tweed jacket that Father Glen Dennagher lost at the circus, and the body is, was, a German from war-time Germany. Was there a German at the circus that night when Father Glen Dennagher lost his jacket? He would not likely be a local resident, but a member of the circus itself. Murf goes to the superintendent's office and borrows a copy of the Connaught Telegraph from District Officer Fox's desk. He consults the schedule of The John Edge Travelling Show. The show was in Killbawn on Sunday, four days ago. It can't be far away. He sees that on Thursday

22 August 1946, the show is scheduled to perform in Swinford. And Swinford is less than an hour away.

At 3:30pm, Murf slips into Cannon's pub in the Market Square and orders a quick bowl of soup-of-the-day and a wedge of the usual crumbly cheddar cheese. As he hurriedly slurps his hot vegetable soup ('left-overs soup') at the counter, Danny the Divil sidles up to him. Murf is impatient to be on his way to Swinford and is not welcoming to the Divil's intrusion.

"Guard Murphy. You are slurping your soup in a helluva hurry. Where are you off to at all, at all?"

Murf responds through a mouthful of cheese. "Sorry, Danny. I've no time for talking. I have to rush off."

It is hard to shake off a friendly drunk. The Divil is both drunk and friendly, and he is curious. "Off to where?"

"Swinford."

"And sure what's in Swinford?"

"The circus."

"Well, it's about time you woke up and went to the circus. Sure haven't I been telling you all along about the leper. And who knows lepers better than other lepers. And where do find lepers, you ask? At the circus of course." The Divil slides along the counter back to his stool and focuses his attention on his whiskey.

Murf stops swallowing and looks sideways at the Divil. "What do you mean by 'lepers at the circus'?"

The Divil edges his way back to Murf and breathes whiskey-breath on his face in an attempt to whisper into his ear. "Sure have you never been to a circus? And have you never seen grown men dressed up in women's knickers like, leppin' around the place and up and over each other? That's lepers, that is."

Murf slaps the counter, spilling some of his soup. "Danny, you are a genius," he shouts. It dawns on Murf with sudden lucidity – the Divil's 'leper' is his mispronunciation of 'leaper' – he means 'tumbler', a quaint term for an acrobat. He realises now that from his first glimpse of the cadaver in the Famine Field, Danny the Divil recognised it as a circus acrobat. Murf rushes off with serious haste. The circus, actually The John Edge Travelling Show, has suddenly assumed a pressing priority.

As Murf runs out the doorway of the pub, the Divil shouts after him, "Hey, Guard Murphy, are you going to finish your cheese?"

Murf takes the R314 to Ballina, and the N26 thereafter. As he crosses the Moy River in Foxford, he considers how all clues point to John Edge's travelling show – Father Glen Dennagher's lost jacket, the acrobat's unitard on the body, and the timing coincides with the presence of the travelling show at Killbawn in late August of last year. He muses that a high-wire artist may possibly have killed a trapeze artist using a prop from the knife-thrower. He smiles at this unlikely scenario. But strange things happen. He feels confident that he is on a fruitful trail.

At 4:20pm, Murf drives into the circus field, off Park Road, on the outskirts of Swinford. He enters the big buff-coloured tent of The John Edge Travelling Show in time to catch the closing act of the matinee performance.

Unlike a traditional ring circus, the performance is conducted on an elevated wooden stage at the far end of a rectangular tent. The seats for the audience are the usual hard wooden circus seats, but they are arranged in theatre-fashion to face the stage. The canvas of the tent imparts a faint clean smell of bleach. There is no odour of mould or dampness from it, notwithstanding the moist conditions it must surely endure in Mayo. There is the clean aroma of wood everywhere, from the wooden seats to the wooden stage. All these fresh smells are assaulted by the competing reek of smouldering cigarettes and pipe tobacco. The smoke drifts up and hangs lazily in the 'V' of the tent. Nevertheless, the electric lights adequately penetrate the drifting smoke and the stage lights illuminate the stage with clarity. Murf concludes that the show has successfully connected to Swinford's electrical supply. In front of the stage, at ground level, is the 'orchestra pit', where the brass band supports the acts with fitting music to excite the audience and create suspense. And the audience participates with appropriate 'oohs' and 'aahs'.

There are nine performers on stage. They are costumed alike in almost-white light-blue unitards. A burly acrobat stands at centre-stage facing the audience. Another performer climbs a nearby step-ladder and launches himself from the top of the ladder. He lands forcefully on a lever that pivots on a fulcrum thus propelling another acrobat into the air. The level and fulcrum are a simple seesaw mechanism. The acrobat thus propelled aloft, somersaults gracefully to land beside the burly man. This is repeated rapidly. Performers are propelled and somersaulted to land beside the burly man, and to land astride the three men standing side-by-side. As the jumping and propelling progresses, a pyramid of six bodies is formed – three at the base and, above that, two and one.

At this point, there is a drum-roll. Two acrobats stand atop the ladder, arms about each other. They drop as one onto the lever. The acrobat on the opposing side of the lever, a young girl of slight build, is launched high into the air. She performs a double somersault and lands on the shoulders of the uppermost acrobat of the pyramid. The drum-roll continues. The performers suddenly lean outwards to the left and right. The audience gasps. The pyramid of bodies appears to collapse outwards at the sides. But the two forces equalise in a counter-balance and the group holds together firmly. The acrobat at the top remains unmoved by this change in the formation. Coincident with this, the two end-performers at ground-level place their inner feet squarely on the feet of the burly man in the centre and raise their outer legs to the side. This is performed in one smooth action coordinated to afford maximum theatrical effect. The pyramid is thus transformed by a fan-like motion into an inverted arrow-head shape, supported solely by the burly man in the centre. 'Burly man' holds his breath; his cheeks puff out and his face turns red. After a brief moment, the drum-roll ends with a cymbal crash. The acrobats bounce lightly back to the floor and they bow to the audience's thunderous applause. Then they tumble and cart-wheel off stage. Murf turns his attention back to the purpose of his visit and goes in search of John Edge or the performance director of the show.

At 4:50pm, Murf is in John Edge's caravan-trailer. John Edge is polite and businesslike. They accomplish the initial introductions more speedily than is customary for Mayo. This pleases Murf who is content to dispense with unnecessary chatter. The caravan is Edge's office-on-the-road. Edge directs Murf to a small wall-mounted folding table that serves as a desk. The two men sit on small collapsible chairs at each end of the table and face each other. John Edge appears sincere and is willing to be of assistance to the police. Murf detects a faint, but unmistakable, English West-Country accent. "You are English, I see. Are you a resident of Ireland now?"

"Since 1935 my abode is in Cabinteely, County Dublin."

"And how long have you been running the travelling show?"

"This is the third year. I was previously a circus manager. However, I left due to my objection to the presence of performing animals. You see, there are no performing animals in The John Edge Travelling Show."

Murf raises a finger in acknowledgement and comes to the point of his inquiry. "I am attempting to trace a person in connection with a case, a person who may have been a member of your travelling show a year ago. I am hoping that you can help us with our inquiries." John Edge nods in understanding. Murf describes the person he is looking for. "Male, a young adult, five feet seven inches tall, likely foreign, perhaps German, dressed in a unitard when last seen, last seen in August 1945."

John Edge nods as Murf imparts each detail of information. But he remains silent. Murf wonders if he truly understands the import of the inquiry or if he is searching his memory. After a moment's thought, John Edge speaks. "We have ninety-eight people employed in The John Edge Travelling Show. Most of the workers are English or Irish. On the other hand, all the artists and performers are displaced persons – refugees, stateless people and homeless people. Europe was ravaged by the conflict of the war, and these are the resulting flotsam and jetsam of humanity – not a large representative number of them, just a few of them. We have two Germans currently engaged here. But we had no Germans employed in the show last year. We almost had, though. For a short while…" John Edge stretches his hand up to an overhead shelf and takes down a hard-cover appointment book. He places it on the table and flips it open. He continues talking "…we had a German travel with us – a young 17-year-old. Ah, here it is. He was with us from Thursday 10 May 1945, in Inver Eske, to Sunday 19 August 1945, in Killbawn. I had hoped to find a spot for him. He was agile and keen. When Annie sprained her ankle, he filled in for her for a couple of months on the human pyramid of the 'Marvellous Magyars'."

Murf gathers from this, that the act he had observed a few minutes earlier was the 'Marvellous Magyars'. He notes that the newcomer had joined the travelling show in Inver Eske, a coastal town and seaport in Donegal. "You say that he performed with the Marvellous Magyars 'for a couple of months'. Then what?"

"When Annie resumed her role in the act he was no longer required in the Marvellous Magyars. Subsequently, I had hoped to train him to become part of the trapeze act. He had the skills and he could climb a rope like a sailor. What he lacked was stage presence – the charisma to draw in an audience and command their attention. But then, just as suddenly as he had first appeared, he left unexpectedly. No note, no explanation, no good-bye."

"On Sunday 19 August 1945? In Killbawn?"

"Yes. He was there on Sunday night at the late show. On the next morning, he was gone."

"Were you not concerned at his sudden departure?"

"Not really. He had difficulty fitting in. He was not cut out to be a showman. Furthermore, he appeared to be on some personal quest which I presumed he had resumed."

"And you know his name?"

"He was the only one who insisted on using his real name – 'Edmund Ludwig'."

CHAPTER TWELVE

EDMUND LUDWIG'S LIFE IN IRELAND

County Mayo, Ireland
Thursday 22 August 1946

"So, tell me about Edmund Ludwig." Inspector Murphy, 'Murf', poses this question to John Edge in John Edge's caravan-trailer, the office-on-the-road of The John Edge Travelling Show, in Swinford, County Mayo. Edmund Ludwig fits the description of the corpse found in the Famine Field. Therefore, he is a person of significant interest. Murf is intent on acquiring all relevant information on this person as it pertains to his case.

John Edge consults the opened appointment book on his desk, on which he has recorded the annual schedule of the show. He flips the pages to May 1945. "There is not much to tell. I wrote notes about him in the schedule book. I see where I have noted that Edmund Ludwig appeared suddenly and without warning on the night of the ninth of May last year. I met with him on the following morning. We were preparing to move from Inver Eske to Belashanny that morning." John Edge shuts the schedule book and continues talking. "Edmund Ludwig could not speak English, except for a few rudimentary phrases of greeting. I don't see how he could have coped in Ireland travelling by himself."

"How did he come to be in Inver Eske and him not able to communicate or converse with the populace?"

"I don't know. He spoke German. Marvin the Magyar, who speaks Hungarian and German, took him under his wing. That's who he stayed with during his time with us. And furthermore, when he arrived, he was without clothes or belongings."

"He arrived naked?"

"I don't think he arrived naked. More likely he disposed of his clothes and was provided with replacement clothes by Marvin. Marvin can tell you a lot more about Edmund than I."

"He disposed of his clothes? Perhaps he did not want to be recognised. Inver Eske is a port. And the date of his arrival coincides roughly with Germany's surrender two days earlier. Could he have been a deserter from the German navy, the Kriegsmarine?"

"Probably. A deserter, or a refugee, or just misplaced until he connected up with, with… he appeared somewhat lost. He was shy and young – only seventeen. I don't believe he could have experienced any normal life serving in Hitler's Kriegsmarine from a young age."

"You have many performers here who fled the war in Europe. Could any one of them have had a reason to hold a grudge against a German serviceman? Did Edmund pose a problem? Was he resented?"

"I don't believe that to be the case. Edmund was well-liked. He was helpful and cooperative, and he was always courteous. If anything, he was withdrawn – a loner of sorts. Everyone chipped in to help him with clothing. His unitard was actually Antonia's – Antonia is my wife and is a trapeze artist – because he was of such a slight build, a man's unitard was too big for him."

"And a unitard is worn skin-tight?"

"Of course."

"Mr Edge, you say that Edmund disappeared on Sunday 19 August last year. According to your performance schedule, that is the date you were in Killbawn."

"That is correct."

"Have you any idea where he intended to go?"

"Not really. He appeared without warning, and so he disappeared in like manner. I presumed that he had continued his journey to connect with… whoever he was attempting to reach."

"I see." Murf considers this unlikely. Who in north Mayo would be of any practical assistance to a deserter from the German forces? Edmund Ludwig would need to be closer to Dublin to achieve any success. Following this sequence of thought, Murf asks, "Could he have driven off in one of the circus cars?"

"In one of our cars? Impossible. I have all the keys under my control. And anyways, that would have been futile as a clandestine exercise. Have you seen how brightly coloured our cars are?"

Murf nods in understanding. All the circus vehicles are highly decorated with the name of the travelling show prominently displayed like billboards. A person could not sneak off unnoticed in one. "Mr Edge, I need you to provide me with a list of names from August of last year – all the members of your travelling show. You understand that in a case such as this we need to question witnesses that could help us in our inquiries, all who could have interacted with Edmund Ludwig prior to his disappearance."

"I have the list right here in my performance book and in my employment book – everyone from last year. It is the same as our current list. We have the same people with us for two years now – except for the additional performers. New to us this year are the contortionist, Teresita; and the photographers, Horst and Greta. Ninety-four people, including myself, are still here from last year. But, tell me, how long will it take to question all ninety-four? We are due to leave Swinford first thing tomorrow morning and travel to Castlebar for an afternoon performance."

"Perhaps we can conduct the questioning without upsetting your schedule." Murf continues with John Edge. John Edge is quite cooperative. He copies all information onto a sheet of paper – names with relative functions in the show. Murf makes a mental note to pay special attention to Marvin and the other members of his team – the 'Marvellous Magyars'. How close a relationship did Marvin provide to Edmund Ludwig while 'under his wing'?

"Mr Edge, you appear to have comprehensive records in your files. Perchance, have you a picture or photograph of Edmund Ludwig?"

"Alas, no. I ensure that all performers are photographed and depicted in costume for publicity purposes. You must have seen our posters displayed prominently a week or two prior to our arrival in a town. But we did not include Edmund in any of our promotional advertising. He joined us towards the end of the season, and he had not actually been placed in a long-term performance role. We had no reason to obtain a picture of him. Is this important?"

"A photograph is helpful in an inquiry of this nature. I'll work with the information you have provided. Expect police officers to arrive to question the staff. One more thing, in case I need to conduct follow-up questions, what is your schedule for the next few days?"

"Monday 26 August, we are in Claremorris. And on Tuesday, Castlerea… Here, I'll write it down for you." John Edge transcribes the information onto a blank sheet of paper and hands it to Murf.

Murf scans the information. "Naas, 16 September 1946 – that is your last date. Is that the end of your season?"

"The end of the season? No, Inspector, that's the end of The John Edge Travelling Show. After three years on the road with my own show, I'm getting out of the business. I have formed a new company, a photographic company, with Horst and Greta Müller. There is a demand for promotional pictures – travel posters, postcards and the like – and I am getting in on the ground floor."

"And the ninety-three others who are employed here?"

"The workers and equipment will be acquired by Fossett's circus. The performers, those who had been displaced by the war in Europe, are required to be repatriated to their home countries or acquire legal status of domicile. That is mandatory now that the war is over."

This information unsettles Murf. An investigation of the circus personnel will require urgent and speedy attention to be concluded promptly. "Thank you, Mr Edge. That's all for now." Murf departs from John Edge and the travelling show.

It is a two-minute drive from the circus site to Swinford District Garda Station at the corner of Kiltimagh Road and Fraunhill. At 5:35pm Murf enters the Swinford Garda Station. He quickly meets with District Officer Superintendent Patrick Kenny. With DO Kenny's cooperation, Murf contacts Divisional HQ in Castlebar and arranges for sufficient manpower to assist in the next stage of the investigation – gathering valuable information from the transient circus staff of The John Edge Travelling Show. Chief Superintendent Ultan O'Neill at Castlebar Garda Divisional HQ is supportive. He is fully aware that in a few more weeks the travelling show will have disbanded. A systematic questioning of the circus personnel should be conducted promptly while the travelling show is still together.

Next, Murf contacts Divers in the divisional forensic section. He informs him of what he has learned about the hitherto unidentified cadaver. Divers undertakes to contact Germany to obtain dental records on Edmund Ludwig from the Kriegsmarine in order to confirm the identity of the body. This may prove difficult. There is no operational

Kriegsmarine anymore, not since Germany's surrender and subsequent occupation. International protocol requires that Ireland's Department of External Affairs contacts the Allied Occupation military government in the appropriate occupied zone. Currently, the Kriegsmarine and its appropriation by the Allies are under the command of Lt. Gerald Ivers of the US Navy. A request to help identify one dead seaman, when many thousands have been lost and are unaccounted for, might be rejected as trivial and unimportant by the Allied occupation administration. Still, such a request is the correct procedure between countries that share diplomatic relations. Will the Allied administration in occupied Germany comply?

Murf remains in the garda station and processes the recently-acquired information while it is still fresh in his memory. He records pertinent points in his notebook, and then considers the import of what he has learned so far today. Edmund Ludwig left the circus field in Killbawn and his deceased remains were discovered a year later in the Famine Field just a few miles distance from there. Could he have suffered an accident in performing acrobatic tricks and died as the result? Not likely. The medical examiner confirms that there are no signs of injury on the skeleton. A severe fall would have broken some bones. Unless he suffered accidental death by non-violent means, and the circus did not want the inconvenience of a medical examiner's visit upsetting their schedule. No, that too is unlikely. If such were the case, the circus would have employed its adequate manpower to swiftly bury the body deep in the circus field. The circus vehicles and equipment would have provided sufficient concealment to conduct the burial without detection. Murf then considers criminal intent. The body was buried in the Famine Field to conceal it from everyone, including the circus personnel. Who would have sufficient motive to kill a German deserter? Someone with a grudge against the

Germans? Someone who suffered at the hands of the German forces, and who later confronted the vulnerable German serviceman?

Murf is convinced that the current course of action is correct – investigate the circus personnel for evidence of **motive**, **means** and **opportunity** to inflict injury on Edmund Ludwig.

Murf is anxiously concerned about one big gaping hole in his premise – what if the cadaver from the Famine Field is someone other than the elusive Edmund Ludwig? And Edmund Ludwig is living contentedly under a new identity in the security of the haven he so longingly sought? Murf twirls his pencil through his fingers. Investigate. Gather facts. Assemble relevant data. Evidence, not speculation, will ultimately provide the answer.

Friday 23 August 1946. At 0800 hours, ten uniformed gardaí descend on The John Edge Travelling Show in Swinford. This is 8:00am, the time when the travelling show is a hive of activity. It takes two hours to dismantle the big top and place it on the lorry for transportation. Coupled with this, all the props are sorted and catalogued for the next location. The travelling show is scheduled to leave Swinford at 11:00am. It is a half-hour journey to Castlebar where the big top ought to be erected and ready for warm-up rehearsals by 1:30pm. This leaves enough preparation time for a 3:00pm performance. The circus staff are prepared for the arrival of the police. A forewarning of their arrival was relayed throughout the circus personnel on the previous night. The gardaí have been provided with the list of all circus staff, and they are instructed to ascertain two overriding primary objectives:

    1) Note the names of all persons who had a relationship with Edmund Ludwig – fellow

performers, friends, confidants. Pay particular attention to unusual and unsympathetic relationships.

2) Note the names of the persons who observed Edmund Ludwig prior to, or at, the time of his disappearance; the last person to have seen him would be of special interest.

This exercise should narrow the list of names to a smaller number of persons of interest, people who will warrant further in-depth investigation.

The inquiries progress favourably. All the circus people cooperate fully, partly due to their desire to keep the show on schedule, and partly due to the dearth of work permits for the refugee-performers. The gardaí conduct their questioning in Swinford, some on the road, and conclude in Castlebar by mid-evening. The show succeeds in opening on time for the afternoon matinee event and the gardaí leave before the start of the evening performance.

At 8:00pm, Murf meets with the ten garda officers in the divisional HQ. During the succeeding hour, he ascertains from them the results of their inquiries. He is provided with written notes and clarifying remarks where they are warranted. Of particular interest are the last people to have interacted with Edmund Ludwig prior to his disappearance. One interaction was of an antagonistic nature. According to Garda Lynch, the acrobat Marvin had 'words' with Edmund at the conclusion of the circus performance on the night in question. Murf queries Garda Lynch, "Garda Lynch, what 'words' of an 'antagonistic nature' occurred?"

Garda Lynch consults his notes and responds. "This is what I learned. I spoke with the acrobatic troupe. Stan, one of the tumblers, informed me of a verbal confrontation between Marvin and Edmund Ludwig. It occurred after they had completed their act that night. Marvin was upset at Ludwig crashing the act unexpectedly. An intense argument ensued between them."

"You say 'words'. Do I understand that this was purely verbal and that there was no actual threat of violence?"

"That is what Stan told me."

"So, what 'words' were used?

"I don't know. And neither does Stan. The argument was entirely in German. It was clear to Stan from the tone of the argument that they were both upset with each other. Perhaps an argument sounds harsher in German. Nevertheless, Stan picked up on one word that was repeated – 'ouse-tygen' (aussteigen). And one other word – 'abhoun' (abhaun)."

"Meaning what, exactly?"

Garda Tynan interrupts, "I can help with this. I was Garda Lynch's partner during the inquiry. I followed up on Stan's account when I subsequently interviewed Marvin. I asked him, Marvin, to explain the verbal exchange he had with Edmund Ludwig. He informed me that Ludwig had intruded on his act unexpectedly. It appears that Ludwig was previously part of the act when it was one acrobat short, but he was dropped when it returned to full strength. Marvin reminded Ludwig that he was no longer a part of the act and that he must leave. That's what the argument was about."

"Leave?" Murf picks up on this word. "What did you understand by 'leave' in the context of the argument?"

"It was in German. And Marvin did not qualify the implication of the word other than in the context of the disagreement."

Murf quickly notes this in his jotter – *'leave the scene of the argument', 'leave the act,' 'leave the circus', 'leave what'?* Murf spreads the garda notes on a table and addresses the assembled men. "Garda Lynch and Garda Tynan estimate the time of the argument as occurring at nine o'clock, give or take five minutes. Could that be the last sighting of Edmund Ludwig prior to his disappearance?"

The men refer to their notes and concur. Garda Lynch speaks. "Stan says that he was the last to speak with Edmund Ludwig. But not necessarily the last to have seen him. Stan and Mario were with Ludwig after the argument for a short time. But Ludwig wanted to be alone. Stan did not press him, so he left him. Mario, on the other hand, left and returned some moments later. Only by the time he returned, Ludwig was not at the spot where he had left him. Mario stated that he looked around hoping to see him and remembers seeing Father Ambrose standing close by at the time."

Murf looks from Garda Lynch to the assembled men. He poses the question to them, "This person, Father Ambrose, may have been the last to have seen Edmund Ludwig. Well then, who interviewed Father Ambrose?" After a few minutes of shuffling papers and scratching heads and scraping feet, Murf realises that no one interviewed Father Ambrose. "Come on men, who has Father Ambrose on their list of persons to be interviewed?" Again, there is no response. Murf is annoyed at this. He consults the master list to ascertain which garda was assigned 'Father Ambrose' and, hence, who is responsible for this oversight. He is stunned to find that Father Ambrose's name is absent from the master list, the list that John Edge gave to Murf with the assurance that it contains the names of all members of The John Edge Travelling Show. This disturbs Murf. The last person to have seen Edmund Ludwig is of paramount importance to the investigation. And Father Ambrose, the most likely person, was missed in the execution of today's sweeping police inquiry.

At 9:00pm, Murf thanks all the officers and dismisses them. He studies the resulting notes. Murf narrows down the list to a few persons of interest. Murf needs to ask the really important questions of the right people. From these reports, and as indicated previously by John Edge, he learns that Edmund Ludwig was a withdrawn loner. In the opinions of those questioned, he was regarded as polite, but he kept to himself and avoided social interaction. He spoke only German. His inability to speak conversationally in any other language could have contributed to his privacy.

From the garda questioning of the circus members, Murf determines that the last people Edmund Ludwig interacted with on the night of his departure were Marvin and the acrobats of the Marvellous Magyars, and possibly the mysterious Father Ambrose. Murf assembles his notes from the meeting and places prominent importance to these key parties. He resolves to investigate them thoroughly as a matter of priority. This entails a second round of questioning but, this time, by Murf himself.

He proceeds to place relevance on these persons. Did any of them interact adversely with Edmund? Marvin did, but what about the others? What is the timeline of these exchanges relative to other happenings within the locale of the circus? Who was the last person to have seen Edmund prior to his disappearance? Could it have been Father Ambrose? Murf consults the list of names he obtained from John Edge. Although there is no 'Father Ambrose' listed, he cross-references the names in the hope of finding a suitable nick-name – a name other than a 'real' name? Most of the performers' names are stage-names. Many have reason to conceal their actual names. Could 'Father Ambrose' be one of the performers under a different name, or is Father Ambrose a non-circus person – a priest who frequents the circus? Suddenly the name 'Father Barry Glen Dennagher' flashes through his mind – the priest who admires acrobats.

CHAPTER THIRTEEN

WHAT MURF LEARNS AT THE CIRCUS

County Mayo, Ireland
Saturday 24 August 1946

Murf arrives at The John Edge Travelling Show at 8:00am. John Edge is not surprised to see him. On this occasion, they are joined by Antonia Edge. Antonia is striking rather than attractive. She moves gracefully. Like a number of circus performers, her attire is influenced by her profession. Her blouse is vanilla-white. Her skirt is short and is a pastel-pink colour and is worn over ballet tights that match her blouse. Her shoes are flat-soled pink slippers. Murf thinks of flavoured ice-cream – vanilla and strawberry. Her long blond hair is tied in a ponytail (not her natural colour) and her complexion is tanned (enhanced by make-up). Thus, her face is darker than her hair. She smiles easily, displaying perfect teeth (more perfect than what God designed). Notwithstanding, she conveys a pleasant and intelligent personality.

Murf is on a quest to complete the details of the previous interview and to clarify some of the information obtained on the previous day. "How long will you remain in Castlebar?"

John Edge responds, "The travelling show has two more performances in Castlebar, an evening show today and a matinee show on Sunday."

"I see. Tell me, do you know a 'Father Ambrose'? His name came up, but he is not on your list."

John Edge informs him, "Indeed, there is a Father Ambrose travelling with us. He is not on staff, either as a worker or as a performer. Consequently, his name was omitted from the list I provided to you. I'm sorry, Inspector. Is this important?"

Clearly, if Murf is inquiring, then it is important. Antonia explains. "Friar Ambrose is *un frate mendicante*. How do you say that in English? A begging friar?"

John Edge interjects. "A mendicant. Father Ambrose is a mendicant friar who relies solely on alms. His vocation is in serving the spiritual needs of travellers and itinerants. Here, in The John Edge Travelling Show, he conducts Mass and prayer sessions and provides counselling. Antonia is a frequent participant in his services – attending Mass and availing of the Sacraments. Furthermore, Father Ambrose has undertaken Annie Magyar's education and he provides the Magyar orphan with instruction on Christian doctrine. He blends in with the labourers in the circus in his attire except for his distinctive bare feet which he thrusts loosely into floppy open-toed sandals."

Antonia takes advantage of a breathing pause by John Edge and continues to describe Father Ambrose. "He wears a plain wooden cross hanging from a string around his neck. And he DOES beg. He is probably off in Castlebar as we speak, where he will go door-to-door begging for alms..."

"...which he gives away as promptly as he receives them." John Edge has recovered his breath.

Murf considers the significance of this piece of information. Father Ambrose's insight into life in the travelling show may provide an understanding of Edmund Ludwig's situation and, thereby, what precipitated his sudden disappearance. And if this same Father Ambrose was the last person to have seen Edmund Ludwig on the night he disappeared, he may prove to be the most important link in the investigation to date. Murf controls his expression to one of neutral interest. He asks matter-of-factly, "Where could I find Father Ambrose at this time?"

John Edge frowns in concentration. "Father Ambrose comes and goes. He is never far away. But on the other hand, he is seldom in the midst of things. If you ask around, some of the workers will locate him for you."

Antonia interjects with slight annoyance. "No, they won't, John. Friar Ambrose went off to town after saying Mass this morning. I already told you, he is off begging at this time. Don't expect him back here until after lunchtime. I know that it will be after lunch. He will undoubtedly manage to find a free meal in some establishment. He always does."

Murf thanks the Edges for their assistance and cooperation. He takes his leave as hastily as politeness permits. Outside in the circus field, Murf mentally enumerates his list of priorities. Of the four parties of special interest at the circus, he decides to turn his attention next to Marvin and the Marvellous Magyars. Thereafter, he will seek out Father Ambrose and determine to what extent the mendicant friar is relevant to the case.

Murf locates Marvin's caravan trailer, identified by the red-white-green trim painted on the sides. Marvin permits him entry. Marvin is dressed in grey flannel trousers and a navy-blue polo-neck pullover. The caravan is a cramped abode for two occupants. And Edmund Ludwig was the third occupant here at one time. Murf realises that in a travelling show it is not uncommon to have four occupants share a caravan of this size. There is a distinct smell of sweat from unwashed clothes. This is understandable. Acrobatics is a sweaty activity and laundry facilities are difficult to avail of while on the move. He glances around. A girl is sitting at the small drop-down table. She looks about thirteen. She is dressed in a unitard, over which she wears a floral wrap-around skirt. Marvin introduces her as 'Annie'. Annie avoids eye contact. She does not look at Murf or acknowledge him in any way. She focuses her attention on an album spread on the table. Murf wonders if it is a photograph album or a stamp album. On closer observation, Murf realizes that the album contains a collection of knotted pieces of fine string gummed in place on the pages. Marvin, noticing Murf's curiosity, explains. "Marine knots. This is Annie's collection of marine knots. She learned marine knots from Edmund Ludwig. She has a sample of each one in her album."

Murf addresses Annie, "Hello, Annie. My name is Inspector Murphy. But you may call me 'Murf'. Everyone does."

Annie continues to peer at the album. She glances quickly and furtively at Murf, but she does not respond to his greeting. Marvin mouths silently to Murf – 'Trauma'. Murf understands. Annie is a child refugee. She must have experienced untold horrors resulting in emotional scars. Murf understands that traumatised children are withdrawn and are reluctant to speak. Marvin gently addresses Annie. "Annie, tell Murf about your knots. How many knots have you mastered? And how many are in your album?"

Annie continues concentrating on the album, slowly and delicately turning the pages. She flashes three fingers on her left hand, followed by three fingers on her right hand, without taking her eyes off the album. Marvin interprets for Murf's benefit. "Thirty-three marine knots. That's a lot. I never realised there were so many knots." Murf wonders if there should be thirty-seven knots in total, adding the four knots found with the exhumed remains of Edmund Ludwig.

Over the next half-hour, Marvin describes his relationship with Edmund Ludwig and how Edmund became part of the Marvellous Magyars for a brief time. "Edmund Ludwig," he relates, "departed from a U-boat in Donegal Bay while it was undergoing repairs en route to surrendering in Northern Ireland. Edmund acted with no clear plan of what he was about, except that he did not wish to be repatriated to

Germany. It was his good fortune that I was the first person he encountered face-to-face after departing from the U-boat. You see, I am proficient in German, the only language in which Edmund could communicate. Furthermore, I quickly discovered that Edmund was a skilled gymnast, a valuable talent that I could take advantage of. At the time of Edmund's arrival, Annie had suffered a sprained ankle. I availed of Edmund's skills. I placed him as a substitute in place of Annie in the human pyramid of the Marvellous Magyars. Annie, of course, rejoined the act when she had recovered completely. Whereupon Edmund requested that I modify the human pyramid to increase the height by one more person, placing him second from the top with Annie on his shoulders."

"So, did you accommodate his request?" Murf asks.

"I attempted to, but the pyramid kept collapsing when we executed the final move."

"The arrowhead shape?"

"Oh, you've seen it, then?"

"Yes. And what was the problem with adding an extra person?"

"Inspector, I am not strong. I am unable to bear the weight of two people unless they are very light."

"Surely not. I saw you myself just last night…"

"It's a trick. You see, my health was damaged during my escape from the Nazis. I puff and strut and appear strong, but it is an act – a trick to entertain." Murf looks incredulous. Marvin laughs. "Come. Let me show you."

Marvin takes a tin box from out of a drawer. He empties the contents on the table beside the album. Annie smiles. It is a child's collection of building blocks, not cubes, but blocks of varying lengths and shapes in multiple colours. This is how a child would build a miniature pyramid or temple or bridge, or whatever takes their fancy. Marvin explains. "This is a game Annie and I once played together. She builds a structure against my attempts to remove blocks without toppling the structure." Marvin constructs a shape, a combination of a pyramid and a Grecian temple. "That's me there," pointing to a vertical block, "and that is the weight borne by my shoulders," pointing to a small horizontal block. "Now, if I am unable to bear the weight of all those higher blocks, watch what happens." Marvin pushes the 'shoulder block' and removes it, whereupon the entire structure collapses. Marvin commences building the structure a second time. "Now watch. When I place additional blocks – one here and one here – at the extreme right and left of the structure…" Marvin again removes the 'shoulder block. "… the structure remains standing. The weight is borne by the extremities rather than by the centre."

"But in your act, the two acrobats – the one on your left and the one on your right – placed their weight on your feet. You still bore the entire weight of the acrobats one way or another."

"When the shape changed from pyramid to arrowhead, did you notice the shift?"

"Yes, the shape bulged slightly at both sides, At that point, I thought that the right and left sides were going to collapse outwards and tumble to the ground."

"What you witnessed was the shift in weight to the outside." Marvin points to the two additional blocks he had placed at the right and left sides of his model structure. "And here are my 'feet'." He points to two little square blocks supporting two pillars. These 'feet' bear the entire weight of the structure. Watch." He removes two more blocks from the base. The structure wobbles but remains standing. Murf looks at the roof-shaped structure supported by two columns situated one-third the distance from the extreme edges. The two columns rest on the 'feet'. Marvin walks away from the table. The little structure remains intact. "Now this is the secret of my trick. Look at this." Marvin takes a one-inch-thick sheet of plywood from where it is leaning against the wall. He places it flat on the floor. Then he places two large boots on the plywood. The boots land heavily on the plywood with a loud thump. "All acrobats, including me, wear light dancing-pumps. But when I perform at the pyramid base I wear these boots. Slip your feet into them and try them out."

Murf is curious to know the secret of the trick. He complies. He removes his boots and places his feet inside Marvin's boots. He is surprised to discover that Marvin's boots are actually hollow iron blocks shaped with toecaps. Marvin steps heavily on Murf's toes. There is no resulting sensation of weight on his toes. All the weight placed on Marvin's boots is borne by the hollow iron blocks and by the plywood underneath. Satisfied that Murf understands the trick, the secret behind the theatrical act of pretending to bear an immense weigh, Marvin invites Murf back to the table. "Now observe, Inspector, when another body is placed on the structure." Marvin takes a small block and places it on top of the structure. "Watch what happens when Edmund Ludwig is added. The weight distribution shifts back towards the centre." The structure of wooden building blocks tumbles onto the table. Annie laughs in childlike glee and claps her hands.

Murf looks at the scattered blocks. He understands the point of the demonstration. With Annie back in the Mighty Magyars, there was no place for Edmund Ludwig. Murf inquires of Marvin, "How was your decision received by Edmund Ludwig?"

"He was sorely disappointed and felt hard done by."

"He regarded your decision as unfair."

"Yes."

"What happened on the evening of his disappearance? Did anything of significance occur? Anything to strain the security of your relationship?" Murf is distracted by the thump of a book being placed heavily on the table. Annie opens a blue hardcover book to an inside page and rotates the book until it is aligned with Murf's line of sight. It is Annie's personal diary. Murf sees the date at the top of the page and, at a quick glance, he perceives Annie's account of the evening of Edmund's departure. Murf quickly reads the open page. It contains one significant sentence in Annie's handwriting – *'Marvin and Eddie spoke German harsh words to each other and Eddie left in a huff'*. Murf looks at Annie and asks, "Edmund left just like that, never to return?"

Marvin, by way of explanation, says, "Children don't understand the ways of adults. Moreover, German sounds harsh and threatening to Annie. She associates it with a period of fear and suffering."

Murf wonders to what extent Annie understood the argumentative exchange. Children have an instinctive understanding of vocal tone and body language. Murf sees that Annie's writings are exclusively in English, albeit with many misspelt words. If Annie communicates in English and Edmund spoke only German, how did they converse? Murf inquires. "Marvin, in what language did Annie and Edmund communicate – English or German?"

Marvin scratches his chin before forming his reply. "Neither. They seldom spoke at all. They would sit together in silence for long spells. Edmund would demonstrate marine knots, and Annie would show him her English exercises."

While Marvin is thus speaking, Annie lifts a jotter from the corner of the table. She opens it. Murf perceives that it is Annie's English exercise notepad. Annie extracts a pencil from the spine of the book and writes on the opened page so that Murf may read it:

I teeched him 100 wurds

Annie resumes studying the knots in her album. She turns over the page. Rather than revealing an expected marine knot, the new page contains a photograph of a smiling Annie with Edmund Ludwig. In it, they are playing with string and tying knots. Once more, Annie writes in her jotter and turns it towards Murf. She has written:

Edmund promised me fore more nots.
He was coming back.
Somthing bad happened.

Marvin intervenes. "Come now, Annie. The inspector is a very busy man. It is time for you to clear the table and attend to your tasks. The inspector and I will talk."

Murf has a lot to digest. He is connecting dots in his mind. A picture is forming, and Marvin is a significant factor in the picture. Did Marvin resent the close bond that was forming between Edmund and Annie? Could he have been jealous of their friendship, fearing that it undermined his hitherto unique exclusive close relationship with the child Annie? Edmund may not have been a danger to the human pyramid collapsing so much as a threatening wedge interfering in Marvin's close relationship with his young ward. Murf surmises that Marvin had motive to be rid of Edmund. And when the opportunity presented itself, Marvin acted. Was Marvin capable of actually harming Edmund? He had the means and opportunity to cause mischief to Edmund. Yet, there is something amiss in the picture.

Murf continues with his questions without any noticeable pause. "Annie, do you mind if I take that photograph of Edmund?" Annie slams the album shut and slides it off the table onto the security of her lap. Annie is possessive of her personal property and clearly will not part with it. "Or perhaps there is another photograph?" Annie glances at a drawer and holds her gaze.

Marvin speaks. "I believe we have a few photographs in here." He slides open the drawer and extracts another photograph. It is similar to the one in Annie's album but without the pronounced smile.

Murf now has a much-needed picture of Edmund Ludwig. "Thanks, Marvin. I have just a few more questions and I will be finished. But not here. Would you mind coming with me, Marvin?"

"What? You're taking me to the police station? Surely you don't think that I…"

"Don't jump to conclusions. I need to show you something, and then we're done."

"Where? Will it take long?"

"Will Annie be all right for an hour or two here on her own?"

"An hour or two?" Marvin recovers somewhat. He realises that this is a serious police investigation, and he, Marvin, is a 'person of interest' required to help in the investigation. His best option is to cooperate fully. "Yes, of course." And turning to Annie, "I'll be back shortly. In the meantime, get on with your tasks. You can start with the laundry." He kisses her gently on the forehead, turns around, and departs quickly with Murf.

It is 10:30am. Murf is driving east on the N5. Marvin is seated next to him in the front passenger seat. "Now, Marvin, take your time. I want you to walk me through all that transpired from the time you had the argument with Edmund Ludwig, starting with the unexpected encounter during the acrobatic act, up to when you last saw him on the night of August nineteenth last year – all the details."

"Here in the car? You think I will talk more freely with Annie absent?"

"Marvin, I am bringing you to the location of Edmund's disappearance, where you claim to have seen him last. Revisiting the site may refresh your memory. Meanwhile, recount to me the details to the best of your recollection."

Marvin relates how on 19 August 1945, during the evening performance of the Marvellous Magyars, Edmund unexpectedly joined them. Edmund was no longer a member of the act and was not scheduled to take part in the performance that evening. Marvin was unsure of Edmund's intentions and feared that they might be detrimental to the performance. Throughout the act, Marvin was anxious and distracted, fearful that Edmund might do something unexpected to cause an upset to the pyramid. Afterwards, offstage, Marvin gave Edmund a severe scolding in which he instructed him to stay away from the acrobatic act. This was an appropriate dressing-down by the troupe leader. Unfortunately, it was received badly by Edmund who over-reacted. He challenged Marvin's authority over the troupe. That's when the row ensued.

Marvin interrupts his narration when Murf stops the car at a field. Marvin looks at the site and takes his bearings. "Inspector, this is the circus field in Swinford. This is the wrong place. Edmund disappeared in Killbawn, not here in Swinford."

"Not to worry. I'll just take the Kiltimagh Road to Main Street and proceed up the Swinford Road to the N26." Marvin picks up his narrative from where he left off. Murf listens to Marvin's account as he continues on the N26 to Ballina, and thence on the R314 through to Killala. Throughout, Murf attempts to read Marvin's expression to determine if he recognises the road or its surroundings. Marvin displays no interest in the route. Murf swings off the R314 and proceeds towards Killbawn by way of the longer coast road, thus to approach the town from the north. Marvin appears unconcerned.

Marvin continues to enlighten Murf on the details of the events leading up to Edmund's disappearance. When the row between Marvin and Edmund came to a head, Edmund stormed off, still dressed for the acrobatic performance. Stan and Mario, two other members of the troupe, ran after him to catch up with him for the purpose of pacifying him. Marvin does not know if they succeeded in speaking with him or not. Marvin claims that this was the last he saw of Edmund Ludwig. He heard not a word of news about him until confronted by the current police inquiry.

Murf drives slowly on the coast road. Shortly, he brings the car to a halt at the bend at the two-mile stone. Puzzled, Marvin looks out to the right and to the left. There is a river on one side, and there is a hill sloping away on the opposite side. Marvin notices the little pink ribbons staked into the ground and little mounds of sand at intervals on the hillside, and just inside the wire fence is an unsightly hole – an unfinished pit or trench.

Marvin is agitated. He asks, "Why are we stopped here? This is not Killbawn. And this is no circus field. It's not an 'anything field'. Why are we here?"

"We are about three miles from Killbawn. And this, Marvin, is the Famine Field."

"And what is significant about the Famine Field?"

"You see yon trench?" Murf asks. Marvin sees where Murf is pointing. Marvin stares in puzzlement at the unsightly hole beside a mound of sand and dirt. Murf continues, "That is where we found the remains of Edmund Ludwig on Monday, five days ago." Murf tries to judge Marvin's reaction. He appears to be genuinely surprised.

Murf slips the car into first gear, but before he releases the clutch, Marvin lays his hand on his arm and asks, "Did you see him? Did he look at peace?" Marvin pictures a dead Edmund with recognisable features. Murf has not the heart to tell him that, after a year buried in the Famine Field, Edmund Ludwig had decomposed to skeletal remains. Marvin continues, "Would you permit me to go to the spot where…?

Murf engages the hand-brake. "Very well. You may spend a few moments here." Marvin exits the car and enters the field. Standing at the edge of the pit, Marvin appears to be praying. Murf looks at Marvin. This paternalistic man, who rescued a war-orphan, was once a trained soldier in the German army. Murf wonders how many people Marvin may have killed in service to the Nazis and later in fleeing from them after his desertion. Marvin had been a killer at one time, but that was then and this is now. Notwithstanding Marvin's lethal capabilities, Murf is dissatisfied with the picture he has formed regarding Marvin's hand in Edmund's death. If Marvin killed Edmund, why would he have chosen this specific out-of-the-way spot to dispose of the body? How would he even know to come here? Only someone with local knowledge would know of this dolmen field's suitability for hiding a body. Marvin may have had the motive, means and opportunity to murder Edmund. But for Marvin to have transported the body to this place, together with the required digging tools, he would have required an accomplice familiar with the area. As a suspect, Marvin fits the picture, except for any part in actually disposing of the body. Murf considers the possibility that Marvin may have committed murder or manslaughter and then engaged someone local to dispose of the body. Marvin and a local accomplice? This is possible but is extremely unlikely. Until, and unless, Murf can connect Marvin to the burial of the body in the Famine Field, he has no grounds to make an arrest. He realises that the investigation must continue deeper and wider until all pertinent facts are accumulated. Murf requires irrefutable evidence to firmly establish a connection between Marvin and Edmund Ludwig's actual demise. Conversely, fresh evidence may vindicate him entirely. Murf has more dots to add and put into context before the picture is complete.

Marvin returns to the car and they resume their journey. Murf visits 'The Home', the sports field in Killbawn where The John Edge Travelling Show performed. Marvin acknowledges the location with a grunt. Murf invites him to enter the field. Marvin walks around the field and points out to Murf all the places associated with events as they pertain to Edmund Ludwig on the night of his disappearance. Murf notes each position in his notebook, detailing their relationship to each other. He paces the distance between the big top and the place where the argument occurred, and he paces back to the car park. Thus he has an understanding of the proximity of the events in terms of physical distance and time intervals. While Murf is thus engaged in writing, Marvin is silent. He is no longer talking and considers that nothing more needs to be said. They drive back to Castlebar in silence and arrive at the circus field in the convent grounds at 12:50pm.

After he leaves Marvin at his caravan abode, Murf walks from the travelling-show encampment to the garda station in five minutes. He checks for any pending messages. There are none. He is anxious to recommence his inquiries. He walks back to Castle Street and quickly grabs some fast-served pub grub.

At 1:30pm Murf resumes his interviews at the travelling show. He wonders if Father Ambrose has returned yet. He intends to seek for him among the workers. Murf wanders around the circus field. After a thorough search and frequent enquiries, Murf determines that Father Ambrose is not in the circus field and has not returned from his begging foray in Castlebar.

He encounters the entire troupe of Marvin's Marvellous Magyars – except for Marvin and Annie – socialising together. The seven acrobats are taking advantage of the rest afforded by the absence of a matinee performance that day. With the arrival of Murf, they cease talking. Murf surmises that the topic of conversation is Edmund Ludwig and the police interest in Marvin. Murf engages them and elicits the details of the brouhaha between Marvin and Edmund insofar as they witnessed the incident. They sympathise with both parties to some extent, but they express the view that the situation was badly handled.

One member states, "They were both out of line, you know."

Another adds, "Edmund was no longer part of our act. He was not needed. If he had joined the pyramid that night it would have tumbled and collapsed."

And from another, "Edmund's intrusion into the act was disruptive and could have caused an embarrassing and precarious situation for us all. But Marvin had no cause to go off the deep end about it either."

"Yes," from another, "it would have been prudent of Marvin to insert an interlude into the act to give sufficient time to placate Edmund and, if necessary, we could have removed him quietly."

Murf wonders if Marvin was itching for a fight with Edmund and this incident afforded him the justification.

The troupe members continue to interrupt each other in order to give a full account to Murf. Murf notates the information being tendered by the acrobats. From the information thus received, he understands that at the end of the argument between Marvin and Edmund, Edmund ran off. Stan and Mario went after him to calm him while the other members pacified Marvin. Undoubtedly, Edmund was in a huff. Stan and Mario caught up with him near the car park. Stan advised him to take a walk and cool off. Mario endorsed that suggestion, and being of the same slight stature as Edmund, he offered to give him a coat to wear due to the coolness of the evening. Edmund shrugged off their offers of assistance and turned away from them. Stan stood speechless. Mario ran off and fetched a coat for Edmund, but upon his return, Edmund had disappeared. So, too, had Stan.

This information supports the report tendered on the previous night by Garda Lynch and Garda Tynan. Murf prompts Stan and Mario to confirm their statement regarding the presence of Father Ambrose. Murf enquires, "So you, Stan, or you, Mario, were the last to see Edmund Ludwig prior to his disappearance?"

Stan and Mario exchange a few words as they attempt to remember. Stan comments, "It's like we told the police officers yesterday. After Mario left, there were a few people still hanging about – the dawdlers from the late show, you know – talking together and smoking and cracking jokes. Young people, you know."

Mario adds, "When I returned with the coat, there was no sign of Edmund. Instead, I saw Father Ambrose at the spot where Edmund had been. Maybe **he** saw something."

This is consistent with their statement of the previous day. Murf reaffirms his resolve to contact Father Ambrose as a matter of primary importance. It is now early afternoon and the friar ought to be back. Murf moves to conclude his interview with the acrobats. "Was it out of character for Edmund to go off at night by himself?"

Stan replies, "Edmund often took off by himself, but always within the vicinity of the encampment."

Mario comments, "He never went off in a huff like that…"

Other members of the troupe express their opinions. "He was lithe and light on his feet. He could steal off quietly in the blink of an eye."

Some of the troupe laugh at this. "Ah, he was light on his feet, all right; light as a fairy." At this, they all laugh, but not Mario. Mario makes eye contact with Murf for a second and walks away.

Murf has concluded his questioning of the Marvellous Magyars and is impatient to question Father Ambrose. There was an unspoken communication from Mario. Murf looks around for him. Perhaps Mario can shed some light on the character of Edmund, something that might be a clue to his behavioural peculiarities and, hence, a clue as to where he may have gone, or to what he intended to do. Murf makes a mental note to speak with Mario alone later on.

Murf leaves the group of acrobats and eagerly resumes his search for Father Ambrose. He walks a few steps and Mario appears at his side. Mario speaks to him as they walk slowly side-by-side. "Edmund had a disposition. I recognised it the instant I met him."

"Like what?"

"It affected his behaviour around people. They regarded him as shy, but... Inspector, you have a saying in Irish – 'Aithníonn ciaróg ciaróg eile' (One cockroach recognises another)."

"That's very well-rendered, Mario. Do you understand it?"

"The words, no; the adage, yes."

"And what 'ciaróg' are you referring to?"

"A 'nance'."

Murf stops walking and turns to face Mario.

Mario reaffirms his statement so that Murf clearly understands him. "Edmund Ludwig was a 'nancy boy'."

Murf understands what is meant. Edmund was effeminate, possibly a homosexual. "You are telling me that Edmund was a, a…?"

"You can say it – 'a homosexual'. There is more than one of us here in The John Edge Travelling Show. Edmund was in denial about his 'peculiarity'. No, that's not correct. Let's say he was confused about his sexuality. He was seeking answers, but he did not know where to turn. Back in Germany, the Nazis would have locked him up or worse."

Murf considers the similarity of conditions in Ireland, where homosexual men are sent for treatment to be 'cured'. He thanks Mario for his honest and helpful contribution. This information could have major significance in placing data into perspective – in arranging Murf's dots in the picture of his case. Murf is alerted to a possible connection, one that he strongly considered a day ago – Father Barry Glen Dennagher and his outreach ministry. Murf has a lot of dots to arrange and rearrange.

Murf is anxious to get back to his office. He is eager to review the information and put the data into perspective. But first, it is important to connect with Father Ambrose. This is his current pressing priority. From what Murf has learned, and further confirmed today, Farther Ambrose might be the last known person to have seen Edmund Ludwig alive.

It is after 2:00pm. Murf asks around for Father Ambrose. He inquires of a group of circus workers if they know Father Ambrose. As it so happens, Father Ambrose is well known to them and Murf is directed to where he is likely to be. This time, Murf succeeds in locating Father Ambrose. He finds him in conversation with the men who erect the big tent and who perform the manual work for the operation of the travelling show. He identifies Father Ambrose by his feet – by his open-toed sandals. Father Ambrose instantly recognises Murf as the investigating police officer in the

Edmund Ludwig missing-person case. He makes eye contact with Murf. Murf gestures to him and the friar extricates himself from the group. He approaches the detective.

Murf immediately questions Father Ambrose, who is accommodating to Murf's inquiries. He quickly learns that the humble friar is particularly astute and observant. Father Ambrose informs him, "Sure I was cognisant of Edmund's discomfort in interacting with people and of his reluctance to engage with people his own age. Nevertheless, in my opinion, Edmund had insufficient cause to run off and disappear that night. Yes, he had a row with Marvin. That is not unusual. Marvin is tense when performing and is apt to exhibit annoyance when the act performs below his expectations. I witnessed the row between Marvin and Edmund and how Edmund had stormed off as a result. But where could Edmund go? Marvin was his mainstay on whom he relied for his welfare. I expected Edmund to return once he had cooled off and things had settled down."

"You are saying that you saw him actually leave the circus?"

"After the incident, I saw him part from Marvin, and I saw him turn away from Stan and Mario. Thereafter, I observed him walk towards the parking lot. He did not depart from the circus field itself. He stood next to the parking lot and stared out towards the roadway. Fearful that he may be considering something rash, I approached Edmund to offer him solace. However, someone else beat me to the punch."

Murf remembers that Mario had come looking for Edmund to provide him with a coat. "You mean Mario?"

"No. Father Glen Dennagher."

There it is again. Father Glen Dennagher's name keeps popping up. "Father Glen Dennagher was with Edmund? Did you see what transpired between them?"

"Father Glen Dennagher, I presume, was consoling him. It would be in keeping with his calling, his outreach ministry, to console and comfort."

"What did you hear them say?"

"Oh, I was not sufficiently close to hear what they said. I deduced my opinion from their gestures and body language."

"And then what?"

"I considered Edmund to be in good hands so, not wishing to intrude, I left."

"You left. And Father Glen Dennagher and Edmund Ludwig were in conversation in the car park?"

"Next to the car park."

Murf mentally pictures the scene. "Father Ambrose, did you notice how Father Glen Dennagher was dressed?"

"Sure. He was dressed like most priests in Mayo – very priest-like in black shoes, black trousers, black shirt and black jacket, a French-style black beret on his head, and the clerical collar of course."

"He was wearing a jacket? Could it have been a tweed jacket?"

"Oh, no, not a jacket like a sports coat. It was a sleeveless woollen cardigan, or it could have been a sleeveless pullover. They are popular with rural clergy, worn in place of a waistcoat."

With that, Murf concludes his interview with Father Ambrose. This last piece of information concurs with Father Glen Dennagher's account. In attempting to locate his lost tweed jacket, Father Glen Dennagher enquired of the people he randomly encountered between his vacated circus seat and his parked car. Was Edmund a 'random person' he chanced upon during his search? Being familiar with the members of the Marvellous Magyars, Glen Dennagher would have known Edmund and would have recognised him at the car-park. It would have been fitting for him to ask him Edmund about his lost jacket. Thereupon he would have learned about the row and, as Father Ambrose observed, he would have tendered some comforting words. Father Glen Dennagher is squarely back in the picture. But Murf is unable to place him in a relevant context other than his having lost his jacket, the one later discovered with the dead body of Edmund Ludwig. Except that now he is the last known person to have seen Edmund Ludwig alive – and the last known person to have actually been with Edmund Ludwig prior to his death. There is no doubt – Murf needs to have another talk with Father Glen Dennagher. This is his new priority.

Murf decides to return to Killbawn via Ballina. His first priority has shifted from questioning Father Ambrose to obtaining more information from Glen Dennagher. Murf thinks back to when he previously interviewed Glen Dennagher. He wonders if Glen Dennagher deliberately concealed information. Or did he, Murf himself, fail to pursue a thorough line of questioning with him? For the inquiry to progress, it is crucial to fill in the final moments at the circus prior to Edmund's disappearance.

Murf drives with haste to Ballina. He glances at the clock on the car's dashboard. It is 4:45pm. He remembers that it is Saturday evening. Today is a busy day for Confessions in rural churches. He speculates on where Father Glen Dennagher might be at this time of day. He drives to the cathedral in Ballina on the chance that Glen Dennagher might be one of the confessors on duty at 5:00pm. If not, he will continue to Glen Dennagher's house in Kilglass, County Sligo. Murf remembers the bishop stating in Killbawn last week that Father Glen Dennagher lives in Kilglass. Murf knows Kilglass. It is a small village of ten houses, plus some neighbouring farmhouses, not far from Ballina.

Murf parks his car at the cathedral. He notices that Glen Dennagher's car is not parked in its previous spot, nor is it anywhere in sight. Murf considers the possibility that Glen Dennagher may later attend The John Edge Travelling Show in Castlebar. If so, Murf could be faced with returning back to the circus.

Murf sees a priest approach the cathedral's sacristy door. Murf hails the priest before he enters the building. "Excuse me, Father. I'm looking for Father Glen Dennagher. Is he here this evening?"

The helpful priest informs Murf, "Oh, Father Glen Dennagher frequently hears Confessions at the cathedral at this time. But he is not scheduled for today. Father Glen Dennagher is visiting the Archdiocese of Tuam. He has a meeting there tonight with fellow priests involved in various outreach ministries. However, if you are here for Confessions, we have two priests available this evening."

"Thank you, Father, but no thanks. I was hoping to see Father Glen Dennagher."

The priest gives Murf a friendly smile and continues into the cathedral. Before he shuts the door, the priest turns to Murf and says, "Monday morning at nine, in the Pastoral Centre. That's where you'll next find Father Glen Dennagher." With that, he shuts the door and is gone to proceed with his business.

Murf calculates that Tuam is an hour and a half away. Glen Dennagher might not yet have left on his journey and he may still be at home. Kilglass is only twenty minutes from Ballina, so Murf enters his car and proceeds onwards to Kilglass.

In Kilglass, Murf inquires of a farmer where Father Glen Dennagher lives. The farmer gives him directions to the townland of Lacken, between Kilglass and the sea, to a solitary one-story house near the seashore. When Murf arrives at the house, he snoops around. He confirms the absence of Glen Dennagher's car. The shed, which might serve as a garage, contains gardening tools and bar-bells and keep-fit equipment. Furthermore, there is no smoke emanating from the chimney, and there is no smell of a cooking fire. The only smell is from the sea wrack, the odour of which wafts inland from the rocky beach. Murf slowly rotates his body to view the surrounding fields. He sees a half-dozen grazing Friesians but not another living soul. Murf is satisfied that Glen Dennagher is not at home.

It is close to 6:00pm when Murf arrives back in Killbawn. He parks his Ford Prefect at the garda station and walks the short distance to Cannon's pub in the Market Square. He enters the pub and proceeds through the bar's saloon and into the kitchen. The Divil, perched on his usual stool at the bar, pays no heed to Murf as he passes by. The inebriate is focused on crooning a love song to his whiskey glass. In the kitchen, Murf avails of a quick fry from Mrs Cannon. At 6:35pm he wipes the bacon fat from his chin and departs from the pub. He strides to the garda station with deliberate purpose, blusters in noisily, ignores the startled duty officer, and ascends the stairs two at a time.

Murf works for another three hours arranging his notes. He sticks more pages to his evidence wall, and he attaches coloured threads to wherever he makes a cross-connection. He sits down at his desk and jots additional notes in his pad. He glances from his pad to the wall, and back again. He shakes his head. He scribbled on his pad the following:

19/08/45 Circus at Killbawn. C21:00 – 21:10hrs.
E.Ludwig learns that Fr GD lost his tweed jacket.
E.Ludwig finds the jacket and disappears from the circus.

Murf crosses the sheet with an 'X' and speaks aloud. "No, Murf. Edmund walks through Killbawn village to the Famine Field without being seen? Not likely. And then, Edmund reaches the two-mile stone and is disorientated by the sea fog, and a vehicle runs over him? Again, no. Even in the dark fog, Edmund would hear a vehicle approach and would step off the roadway onto the grass verge, and into the brambles if necessary. No, that does not fit. And even if a vehicle hits him, killing him, would it remain stationary, blocking the road, while the driver/occupant disposes of the body? And he just happens to have a spade? The driver would either quickly fling the body into the reeds of the sea marsh, or transport the body to a secluded place." Murf tears the sheet off his pad and crumples it. He tosses it towards the trash basket and misses. The crumpled ball of paper rolls against the wall.

Murf commences writing on a fresh page. Again he shakes his head and views his notes:

19/08/45 Circus at Killbawn. C21:00 – 21:10hrs.
E.Ludwig learns that Fr GD lost his tweed jacket.
E.Ludwig finds the jacket and returns it to Fr GD before he departs from the car park.
No other cars at the circus – just Fr GD's and circus vehicles.
E.Ludwig departs from the circus in Fr GD's car – that's how he disappears from the circus unobserved.

Again, Murf scores the page with a large 'X' and speaks aloud a second time. "Murf, you are still wrong. If

Edmund finds the lost jacket and successfully returns it to Glen Dennagher, then it is no longer 'lost'. Glen Dennagher would have it back. And if Edmund requires insulation from the coolness of the night, Glen Dennagher would likely proffer him his cardigan knit jacket rather than his expensive tweed jacket." Murf scrunches the page, ripping it from the pad, and casts it away to join its crumpled companion on the floor.

Murf stares at the blank page on his jotter. The empty page clears his mind. Suddenly he stands erects and exclaims, "What if Edmund did not disappear FROM the circus, but disappeared WITHIN the circus?" This re-establishes his focus on Marvin as the most likely suspect in the demise of Edmund Ludwig. Murf's euphoria is short-lived. He sits down once again and thumps his head repeatedly, shouting "Wrong! Wrong! Wrong! Murf me boy-oh, you are putting the cart before the horse." A fundamental rule of police detective work is to 'follow the evidence'. A common trap, and one which Murf has been toying with for the past few hours, is to contrive a scenario and attempt to force the evidence to fit the conclusion. This is an irresponsible exercise which, in some cases, has resulted in charging the wrong person for a crime.

Murf rises from his chair and retrieves his discarded papers from the floor. He flattens both pages and pins them to the wall, but outside the vicinity of his evidence notes. These crumpled sheets are his flags, his cautious reminders, to stay on track with the facts. He sits back against his desk and objectively views the data displayed on the wall. He weighs the data and considers the import. Marvin is the most likely suspect. Marvin had two motives to get rid of Edmund – one being a very strong motive. He and Edmund had disagreed about the performance routine and he feared that the German might sabotage the act. But, more importantly, Edmund had intruded too deeply into Marvin's life by undermining Marvin's relationship with the young girl, Annie. Furthermore, living in the same cramped caravan aggravated the situation. Did it become intolerable for Marvin, Murf wonders?

Murf considers homophobia as an added pertinent motive. This widens the field of suspects to other members of the circus, and even to denizens of Killbawn, the stragglers in the car park. And where does Father Glen Dennagher fit into this? Murf is fatigued. He concentrates hard on the wall. He is missing something significant in the picture before him — something that is staring him in the face which he fails to see. Murf rubs his tired eyes. He flings his pencil on the desk and calls it a night at 9:45pm.

CHAPTER FOURTEEN

DEATH IN IRELAND

County Mayo, Ireland
Sunday 25 August 1946

Sunrise is 5:30am. Murf is driving north from Ballina on the R297 to Kilglass. The journey from Killbawn to Kilglass takes forty-five minutes, but it is only a short distance across Killala Bay and the mouth of the River Moy if Murf were to fly or take a boat. He remembers the directions from the previous day – take the R297 to Kilglass, turn left after the GAA pitch onto an unnamed boreen which ends at the seashore. Father Glen Dennagher's cottage is the last house before the shore.

At 5:50am, Murf parks his car in the boreen. This is actually the townland of Lacken, the farmland between the village of Kilglass and the seacoast. Murf steps out of the car. The breeze from the sea hits him unexpectedly. He peers around, rotating his body a full circle. The land here by the sea is bereft of trees and shrubs. Murf has a panoramic view of coastline for a considerable distance. The adjacent seashore is rocky and is slick with glar. It is not like the beach in Enniscrone, an hour's walk from here. No one is likely to come to the Lacken shore except in springtime to gather wrack for fertiliser. There is a rough track, wide enough for a farm vehicle, running along the shoreline and bordering the farmland. Murf continues to turn his body and fixes his sight on his destination. There it is, Father Glen Dennagher's neat little single-storey cottage, sitting isolated from other habitations. Murf casts his eye on the cottage and turns to view the length of the curving shoreline. It is the priest's habit to jog along the shore at dawn every morning. It should be easy to spot a solitary jogger on the track at the seashore. There is no one in sight. Father Glen Dennagher could have jogged out of sight if he chose to go as far as the beach in Enniscrone, a fifteen-minute easy jog from here.

Murf turns his attention to the cottage once more. Nothing appears to have changed from when he visited here on the previous evening. The adjacent shed looks the same. Murf does not expect to see a change in the twelve hours since he last visited the cottage, except for some sign that Glen Dennagher has returned home. He notes that there is no smoke emanating from the chimney. Murf deduces that if in fact he has returned, he has not yet arisen from sleep. That would be uncharacteristic of him. Murf leans back against the side of his car. He considers the wisdom of coming here so soon after his previous unfruitful visit. He is anxious to question Glen Dennagher as a matter of priority. Furthermore, he needs to question him without the bishop interfering with obstructive intrusions. Hence, confronting him on his home turf so early in the morning affords Murf the element of surprise and is free of unwelcome distractions.

Murf waits until 6:00am. Then he walks slowly towards the cottage. He arcs through the adjoining field in order to observe the house from all sides. He registers the absence of a car. He walks as far as the shed beside the house and peers inside. The shed, which may serve as a garage for Glen Dennagher's car, appears as before. It is empty except for the same gardening tools and a dumbbell and some scattered keep-fit equipment. Murf concludes that Father Glen Dennagher is not at home. Perhaps he has not yet returned from Tuam. He considers that Glen Dennagher's business in Tuam may include Sunday Mass there.

Murf had intended to pounce upon the unsuspecting cleric in a surprise visit. The only surprise now is his failure to actually meet with him. Murf hopes that this is only a temporary failure. An unpleasant thought suddenly strikes him – what if the bishop made good on his threat to send Glen Dennagher to 'Krilly Island'? Deflated, he returns to his car and drives back the way he came.

Murf passes through Ballina. On a hunch, he drives to the cathedral and enters the adjacent parking lot. It is 6:20am. The lot is empty. No car with number plate EI 4493 is parked here. Murf attempts to gain access to the cathedral and to the pastoral centre. Both are securely locked. He reads the Mass times on the exterior notice board. It is Sunday and the first Mass of the day is scheduled for 8:00am. Disappointed, Murf accepts that Father Glen Dennagher is not at the cathedral – no one is at the cathedral, hence there is no one of whom to inquire. Murf is worried that Glen Dennagher may have flitted or has been 'sent on sabbatical'. Dejected by this possibility, Murf resumes his journey back to Killbawn.

At 7:00am, Murf enters the garda station in Killbawn. He is tired, but he is too agitated to relax. Instead, he shuffles files on his desk and rearranges the papers stuck to the wall. He sits on his desk and stares at the wall. Is there an answer there, staring him in the face? Only God knows. It is 10:40am. Murf decides that if God alone knows, then perhaps he should go to 11:00am Mass. Murf is an usher at St Bawn's. He ought to be there in any event from 10:30am. He walks from the garda station and he enters the church at 10:45am. He silently prays that God might share a little of his all-knowingness to disclose a clue to him or reveal to him some insight into solving the case.

Upon entering the narthex, Murf is confronted by Jack Gilban, the sacristan. "What's wrong with you guards at all, at all? You turn up late, and Guard O'Reilly has not shown up yet. Urgent police business, is it? We're short an usher for the collection."

Murf apologises to Jack, who is obliged to exercise double duty whenever ushers fail to show. Murf wonders where Seamus O'Reilly could be. He sees Patrick Gildea, the county councillor, arrive with his family. Murf quickly engages Gildea and employs him as a substitute usher for the Mass. Gildea, the amiable politician, graciously obliges. Mass commences at 11:00am. Murf is so distracted that he forgets to pray for enlightenment on the case. During the collection, Murf see Seamus O'Reilly tiptoe quietly into the narthex. Murf resolves to speak harshly to O'Reilly at the first opportunity, that is, once the collection is concluded. Guiltily, he considers his own tardiness and relents. After the collection, Murf joins O'Reilly in the narthex. He enquires of O'Reilly as to why he arrived so late to Mass.

As O'Reilly tenders an explanation, Murf ponders whether God answers prayers even when you neglect to pray. His attention is focused on O'Reilly's narrative. Garda O'Reilly and the entire county team went to Croagh Patrick that morning. Murf knows that the pilgrimage to the holy mountain is held annually on the last Sunday in July. Today is the last Sunday in August. So why today? O'Reilly elucidates. It was a special event for the County Mayo Gaelic Athletic Association. The entire football team climbed the Reek. They attained the summit at dawn, whereupon they attended a special dawn Mass. Murf deliberates aloud that Croagh Patrick is an hour and a half journey from Killbawn, and it takes two hours to climb the Reek. O'Reilly would have needed to depart Killbawn at 2:00am. Not so, O'Reilly explains. The ascent was conducted by jogging and walking vigorously, not in the slow plodding manner common to pilgrims who stop to pray (and rest) every few steps. The county football team is fit, and they climbed the Reek in one hour. "You see, Murf, I left Killbawn at 3:30am and met up with the team at 4:50am. And we all started up the mountain at 5:00am."

"But sunrise is at 5:30am. You must have missed dawn at the summit."

"I know. And that's the funny part. We had Mass starting at 6:00am in the chapel at the summit. And Father Barry informed us that, according to Old Moore's Almanac, sunrise was actually at 5:32am. He told us that we were all twenty-eight minutes late…"

"Stop there! Father Barry? Which 'Father Barry' was that?"

"Father Barry the athlete, of course – Father Barry Glen Dennagher."

"Father Barry Glen Dennagher was at the Reek at 6:00am this morning?"

"And he was still there at 7:00am. And at 8:30am he was down at the bottom of the mountain on Reek Road. After that, we were all in Castlebar, where, by 9:00am, we were all tackling a big breakfast of…"

"When did you leave Castlebar?"

"Well, I lost track of time. It was past 10:00am when I remembered that I should be back here in Killbawn."

"And Father Glen Dennagher?"

"And Father Glen Dennagher what?"

"Where did he go?"

"Now how would I know that? I was the first to leave. For all I know, they could still be in Mooney's at the minute – Father Barry and the rest of them." Garda Seamus O'Reilly continues to relate to Murf his experience with Father Glen Dennagher that morning. The energetic priest's sermon was the usual – 'if your foot causes you to stumble, cut it off and cast it away'. "Imagine that, Murf, a footballer cutting off his foot if he stumbles. And then at breakfast, we got to ribbing Big Frank the full-back. Stevie the goalie says to him, 'Well now, if that sweet colleen, Mary-Anne, causes you to stumble, cut her off and cast her away. I'll be there to catch her if you do.' To which Big Frank responds, 'You shut your mouth, Stevie boy, or **I'll** cut **you** off and cast you into the Castlebar River.' And so the *craic* went on, and I clear forgot the time…"

The bell for the consecration sounds. Murf thumps O'Reilly on the shoulder to stop his talking. "O'Reilly", he whispers, "have respect while at Mass. Now kneel down and pay attention." Both men kneel on the bare flags of the porch and O'Reilly turns his attention to the Mass.

Murf, on the other hand, is unable to concentrate on the Mass. O'Reilly has disclosed important information to him – Father Barry Glen Dennagher is still around. He has not flitted nor has he been sent to 'Siberia' or to 'Krilly Island'. Now that Seamus O'Reilly is here, albeit late for Mass, Murf delegates to him the job of counting the collection money and preparing the bank lodgement. 'Ita missa est,' followed by a quick 'Deo gratias,' and Murf is off and running to his car. He can still catch Glen Dennagher by surprise before the day is out.

For the second time that day, Murf drives on the R374 to Ballina. This time, on his third visit to Kilglass within twenty-four hours, he expects to finally meet Glen Dennagher. Thinking ahead, he questions in his mind what reason Glen Dennagher could have to choose Castlebar for breakfast with the County Mayo Gaelic Football Team. Westport, being closer to Croagh Patrick, is the obvious choice. And what is an athletic priest likely to do if he returns to Kilglass in the middle of the day? Spend time alone? Murf once saw Glen Dennagher's car parked at *An Chúilfhionn*, the club outside Castlebar on the Westport Road. Maybe he went there again today. Murf speculates on other possibilities. He considers the keep-fit cleric's admiration for acrobats.

Perhaps he went to The John Edge Travelling Show. That's it, Murf decides. The travelling show has a final performance in Castlebar at 3:00pm today. That is where he will find Father Glen Dennagher.

In Ballina, Murf changes direction. Instead of heading for the R297 to Kilglass, he turns onto the N26 and heads for Castlebar. At 1:00pm. Murf parks his car at the garda station in Castlebar. He walks around the corner to Spencer Street and slips into Tolsters *teach tabhairne* where the sign at the door states that 'food is served daily'. Later, refreshed and fortified by black pudding and sausages, Murf exits the pub at 1:50pm.

The most likely place to park a car, if one is going into the convent grounds to attend the circus, is either Rock Square or The Mall. Murf walks around the curve of The Mall. He sees it – EI 4493 parked at the kerb. He scans the garden area of The Mall, checking to see if Father Glen Dennagher is sitting on one of the benches. There is no sign of him in the vicinity of The Mall. A garishly-coloured car captures his attention. It drives out from Rock Square with a loud-speaker fastened atop. The voice from the loud-speaker recites all the reasons one should attend The John Edge Travelling Show – enumerating the exciting acts that should not be missed. The car circles The Mall and enters Ellison Street. The barker's voice fades into the distance. Murf walks in the opposite direction and enters Rock Square. As expected, he is confronted by two gates at the farthest end – the entrance to the military barracks and the entrance to the convent grounds. Lest there is any doubt as to which is the location of The John Edge Travelling Show, a brass band strikes up a lively tune to draw patrons to the designated spot. It is 2:10pm. Murf enters the convent grounds and proceeds to the show.

Murf walks up to the ticket booth and purchases a ticket for admission. He surprises the attendant at the booth by choosing a seat with the least favourable view of the stage – a seat up at the front, but well to the side, with only a partial view of the stage. The crowds have not yet arrived, so the prime seats are still available. But Murf chooses a seat that affords him the best view of the audience rather than the performers. From his seat, a short time later, he observes Father Glen Dennagher enter the big top. He is easily recognisable in his distinctive black brier-proof tweed jacket. Not surprisingly, he sits front and centre. He does not notice Murf sitting with the penny-wise people in an insignificant dim corner of the one-and-sixpenny seats.

At the conclusion of the show, Murf stands up concurrent with Father Glen Dennagher and moves to follow him to the exit. Unexpectedly, the priest walks to a flap in the tent and enters the back-stage area. Murf hurriedly follows him, whereupon a stagehand blocks his progress and directs him back to the public exit. Murf utters one word – 'Garda'. The stagehand recognises him from the recent police investigation and permits him entry. Murf peers around. He perceives Glen Dennagher with a troupe of acrobats, Marvin and The Marvellous Magyars. Murf tunes his ears to their voices. The acrobats are relating the events of the police inquiry. The curious cleric is keenly attentive to the news. Murf steps forward. Seeing him approach, the group falls silent.

"Father Glen Dennagher, a moment of your time, if I may." There is no doubt that Murf's intrusion is unexpected and is unwelcome. The apprehensive cleric steps away from the troupe, hoping to get out of earshot. Murf shows to him the picture of Edmund Ludwig, the one taken with Annie. Glen Dennagher readily identifies him. "That is Edmund, one of the Marvellous Magyars from last year." When Murf poses more questions, Glen Dennagher admits to having seen Edmund and to have spoken with him when he was searching for his lost jacket. As to why he did not mention it previously he explains that the inquiry centred on the lost jacket; there was never any suggestion, at the time, that Edmund Ludwig was relevant to the inquiry.

"Father Glen Dennagher, I want you to think very carefully. What do you remember of that night – the night you spoke with Edmund Ludwig after having lost your jacket? I want ALL the details." The anxious priest swallows. He is nervous and agitated. Murf prods him. "You realise that this is an inquiry into a suspicious death, and hence a criminal investigation. Edmund Ludwig's body was discovered in mysterious circumstances and clothed in your jacket. And you, Father Glen Dennagher, are the last known person seen with him."

Father Glen Dennagher repeats to Murf the same explanation he first tendered – he lost his jacket at The John Edge Travelling Show in Killbawn, and he asked people at random if they had seen it. Edmund Ludwig just happened to be one of the random people at the car park at the time. Accepting the loss of the jacket, he drove home without it.

"Can anyone confirm that?"

"Are you are asking if anyone can corroborate my account? Am I a suspect?"

"Father Glen Dennagher, if someone witnessed your exchange with Edmund Ludwig and your subsequent departure in your car, then someone other than you would have been the last person to have seen Edmund Ludwig. Now think. Who else was present in the car park at the time you departed?"

"There were eight young adults there at the time, four boys and four girls, in their twenties. The four lads were country boys, the four girls were town dwellers."

"Did you recognise them? Or could you identify any of them?"

"No. They were too far away to distinguish their features."

"But they were in their twenties?"

"They laughed loudly and flirtatiously. They sounded young."

"And they were country boys and town girls? How could you tell?"

"The four lads were wheeling bicycles, and the four girls were dressed in high-heeled shoes."

"I see. So you left at that point and drove home?"

"That is correct."

"And at what time did you arrive home that night?"

"I drove home, but I don't know at what time I arrived. But it is a forty-five-minute drive. Maybe at ten-thirty or eleven o'clock."

"Is anyone able to confirm that?"

"Inspector, I live alone at the end of a quiet laneway. No one would have observed my arriving home."

Murf concludes his questioning. Glen Dennagher is sticking to his story, and his story is plausible. But it would be preferable to confirm the details. Until he can corroborate the details, Murf decides to keep Glen Dennagher's name posted as a feasible suspect.

Monday, 26 August 1946. It is 8:00am in Killbawn Garda Station. Murf studies his case notes. He enters new data on his evidence wall. His chief suspect, the only one to have motive, means and opportunity, is Marvin the Magyar. Murf decides to bring him in for interrogation. By employing subtle techniques, Murf will attempt to elicit a confession from him. Murf decides to swing past the Famine Field once more to help sort the assembled data in his mind. Afterwards, he will phone the divisional HQ and speak to Finbar and Divers to check for any updates. He feels that he is missing a key piece of the picture. This last step may trigger a small but significant 'dot' in his picture, enough to put the entire picture into perspective.

At the Famine Field, he notices that the archaeological team is back at work executing non-intrusive bores into the ground. Sean Macilmyra, the county engineer, is on-site and is checking on their progress in the hope of getting the work back on schedule. Sally Plunkett, the archaeologist, is present and is busily engaged with her two student assistants, B Tobin and Sandra McCurry. There is no new evidence to report from the Famine Field.

Back at the station, Murf contacts Finbar Dorrian, the medical examiner. Finbar has nothing further to tell him about the case, and why would he, he asks Murf, considering that he had provided a detailed and comprehensive report? Murf contacts the last name on his list, Phil Divers, the head of the forensic section. Divers has nothing to add either, and he has not heard back from Germany yet on the dental files.

"O'Reilly!" O'Reilly, standing at the front counter of the garda station, quickly hides the sports page of the district officer's Irish Independent. He had not heard Murf approach in his rubber-soled farm boots.

"Lord, Murf, you gave me a scare."

"At two o'clock you will accompany me to Claremorris, where we will arrest Marvin the Magyar for the murder of Edmund Ludwig. So, sort your papers and grab lunch, and have the garda car ready."

"Claremorris?"

"Yes. That is where The John Edge Travelling Show is performing. Except that Marvin will not be appearing with the Marvellous Magyars today. It is twelve o'clock now, so have the car ready on time."

At 2:00pm O'Reilly has the garda car parked at the kerb outside the station. Back inside the station, he leans on the front counter while waiting for Murf to arrive from his upstairs office. Garda Caldwell is manning the front counter. Murf arrives and nods to O'Reilly. Just then, they are disturbed by the blustering entrance of Danny the Divil. The three police officers look at him in surprise. It is two in the afternoon and Danny the Divil is still sober? Something is truly wrong. By now he would have exhausted his maintenance dose and is apt to be cantankerous until he imbibes his afternoon requirements – but not until he is first relieved of his driving duties for Doctor McBratt. Something serious has disrupted Danny the Divil's routine.

Garda Caldwell asks, "Not another car stuck in the ditch at the two-mile stone, surely?"

"No, it's not!"

Garda O'Reilly enquires, "Or they found another leper in the Famine Field?"

"No, not a leper. This time, they found a giant buried in the Famine Field."

Murf attempts to make sense of the Divil's report. After all, his previous account was accurate, albeit confusing. But a 'giant' is a stretch. "Describe to me what was found, Danny."

The Divil paces out a measurement on the floor in an oblong three feet by twelve feet. "They put a probe down here – the arsy-ologist woman did." The divil stamps his foot to indicate the spot. "And then here, and here…" The Divil stomps twenty-one times. "Here and here they found nothing down to the stone bottom. But here, and here, and all the way up to here, the probe stopped at two and a half foot. You know what that means? A giant, that's what."

"Or it could be two bodies, or it could be where Delahunty buried a dead heifer."

"Well whatever it is, Guard Murphy, the arsy-ologist will do no more probing or poking until the guards come"

Murf views the floor area stomped out by the Divil, the imaginary area on the station floor, and considers the wisdom of Sally Plunkett in ceasing the archaeological probes. If this were a mass burial site from the Great Famine, the area yielding evidence of a burial would be much wider. Murf addresses O'Reilly, "Come on, O'Reilly! We're going to the Famine Field!"

Ten minutes later, Murf arrives at the Famine Field. O'Reilly drives the garda car around the bend and parks it in Delahunty's farmyard. Sally Plunkett is sitting on the Divil's plank of wood, close to the previously excavated trench. And like the previous time, she has her knees drawn up and is leaning her elbows on them. Her hands are caked in mud, most of which she has rubbed into her hair as she continually slaps her palms onto her crown. Her two assistants are standing close by in silence. Clearly, all three are distressed. It is apparent to Murf that although new probes have been conducted, no actual digging was executed today.

"Hello, Sally. So tell me, have you encountered another body?"

Sally looks up at Murf and shifts her gaze to indicate an area close to the fence, a location a mere four feet in distance from the previous find. There is a little mound of sandy dirt at each borehole. In the area of the find, Sally has inserted rods into the ground and she has marked each rod with a line of chalk to indicate the depth at which she encountered obstructions. The bore-holes are concentrated in one-foot squares rather than the two-foot squares employed elsewhere. Sally is conscientious in marking her work accurately – she shortened the distance between the bore-holes to achieve a precise mapping of the area. The mapped area is rectangular in shape, three feet by twelve feet.

Murf waits for her response. There is none. Murf coughs and attempts to get an answer. "Are you sure that you encountered a body?"

"No, Inspector. I am not sure; I am fearful."

"That there might be…"

Sally suddenly stands up and walks to the marked area. "I fear that there may be two bodies here under my feet. And they are not from the Great Famine." She returns to the plank and resumes her dejected position.

Garda O'Reilly, having parked the car, joins them. He walks down from the spine of the hill. He is accompanied by Pat Delahunty. Murf hails them and addresses Delahunty. "Pat, have you ever buried anything in the field here – a dead animal or the like?"

"Here? Buried a beast? Lord, no. Ever since my family owned the farm, the sod here has never been pierced by a spade, not until the excavation here last week. But you know, Guard, there was the time when the county council dug out the scrub."

"Tell me about the scrub."

"Well, in the spring of last year the county council requested permission to remove scrubs and bushes from the bend. They said it was to give traffic a better view when rounding the corner. There was hazel growing over there and, a bit past it, there was a sloe bush. They removed the scrubs and bushes, but they did not remove the briers. In the autumn, after the blackberry season was done, I got me lads to hoke out and remove the intrusive briers all along the roadside. You can see how clear the whole area is now."

Murf sees that the area along the wire fence is clear of briars and shrubs. But with this information, he realises that the roadside area was not always so clear. "So, Pat, where exactly was the scrub?"

Delahunty walks to the spot, the same spot that Sally had identified as the location of two buried bodies just moments earlier. He points to the grass verge of the road. "From the fence here, out to the roadside, there was a hazel scrub. I mind it from when I was gossoon. Once upon a time, I would gather nuts here for Halloween. But diggin' in the Famine Field? No, Guard Murphy, never."

Murf turns to Garda O'Reilly and draws him aside. "O'Reilly, go back to the patrol car and radio the station. Get them to contact Castlebar urgently."

"And tell them what?"

Murf grips O'Reilly's arm and lowers his voice. "This might be a serial murder. We need the medical examiner and the forensic team here with due haste."

O'Reilly shivers as he considers two bodies – three if you count the 'leper' – lying a few feet below the ground and stretched out along the fence. And could there be more? He shakes himself and runs off to the garda car.

Delahunty walks away. He cannot afford to let his work lag. He has satisfied his curiosity for the moment, so he returns to his tasks on the farm. Murf sits down beside the archaeologist and awaits the arrival of the medical examiner and forensic team from Castlebar. The two student-archaeologists join them on the plank. Murf hardly notices the arrival of the Divil who also sits alongside. No one speaks.

At 2:40pm, Murf turns to the three members of the archaeological team and addresses them. "There is nothing more you can do here now. Take the rest of the day off. Actually, you will not be permitted to continue your investigative probes during the police investigation of the field. That could take a few days. You will be absent from the

Famine Field until you are notified to recommence your work here."

Sally Plunkett is staring blankly ahead. She blinks and comes alive at Murf's instructions. "You are right, of course. The car is parked in the farmyard. We'll be off then." She turns to her young assistants. "B Tobin and Sandra, gather up the tools and equipment. Make sure to clean the tools at the tap in the farmyard. Sort them all and store them back in the toolbox. Then, we are leaving."

Murf watches them clear up and retrieve their tools. "Sally, I know where to contact you if needs be. When you get back to Castlebar, report to the county council office and advise the county engineer. He needs to be informed. Later, when the site is cleared and the project can resume, I will advise him so that he can reschedule the work."

Sally, B Tobin and Sandra walk away to the farmyard and to their car. Garda O'Reilly returns from having contacted the station on the car radio. He paces impatiently back and forth along the fence by the roadside. The Divil remains seated quietly on his plank. The silence is broken only by the sounds of his whiskey consumption – swallowing loudly and smacking his lips every few minutes. Murf sits beside the Divil. He is anxious to learn the state of the bodies – if indeed there are two additional bodies buried here. This discovery could have a major bearing on the Edmund Ludwig case. If there are three victims instead of one, it could point more strongly to Marvin and his circus associates. Or it could direct the investigation in an entirely different direction. Or this new discovery could be totally unrelated to the death of Edmund Ludwig. Murf sighs. The arrest of Marvin the Magyar is delayed for one more day.

At 3:30pm, Murf hears the sound of an approaching car. As it nears, the sound is identifiable as a number of cars. Three cars and a van arrive and they are directed by Garda

O'Reilly to park in the farmyard. Minutes later, a team of eight invades the Famine Field. Murf is thankful that they have taken the report seriously and are here in force. The first to appear over the spine of the dolmen are Finbar, the medical examiner, and Divers, the head of the garda forensic section. Divers carries his little step ladder which he needs if he is to climb any farther than two feet. They are followed closely by the six remaining members of the team who are laden with spades and equipment and boxes of tools. From their previous visit last week, Divers is familiar with conditions in the Famine Field and he prudently determined the most appropriate equipment to employ.

Divers, panting from the unaccustomed exertion, addresses Murf between breaths. "Well, Murf, you think you may have more bodies buried here?"

Murf directs him to the area distinctly marked by Sally Plunkett. Divers and Finbar understand without the need for explanation. Murf repeats Sally Plunkett's expert opinion, "We are not sure of what is down there, but I am greatly apprehensive of what you will uncover. The archaeologist was careful not to intrude beyond making the discovery, so you should find the evidence undisturbed and intact."

Finbar views the location of the area of interest. "Inspector, have your man stand by the roadside and direct people away from the area. I don't want curious civilians poking their noses into the site." By 'your man', Finbar makes reference to Garda Seamus O'Reilly. Finbar notices an unkempt man sitting on a plank close by. "And that shabby fellow over there, ask him to leave the area."

"Ah! The 'shabby man' is 'Danny the Divil'. He unexpectedly displays uncanny insight into unlikely situations. Leave him be. Regard him as my assistant."

Finbar shakes his head. He glances from one to the other, from one almost-shabby man to a totally shabby man.

He recognises and accepts Inspector Murphy's characteristic eccentricity. He is cognizant that Murf's pitiable attention to dress in no way inhibits his exceptional detective skills. "Fine. But he better not get in the way. He is to stay outside the police tape that we are erecting around the site." The Divil takes another slug from his bottle and looks glassily at nothing in particular. He has consumed the last of his whiskey, but he is resolved to stay until the end.

The six younger members of the team throw themselves into serious digging. Once through the surface sod, the soil is sandy and easily excavated. They dig a trench on three sides of the marked area – three feet long, ten feet long and three feet long to a width of two feet. At 5:30pm, the trench is excavated to a depth of four and a half feet. At this point, the delicate work begins. Four of the team undertake to scrape and brush the wall of the pit, slowly and delicately closing in on the object of their interest. Concurrent with this activity, Divers directs the two remaining members to conduct a series of probes in the area left untouched by Sally Plunkett and her team. Within an hour they confirm that they discovered nothing of additional interest below ground to the depth of the bedrock. Thus, Sally's marked area is the sole focus of their concentrated investigation.

At 7:12pm, one of the team members in the trench shouts, "I think this is something. Right here." He points to a bump protruding from the wall of the trench at a depth of two and a half feet.

Finbar enters the trench and gently brushes the bump. Divers lies on the surface ground and peers down at the bump. It is beyond his reach. He estimates the width of the trench. It has been widened to two and a half feet by this time. This is just enough space for him to fit. He places his little ladder in the trench and joins Finbar inside the pit, forcing two members of the team to climb out in order to accommodate him. Finbar and Divers work cheek-by-jowl in the close confines of the pit, both peering closely at the bump. Finbar continues to labour delicately in an attempt to identify the nature of the bump. He determines that it is not bone. After a few more swishes of his brush, they recognise the shape – the heel of a shoe. Just then, one of the team shouts from the opposite end of the trench, "There is something here too. And THIS looks like bone."

Finbar, in his haste to navigate to the location of the second find, climbs over Divers' portly body that is blocking his path. He examines the second exposed object and instantly recognises a section of skull. Everyone is fixated by these two finds. Murf and the Divil relinquish their seat of relative comfort on the plank, and Garda O'Reilly abandons his post at the roadside. The Divil looks at Divers' progress as he exposes more of the shoe. The width of the sole indicates a man's shoe and the heel is an elevated heel. The Divil nudges Murf and utters, "A dandy."

Finbar is working around the skull, exposing the crown down to the forehead. At this point, he encounters spectacle glasses. He brushes around the frames until the shape and style are apparent. Again, the Divil makes a quiet comment to Murf, "Cary Grant glasses. That reminds me of 'The Dazzler Fegan' who left and went to England five year ago."

Murf is anxious to know if these two finds can be dated to a year ago, and hence to the possibility of a triple murder. Neither Finbar nor Divers is so reckless as to make a pronouncement.

"It is impossible to say at this juncture how long the bodies have been buried here…"

"A year? More than a year? Less than a year?"

Divers looks up at Murf and says, "Tomorrow, Murf. Give us until tomorrow at least."

They work for another hour. They expose sufficient bone to confirm that the site contains two bodies. Finbar removes his glasses to wipe off splatters of sand and dirt. "I am unable to conduct a thorough preliminary examination. These are skeletal remains of two cadavers. That much, I can confirm, but no more at this time. I will conduct a pathological examination tomorrow."

The team works for another hour. They remove the two bodies, including the underneath soil to a depth of three inches, and they place them in the van for transport to the crime lab. Divers obtains soil samples from the surrounding area at varying depths. He places the soil samples in glass jars and writes on the outer labels. It is close to ten o'clock, with nightfall fast approaching, when the last of the forensic team packs up and leaves the Famine Field. Garda O'Reilly promptly departs close behind, eager to vacate the foreboding place before darkness descends. He crosses his fingers in prayer, hoping that he will not be ordered to remain behind to guard the crime scene. Murf and the Divil are the last to leave. Murf takes a final look at the site – at the two open pits side-by-side. The Divil speaks. "A dead leper; and now a dead dandy and a dead dazzler."

CHAPTER FIFTEEN

THE LEPER, THE DANDY AND THE DAZZLER

County Mayo, Ireland
Tuesday 27 August 1946

8:00am. Murf is half-sitting/half-leaning back against his desk. He twirls pencils through the fingers of both hands and studies the papers pinned to his investigation wall. He is troubled that the picture – his mental perspective of the case – is out of focus. This bothers him. It played on his mind all night. Murf was so distracted this morning that he overlooked attention to his attire. His pin-striped shirt is styled for a detachable collar. Murf has forgotten to attach one. Also, he neglected to check that his shirt buttons line up. They don't. He is dressed in his usual dull rubber-soled boots, the kind that (according to Murf) don't require polishing. One woolly sock is grey with white dots; the other is white with grey dots. The ends of his grey-flannel trouser legs are tucked into his mismatched socks. This is not totally out of character. Murf, when focusing on a case, frequently forgets to attend to his appearance. He is anxious to learn the outcome of the forensic examination on yesterday's two additional cadavers.

Murf is not a believer in coincidences. Things either connect or they don't. The three cadavers from the Famine Field are either connected, or they are not connected. He urgently requires the results of the medical examiner's pathological examination in order to confirm or reject a connection. And he needs to examine any and all evidence found with the bodies. Murf realises that he should not expect a report today. But perhaps he should phone, regardless, just to emphasise the urgency.

Murf considers his prime suspect, Marvin the Magyar. And Marvin is travelling farther away each day. Today he is in Castlerea in County Roscommon. Wednesday and Thursday he will be in Athlone in County Westmeath. After Naas on 16 September, Marvin will likely leave Ireland. Murf considers how Marvin the Magyar fits into the case. Will the new evidence implicate him more strongly? Or perhaps the evidence will lead in a new direction. If Murf is to arrest Marvin, he must act within twenty days.

Murf turns his attention to what the Divil said upon seeing the corpses yesterday. The Divil was quick to voice his opinion notwithstanding how little was revealed – the sole of a shoe belonging to one cadaver, and the upper skull and heavily-soiled glasses of the second body. How is the Divil so quick to form an opinion and be so certain? Is he that astute? Or is he in possession of some foreknowledge? Murf decides to question the Divil and get an understanding of his reference to 'the Dandy' and 'the Dazzler'. The Divil may prove to be pivotal in leading to the identity of the two recent bodies.

Murf takes a clean sheet of paper from his desk. He writes on it and pins it to his investigation wall. The sheet is entitled 'Danny the Divil Begley'. Marvin is the prime suspect. But there is a weakness in this premise due to Marvin's unfamiliarity with the Famine Field. The Divil, on the other hand, appears to have intimate familiarity with the location. He is comfortable with the ghosts that haunt the place; he is at ease in a setting which others consider unsettling; he has a make-shift seat at the field in order to study the progress of the ongoing excavation there, and he is not bothered by the malodorous fog that drifts in from the marsh. Who is most likely to conceal an article by burying it the Famine Field? Danny the Divil Begley, that's who. However, the Divil's interests are very limited. Other than concealing a stash of 'poteen' or some personal treasure, what would he need to bury? Murf considers how the Divil, when intoxicated, is accommodating to spirits and ghosts. In that state, his grip on reality is somewhat tenuous. As one who is at ease in the Famine Field, could the drunken Divil have been an unwitting accomplice or a bewildered witness to what occurred there?

Murf telephones Castlebar. He leaves a message for Finbar and another for Divers, requesting them to relay information on the two new cadavers as soon as valuable and relevant data are uncovered. At 10:00am, neither has phoned back. This is not unexpected. Murf will give them twenty-four hours to come up with something.

Murf turns his attention back to Danny the Divil. To question the Divil, Murf must first wait until the Divil concludes his morning driving duties for Doctor McBratt's professional rounds. The Divil could be anywhere in the parish at the moment. Doctor McBratt is due at the dispensary for patient visits at 3:00pm, and she customarily arrives an hour early. That is when Danny the Divil will be back in Killbawn. There is no activity at the Famine Field today, so the Divil is unlikely to go there. More than likely, he will go to Cannon's pub in the Market Square as soon as the doctor relieves him of his duties. That will not be until 2:00pm.

At 1:45pm, Murf enters Cannon's pub. Mick Cannon greets him as he enters. "Good-day to you, Guard Murphy. And is it a drink you'll be having?"

"Ah no, Mick. I came to work today without breakfast. I'm so hungry I could eat a horse. What's your fare for today?"

"What? No breakfast, Guard Murphy? Sure it's almost two in the afternoon, and haven't had a bite yet? Go on back into the kitchen and the missus will fix you up with something."

Murf opens the kitchen door. The unmistakable smell of boiled cabbage hangs heavily in the air and beckons Murf into the inner sanctum of the kitchen. Mrs Cannon directs him to the large wooden table bleached white from constant scrubbing and cleaning. "Today is Tuesday. Tuesday is boiled bacon and cabbage. If it's stew you're wantin', you'll need to come back tomorrow. And on Thursday it's…"

"Bacon and cabbage sound great, Mrs Cannon." Mrs Cannon prepares a platter of food for Murf. Murf enquires, "Any sign of the Divil today?"

Mrs Cannon glances up at the mantle clock. "I don't expect him until ten after two – that's after he drops the doctor off at the dispensary. And I hardly ever see him these days anyhow. I thought he was spending time with you out at the Famine Field – he's turnin' into a right detective he is now. Lord, Guard Murphy, it's **meself** what should be askin' **you** about his whereabouts. But if he's back to his old routine, you'll see him in here in a few minutes."

At 2:10pm, the Divil saunters into the pub. He leans on the counter and grabs the glass of whiskey that Mick offers him without prompting. He downs the contents, four liquid ounces, in one swallow. Simultaneous with his swallowing, the Divil holds up four fingers and Mick passes him four Baby Powers, 9.6 ounces of whiskey, which he inserts into his jacket pockets. He exclaims an audible 'ah!' to express his contentment in consuming the fiery liquid. He shuts his eyes and concentrates on the creeping relief washing over his body. His craving thus addressed, the Divil enquires, "And how's the good woman today?"

Mick is busy polishing a glass. He nods in the direction of the inner door. "Mrs Cannon is back there in the kitchen. Go on in there and visit her." Mick is fully cognisant that the Divil is seeking a bite to eat. And depending on Mrs Cannon's mood of the day, the Divil might be proffered boiled potatoes and buttermilk. Today he is in luck – he is provided with bacon and cabbage.

The Divil sits at the kitchen table beside Murf. Mrs Cannon serves him a dish of food and a mug of buttermilk. "There you go, Danny. Mick needs to go out a bit, so I'll be working the bar for a while. Give me a shout if you need me. And don't you two men be stealin' stuff out o' me larder while me back is turned," and she goes out through the doorway and into the saloon.

The Divil looks at Murf. "I didn't know you came to Cannon's to eat. When did that start?"

"It's not my custom. I'm here today to see you, Danny."

"To see me? About what?"

"The bodies in the Famine Field."

"Ay, and what about the bodies in the Famine Field?"

"You were very quick to identify the first body."

"The leper."

"How were you so sure, so fast? It took the rest of us over a day to come to the same conclusion."

"And you a detective, Guard Murphy. Let me ask you something to see if your detectivating is working proper – 'Brothers and sisters I have none; but this man's father is my father's son'. Who is it?"

"It's yourself."

"And how did you come to that right conclusion?"

"Sure you just told me that, Danny, in a round-about way."

"Ay, and so I did. Just like the leper told me when the arsy-ologist dug him up."

"Are you telling me that it was so obvious from your first glimpse of the cadaver?"

"I don't know anything about no cavi-dar. But I sure know a leper when I see one. Now, who else dresses in knicker-togs – the stuff that circus lepers wear that's like women's knickers with tight stockings attached?"

"It's called a 'unitard'. A circus acrobat dresses in a unitard for a performance."

"Well, whatever you call it, that unitog thing told me more certain than words. Sure it was like reading a dashboard."

"How is it 'like reading a dashboard', Danny?"

"The clothes tell you how a person moves. You wear a unitog thing for leppin' about, so you must be a leper."

Murf is impressed that Danny the Divil is able to deduce from a person's clothing what that person might engage in, and hence a clue to his identity.

The Divil is focused on his bacon and cabbage. Between bites, he pauses to direct a question, "Guard Murphy, do you know the differ in a hare and a rabbit?"

"Of course."

"Some people don't. The biggest differ is in how they move. You never hear a body say 'he ran as fast as a rabbit'; but 'to run like a hare' is fast. Am I not right?"

"Yes, Danny. But I would like to ask you a few questions about the two recent bodies."

"And tell me, Guard Murphy, can you tell the differ in socks – which is the right and which is the left?"

"Danny, socks don't have a 'left' and a 'right'."

The Divil ceases chewing and raises an eyebrow at Murf. "Except…"

"Except what, Danny?" Murf is eager to get off the topic of socks and focus on the two recently-exhumed bodies.

"If you wear your socks all day long, and then take them off and throw them on the floor, can you tell the right from the left?"

"In that case, Danny, yes there is a difference between the two socks because of the stretching caused by the big toe…"

"And then on the next day, you put them on different feet. What does that tell you?"

It tells Murf that the Divil doesn't change his socks frequently. "It alters the shape. The left becomes the right and vice-versa."

"And that is what a detective can tell. You see, evidence can change shape. When did it change? Was it accidental or deliberate?"

Murf is surprised that the Divil is warning him about altered evidence, misinterpreting evidence, and tampering with evidence. "Danny – 'the Dandy'. Tell me why you said that one of the bodies was 'a dandy'."

"A man's shoe with a high heel? Have you ever seen one, Guard Murphy? Or more important, have you ever heard one?"

Murf thinks back. He remembers a young man who once came to Mass wearing shoes with elevated heels. He walked loudly in mincing steps, 'clip-clip'. Murf steered him to a pew near the back so as not to distract the worshippers with his distinctive attention-seeking bearing. Everything about him was flamboyant – his strutting walk, his stylish clothes, and his flashy tie. This was a young man who wanted to be seen – and heard. Murf admits that the Divil is correct, this was a dandy. But could the dandy at the church be the same dandy as the exhumed cadaver? Murf responds to the Divil, "Yes. I encountered a dandy once, a few years back. And you are correct. A young man in elevated heels is an ostentatious dresser."

"Not something you'd expect to see often in Killbawn, now is it?" The Divil has finished his bacon and cabbage. He drains the last of the buttermilk from his mug. He wipes his mouth with the back of his hand and says, "Ask me another."

"What about 'The Dazzler'?"

"Ah. The glasses put me in mind of 'The Dazzler Fegan' who left for England in 1941, during the war with Germany – that was England's war with Germany. We had no war with Germany. The Dazzler liked to dress like Cary Grant. Don't you mind him from back then, Guard Murphy? The Dazzler was always nattily dressed. You wouldn't know that he was a country boy from Ballycorry."

"Yes. I remember a Fegan boy who dressed neatly. He had a penchant for double-breasted blazers. But I would not have described him as a 'country boy', perhaps more aptly referred to as a 'county boy'."

"Ah, 'country' and 'county', like a 'hare' and a 'rabbit'. Either way, he was from Ballycorry. Well, before young Fegan left for England he got new glasses. And he insisted on frames like Cary Grant in that picture with the lion."

"'Bringing Up Baby'. And it was a leopard in the motion picture."

"A leper? No, Guard Murphy, there was no leper in that picture. But there was a big cat."

"And you think that the body found in the Famine Field might be him?"

"I said that it put me in mind of The Dazzler. But if The Dazzler is in England, he can't be in the Famine Field. Now, can he?"

"Unless he returned."

"Lord, no. If The Dazzler ever returned from England we would surely know."

"Or perhaps he never left."

"Well, if the body dug up in the Famine Field is The Dazzler Fegan, check his glasses. He got his new glasses from McNiff in the Market Square way back then. So, bring them to McNiff and he'll be able to tell you if they're the same glasses or not."

Murf nods in agreement. He continues to question the Divil. "Danny, you are an astute person. Who do you think would hide a body in the Famine Field?"

"Well, it can't be an outsider. Who, besides us people here, would know of the out-of-the-way Famine Field outside Killbawn halfway to the coast? So then you think that it must be a local what done it. Now, the country people and most of the town people are a superstitious lot. They stay clear of the Famine Field during the day, and they are afeared to go into the Famine Field after dark. It's not likely to be any of them."

"What about the people who are **not** superstitious?"

"Them ones? No. They may have no fear of ghosts and the like, but they are afeared of the foul gasses what drifts in from the marsh."

"What about you, Danny? Are you not afraid?"

"Of the ghosts? Oh, I see them spirits floating about all the time. But they pay me no heed, and **I** pay **them** no heed."

"And what about the foul odours and marsh gases?"

The Divil laughs. "There's people what say that I smell just like the marsh. I fit right in with the gases. And anyways, after a few swallows of whiskey, I don't smell a thing."

"So let me understand you, Danny. You are the only person you know of, who would be daring enough to hide a body in the Famine Field?"

"That's right, Guard Murphy. If you are looking for the one person who would hide a body in the Famine Field, it's meself. Now, all you have to do is find the man who dug the holes, and your case is solved."

Murf tries to picture the Divil wielding a spade, and he concedes that the likelihood of the Divil digging a hole is remote. And three and a half feet deep? No, not the Divil.

"Maybe those cavi-dars dug their own holes."

Murf realises that the Divil is taking the mickey with him. It is past 3:00pm. Murf returns to the garda station to check his messages – if there are any – and to place this new information in perspective. Every detail adds another dot to the picture. What is the common thread that connects the three bodies – and to use the Divil's terms – the Leper, the Dandy and the Dazzler? Back in his office, Murf assumes his familiar pose – half-sitting/half-leaning back against his desk – twirling pencils through his fingers while considering the data on the papers stuck to the wall.

Wednesday, 28 August. Murf drives to Castlebar. He enters the Garda Divisional HQ at 9:00am and proceeds to the crime lab. His first visit is to Finbar Dorrian, the county medical examiner (coroner), in the autopsy room. Finbar is not happy to see Murf, but neither is he surprised. "Lord, Murf, you'll have my report in three days' time. Now give me space to conduct my examinations."

The three cadavers are lying on three metal tables side by side. The autopsy room is on the ground floor on the north side of the building. The smell of sterilisation adds to the coldness of the room. Murf subconsciously checks that the upper button of his shirt is fastened against the chill. He peers intently at the three cadavers. The dirt and sand have been brushed off. Consequently, the skeletal remains are clearly revealed. "Finbar, just tell me this for now. Are the three bodies related?"

"From the same family?"

"No. I am asking about the circumstances of their death and interment."

Finbar points at the three cadavers. "Let's see. Three bodies, all buried in the same place, at the same depth, all laid out prone in the supine position, all facing the same direction… That is not likely to be by chance."

"They appear to be arranged orderly. Were they buried at the same time, or about the same time?"

"No. This one, the first cadaver, was buried one year ago; this one, two-and-a-half to five years ago; and the third one, five years or more."

Murf is taken aback. "YEARS apart? This is very significant. And it throws the inquiry in a totally new direction." Murf turns to face the medical examiner. "Are you sure of this, Finbar? How accurate is your assessment as to how long they have been in the ground?"

"Really, Murf! Are you challenging my findings…?"

"Easy on, Finbar. This information has taken me by surprise. I need to consider the significance of it. So tell me, how precise is your assessment?"

Finbar is miffed. Regardless, he resumes a professional manner and responds to Murf. "Very accurate for number one, fairly accurate in the case of number two, and… after five years, there is a slow decay of the bones: five years to fifty years looks much the same. Of course, the items found with the bodies are much easier to date. Divers, next door, can give you a more accurate assessment based on his forensic examination of the accompanying articles."

"Anything else I should know?"

"The bodies were all male of medium height – Five feet seven for #1, five feet seven-and-a-half for #2, and five feet eight for #3. And they show no signs of injuries. I'll send you a detailed report in a few days when I have concluded my examination."

"One more thing. You say that all three cadavers were discovered lying in the supine position. Is that 'supine position' as in a wake – lying face up with hands crossed at the chest?"

The medical examiner is impatient for Murf to leave. He answers curtly, "Yes, that's 'supine position'. Are you finished with your questions now, Inspector?"

"Thanks, Finbar. I'll go visit Divers next door and see what he has uncovered."

Some minutes later, Murf is speaking with Divers in the forensic laboratory. Murf is glad to be out of the cold autopsy room. Divers is perspiring from the exertion of his work. He directs Murf to put on rubber gloves and he brings him to the tables which contain the articles and samples recovered with the cadavers.

"Here is table number one, Murf. Now we know that this table contains the items associated with Edmund Ludwig. We are still waiting for confirmation on his dental records from Germany."

Divers ambles to the second table. "Table number two. No identification as to the identity of cadaver #2. Nevertheless, we have some interesting items that could yield you favourable results – shoes, a belt, buttons of course, and coins. First, the shoes. Look at the soles, Murf." Divers positions his glasses securely on his nose and points to the shoes with his pencil. "These are a fine pair of shoes. Pre-war, I would say. Irish-made after independence. But note this," he gently taps the sole of one shoe, "these are not the original soles. These soles were hand-crafted as evidenced by the edges. The edges were hand-pared by a craftsman – a well-practised cobbler. And the heels were replaced, probably modified, after manufacture."

"These shoes have been modified by a cobbler? Why would someone do that? If you choose a pair of shoes to your liking, why alter them later other than to maintain them in good repair?"

"Well, Murf, that is where you need a detective to find the answer." Murf accepts Divers' customary wit which could be tendered as sarcasm or in jest. Divers directs Murf's attention to the other objects. "The belt and the buttons are regular common items. But look at the coins. The total value is sixteen shillings and eight-pence. The oldest coin in the lot is a 1922 George V penny; and the most recent coin is an Irish sixpence dated 1942."

Murf considers this information. If coins are present, then robbery was not a motive. He combines this information with what he learned from Finbar and puts it into the context of the orderliness of the interment. "That is quite revealing. The body, cadaver #2, was interred in the Famine Field between 1942 and early 1944 – some time within a period of twenty-eight months."

"That would be consistent with my findings."

"So, what about the items from cadaver #3?"

"We retrieved a pair of shoes, an empty wallet, buttons, coins and a pair of spectacles. See, the spectacles are intact, and they were correctly positioned over the cadaver's eye-sockets when we uncovered them."

"Are you saying that the body was wearing eye-glasses when he was buried?"

"Yes. And look closely. They are not scratched."

"Surely, if sand and gravel are thrown onto a dead body two feet down, the glasses would get scratched."

"That is correct."

"But these glasses are not scratched?"

"Correct again, Murf."

"How do you explain that?"

"What do YOU think could explain it, Detective?"

Murf pictures a dead body laid out as in a wake. He is familiar with wakes. At the conclusion of a wake, the corpse is shrouded. "A shroud!" he exclaims. "The face was shielded by a covering."

Divers snorts at Murf. "Ah yes, that could explain it. And…"

Murf waits for Divers to finish the sentence. Divers stares with eyebrows raised, prompting Murf to the next logical step. Murf concludes Divers' unfinished remark. "And the covering on the face has since decayed without a trace."

"That could explain it. If the face was covered by a cotton or linen cloth, the covering would have decayed within weeks in the moist moraine soil. Mind you, Murf, there is no **evidence** that the face was shielded by a covering."

"There is no evidence, but it is an explanation, nevertheless. Anything else of special significance in the items?"

"Ordinary shoes, size eight. The wallet is inexpensive leather; there are no identifying markings on it – and it is empty. If it contained any photographs or papers at the time of burial, they have disappeared through decay."

Murf considers another possibility – personal identification may have been removed prior to burial.

Divers continues. "The buttons are interesting though. They are brass and have anchor-design imprints and, judging by their location to each other, they belong to a double-breasted jacket."

"A nautical-style blazer perhaps?" Murf is picturing Cary Grant lying in the supine position.

"From the position of the buttons and the undamaged state of the glasses, it appears that the body was placed in the ground with care."

This is consistent with Finbar's account that the skeletal remains show no signs of injury. Someone buried three bodies free of injury (at least, with no **evident** signs of damage), and laid them to rest considerately with clothing properly in place. Murf considers the possibility that the responsible party might be an enabler assisting in suicides, one who subsequently interred the bodies with some semblance of dignity. A caregiver, perhaps?

Divers is still speaking. "There are four coins to a total value of four shillings and sixpence – a florin, two shillings and a sixpence. They are all Irish and dated between 1938 and 1940."

"That narrows the time of the internment to 1940 or 1941."

"But this, Murf, is the real piece of evidence." Divers points to the pair of glasses. "The spectacles are high-quality and have bakelite-frames with brass screws. They are still in perfect condition. These are prescription glasses that could only come from an optometrist."

"An optometrist like McNiff in the Market Square?"

"I don't know McNiff. But that's your job, Murf, to locate an optometrist who can identify the prescription and the glasses."

"And thence to the identity of the body," Murf says aloud to no one in particular. He considers the similarity of this information to the opinion expressed by the Divil on the previous day. Murf decides to investigate the current whereabouts of The Dazzler Fegan.

"Ah, good, Murf. You're catching on."

"Divers, when you are finished examining the items of evidence, I would like to take them."

"Give me until the end of the day. Then I'll pack them up for you – except for the soil samples. I need a few more days to conduct a thorough examination of the soil."

"The coins and the shoes and the glasses – will you be able to release those?"

"Sure, Murf. Come back at nine tomorrow morning."

At 2:00pm. Murf is in his office in the garda station in Killbawn. He busies himself in updating the information on his investigation wall. He scribbles notes and sticks additional papers to the wall to include the information pertaining to the two recently-found bodies. The three cadavers reveal similarities that could not be coincidental. Murf considers what they have in common – laid out in the same location, in the same manner, and at the same depth. This indicates that the burials were executed by the same person (or persons). Murf considers the significance of the point in time of each burial. Working backwards: 1945, 1942-44, and 1940-41. Murf wonders if this is a pattern – every two years.

Three things strike him as particularly peculiar, three things that render the case at odds with text-book cases. One, there are no signs of injury on the cadavers; two, the bodies were laid out with clothing neatly in place; and three, they were not robbed of their money. The manner in which the corpses were interred fits into the custom of a mid-nineteenth-century wake-and-burial – whereby a corpse is dressed in his best clothes, wrapped in a linen shroud, and buried in sacred ground. No, not quite the same. The Famine Field might be revered, but it is not 'sacred ground' in the sense of a consecrated cemetery. And all funerals in Killbawn, Catholic or Protestant, conclude with burial in the abbey graveyard. Notwithstanding whatever custom was observed, interment in an unmarked site in the Famine Field amounts to concealment of a corpse and improper interment of a body. So, why hide a body? To conceal a death. And why conceal a death? Murf sighs and rubs his blood-shot eyes. He is fatigued. He fights to stay alert. Dots are dotting and strings are stringing as Murf arranges the information on his wall according to relevance.

Murf focuses his attention on the sheet marked 'Marvin'. The circus (or travelling show) arrives on a yearly schedule. Could Marvin be the murderer, hitting only on alternating years? However, John Edge acquired Marvin at the initial commencement of the travelling show. The show first toured in 1944. Marvin would have joined the show in late 1943 or in early 1944. And the show first came to Killbawn in August 1944. Murf concludes that Marvin is not the link to cadaver #2 or to cadaver #3. Furthermore, had Marvin killed Edmund Ludwig, whether deliberately or accidentally, the victim would likely have sustained visible signs of injury. In the context of the three related deaths, Marvin is an unlikely link to the murder of Edmund Ludwig. Murf shortens the coloured threads linking Marvin to the Edmund Ludwig victim – thus shortening the probability of his being the prime suspect.

Murf sits back against his desk. He considers the information on the wall. There is no clear strong suspect. Danny the Divil? No. If the Divil killed someone, he would be unable to dispose of the bodies so neatly. And there is no clear motive. Unless, when driving the doctor's car, he collided with them and killed them accidentally. But then Doctor McBratt would have noticed damage to her car. Murf knows the doctor quite well, and he knows her car – and her previous car. Her car never suffered any damage since the first day the Divil drove it. Murf exhales loudly. Realistically, the Divil is not a likely suspect.

Murf scans the other sheets on the wall. His eyes rest on 'Father Barry Glen Dennagher'. Glen Dennagher knew Edmund Ludwig, just as he knew every circus acrobat that came to Sligo and Mayo. And his car is occasionally spotted in strange places. Surely his outreach ministry must bring him to unusual places. Regardless, what possible motive could Glen Dennagher have to kill an acrobat – or kill anyone for that matter?

Murf sighs again. He reaches out to the wall and re-adjusts the coloured threads. Three names have threads attached, and all threads are exceedingly short. This indicates that Marvin, the Divil and Glen Dennagher are an important part of the picture. Although, they are not considered likely suspects, neither are they discounted completely. What is the relevance of their connections to the case – either to the victims or to the burial site, or as witnesses or abetters?

Murf comes to an undeniable conclusion. He has insufficient information at this point. His immediate focus is to identify the two new bodies – cadaver #2 and cadaver #3. The investigation must continue and intensify. Once he accumulates additional information, he will determine relevance and see if a clearer picture emerges when he reconnects the dots.

Thursday 29 August 1946. At 9:00am, Murf enters the crime lab in Castlebar and seeks out Divers. Divers, of course, is expecting him. Divers has prepared two heavy-duty corrugated boxes appropriately marked 'Famine Field Cad #2' and 'Famine Field Cad #3'. These sturdy cardboard boxes are able to withstand two hundredweight and, therefore, are Murf-proof for rough handling. Murf will add these two evidence boxes to his previously obtained 'Famine Field Cad' box.

"Now see here, Murf, handle the items with cloth gloves so as not to contaminate them."

"Are you saying that there are fingerprints in evidence after so many years in such a dirty environment?"

"Murf, I've seen a good set of prints after ten years or more. As against that, I have failed to lift a clear set of prints from an item after only six months. It depends on how sweaty the fingers were when leaving the print, and the surface condition of the object – how porous it is, and how the object had weathered or the degree to which it suffered decay."

"But regarding these items here, did you obtain fingerprints from them?"

"Yes. But don't get excited. All the objects here, those that have survived free of decay, bear fingerprints. But because of multiple handling and smudging, there are no clear prints. All I can say with certainty is that they were handled multiple times – the buttons, the coins, the belt buckles, the shoes, the wallet, the frames of the glasses. Just don't add any new prints to them. I don't want to hear that Inspector Murphy's fingerprints are the only clear prints on the evidence objects."

"Come on, Divers, you know that I never touch an item of potential evidence with my bare hands." Murf removes the lids from the boxes and peeks inside at each one in turn. "Is this all you have for me, Divers?"

"That's all for now, Murf. But there's more to come. I await the results of the soil analyses. That could indicate the presence of decayed materials which have leached into the soil."

"And you are waiting for a response from Germany on Edmund Ludwig's tooth filling?"

"Yes – the dental records to confirm his identity. And that could be a long wait."

"Right-oh, Divers, I'm off. I have my work cut out for me with all this stuff here."

An hour later, Murf enters McNiff's optometrist's office in the Market Square in Killbawn. Murf shows the Dazzler's glasses to Val McNiff, the optometrist. McNiff laughs upon seeing them. Murf asks him, "So you recognise these glasses?"

"How could I forget them? Young Fegan obtained them from me in… let me see."

"Val, these glasses are evidence in an investigation. Don't handle them with bare hands."

Val McNiff puts on a pair of medical gloves and takes the glasses from Murf. He enters his inner office and examines the glasses. Then he refers to a file. "Inspector Murphy, it is just as I thought. These are the very glasses I got for Bobby Fegan on 19 March 1941. He was a young lad of about 20, and he wanted to look like Cary Grant from the motion pictures. He showed me an advertising poster for one of his films. He pointed to the glasses worn by Cary Grant and asked me to get him the same frames. I was required to submit a special order to Dublin to obtain the requested frames. Oh yes, I remember him well. The lads around here called him 'The Dazzler' on account of his emulating Hollywood film stars and actors in his manner of dress – not that he succeeded, but he sure tried."

"I know of one Fegan family here – the one in Ballycorry."

"That's the family, all right. Actually, since Bobby left, it is just one old lady living alone now. She lives in a big old house next to the Fitzpatrick farm in Ballycorry. They say that young Bobby went off to work in England shortly after that."

"Is that a fact?"

"Of course, I don't know that for sure, but a lot of the lads from here, lads of that age, went off to England at that time to assist in the war effort."

Murf departs from McNiff's office. He is pleased with his progress today. Where skeletal remains are unable to provide conclusive proof of identity, Murf must rely on the personal objects found with the remains. These are his sole means of identification. He is satisfied that he has identified one of the two bodies – Bobby Fegan of Ballycorry townland. And the timeline is consistent with the forensic evidence – 'shortly after 19 March 1941'.

At 12:00 noon, Murf enters Paddy McCafferty's shoemaker's shop in Church Street. Upon entering, Murf inhales the pleasant smell of leather. Paddy is seated, dressed in a leather apron, and is busy hammering nails into the sole of a shoe held in place on a last. "Hello, Paddy!" Murf shouts over the noise to get his attention.

Paddy stops hammering and looks up. "Guard Murphy. So what can I do for you?" Paddy has no shoes belonging to Murf that are scheduled for pick up. And Murf is not carrying any shoes in need of repair. Instead, Murf places a corrugated box on the floor and flips off the lid. This is an unusual way to request a service. Paddy places his hammer on the lapstone at his side and peers into the box with curiosity.

"Paddy, have a look at this. But don't touch anything. What do you see?"

"I see the shoes I mended for Tunnery a few years ago. That's my work, all right. Them shoes belong to Big Bill Tunnery of Tubberbawn. He hardly ever wore them. After more than ten years they were still like new."

"Big Bill Tunnery, the ganger of the county council work crew? Sure I saw him at Mass last Sunday."

"You may have, Guard Murphy, but he was wearing no shoes. He would have been wearing his boots."

"So, Paddy, why did you mend Big Bill's shoes if they didn't need mending?"

"Ah, it wasn't him. It was for his cub, Liam. Liam came in with his dad's shoes one day. He told me that Big Bill will never wear them again and that he, Liam, was to have them. Now, young Liam was a natty dresser and he wanted to appear taller than his five feet seven-and-a-half inches."

"So he had you replace the original heels with elevated heels?"

"Exactly."

"And when did you do the work, Paddy?"

Lord, Guard Murphy, I can't mind when I did the work. One day is like another to me. But surely it must have been afore he went off to… well, wherever he went off to. The story is that Big Bill hires his own boys to work in the work crew – two of his lads work with him now. But Liam did not want to do county council work filling potholes in the road and slashing hedges with a billhook. So he took off. Well, that's the story what's goin' 'round, anyhow."

"But you are sure that these are Big Bill's shoes?"

"No doubt. But I fixed them up for young Liam, I did."

Murf now has a name for each of the three cadavers:
#1, Edmund Ludwig, the Leper
#2, Liam Tunnery, the Dandy
#3, Bobby Fegan, the Dazzler

CHAPTER SIXTEEN

MURF CONNECTS THE DOTS

Killbawn, County Mayo, Ireland
Friday 30 August 1946

8:00am. Murf is busy jotting notes and drawing shapes on his investigation wall. He runs out of space on the papers stuck on the wall but, undeterred, he extends his writing onto the bare wall itself. At length, he sits back against his desk, half-sitting/half-standing. He twirls two pencils through his fingers and he studies his work. Murf has a good feeling, deep down inside, that a picture is forming at last. To any other observer, the writings and drawings on the wall might suggest chaos rather than order. Murf exhales a sigh of contentment. Just then, his phone rings. Garda Eddie Caldwell from the front desk informs him that Divers from the forensic crime lab wishes to speak with him. Murf accepts the call. "Divers, you bringer of jollity, you have news for me?"

"It's a fine day when the postman brings a surprising gift. You'll never guess what arrived in the morning post."

"No. You won the Sweep?"

"Post from Germany, Murf. The dental records obtained from the Kriegsmarine confirm the identity of cadaver #1 as Matrose Edmund Ludwig."

"'Seaman Edmund Ludwig'. Thanks, Divers. That's good news and, hopefully, it is a good omen." Murf hangs up the receiver and lifts his casebook from the desk. He writes a checkmark next to the first name:

#1, Edmund Ludwig, the Leper √
#2, Liam Tunnery, the Dandy?

The identity of the first cadaver is confirmed. His next task is to confirm the identities of #2 and #3.

At 10:30am, Murf drives up to the Tunnery cottage in Tubberbawn. Mrs Tunnery is outside feeding the hens. She is dressed in black wellington boots and a yellow wrap-around apron. She has tied a red-and-white-checkered cotton scarf around her head due to the breeze from the Atlantic. Out here on the headland, the land is exposed to the sea breeze more so than in Killbawn. Mrs Tunnery lowers her pail of wet oatmeal mash in surprise as she observes Murf's car approach, bouncing up the rutted laneway. She wipes her oatmeal-encrusted fingers on her apron and shoos away the pecking hens to clear a space for the advancing car. Murf brings his car to a halt in the front yard in the space cleared between Mrs Tunnery and the low stone wall encircling the yard. The perceptive woman recognises him – she is familiar with Murf from seeing him at Mass every Sunday with the collection box. She is curious as to why he would be visiting this remote part of the parish. As Murf steps out of the car she addresses him. "Guard Murphy, and what do ye be wantin' out here in the back-of-beyond at all, at all? If it's the holy well you're lookin' for, you just past it a half-mile back there at the bend, in that wee stone circle at the foot of the hill."

"Ah, no, Mrs Tunnery, I am just coming around to see how things are."

She gawks at Murf with a look that says, 'I don't believe that'. She waits for Murf to recommence speaking.

Murf leans back against the bonnet of the car and scans the land in feigned admiration. He brings his focus back to the cottage and to the foraging hens that have since returned and are attempting to peck at the contents of the pail. For a moment both Murf and Mrs Tunnery take some relief in the inconsequential distraction of the hens. Murf rubs his eyes as a gust of wind whips against him unexpectedly. He speaks. "So, how's the family, Mrs Tunnery?"

"Fine, fine, thank God."

"And Big Bill? He is well, I trust?"

"Big Bill is workin' the coast road the day. Fixin' potholes he is – at least I think he is. He sent Pat off with the donkey to bring the tar-boiler. Then himself and Mick followed on their bicycles. If they are boilin' tar, then they must be fixin' holes in the road."

"Ah yes. With Pat and Mick?"

"Well, there is a whole crew of them – I don't rightly know the whole of them. But, it's a county council work crew what does be doin' the road repairs."

"It must be nice for Big Bill to be working alongside his sons, Pat and Mick."

"Ay. I have two sons, you know. That's them, Pat and Mick."

"Is that right? I thought you had three sons. Isn't there one called after his father – Liam?"

Mrs Tunnery stands stoically still, struggling to maintain a neutral expression. After three seconds, she responds in a low whisper, "Liam left. And I blame Big Bill. They had a hell-of-a row at Easter three years ago. Big Bill told him to leave. And he did leave, by God, on Easter Monday. And we never heard from him again." With that, she lifts the pail and scoops the remaining oatmeal up in her hand. She flings it to the far side of the yard. The hens scurry after the meal and they pounce upon the scattered mash. She then enters the cottage. She turns and speaks over the half-door to Murf. "When Liam went, it broke my heart. I have not smiled once since that day, Monday 26 April 1943." With that, she disappears into the interior of the cottage. Murf has no opportunity to tell her of the corpse found in the Famine

Field, the corpse which may be the remains of her dead son, Liam. He could go after her, but he chooses not to follow her. Until he himself is certain as to the identity of the body, he decides to withhold this information until a more suitable occasion.

Murf rubs his eyes once more and re-enters his car. He drives off, scattering the hens, and considers the information thus obtained. Speaking of Liam is a painful experience for Mrs Tunnery. He considers engaging the assistance of Doctor McBratt when he next broaches the subject of Liam Tunnery with the distraught mother. Regardless, the investigation needs to be conducted thoroughly. He decides to continue the current inquiry with Big Bill. And Big Bill is working somewhere on the coast road.

Murf drives back down the rutted laneway and turns onto the coast road. Within a few minutes, he spots bicycles leaning against the roadside bank. Each bicycle has an olive-green canvas bag either secured in the carrier or draped over the handlebars. These bags are the standard-issue satchels allocated to county council workers. This is a sure sign that the work crew is close by. Murf rolls down the side window. Immediately, he gets the whiff of boiling tar. He rounds the bend and sees two donkeys grazing on the roadside grass. The donkeys are part of the work crew − one to draw the cart of stone chips, and the second one to pull the tar boiler. The smoke from the hot tar whips around in the breeze and disturbs the two donkeys. They shake their heads in protest and resume chomping the grass according to the whimsical direction of the changing breeze. He hears the crew before he sees it. The men shout and laugh. They strike their shovels on the ground and scrape them against the loose stone chips. There are ten workmen in evidence and, amongst them, in the thick of it, is Big Bill Tunnery.

Big Bill is the ganger. It is usual for the ganger to wear a hat rather than a soft-cap, and to issue orders to the crew rather than engage in the physical labour himself. Big Bill is different. He dresses in denim dungaree overalls and wears a soft-cap just like the workers, and he leads by example – setting the pace and maintaining a high standard of work. As one, all the men cease their activity upon perceiving Murf's arrival. They lean on their shovels and scratch their heads through tilted caps. Murf's unexpected presence arouses their interest.

Big Bill passes his shovel to young Mick and addresses Murf. "Guard Murphy, and what brings you out this way?"

"Hello. Big Bill. I need to ask you something. It's part of my investigation. And you know these parts around here right well."

"Aren't you investigating the holes in the Famine Field and what was dug up?"

"Ay, it's to do with the Famine Field and what was excavated there. If you come to my car…" Murf walks back to his car, followed closely by Big Bill. Bill turns back and addresses the crew lest they follow him in their curiosity. "Don't let the hot tar set. Fill in them holes with chips while the tar is still runny. Now get back to it, men."

Back at the car, Murf and Big Bill hear the sounds of the work resuming. Satisfied that they are out of ear-shot, Murf speaks to Big Bill. "Bill, it is true. This has to do with the Famine Field. Brace yourself for what could be bad news."

"Bad news for me from the Famine Field?"

"Yes. You know that we exhumed three bodies from the field?"

Big Bill reads Murf's expression. "Guard Murphy, it's not about Liam. No. Don't tell me…"

"I'm not sure. I need you to look at some things and tell me if you recognise any of them. These are things that we excavated alongside one of the bodies found in the Famine Field. Tell me when you are ready, Bill. Take your time."

"You have them here? The items?"

"In the boot."

"Let me light a fag first." Big Bill takes a 10-pack of Woodbine out of the breast pocket of the bib of his overalls. He places one of the thin loose-leafed cigarettes between his lips and applies a flaring match in a smooth well-practised coordinated motion. He drags deeply. Pauses, and takes a second drag. He speaks as the smoke is expelled from his lungs rendering his words in a low muffled sound as if speaking through a blanket. The words are indistinct but clear enough for Murf to understand that Big Bill is ready.

Murf flips open the lid of the boot. Big Bill walks around to the back of the car and peers into the interior of the boot. He sees a folded brier-proof tweed jacket. Alongside the jacket are three heavy-duty corrugated boxes. Murf rests his hand on one box and looks into Big Bill's face. "Are you ready?"

"Open the box, for God's sake. Show me what is in there."

Murf flips the lid off the box. He keeps his gaze on Big Bill's face. Big Bill's face registers a pained look of distress as he recognises the contents within. He staggers forward and grips the raised lid of the boot for support. The boot lid would surely have fallen shut had Murf not been alert to Big Bill's reaction. Murf holds the boot lid safely propped open with his arm.

"My shoes. Those are my shoes. The ones I gave to Liam. But wait. Could not the shoes have been buried in the Famine Field by someone else – someone who stole them?"

"Yes. That is possible. But, Bill, they were found on the feet of the deceased. He was wearing them when he was buried."

"But it still could be someone else. Couldn't it?"

"Bill, did Liam have anything that was unique to him – something from which he would not be parted?" Murf puts on a pair of cotton gloves and passes a pair to Big Bill. "This is evidence, Bill. You are not allowed to touch any of the items; not yet, but later."

"Liam had a lucky penny. It was a penny with the date of his birth. He always carried it in an inner pocket."

"What penny was that, Bill?"

"1922. An English penny dated 1922."

"Could this be it?" Murf shows Big Bill the coins that were discovered with the body. One, in particular, is a penny showing the profile of George V on the obverse. Murf turns it over to reveal Britannia and the date – 1922. The smouldering Woodbine drops from Big Bill's mouth. Murf catches it before it lands on the floor of the boot and he throws it onto the roadway.

"Liam. Lord knows this can only be Liam. So where is he?"

"Liam is in the forensic lab in Garda Division Headquarters in Castlebar."

"He is? Could I go see him? Would I recognise him?"

"Bill," Murf says softly, "Liam was lying in the Famine Field, three-and-a-half feet down, for three years. There are only the skeletal remains now. You will not be able to recognise him. But, of course, you are permitted to see him. Just be prepared."

Big Bill retreats from the car and sits on the roadside embankment. Murf secures the evidence box and closes the boot. Big Bill replaces his lost cigarette with a fresh one. He is quiet for a time, blowing smoke and examining the glowing tip of the smouldering Woodbine. Woodbine is a loosely-packed cigarette. It burns down quickly. Big Bill shifts the positioning of the cigarette to grip it by his thumb and the tips of his fingernails. When it becomes too hot to hold, he drops it onto the roadside gravel. Watching the last wisps of smoke rising from the dirt, Big Bill speaks. "I blame myself. Every morning I wake up, and I blame myself. And lest I forget, the missus reminds me. She blames me too."

"Blames you for what, Bill?"

"For sending Liam away. I know I said what I said – but I did not mean it. Lord knows I did not mean it. But he went, so he did. At first, I expected him to show up later in the day or, at worst, on the following morning. But… Liam did not return." Big Bill fumbles in his bib pocket and extracts his pack of Woodbine. He removes another cigarette. He realises that it is his final cigarette. He taps it on his knee to settle the loose tobacco. Then he places it in his mouth and crumples the empty pack, tossing it carelessly over his shoulder.

Murf decides to let Big Bill continue speaking. No prodding or prompting is required. Murf leans back against the side of the car and stands facing Big Bill, who is sitting on the embankment of the roadside sheugh.

"It was back in 1943. The row was brewing from St Patrick's Day. Liam was reading about how the blitz had recently ended in England. And he saw an announcement that they wanted workers to help in the war effort over there. You see, Guard Murphy, the Englishmen were mostly off fighting and there was a big push to manufacture things and to produce food what with no ships being available to bring stuff in and all. Women joined the workforce over there to do a man's work, and there was a great demand for Irish labour."

Murf nods. He knows the nature of the situation in the spring of 1943. Many men from Mayo went to England that year. So many that there were Irish work gangs made up exclusively from a single Irish community. So, like many young men in north Mayo, young Liam Tunnery wanted to go to England – or so it seemed.

"I said to Liam that he had no business going to England. I could land him a job right here at home working for the county council, I said. Then he got angry and he told me that he wanted no work filling holes in the road or draining sheughs. He was going to do clean work – like working on the buses in London just like Sean Meehan done. Can you imagine that, Guard Murphy? Him telling me that this work here is too dirty a job for him when this job here put food on his table for all these years."

Big Bill takes a final drag on his cigarette and tosses the butt on the ground. He stamps on it loudly and says, "So I cuffed him one on the ear. And that should have put an end to his nonsense. Then, on Easter Monday, I announced to the family that Liam would be starting to work alongside me the following day. I was able to get the job I promised – and it took a bit of pull, I can tell you. Well, the row blew up again. This time Liam tried to draw in his mother to back him up. But she kept her quiet. Anyways, Liam said that he was leaving for England. And I said to him that I expected him at the worksite on the following day. And that's when I said the wrong thing. I said to Liam that if he failed to show up for work, then go to England and be damned. He shouted back, 'I'm leaving, I'm leaving right now'. And he ran out the door. I shouted after him 'Then leave! I never want to set eyes on you again!' Right away, I knew it was the wrong thing to say. But Liam was already gone. I sat by the fire all day, and I sat up all night waiting for him to return so that I could make things right by him. The hours passed, but he did not show up – not that day; nor that night; nor at the work site the next day; nor ever again. If Liam is dead now because of that row, then I am to blame, just as sure as if I struck him down myself."

There is silence for a moment. Murf speaks to Big Bill. "Bill, I want you to come with me."

"Ah, you're arresting me. And I deserve it. Any man what killed his own son…"

"I'm not arresting you, Bill. I'm taking you to visit Doctor McBratt."

"To visit the doctor? What for? I'm not sick or nothing."

Murf realises that Big Bill is in shock and is in grave need of grief counselling. And Doctor McBratt is the Killbawn expert in that field. "Bill, it's not just for yourself. I need to inform the rest of your family. Doctor McBratt will be able to handle this and help break the sad news to them better than I can. So, Bill, tell the men here to finish up and go home. And tell the lads, Pat and Mick, to be at home this evening when we arrive with the doctor."

This makes sense to Big Bill. It also motivates him to some purpose other than to sitting steeped in guilt and regrets. He rises from the bank and walks to the bend. He shouts instructions to the men. And he tells his two sons to be at home for when he arrives later with Guard Murphy. Pat and Mick are puzzled as to why Big Bill is going off with Murf. They agree to meet him at home later, and they inquire as to what they should do with his bicycle. Big Bill is not concerned about the bicycle, so Pat decides to bring it back with the donkey.

On the way to Killbawn, Murf tries to console Big Bill. "You know, Bill, whatever tragedy befell Liam was not at your hands. But you could help us, and help Liam, by bringing closure to this. Help us find the person responsible."

"You don't think **I'm** responsible?"

"Bill, you had no hand in Liam's death – not in any way. But you **can** have a hand in solving his death and in bringing the party responsible to justice. That is something you can do for Liam. Now listen to me…"

Murf and Big Bill enter the dispensary at 3:00pm. Murf provides a short explanation to Doctor McBratt. She instantly assesses the situation and takes control. A country doctor regularly sees death, and comforting a grieving family is a duty that Doctor McBratt frequently performs with tender skill. Surviving family members frequently experience guilt. Big Bill's condition is not unique. She pulls Murf aside and instructs him to fetch the Divil from Cannon's bar while he is still able to be of service.

Murf leaves Big Bill in the capable care of Doctor McBratt. Moments later, he enters Cannon's pub. Mick Cannon is behind the bar. Murf sees that the Divil's stool at the counter is vacant. "Mick," he shouts, "where's the Divil? Is he not here?"

Mick does not register surprise. Both Murf and the Divil are given to unexpected behaviour. Mick tilts his head and says, "He's in the kitchen eating mashed potatoes and buttermilk. Go right in."

Inside the kitchen, the Divil is sitting at the table and is wiping his mouth. "Danny! Get yourself up! The doctor wants you urgently. And I need you."

"What? Is it about the Famine Field stuff?"

The Divil grabs his soft-cap from the table and jams it on his head as he rises. Mrs Cannon, who is washing dishes in the sink, shouts at him as he exits the kitchen, "There you go, Detective Danny. You're back on the case."

Back at the dispensary, Doctor McBratt instructs the Divil to fetch her car. She declines to travel to the Tunnery house in Murf's car lest she ladders her stockings on Murf's untidy back seat. She addresses the Divil, "Danny, let me look at you. Are you sober enough to drive?"

"Oh, I am indeed, Ma'am."

"Good. Now, hand over your travelling supply of whiskey."

The Divil hands her four miniature bottles from his outer pockets. "That's the lot there, Ma'am."

Doctor McBratt slaps the Divil on the chest and on the rump. The Divil winces at each slap. "Danny, I can see the bulge of bottles. Now hand over the remaining four bottles."

Having settled the order of travel, Murf and Big Bill set off in Murf's car. They are closely followed by Doctor McBratt, armed with her medical bag, driven by her faithful Divil. They arrive at the Tunnery cottage at 4:30pm.

Inside the cottage, in the kitchen of their three-roomed abode, Mrs Tunnery and the two sons greet them as they enter. From Murf's earlier visit, the astute Mrs Tunnery construed correctly what is in store – some bad news about Liam. And not just any bad news, but the worst news.

Murf describes the nature of the find in the Famine Field. He explains how the police determine the identity of a body. In the case of skeletal remains, such as this, the accompanying personal items are the most reliable identifiers. He opens the evidence box and reveals the contents. Mrs Tunnery glances inside the box and nods. It confirms what she long ago suspected, that Liam had departed this life. She knows that, because no card ever came from him at Christmas; no letter arrived; no news sent via any of the neighbours' boys from England; nothing. The two brothers peer inside more intently. They enumerate the contents visually, noting, in particular, the presence of Liam's 'lucky penny'.

Doctor McBratt takes over. She speaks her consoling wisdom and comfort. The two boys are bewildered. They attempt to put this newly-acquired information into perspective. Mrs Tunnery busies herself by making tea – really strong tea.

Big Bill, who has been silent since he entered the cottage, asks Murf, "So, tell us, Guard Murphy, what now?"

"Liam will be released to you in about three days. That's when the county medical examiner will release the body. You may wish to have a requiem Mass and funeral, and have Liam laid to rest in Killbawn Abbey."

Mrs Tunnery turns from the hearth and addresses Big Bill. "First thing on the morrow, go visit Canon MacMorrow and arrange the funeral."

"Oh, I will, yes." He turns back to Murf. "Guard Murphy, you said that you have a police case arising out of this?"

"Yes. We are determined to find the person, or persons, responsible for Liam's tragic death. My immediate focus is on Liam's last known movements. So tell me, to the best of your knowledge, who was the last person to see Liam?"

"Sure that was the whole of us. We were all here when he ran out through the doorway. That's the last we saw of him."

"Well, did he walk away from here; or did he cycle?"

"He left his bicycle here by the gable. So he must have walked."

"At what time?"

"It was half four when he left."

Mrs Tunnery interjects. "It was 4:28pm on Monday 26 April 1943."

Murf nods in acknowledgement. "It was daytime. So someone might have seen him. Perhaps he got a lift. If so, someone would remember." Murf pieces together the final moments of Liam Tunnery's departure from home.

An hour later, Murf is finished assimilating information. "One last thing, have you a photograph of Liam? It is important that we find the last person to have seen Liam after he left home. Someone at the bus station, or at the train station in Castlebar, may recognise him – assuming that he was on his way to England."

Mrs Tunnery removes the family pictures from the mantle. "This is Liam's First Communion photy, and this is him at his Confirmation. But I won't part with them picturs."

"I understand, Mrs Tunnery. But I was hoping for a more recent photograph – one taken close to his departure."

Pat and Mick interject. "There's the one what was took on St Patrick's night that year. The one with him and a bunch of lads." Pat goes off in search of the photograph. He returns shortly and gives the snapshot to Murf. It is a picture of six young men laughing and smoking, and leaning against the side of a car. "See here, Guard Murphy, this one is Liam."

"And who are the others?" Murf takes special note that Liam's friends may have access to a car – a car that may have accommodated his departure from home.

"Well, we don't know who these lads are. We never seen them around here nor in Killbawn nor anywhere else forbyes."

Murf turns the photograph over. Written on the back is the date – 17 March 1943. Six letters are inscribed beside the date, all in different handwriting – J, L, P, N, T, B. Murf asks, "Do you have any idea what the writing means?"

"No."

Murf turns the photograph back to face him and examines the scene. "…or where the photograph was taken?"

"No, Guard Murphy. We have no idea."

Big Bill adds, "Liam was knocking around with a different lot back then – boys from God knows where. They were putting ideas into his head – talk about England, no doubt. But he would not tell us anything about them."

"Thank you for the information. It may be of help in the investigation. And if you can think of anything, anything at all, please get in touch with me. And should something come to light at my end, I'll let you know. I may have more questions later. But this is all for now. I bid you all *oíche mhaith.*"

Murf and Doctor McBratt take their leave. As Murf replaces the evidence box into the boot of the car, McBratt whispers to him, "The photograph. You went quiet when you looked at it. You recognised something in it. Didn't you, Murf?"

"Yes."

"What was it, Murf?"

"Ah…" Murf shuts the boot lid and enters the car by the driver's door.

"So you won't tell me?"

"Good-night, Doctor McBratt." Murf shuts the car door and starts the engine. He drives off, bumping over the ruts in the laneway. Upon reaching the coast road, he heads back to Killbawn. He removes the photograph from his pocket and looks at it again. He recognises the location. The snapshot was taken in a car park – the car park of 'An Chuilfhionn', the private club in a secluded wooded area near Islandeady Lough, located off the Westport Road, a short distance from Castlebar.

Back in his office, Murf makes a quick checkmark in his casebook:

#1, Edmund Ludwig, the Leper √
#2, Liam Tunnery, the Dandy √
#3, Bobby Fegan, the Dazzler?

The identities of two cadavers are confirmed. Murf then hurriedly attaches a fresh sheet of paper to his wall. He entitles it 'An Chuilfhionn'. This club now features as a link to Liam Tunnery. It is also linked to Father Barry Glen Dennagher. And Glen Dennagher is linked to Edmund Ludwig. The dots are connecting and a picture is forming. Undoubtedly, Murf must investigate the club in light of this recently acquired information. And how does the priest feature in this? Even if he is not considered a suspect, he may provide invaluable information relative to the other participants, and hence lead to the identity of the criminal offender. More investigation on Glen Dennagher is in order, and Murf wonders if there could be a direct link from him to Liam Tunnery.

According to the premise held by Murf and the forensic investigators, all three murders are linked. This implies a serial killer. Did the serial killer stop at three victims, he wonders? Are there more victims yet to be discovered? And if the killer is not apprehended, could there be additional future victims? Who is being targeted? Murf brings his eyes to rest once more on the page entitled 'Barry Glen Dennagher'. Previously regarded as a suspect, Murf now regards Glen Dennagher as a possible target of the serial killer.

Although tempted to pursue this line of inquiry as a priority, Murf decides to press on with the current task of confirming the identity of cadaver #3, Bobby Fegan. Three murders – one case. Bobby Fegan may prove to be a crucial link to the picture. Murf expects to uncover more common elements in the three murders by investigating Bobby Fegan.

At first, Murf considered three murders to be an overwhelming investigation – three murders, hence three times more difficult to solve than a single murder. He realises now, that with three inter-connected murders, each victim may afford clues relative to the other two, and hence contribute a lot of supporting data to the case – more interconnecting dots for Murf's picture.

It is almost midnight. Murf's blood-shot eyes are smarting from fatigue. He flings his pencil on the desk. It bounces once and tumbles to the floor and rolls out of sight. Murf grunts in reluctant acceptance of losing a pencil. He yawns and calls it a day.

CHAPTER SEVENTEEN

BOBBY FEGAN OF SCOTT MANOR

County Mayo, Ireland
Saturday 31 August 1946

8:00am. As in most days, Murf is busy jotting notes and drawing shapes on his investigation wall. He has a feeling that his understanding of the case is now more clearly formed. Previously, he had been unable to link a possible motive to the actual crime. The disposal of Edmund Ludwig's body lacked any clear linking of motive to means. The condition in which the second body was found suggests a pattern. Therefore, these are not two random killings. The combined background information on Ludwig and Tunnery fills in a number of missing dots in the picture. For the first time, Murf recognizes a pattern that may be a common link. He refrains from notating it on his investigation wall at this juncture. That would be premature. The inquiry into the third cadaver, Bobby Fegan, 'The Dazzler', should provide information to strengthen his theory on connecting motive to opportunity to means – or point him in a new direction. Murf sits back against his desk and twirls his pencils as he formulates his thoughts. If he can establish motive, one common to all three killings, he will be able to focus the inquiry to a narrow field of investigation. Therefore, he intends to collect information pertaining to Bobby Fegan in the forthcoming hours. He hopes that the added information will prove to be a valuable component and provide a clearer picture of the case.

Murf slams the pencils carelessly on his desk and moves purposefully and deliberately out through his office doorway. He walks down the corridor and enters the district officer's office. Superintendent David Fox is inside sitting at his desk and is studying the morning edition of the Irish Independent. "Foxy, I need a garda to run an errand for me. It will take a couple of hours."

Superintendent Fox glances up from his reading. Murf has entered without knocking, but Murf seldom adheres to respectful protocol. Fox overlooks Murf's characteristic absence of formality and the unorthodox use of his familiar name 'Foxy'. "So, Murf," Fox responds with an equally familiar form of address, "is this to do with the triple-murder case?"

"Of course. I need an officer to take a photograph to forensics in Castlebar, to have them enlarge it and isolate one of the people depicted on it into a separate picture. It is a picture of Liam Tunnery with five other lads. But I require the original photograph returned to me immediately. It has interesting writing on the back."

"They can do it that quickly – there and then?"

"I believe they take a high-resolution photograph of the primary photograph. They subsequently develop and enlarge it, and crop the secondary photograph to the desired result. The second picture will not be available until Monday, but I will have the original back here within two hours."

"Very well, Murf. Send Garda O'Reilly to Castlebar. But first, check that the forensic lab is staffed on a Saturday."

"Thanks, Foxy. I'll do that."

"And Murf, you appear to be overwhelmed with this inquiry. As of now, I'm assigning Garda O'Reilly to assist you for the duration of the investigation."

Moments later, Murf enlists the assistance of Garda Seamus O'Reilly. O'Reilly is pleased that he is selected to assist in an important investigation, and he takes to his responsibilities eagerly. Murf has two important assignments for O'Reilly. First, he directs O'Reilly to go to the crime lab with the photograph of Liam Tunnery. O'Reilly understands his mission. He undertakes to telephone Castlebar to inform the lab staff of his intended visit today and to request them to be prepared to accommodate him expeditiously.

The second task is plain old slogging to get information. Murf hands a sheet of paper to O'Reilly. "O'Reilly, here is a list of families who have had a son go to work in England during the war. No doubt, you recognise every name on the list. I have gone over every family I know in the parish, and these twenty-two names should be a complete list."

"It's a closely-knit parish, Killbawn is. Any single name on the list, of those who went to England during the war, would certainly know every other person that went. If there is a name missing, Murf, any one of these would know."

"Precisely. But I want you to concentrate on Liam Tunnery. See if any of these families know anything about Liam Tunnery going to England."

"If Liam Tunnery is one of the bodies dug up in the Famine Field, Murf, sure he couldn't have gone to England. Now, could he?"

"O'Reilly, Liam Tunnery left home intending to go to England on Monday 26 April 1943. Someone must have seen him. Who was the last person to see him alive after he left home, and under what circumstances?"

"Ah, he set out for England, and then something happened to him. Is that what you're thinking? And someone else, also on his way to England at that time, might have seen him or…"

"…or may be able to provide valuable information on his last movements."

O'Reilly understands both assignments. Murf, on the other hand, is off to conduct his continuing inquiry in another area. He checks that he is carrying the correct evidence box –

the one marked 'Cadaver #3' – and he leaves the garda station. He drives to Ballycorry to visit Mrs Fegan at the old Scott Manor. He recites in his mind the local information he has acquired about the Fegan family in Ballycorry. Murf prides himself on his extensive background information on every family in the parish, albeit that he prefers not to openly acknowledge the depth of this knowledge.

Fegan is not a local name. And Mrs Fegan is actually Miss Fegan. She is unmarried. Since Bobby left, she lives alone in the old Scott Manor. This is not exactly true. Tom Buckley, with his wife and three children, live in the servants' quarters of the manor house. Robert Scott is the present owner of the manor. He is currently living abroad.

The Scott family has occupied this site since 1699. The property was gifted to Clive Scott for his loyal service to the Crown – the result of the fortunes of war in which some people gain land while others lose possession. The Scott family constructed the present manor house in 1815 in celebration of Wellington's victory over Napoleon at the battle of Waterloo. Unlike many landlords, the Scotts actually lived here locally, whereas many landowners drifted back to their previous English and Scottish homes and left the management of their Irish holdings in the hands of appointed agents.

During the Great Famine, the Scott family employed local Irish labour to construct follies as a means of providing work-relief.

In 1918, after the Great War, the current Robert Scott embarked on a new venture in Uganda. And during 'The Troubles' in Ireland he sold off his Irish land holdings to a fellow Protestant, his landowner neighbour, Fitzpatrick.

Robert Scott's current Irish property consists solely of his family home, the Scott Manor, a big house with an exotic walled garden and an impressive yew-lined wide avenue. The agent's cottage, previously the abode of his land steward, was sold to Fitzpatrick as part of the farmland sale. Willie Buckley, Scott's former land steward, was thence employed by Fitzpatrick as his farm foreman, and he continues to live in the agent's cottage. Willie Buckley's brother, Tom, is retained by Scott as caretaker of the family's manor house and gardens.

Mrs Fegan was ensconced in the house as house-manageress and housekeeper in 1920. She had previously lived with the Scott family on their plantation house in Uganda as a lady's companion to Robert Scott's wife, Elizabeth. She was later relocated to the Ballycorry house in anticipation of Robert Scott's return home to Ireland. Shortly after her arrival in Ballycorry, Mrs Fegan gave birth to a boy. She would have been well into her pregnancy at the time of her arrival here. She named the boy 'Bobby'. Murf wonders if Bobby Fegan is the illegitimate son of Robert Scott. Perhaps he is, or perhaps not.

The years passed; twenty-eight years since departing for Uganda, Robert Scott has not yet returned to live in the Scott Manor. The once-great house has fallen into a state of disrepair. And the current condition of the once-exotic gardens is unknown. Mrs Fegan lives in 'the house' as befitting her status of house manageress, and Tom Buckley's family lives 'around the back'. Tom Buckley works, if he ever works at all, for his brother Willie on Fitz's farm. He lazes around most of the time.

Murf drives up the wide avenue towards the manor. He stops the car and switches off the engine. The avenue is exceedingly wide, constructed in this manner as relief-work during the Great Famine. He looks at the great house in the near-distance. The 'great house' is no longer great. Murf ponders on the events which contributed to the demise of the once-great Scott Manor, events which, as a consequence, dealt misfortune to Mrs Fegan.

The Bann Royal Academy for Girls
Ballynahinch, County Down, Ireland
Wednesday 25 June 1919

Head Mistress Margaret Graham addresses the senior girls. "In another week, you young ladies will depart from this august establishment of learning. You came here as girls; you leave as young ladies. Today, you are ready to take your places in the world. Great opportunities lie ahead. For example, upon reaching the age of 21 you have the right to stand for election as a Member of Parliament." She smiles at her star student, Yvonne Foster, whose family is actively engaged in politics, and whose father is the incumbent MP for mid-Down. She continues, "Today you will be addressed by Captain Robert Scott from County Mayo…" At the mention of 'County Mayo,' there are audible whispers from the girls that a papist is about to address them. Mistress Graham is swift to assuage their concerns and quickly corrects any misunderstanding. "…a member of a prominent Protestant land-owning family. The Scott family has a number of business interests – in Ayrshire and in Alberta. Captain Scott served in the Great War with distinction and has lately embarked upon an economic endeavour to operate a plantation in Uganda. He is recently married and he requires a white female companion for his wife while in Africa. Pay attention, class. We must impress Captain Scott with our knowledge of geography as it pertains to his family interests. Now tell me, where is County Mayo?"

Instantly, Yvonne Foster raises her hand and, with a nod of acceptance from Mistress Graham, she stands and answers,

"County Mayo is in the Province of Connacht (pronouncing it as 'Connat') in the west of Ireland."

"Excellent, Yvonne. Now, can someone tell me where Ayrshire is located?"

Yvonne remains standing and volunteers the answer. "Ayrshire is a county in the south-west of Scotland."

Mistress Graham smiles proudly at Yvonne. "That is correct, Yvonne. But please give some others an opportunity to answer."

"Yes, of course, Mistress." Yvonne sits down.

"Now, girls, does anyone know where Alberta is located? What about you Sarah? Yes you, Sarah Fegan." Sarah Fegan is the daughter of a Protestant shopkeeper of modest means. Mistress Graham wonders why Sam Fegan bothered to place his daughter in the prestigious Bann Royal Academy for Girls. Alas, Mistress Graham could not refuse him. He is a staunch member of the Orange Order, and he plays the bass drum in the pipe band every Twelfth of July, proudly marching to commemorate King Billy's victory over the papists. But Sarah Fegan, in the opinion of Mistress Margaret Graham, will never make a lady.

Sarah Fegan stands up and attempts to answer the question. "Alberta is in America."

Mistress Graham looks disapprovingly at Sarah Fegan. "Miss Fegan, are you referring to the continent of America, or to the United States of America, or to British North America?"

"Is there not just one America?"

"Really, Sarah." Mistress Graham nods to Yvonne Foster. Yvonne Foster rises and speaks. "Alberta is a newly-formed province in the Dominion of Canada, a member-country of the British Empire."

"Well answered, Yvonne. But I'm afraid that we have no time for further questions. I see that Captain Scott has arrived at our classroom. Be sure to greet him as 'Captain Scott'." Sarah Fegan shuts her eyes briefly in relief. The entrance of the visitor shifts attention away from her discomforting situation. She remains standing, and so does Yvonne. The rest of the class rises to greet the newcomer.

The school secretary-receptionist opens the classroom door to permit the entrance of two men. The first to enter marches with a military stride to the front of the class. The class chimes in unison in pleasant sing-song voices, "Good morning, Captain Scott."

The visitor is dressed in a dark-tan jacket with light-tan cavalry-twill breeches and mahogany-red leather gaiters. He walks loudly. His dark-tan military boots are fitted with steel tips on the heels and toes. He is old – at least ten years older than the girls in Mistress Graham's senior class. Nevertheless, the girls are much taken by his bearing. He slaps the tip of his swagger-stick against the top of his gaiters when making a point, as he does now. "My name is Captain Robert Scott. You address me as 'Captain'. Back there…" he points with his swagger-stick to the entrance door, next to which the second man is standing. This man is dressed in a three-piece charcoal-grey suit and is carrying an attaché case. "…is Mr Vincent Kelly, my solicitor from Killbawn, County Mayo." He surveys the rows of standing girls. "At ease. You may be seated." The girls sit down in unison. This detail to correctness meets with his approval.

Captain Scott explains his purpose in coming to the Bann Royal Academy for Girls. "I operate a plantation in Uganda, a cotton plantation. In May, some five weeks ago, I got married to my wife, Elizabeth. Next month, in July, she will travel to Uganda to take up residence in the great house on the plantation. The plantation is over two hundred miles from the nearest town. While resident in Africa, due to the vast distances between plantations, Mrs Scott will be unable to enjoy customary social intercourse with other white ladies of her social class. Thus, she will have little opportunity to entertain with ladies of equal status. Hence, she requires a white lady companion. The companion will be required to convey Madame's wishes and instructions to the black servants. Madame herself will not address the black servants directly. Her companion will do so on her behalf. The companion, upon assuming the position, will be unable to visit her home country or family for many years – at least for two years or, more likely, five. That will all depend on Madame's desire to travel."

The entire class of twenty-seven young ladies is attentive to every word uttered by Captain Scott. He continues. "Due to the hardship of living in such a remote region, the allowance allocated to the position of companion is £100.00 per annum."

There is an audible intake of breath from the entire class including from Mistress Graham. £40.00 would be considered generous. Captain Scott continues, "I have conveyed my conditions to Mistress Graham. She is fully cognisant of what is required in a candidate and of what factors need to be considered. I have requested interviews with five selected candidates of her choosing. Thank you for your attention."

Captain Scott steps to the side, and Mistress Graham steps forward. "Ladies, here are the names of the young ladies chosen to be interviewed by Captain Scott:

Miss Pamela Bertram;
Miss Florence Flower;
Miss Olive Overend;
Miss Sarah Fegan;
Miss Yvonne Foster.

"These five ladies, please wait in the corridor outside my office. You may be seated there until I summon you.

Captain Scott will conduct the interviews in my office assisted by his solicitor, Mr Kelly, and by myself." Mistress Graham smiles inwardly and thinks to herself how well she has planned this. She chose, not her five brightest students as she had promised Captain Scott, but her star pupil and four mediocre students. In this way, she is certain that Yvonne Foster will shine that much brighter when compared to the other four candidates. And bringing Yvonne in last, after the sub-mediocre Sarah Fegan, is a truly shrewd strategy. Walking down the corridor to her office, Mistress Graham is unable to suppress her smile.

Moments later, Captain Scott is seated at Mistress Graham's desk. Vincent Kelly and Mistress Graham are seated to his right and left. There is a vacant chair facing the desk, the chair allocated for each candidate's use during the course of each interview. Mistress Graham summons Miss Pamela Bertram. Pamela Bertram enters promptly and walks to the desk. She stands with her back to the vacant chair. She waits expectedly for permission to be seated. Captain Scott looks at her briefly and says "Next." And so, she is dismissed. Mistress Graham is taken aback. She never got to enlighten Captain Scott on the merits and qualities of the candidate. The following four candidates are treated in the same manner. All five young ladies have entered and have been dismissed in less than one minute. Mistress Graham looks to the captain for an explanation. He instructs her to recall candidate number four. Mistress Graham assumes that the captain misspoke. Surely he requires her to recall Yvonne Foster, candidate number five. She summons Yvonne Foster to re-enter.

Vincent Kelly leans forward on the desk and whispers across to Mistress Graham, "The captain said 'number four'. That would be Miss Sarah Fegan, I believe." Red-faced, Mistress Graham dismisses Yvonne and summons Sarah

Fegan. Sarah enters and she is granted permission to be seated. Mistress is anxious that the interview will go well and that it will reflect favourably on the academy. She looks at Sarah Fegan. Sarah may not be smart but, thankfully, she **looks** smart. Her navy-blue school blazer is well-fitted and it sits well on her. Her kilt is the school's blue-and-green Hebridean tartan. It is well-ironed and all pleats are perfectly in place. Sarah sits erect in the correct lady-like posture. Her knees are together, and her feet are tucked back under her chair ever so slightly, and she crosses one leg in front of the other at the ankles. Mistress Margaret Graham clears her throat in preparation to enumerate the young lady's qualities and accomplishments to Captain Scott. Unexpectedly, Captain Scott waves her to silence.

Captain Scott addresses Sarah. 'Your name is Sarah Fegan. Is that so?"

"Yes, sir. That is correct." Sarah smiles slightly. The captain pronounces her name as does her own family – 'FEG-an'. (The first syllable is rendered as 'feg' to rhyme with 'leg'.) Mistress Margaret Graham insists on a posh pronunciation – 'FEE-gan'.

The captain notices her smile and the brightness it brings to her eyes. "You address me as 'Captain'. But with regards to your name, I don't like 'Sarah'. It reminds me of a crabbed old aunt I once had. But 'Fegan' I like. So, 'Mrs Fegan' it is."

"Captain, I am not married. Surely you mean '**Miss** Fegan'?"

Captain Scott approves of her forwardness. He responds and tenders an explanation. "I am offering you the position of lady's companion, with some additional duties, in my plantation in Uganda. Do you accept?"

"Yes, Captain. I am delighted to accept."

"In that case, you are to be addressed as 'Mrs Fegan' in recognition of your rank in the household. Mr Kelly will draw up a contract of service. Since you are under 21, your signature of acceptance will be supported by your father's signature of approval. We meet in Mistress Graham's office again tomorrow to execute the contract – you and I and your father and Mr Kelly. Mr Kelly will subsequently explain to you the arrangements for your travel to Uganda with Mrs Scott. You will arrive at the plantation on Friday 6 August."

Captain Scott stands up. Mr Kelly likewise stands. This signifies that the meeting is concluded. Mistress Graham and Sarah stand in acknowledgement. The two men bid 'Good-day' to the ladies and depart hastily. Sarah Fegan is delighted with the position offered to her. It is more than she could ever have dreamed of. Mistress Margaret Graham is pleased and relieved. The result is unexpected. She had some anxious moments during the interview. Fortunately, the conclusion is favourable. Her academy has one more success to boast of.

The journey from Ireland to Uganda is arduous. It is so confusing that Sarah is overwhelmed with all the alien sights and customs. People are unexpectedly numerous and loud and busy. It is hot, and she is frequently assailed by smells of body-odour sweat, animals and unfamiliar cooked foods. She has no clue as to where she is most of the time. Oh, there is a ship, and a canal, and a train for two days, and then an uncomfortable lorry for a day. Throughout the journey, Vincent Kelly shows papers and documents to officials, and he succeeds in getting them passage on every stage of the journey. Mrs Scott, 'Madame', makes the journey particularly trying for Sarah. Madame complains constantly – the weather, the accommodation, the food. The only relief is when Sarah reads to her. She likes 'Jane Eyre' and

'Wuthering Heights'. During these readings, Mrs Scott relaxes and occasionally falls asleep.

At the Scott plantation, life gets off to a difficult start for the ladies. The plantation house is a two-story wooden structure with a white plastered exterior. A verandah runs the entire length of the house in order to afford shelter from sun and rain. Alas, Kabujogera is not prepared to receive white ladies of a genteel nature. It turns out that Captain Scott had arranged for the furnishings and household items to be shipped from Scott Manor in Mayo to Kabujogera plantation house in Uganda. Everything was packed and crated. But the recently-married Mrs Scott, in keeping with her disagreeable disposition, strongly objects. She states that furnishings from Ireland would not be suitable in Africa. As a result, the furnishings from the Scott Manor remain behind, crated and unmoved, in the empty manor house in Mayo. Mrs Scott insists on choosing the household furnishings upon arrival at the plantation. This is exceedingly naïve and imprudent of Mrs Scott. Obtaining furnishings and household items locally for a large plantation house in Kabujogera is impossible. She soon learns that the purchases must be made in Entebbe and that many of the items would not be readily available. She complains strongly to Captain Scott.

After two days of her complaining, Captain Scott storms out of the house and summons a small army of his workers and three lorries. On Sunday 8 August, he drives overnight and overland across the savanna to Entebbe. Being the dry season, the savanna is dusty, but not barren. The forest trees are lush and are growing some distance apart from each other. Hence, there is no tree canopy in the savanna. The convoy travels unhindered on the inter-spaced dry grassland, their progress marked by the cloud of red dust kicked up by the intruding wheels of their lorries. Should Captain Scott wait another three weeks to make this journey, he would encounter mud rather than dust. And heavily-laden lorries would sink into the mud. He is fortunate that he is able to execute this entire trip before the commencement of the seasonal rains.

On the following day in Entebbe, Captain Scott enters one shop after another and points to the first things that meet his eyes. On Tuesday morning, he arrives back successfully and without incident at the plantation house with three heavily-laden lorries. He strides in through the front doorway of the two-story plantation house. His olive-green safari clothes are heavily coated in the red dust of the savanna in stark contrast to the white plaster of the exterior walls of the house. He removes his slouch hat and smacks it against his thigh, spilling red dust onto the highly-polished mahogany floorboards. He shouts for his wife to appear. She stands at the top of the impressive two-level staircase and looks down at her angry husband framed in the doorway. Seeing her, the captain barks, "Elizabeth, you have twenty servants in the house, and twenty more in the grounds outside. Tell them where you want the stuff in the lorries to go." And with that, he storms off to return to his work, notwithstanding that he had slept for just a few fitful hours in the past two days.

Mrs Scott is unable to take command of the situation. She instructs Sarah to look after things. By the end of the day, the house is fully furnished, but with mismatched and inappropriate items. And so, it remains.

Sarah realises that not only does Mrs Scott refuse to speak directly to the black servants; she is incapable of making a decision. Her rash judgement regarding the house furnishings appears to have undermined her ability to take control. She resorts to her sole remaining skill, complaining, which she executes incessantly. Clearly, Mrs Scott is incapable of running the house. This duty now falls to Sarah.

But things are not all bad for Sarah Fegan. Three things occur over the following days that alleviate the stress of managing the household. Even Captain Scott realises that Sarah must undertake a greater responsibility than was originally intended. He arranges for Sarah to have 'per pro' signing authority on the household bank account. He gives her the accounts books and the cheque books.

The second fortuitous feature is in the person of Nyena. Nyena is the elderly woman in charge of the kitchen. But, more importantly, she is respected by all the servants, male and female. She speaks English, and she appears to be skilled and knowledgeable in practical matters. Sarah is at ease in speaking to her. Nyena, in turn, speaks Bantu to the servants and she ensures that instructions are carried out promptly and efficiently.

Throughout the early days of confusion, Nyena manages to prepare and serve food acceptable to Madame. A suitable protocol is established for serving at the dining table. A maid would place the food on the sideboard in the dining room, and Sarah would actually serve Madame and the captain at the table. Except that the captain seldom arrives at the dining room in time for dinner.

The third piece of good fortune occurs when Nyena introduces Sarah to Raj. Raj is a second-generation Ugandan of Indian extraction. He is educated. He speaks good English, and he is able to converse in Bantu and in Swahili. Most importantly for Sarah, Raj comes to the plantation once a week to peddle small household items – pots and pans, and needles and thread, and other common items that he is able to accommodate in his lorry. He accepts payment by cheque and, with sufficient forewarning, he obliges Sarah by cashing small cheques for her. Sarah avails of Raj's services and she establishes a functioning petty-cash box for small local cash transactions.

Within a month the house is running smoothly. Mrs Scott becomes more solitary and seldom appears from her bedroom except to dine. Sarah continues to spend time with her, reading books to her in the evening.

However, not all is smooth in the house. Captain Scott entertains his gentlemen friends every Friday night in his study. Sarah presumes that these are neighbouring plantation owners. Usually, three men attend on a Friday evening, and not necessarily the same men every time. Captain Scott tenders no explanation for these meetings. They involve activities that interest men rather than women. Except that in the course of these Friday evenings, as many as eight young black girls are admitted to the study.

The first time that Sarah becomes aware of these meetings she is upstairs reading to Madame in her bedroom. They hear the sounds coming from the study below, and they discern the unmistakable smells of tobacco smoke and whiskey. At intervals, the sounds are interrupted by loud screams, presumably from the girls present in the study. At first, Sarah is concerned that black girls are being tortured, but she quickly realises that the squeals she hears are squeals of delight. Initially, Sarah is disturbed by these odd activities. Mrs Scott appears to be oblivious to it all and insists that Sarah continues reading to her. Later that evening, Mrs Scott decides that it is time to retire for the night and she dismisses Sarah. Sarah leaves Madame's bedroom. She hesitates outside in the corridor in order to listen to the sounds emanating from the study below. As she stands silently in the semi-darkness, she hears the sound of a key turning and realises that Mrs Scott has locked her bedroom door.

Time passes – one month, two months. Mrs Scott becomes more introverted. She and the captain sleep in separate bedrooms. She seldom appears at the dining table anymore and becomes estranged from human contact, even from her husband. Sarah frequently dines alone in the dining room. Whenever the captain is present, he insists that Sarah occupies Madame's place at the table rather than sit at the side so that 'the balance is right'.

On Wednesday 20 October, Sarah is walking past the captain's study after dinner. The door being open, she glances inside. She sees a bookcase crammed with books. This affords her an opportunity to select a new book to read to Mrs Scott. She walks quietly to the bookcase. The shelves are labelled according to the subject – 'Camellia Sinensis', 'Nicotiana', 'Hevea-brasiliensis'. She deduces that these books are of a botanical nature and must refer to plantation plants. Sarah concludes that she is unlikely to locate a work by any of the Brontë sisters in this bookcase. Casting her eyes to the end of the bookcase, she notices a misspelling in one of the labels which, she assumes, must refer to tropical plants – the subject 'exotica' is rendered as 'erotica'. She laughs audibly and says 'erotica'.

"So, Mrs Fegan, you are interested in erotica?"

Sarah spins around at the unexpected voice. She had not noticed the captain sitting in a wing chair. Has he been watching her all along, she wonders? "Captain, please excuse me. I was looking for a book to read to Madame."

"And did you find one?"

"No, Captain. I see that all these books pertain to plants. Forgive me. I did not mean to disturb you."

"No. Don't leave. You are curious about my study, are you not?"

"Captain, it is not my place to intrude into your private study, or to be concerned with the business you conduct here."

"And what business do I conduct here?"

"Please, Captain…"

"Come, Sarah, I'll show you." The captain describes poker to her. He offers her a cigar. He pours her a glass of whiskey.

Sarah is confused, yet she is pleased with the attention the captain tenders to her. And he did call her 'Sarah'. Sarah wonders if the memory of his crabbed aunt is waning. She permits the captain to introduce her to the exotic mysteries of his study. Over the next hour, it becomes clear to both of them that Sarah will never be skilled at poker, nor will she take to tobacco, and fiery whiskey is unpalatable to her. The captain is amused at her failure in these skills. Both of them laugh. Sarah rises and excuses herself to retire for the night.

The captain also rises. "Wait," he says, "surely there is something here that would interest you. Permit me to choose some reading for you. If you like it, well, good fortune. And if not, there is no loss. Here take this book. You may return it to me here at this time tomorrow and let me know what you think of it." The captain chooses a book from the 'erotica' section of the bookcase. Sarah politely takes the book from him and bids him a good-night.

Later, Sarah places the book on her bedroom chest-of-drawers. She has no interest in botany or in dendrology, and so, she has no intention of reading this book. She decides to return the book as promised and pretend that she has read it. She may even say that she liked it, just to be polite.

On the following day, Thursday 21 October, Sarah decides to return the book to the captain's study prior to dinner. The door to the study is locked, so she is unable to return the book until the appointed time after dinner. Sarah considers that if the captain arrives home in time to sup, he may bring up the matter of the book at dinner. She should be prepared to make some reference to the subject in the book. She returns to her room, and for the duration of the half-hour wait until dinnertime, she leafs through the book quickly in order to get some understanding of the subject matter. What she encounters is unexpected. She is curious and continues reading. She stops upon realising that it is close to dinnertime. She puts the book aside, having read less than ten pages. To prepare herself for her visit to the dining room, she checks her appearance and attire. Thus satisfied, she departs her private room and proceeds to the dining room.

Later, in the dining room, Captain Scott uncharacteristically arrives punctually and sits at the head of the table. And, according to the revised seating arrangement, Sarah sits opposite him. The captain addresses her. "Sarah, dressing for dinner is important. Do you not agree?"

"Of course, Captain." Sarah becomes self-conscious of the modest attire and of her station. "Please excuse my plain attire. I possess few dresses, and I am obliged to dress according to my station."

"Madame must have over one hundred dresses by now. I don't believe she will ever wear more than a few of them. And when, I wonder, considering that she dines alone in her bedroom? I suggest that you obtain some of her surplus dresses. You are her size, are you not? It is a shame that expensive stylish dresses are stored in the attic never to be worn. Do you not agree, Sarah?"

Sarah declines to answer.

At the conclusion of dinner, the captain decides to go to his study, as is his custom, to smoke a cigar. He turns to Sarah and asks, "Shall I see you later when you return the book? I am eager to learn your opinion on it."

"Captain, the book. What I mean is that I have not yet finished reading it. It would imprudent of me to render an opinion on the contents without reading the book in detail first."

"Ah, quite so," and he leaves the room.

Over the next three months, Sarah becomes sure of herself and of her surroundings. The captain provides her with additional books, books that she would not dare read to Mrs Scott. On the other hand, Madame appears to be oblivious to her surroundings and she chooses to spend her entire time confined to her bedroom. Sadly, she is unable to achieve contentment even in her private room. She adds to her list of complaints – the mosquito net around her bed is inadequate and fails to protect her fully; terrifying green lizards run across the bedroom walls in the mornings; at night, there are frightening sounds from wild animals prowling about outside. She believes that fierce beasts are seeking an opportunity to pounce upon her and devour her. Captain Scott explains to her that her fears are unfounded and that these 'hazards' are insignificant. He attempts to reassure her, but his efforts are rebuffed. Elizabeth Scott distances herself from her 'uncaring' husband and retreats further into herself.

Meanwhile, Sarah runs the house efficiently without any guidance from Mrs Scott. Madame's greatest thrill, her only thrill, is to have Sarah read to her every evening for an hour after dinner. At the conclusion of her readings, Sarah customarily visits the captain in his study – except on Fridays when the captain entertains his private guests.

Sarah learns a lot about Captain Scott and his family. Captain Scott is an only child. His father had him enter the army to become an officer in order to learn officer-skills – the same skills required to manage an estate or a plantation. The captain has relatives that operate extensive farms in Scotland and in Canada. Captain Robert has only a token financial interest in the farms in Ayrshire and in Alberta. Similarly, his Scottish and Canadian kin have only a token financial interest in Captain Robert's operations in Ireland and Uganda.

On 15 April 1912, both of Robert's parents perished with the 'unsinkable' Titanic. Robert was 21 at the time. Thereafter, the farm in Mayo was managed by his land-steward and agent, William Buckley. Despite his distaste for papists, Captain Scott recognised the advantage of having a papist land-steward. A papist would be familiar with all the shenanigans that the papists in Mayo might get up to and, hence, he would be alert as to how best to protect the property and the Scott interests. (This is consistent with the similar regard he has for Nyena here on the plantation.) Prudently, William Buckley leased most of the land to Fitzpatrick for cattle-grazing, thus ensuring a steady income until Captain Robert is ready to resume control of his Irish estate. And, for a number of years, this continues as the normal state of affairs with respect to the Mayo property.

The captain's status in Uganda is also quite interesting. He considers the cotton crop to have limited profits. He believes that there are other crops that will reap greater rewards. Tobacco is his prime choice. But to convert his one plantation from cotton to tobacco could be foolhardy without first establishing the viability of a tobacco-growing industry in Uganda. Launching this new crop in Uganda is the prime purpose behind his Friday night meetings. He is organising a group of like-minded plantation owners. He is certain that in five years he will have successfully converted his cotton plantation to harvesting tobacco. Once the plantation is fully operational, perhaps in ten years, he will appoint a white manager to run the plantation. And Captain Robert Scott will return to the family home in Ballycorry, County Mayo.

In March 1920, Sarah is unwell. The captain notices that she has lost her appetite for certain foods. She blames it on the wet season. But she had not suffered any discomfort during the previous wet season from September to October. Fearing that she may have contracted a tropical illness, she consults Nyena. Nyena informs her matter-of-factly that she is clearly with child.

In May 1920, Mrs Sarah Fegan is resident in the Scott Manor in Ballycorry, County Mayo. She is the only occupant of the house. She is the de facto lady of the house and housekeeper. Her previous status, as per her contract, remains intact. Captain Scott arranges with the solicitor, Vincent Kelly, to have Mrs Fegan accommodated in the manor. She is granted the privilege of having per-pro signing authority on the manor's household bank account for operating expenses.

It is strange living in a large house where all the furnishings and household items are crated and stacked in otherwise empty rooms. She has the strength, and the motivation, to organise the kitchen and one bedroom. She reactivates a household account with Casey's General Store. And she visits Doctor Walter O'Toole (Doctor McBratt's predecessor).

In order to keep her condition secret, she avoids contacting her family in Ballynahinch, County Down. To give birth to a baby out of wedlock is unacceptable to them. As far as they know, Sarah remains securely in residence as a lady's companion in the Scott Plantation in Africa. Here, in Mayo, no one knows her, and they have no way of knowing her circumstances. She is simply 'Mrs Fegan' to anyone who enquires. Alone in a big house, Sarah awaits the arrival of her baby.

On Tuesday 29 June 1920, a crate arrives at the Scott Manor in Ballycorry. It contains the items that Sarah had installed in her bedroom in the plantation house in Kabujogera, including a large selection of Elizabeth Scott's stylish dresses and shoes. The captain has sent her personal belongings and the things to which she had become attached. There is no note included with the consignment.

On Monday 20 September 1920, Robert (Bobby) Fegan is born. The delivery is assisted by Doctor O'Toole. The doctor arranges for Nora Buckley, the sister-in-law of the land-steward and wife to one of the estate workers, to move into the manor house's servants' quarters and act as a caregiver to Mrs Fegan during her postpartum recovery.

On Monday 27 September 1920, Vincent Kelly, the solicitor, pays a visit to Scott's land-steward, Willie Buckley. He informs him that Captain Robert Scott fears for the safety of the property and its occupants. The IRA – referred to by Captain Scott as 'savage Irish hooligans' – are targeting British sympathisers. They have burned and destroyed many properties since the collapse of British administration in April 1920. Properties with absentee owners are particularly vulnerable to attack. Consequently, Captain Scott has sold the estate to Fitzpatrick – everything except the manor house and garden. Willie Buckley, the land-steward, will henceforth work for Fitzpatrick. He will continue to live in the agent's cottage, now located in the land owned by Fitzpatrick. Willie's brother, Tom, a worker in the estate, is henceforth retained as a house-steward in the manor. He will move in and occupy the servant's quarters on Friday 01 October. In compensation for being granted living accommodation in the manor, he is required to conduct repairs to the house and gardens as the need arises. Willie will continue to engage Tom as a worker on an as-need basis on the Fitzpatrick farm.

Two days later, on Wednesday 29, a formal letter, with detailed instructions to Sarah Fegan, is delivered to the Scott Manor by registered post. Mrs Fegan is instructed therein to pay Tom Buckley for the costs of any repairs out of the housekeeping account at the bank.

On Wednesday 27 October 1920, the solicitor pays a follow-up visit to the Scott Estate. He drives up the wide tree-lined avenue and parks his car at the front entrance of the manor. Mrs Fegan is sitting in a chair in the portico. She is cradling her baby in her arms. Nora Buckley, having heard the arrival of the car, comes from the back of the house to investigate. Both women recognise Vincent Kelly, Robert Scott's solicitor. Kelly, so as not to intrude, remains standing on the pebbled driveway rather than ascend the steps of the portico. He looks from one woman to the other and addresses them jointly. "Good morning. I am checking that the new arrangements are working out."

Nora responds, "Oh, they are, to be sure, what with the house and all. Tom's over with Willie working on some fence repairs at the moment. Do you want to talk to him?"

"No, Mrs Buckley. I met with your husband Tom on October the first to discuss the new arrangements. You are settled in, I see." Kelly turns his attention to Sarah Fegan. "Mrs Fegan, are you comfortable with the new arrangements?"

"Yes." A monosyllable.

"And you understand your responsibilities?"

"Of course."

"And how is the baby? Bobby, isn't it?"

Sarah lifts her baby and Nora takes it from her and returns to her quarters in the rear of the house. Sarah is not in the mood for redundant conversation. "Bobby is fine. The doctor visited yesterday…"

Kelly waits for Sarah to impart some more information. She falls silent. Vincent Kelly feels awkward. Clearly, Sarah Fegan would prefer to be left alone. He understands that she may not yet have returned to full activity so soon after the birth. To be polite, he enquires as to her state of health. "You are well, I trust?"

"Thank you for asking. I am well. The baby is well. The Buckleys are well. We are all well. Is there anything else?"

"Well, no. In that case, I'll be off." The solicitor considers it unnecessary to intrude any further. He had considered conducting a physical inspection of the house, but he decides against it. In any event, he is not mandated to do so. The housekeeper and the house-steward are entrusted with that responsibility. His business thus concluded at the Scott Manor, Vincent Kelly departs not having proceeded further than the pebbled driveway.

In 1925, Captain Robert Scott completes the conversion of his plantation from cotton to tobacco.

On 01 June 1930, Elizabeth Scott dies in Africa. She was thirty-five. Captain Robert finds himself with no heir, neither son nor daughter, to take over the family affairs when the time comes. At forty years old, he is young enough to marry again. But the development of the new plantation crop is severely demanding on his time and energy – new harvesting skills are required by the workers, and the quality of Ugandan tobacco is still unproven in the lucrative European market. For the moment, marriage is out of the question. He considers turning to his kin in Scotland or Canada in the hope of taking a nephew under his wing. In the absence of a legitimate son, he wonders who he will groom to take over the operation of the Scott interests in Africa. He is anxious.

Captain Robert is unsettled by the news from Ireland. The new Irish government appears to be ill-equipped to deal with anti-Treaty trouble-makers. It is his belief that Britain made a serious error in permitting a savage people to self-govern a country. It is understood by Captain Robert Scott that God ordained different classes of people for a reason. Some people are meant to serve, and some are meant to be served. The Irish peasants are capable workers provided they are controlled and administered by British Protestant taskmasters. Captain Scott breathes a sigh of relief in his certainty that the British will not make the same mistake twice, and that the administration of Uganda will never fall into the hands of the local black population. His original intent was to get the plantation up and running profitably. Thereafter, he would engage a land-steward/manager and ultimately hand over the operation to his son and heir. Upon establishing a solid managerial protocol in the plantation, Captain Robert would then retire back home to Ballycorry. That was the intent, but things have changed. He now views Uganda as his place to reside. Thus, his return to Ireland becomes just a remote and distant possibility.

On Monday 08 September 1930, Vincent Kelly takes Bobby Scott away from the Scott Manor and brings him to boarding school, to Portora Royal School in Enniskillen, as per the instructions he received from Captain Robert Scott. Shortly thereafter, the housekeeping account at the bank runs out of funds. It is no longer replenished by Captain Scott.

Subsequent to October 1930, Sarah Fegan finds herself with no income, and she is unable to pay Tom Buckley. Funds have not dried up entirely though. Bobby's school expenses are paid, as are Bobby's material needs at school. The rates on the house are paid promptly when due. And when the bank account goes into overdraft due to the annual bank charge of ten shillings and sixpence, the overdraft is covered – but no surplus funds are lodged into the housekeeping account. In desperation, Sarah takes to selling off her few possessions in order to make ends meet. Casey, of Casey's General Store, buys articles of furniture and bric-a-brac from her.

At school, Bobby Fegan becomes a noted and popular athlete and excels in English Literature. He returns home briefly during school holidays.

In 1938, Bobby Fegan enters Trinity College. Travelling from Dublin to Castlebar is easy, and he comes home frequently. Bobby dresses quite flamboyantly and expensively, in stark contrast to the poor residents of the dilapidated Scott Manor. Sarah assumes that Captain Robert has established a trust account for Bobby, one probably managed by Vincent Kelly. Bobby does not know, nor care, so long as his expenses are covered. She wonders what will occur when Bobby reaches the age of majority at twenty-one. As a young man, Bobby creates a minor stir whenever he arrives in Killbawn. He is referred to locally as 'the Dazzler Fegan'.

In the summer of 1941, Bobby comes home for a visit. He talks about theatre and whether or not he should go to fight the Germans. And he enquires about the plantation in Africa. Sarah is unable to venture an opinion on any of these matters. She regards Bobby's speculations as just a young man's searching for purpose and adventure.

"Caw! Caw!"

Murf looks up at the three crows perched on the yew tree above him. Some minutes have elapsed since he parked his car in the wide avenue leading up to the Scott Manor. The crows are curious about the immobile occupant of the car. Motionless animal life is of interest to carrion birds. Murf shakes himself and restarts the engine. The crows fly away. Murf drives up to the front of the house. He parks in the wide weed-choked pebbled driveway in front of the main doors. He sees Mrs Fegan sitting outside in the portico, enjoying the warmth of the sun. She is sitting in a high-backed Victorian dining-room chair. The chair is armless and appears to be one of a set, presumably a chair from the dining room of the manor. An opened book is resting on her lap. She looks at

Murf, surprised at this unexpected visit, and waits for him to approach.

275

CHAPTER EIGHTEEN

GARDA SEAMUS O'REILLY INVESTIGATES

County Mayo, Ireland
Saturday 31 August 1946

8:30am. Garda Seamus O'Reilly is readying himself for a visit to the Puckany Johnsons. He has attached the bicycle clips to his trousers in preparation for his foray. This is the closest thing to 'a raid' that O'Reilly is expected to execute. The Johnson family moved into Killbawn Parish after 'the Troubles'. They came from a place known as 'Puckany'. Garda O'Reilly has no knowledge of where Puckany is situated – somewhere up in the north is his guess. The supply of 'poteen', illicit whiskey, increased in Killbawn following the arrival of the Puckany Johnsons in Lough Corry Lower. Illicit whiskey-making has been an off-and-on issue for the gardaí ever since. Periodically, the guards visit the Puckanies to clamp down on their illicit industry.

The Puckanies live in a small stone cottage at the edge of the bleak bog. Anyone intending to visit, or raid, this isolated house is observed by the Puckanies well in advance of their actual arrival at the cottage. The Puckanies are not smart and they are ill-educated. Nevertheless, they possess a low cunning that renders them impenetrable to entrapment by the police. And so there is a kind of stalemate in the struggle between An Garda Síochána (the police) and the Puckanies. Periodically, a garda arrives to snoop around for evidence of distillation apparatus in a futile attempt to expose the Puckany Johnson's prohibited industry. During these periods of garda activity, the Puckanies cunningly conceal their equipment and stock in a bog hole while the garda conducts his investigation. Later, after the garda has safely departed, they retrieve their stock-in-trade from the sanctuary of the peat-filled swallow-hole. The Puckanies are not perturbed by peat contaminating their equipment; the taste of peat actually enhances the flavour of their product. Visits by members of An Garda Síochána may interrupt and impede their production of poteen, but these minor raids never actually stop the creative flow of the liquor. Reluctantly, the gardaí accept this less-than-perfect outcome.

Today, Garda O'Reilly is scheduled to make a visit to the Puckany Johnsons. He is prepared to cycle out to Lough Corry Lower where he will execute his duty. It is a pleasant day. This task should take up the rest of the morning. And O'Reilly is much happier cycling out to the bogland than sorting wanted notices in the garda station. This 'raid' today is expected to produce the usual win-win-win outcome – the flow of illicit whiskey is curtailed for a while, the Puckany Johnsons are assured of an extension to the practice of their prohibited craft, and Garda O'Reilly should come away with a bottle of 'the water of life' in his pocket. He is whistling happily when Murf interrupts him.

"O'Reilly, you are working with me on the triple-murder case." Murf directs O'Reilly to execute two tasks – visit the crime lab in Castlebar to obtain an enlargement on a photograph of Liam Tunnery and, secondly, question a number of people who may have knowledge of Liam Tunnery's last known movements prior to his disappearance. O'Reilly understands. Murf elaborates for the purpose of clarification. "This is approved by the district officer. Now go to Foxy and get official clearance and be on your way."

"What about the Puckany Johnsons? I am about to execute a surprise raid on their illicit whiskey still."

Murf suppresses a smile. "The Puckany Johnsons will have to wait until another day for Garda O'Reilly's tactical surprise visit." Murf is aware that Peter Meehan, in conducting his customary expert job of spreading rumours around the townland, would have forewarned the Puckanies of the impending police raid today. By failing to visit the Puckany Johnsons in a timely manner as expected, Garda O'Reilly will cause them greater disruption than if he were to conduct an actual raid.

O'Reilly's disappointment is short-lived. Working with a detective on a murder case gives him status, a lot more status than the Puckany Johnsons' poteen could ever give him. Murf instructs O'Reilly on what he is required to do to assist with the case. O'Reilly proudly accepts his new responsibilities. He puffs out his chest and feels important. He marches smartly to Superintendent Fox's office and reports for official authorisation to this serious assignment. He remembers to perform a formal salute and waits for Fox's directive. O'Reilly expects to be ordered to change into plainclothes in place of his uniform and be permitted to drive the patrol car. He envisions himself driving around town and waving at the young ladies to impress them. Foxy makes it official; O'Reilly is assigned to assist Inspector Murphy for the duration of the triple-murder investigation. But not all goes as O'Reilly expects. He is to remain in uniform. And Foxy will not forego the use of the station's sole patrol car for O'Reilly's exclusive benefit.

Garda O'Reilly coughs and ventures a request. "Superintendent, if I am not afforded the use of the patrol car, how am I to conduct the inquiries assigned to me by Inspector Murphy?"

Superintendent Fox suppresses a smile. He is aware that O'Reilly is angling for enhanced status. "Garda O'Reilly, I understand that you are a forward on the county team. Now, here is your opportunity to maintain physical fitness – use one of the garda bicycles to get around."

"Sir, you want me to cycle all the way to Castlebar?"

"Don't play smart with me, O'Reilly. Use your head. Have Garda Clancy drive you halfway to Castlebar in the station's sole car. And have Castlebar meet you and take you on the remainder of the journey to your destination. And O'Reilly, if you are serious about assisting Inspector Murphy, you need to sort things out on your own. Be thankful for the opportunity this case affords you." O'Reilly is thus duly reprimanded. Fox concludes with a single word, "Dismissed!"

At 9:10am, Garda O'Reilly is en route to Castlebar. He is elated with the lofty responsibility of assisting a detective inspector in a prestigious case. He taps his pocket for the umpteenth time to check for the presence of the Tunnery picture safely enclosed within a stiff envelope. Satisfied that it is still securely in place, he turns his attention back to the list he obtained from Murf. He carefully examines all the names thereon. He is impressed, but not surprised, with Murf's thoroughness. Murf knows everyone in the parish. As expected, the list contains the names of all those who left Killbawn Parish and went to England since 1939. O'Reilly marks off the names according to their probability factor. The names that offer higher chances of successful results are the names of those who left Mayo in 1943 and who are neighbours of the Tunnerys. Two names top his list – Dunleavy and Gorman, both denizens of Tubberbawn. He remembers that Charlie Dunleavy left home around Easter-time at, or near, the time of Liam Tunnery's departure in 1943. Charlie permanently remained in England thereafter. He returns to visit his family every year during the first two weeks of August. O'Reilly realises that he missed him this time by a couple of weeks. He next considers the second name – Gorman. Ambrose Gorman left Killbawn at the same time as Charlie Dunleavy. O'Reilly remembers hearing that they travelled together. Unlike Charlie Dunleavy, Ambie

Gorman returned to Killbawn about a year ago at the end of the war. Ambie Gorman currently lives in Tubberbawn and assists in running the family farm.

The patrol car comes to a sudden halt. The stopping motion of the patrol car interrupts Garda O'Reilly from placing four asterisks against the Gorman name on the list. He looks out the car window and recognises Chapel Street near the bridge over the Deel in Crossmolina. His patrol car is stationary and parked next to the garda car from Castlebar. O'Reilly requires no prompting. He exits one car and enters the other. Thus, he continues on his journey to Castlebar.

At 10:05am, Garda O'Reilly is in Garda Divisional HQ in Castlebar. O'Reilly is directed by the duty officer to the Forensic Department, where Phil Divers (the head of forensics) is expecting him.

"Hah! O'Reilly. You're here wanting to blow up a picture and isolate one figure on it. Right? Well, show it to me, lad." Divers is busy, but he is also efficient and thorough. He is prepared for the arrival of Garda O'Reilly. O'Reilly takes the envelope from his pocket and extracts the photograph. He points out Liam Tunnery. Divers takes the photograph and leaves the room. He shouts back, "Don't bother sitting down, O'Reilly. This will be done in two shakes of a lamb's tail."

Divers is as good as his word. Within a minute he returns. He delivers the photograph back to O'Reilly. "We have taken a high-resolution photograph of your original. Now you need to wait for it to be enlarged, cropped and developed. It will be ready late on Monday. How many copies do you require?"

"I don't know. Murf never said."

"Three copies should be enough. No, to be on the safe side, I'll print five copies. Pick them up from here on Tuesday morning. Now I'm done with you, O'Reilly. Be off with you." Divers is already tackling his next task, and O'Reilly realises that he is dismissed.

At the front desk, O'Reilly speaks with Garda Jerry Coulter. "Jerry, I need to get to Killbawn…"

"And you want to know where the closest bus-stop is? Well, it's right outside the door. Good-day to you, Seamus."

"Stop taking the mickey, Jerry…"

"Look outside, Seamus. There's your ride. It's waiting for you, and it takes you all the way to Killbawn. Now, how about that?" Sure enough, a patrol car is parked at the kerb outside, and it is prepared to take O'Reilly the entire distance to Killbawn.

O'Reilly reaches the Garda station in Killbawn at 11:25am. He immediately delivers the photograph of Liam Tunnery & friends to Murf's office. Murf is not in, so he places the envelope in the free space in the centre of the desk. O'Reilly is full of energy, and he is keen to direct his enthusiasm to accomplish his second assignment. If his intuition is correct, he expects to obtain the required information on Liam Tunnery long before he exhausts the complete list of names – perhaps even in the first inquiry. His first scheduled inquiry is to 22-year-old Ambrose (Ambie) Gorman. On Murf's list, O'Reilly has flagged Gorman's name with four asterisks to indicate his priority preference.

Garda O'Reilly chooses one of the four garda bicycles from the bicycle shed. It is a simple choice – all four bicycles are identical. They are black, strong and cumbersome. Satisfied with the inflation in the tyres, he chooses the first one. He attaches his bicycle clips and fastens his garda-blue greatcoat securely. Thereupon he sets out on his mission. He cycles out of Killbawn on the Blackwater Road. His destination is Ambie Gorman of Tubberbawn.

At the two-mile stone, he stops to view the scene of the

excavation in the Famine Field. The three unsightly pits give him the shivers. The surveyor's identification stakes are clearly visible. They curve in a line through the Famine Field and out to the edge of the inlet. This is the path of the proposed new road. The sooner they start work on the project the better, so as to obliterate the scarred evidence of where the cadavers were discovered. O'Reilly recommences peddling and continues onward. Once past the shelter of the estuary, O'Reilly is exposed to the sea breeze. The salty air fills his nostrils and he breathes more deeply due to the exertion. At a mile past the two-mile stone, the cross-wind pushes O'Reilly's heavy bicycle sideways and his worsted-serge greatcoat flaps like a torn sail. He has reached Tubberbawn.

Garda O'Reilly arrives at the Gorman farm in Tubberbawn at 11:50am. His cheeks are glowing from the exertion of cycling and from the beating of the wind. He places his big black garda bicycle against the gable wall of the white cottage, and he walks around to the front door. He shouts through the open half-door to announce his arrival to Mary Anne Gorman, Ambie's mother.

Mary Anne is too busy with her kitchen tasks to leave them unattended. She shouts from the hearth, "Who is it?" O'Reilly hesitates, undecided as to how he should explain his presence. Mary Anne's voice is muffled due to her bent position over her cooking tasks. Whereas her voice is weak, the smells emanating from the fireplace are strong and specific. O'Reilly identifies potatoes boiling in a pot that is dripping onto the fire, and there is the unmistakable smell of bread baking in a pot-oven. There is one unusual burnt pungent smell which, for the moment, he is unable to make out.

"Tá fear éigin ag an doras. Is strainséir é. Och, ní hea — is garda é." O'Reilly recognises the voice of Ambie's grandmother, Seanmháthair. "Tar isteach, a mhic." She identifies him as a garda and bids him enter.

O'Reilly unlatches the half-door of the cottage at the invitation of Seanmháthair. "Good morrow, Seanmháthair Ní Gormáin. Good morrow Mrs Gorman." O'Reilly is familiar with the dual languages spoken in the rural areas. The old people speak in Irish; the next generation speaks Irish in the home but English when out and about, and the young ones speak English except when speaking respectfully to their elders.

Seanmháthair Ní Gormáin is sitting in a rocking chair next to a blazing turf fire. She spits tobacco juice into the fire, narrowly missing the assemblage of steaming black iron pots and steaming kettles dangling from hooks over the blazing turf fire. Now he recognises the odd pungent burnt smell; it is the smell of scorched tobacco juice. The old lady places her smouldering pipe back into her mouth. She smiles at O'Reilly through clenched teeth – all four of them – and beckons invitingly to him. O'Reilly decides to conduct his police work in English.

Upon entering the house, Garda O'Reilly secures the latch on the half-door behind him. Mary Anne turns to look at him while still attending to her tasks. She wipes a stray of her auburn hair from her eyes with the back of her hand and lifts a steaming black iron pot from the fire. She carries it to the kitchen table where she spills the contents into a large cream-coloured ceramic bowl. O'Reilly sees that she has unloaded a huge pile of potatoes boiled in their jackets, and each spud is smiling broadly. This confirms the smell he first identified at the half-door.

Mary Anne pauses from her task and faces O'Reilly squarely. This time, she speaks clearly. "Guard O'Reilly? And what do you be wantin' out here in the middle of the day? Well, step away from the threshold and sit here at the table.

The men are about to come in from the fields for their midday lunch." She indicates to the table, which O'Reilly understands is an invitation.

O'Reilly approaches the table politely. The kitchen table is a large wooden table, scrubbed white with bleach each day no doubt. The seating is comprised of two forms (backless benches), one on each side of the table. O'Reilly decides to sit in a spot farthest from the door.

"O for the Lord's sake, Guard O'Reilly, don't sit right at the end. Sure you'll tip the form and send the whole of the praties flyin' off the table." She slaps the form to indicate where he should sit. She continues to set the table. Six white dinner plates with accompanying knives and forks are placed on it, and six white enamelled mugs with blue rims, and a bowl of yellow country butter, and a saucer of salt. As Mary Anne pours buttermilk into the six mugs from a white enamelled jug, O'Reilly hears the approach of the men from the fields.

Packie Gorman enters ahead of his two sons, Ambie and Sean, followed by two of his farmhands. At twenty years old, Sean is younger than Ambie by two years; the two farmhands are in their forties. All five are clad in dungaree overalls with wellington boots. Packie looks at O'Reilly and exclaims triumphantly, "Ha! It's Guard O'Reilly." He turns back to the men. "I told you I recognised the garda bicycle at the gable." The full company of men – six including O'Reilly – sit occupying both sides of the table. They cross themselves and say a silent quick prayer of grace. O'Reilly is familiar with the ritual and does likewise. Then there is a burst of arms and hands as everyone pounces on the bowl of potatoes in the centre of the table.

"Stop!" Packie brings the activity to a sudden halt. "Leave a spud for Guard O'Reilly for God's sake." O'Reilly respectfully selects the smallest potato from the bowl, whereupon Packie nods in acknowledgement. Immediately, the mess of flying arms resumes. The mode of procedure is to slap generous dollops of butter on the hot potatoes, followed by a sprinkling of salt, and wash the lot down with buttermilk. O'Reilly is about to place his first forkful of potato into his mouth when he notices that the bowl at the centre of the table is already empty, and the men are draining the last of the buttermilk from their mugs. Packie then announces, "Right, men, it's back to work – unless Guard O'Reilly here has other plans." He looks at O'Reilly to indicate that he ought to state the purpose of his visit. Otherwise, he and his work team are eager to resume their farm tasks.

O'Reilly realises that from the time he entered the Gorman cottage, he never stated the purpose of his visit. He coughs, and stands up, and quickly comes to the point.

"Liam Tunnery," he says, thus capturing their attention. "I am making inquiries as to the whereabouts of Liam Tunnery."

"Liam Tunnery?" Packie responds questioningly. "Sure Liam Tunnery left these parts to go the England three year ago. Ask Ambie here. He knows all about that."

O'Reilly nods in acknowledgement. Ambrose Gorman, young Ambie, is the focus of his inquiry at this point. "Well, that's just it. We have reason to believe that he never went to England at all. And we would like to talk to the last person to have seen him."

"Well, that's me, I suppose," comments Ambie.

"So, there you go, Guard O'Reilly," says Packie as he leaves the table. "Talk to Ambie. The rest of us are off back to the upper field while the rain holds off." Packie and Sean and the two farmhands depart the cottage to attend to their tasks. Garda O'Reilly resumes his seat, and he and Ambie sit facing each other at the table.

Mary Anne goes to the half-door. She leans out and shouts, "Maura, if you're finished churning, bring a basin in here would you." Maura, Ambie's sister, enters the cottage from the dairy next door. She is carrying a basin. She fills the basin with hot water from the black kettle on the hob and disappears again. Mary Anne clears the table and follows after Maura with the stack of plates and mugs, presumably to wash them in preparation for the next meal.

O'Reilly commences questioning Ambie but is interrupted by renewed activity at the table. Maura returns and proceeds to set the table a second time. She wipes the inside of the potato bowl with her apron and Mary Anne fetches a newly-baked scone of bread from the cooling rack on the windowsill. O'Reilly understands. Having fed the men from the fields, it is the turn of the womenfolk to eat. This time, the fare is different. The bowl in the middle of the table is filled with slices of still-warm soda bread, the butter dish is replenished, a jar of strawberry jam is placed on the table, and strong black tea is poured into the enamelled mugs. Ambie rubs his hands in delight. He gets to have two lunches, and this second one is better. He eagerly snatches a slice of the soda bread from the bowl and spreads a layer of butter on it. His mother raps her knuckles on the table and joins her hands. Ambie's second lunch requires a second prayer of grace. After a very hurried grace, Ambie spoons a generous heap of jam on his bread, followed by a second spoonful. He is about to heap the third spoonful when he is halted by another rap on the table.

The company at the table, three women and two men, assume a quiet rhythm to their eating. O'Reilly sees his opportunity to steer his way back to his police inquiry. "So, tell me about Liam Tunnery, Ambie, and when you last saw him."

Ambie wipes the melted butter and jam off his chin

with the back of his hand. He takes a swallow of tea and begins to relate an account of his last association with Liam Tunnery. "I last seen Liam just after Easter three year ago. If I rightly remember, it was the Tuesday after Easter Sunday."

O'Reilly interjects. "Not Monday 26 April 1943?"

"I can't rightly mind what day of the month it was. But I last seen him on the Tuesday."

Ambie's sister Maura exclaims from the far side of the table. "Aye, but it was on Easter Monday what he came here. Sure I mind it well. Liam came in here about half-four. And I says to him, 'your shoes are muddy' – you know, he couldn't abide mud on his shoes. So I gave him a polishing rag and he buffs them clean…"

"Maura, that has nothing to do with the story. **I'm** telling it to Guard O'Reilly." Maura sticks out her tongue at Ambie. Ambie continues to relate his account to O'Reilly. "That's right. Liam came here at half-four on Easter Monday. He comes in here, right through yon door, and he says to me, 'Ambie, are you still going to England?' Well, of course, he knew that. Sure weren't we talking about that since St Patrick's Day? So I tell him that I was waiting for Charlie Dunleavy. And that meself and Charlie was going into Killbawn with Peter Meehan to catch the last bus to Castlebar. Well, Liam says to me, he says, that he is going to England too – and him with no bag or nothing with him – and that we should wait out by the road for Charlie. And that's what we done. I sling me bag over me shoulder and we go out to the road. Charlie comes and is surprised that Liam is coming too – well, Liam said many-a-times that he was intendin' to go to England and all, but we didn't put much heed in what he said. But here he was, by God. And meself and himself and Charlie were headin' off to England.

"Liam was fierce impatient throughout. He says that Peter Meehan and his stupid donkey, Maeve, would take too long to get to town and that it would be faster walking. Then we see Delahunty come down the road in his tractor. Well, didn't Liam wave him down and convince him to drive us the whole way to Killbawn – Delahunty is right obligin', you know. Delahunty dropped us off at the bus station. Then Liam sees the bus for Castlebar via Ballina parked there at the bus station. He says to get on the bus right away, even though it wasn't leaving for another fifteen minutes. He was in a fierce hurry to get out of Killbawn."

"Did Liam say why he was in a hurry?"

"No. But he must have had a row with his da. It was well known that they were at odds over what Liam should work at and all that. And when things got rough, Liam would threaten to leave home and go to England. So, I supposed that they had one more row and Liam finally left."

"Were you surprised at Liam turning up like this?"

"I was only half-surprised. And sure Liam, if he was acting in haste, would have the next few hours to change his mind – the train from Castlebar wasn't leaving until eight o'clock on the following morning."

"So, then what? You got the bus to Ballina?"

"That's right. We got the bus from Killbawn to Ballina, and from Ballina to Castlebar. Liam was quiet the whole way, but we left him alone. It was after eight in the evenin' when we entered the Railway Bar in Spencer Street in Castlebar. I don't know why they call it the 'Railway Bar' at all. It is a good ten-minute walk from there to the train station. Anyways, we settle in comfortable-like to sit it out until the next morning."

"You got a room for the night in the Railway Bar?"

"Naw. They let us sit it out in the backroom for no charge. At seven the next morning we left the Railway Bar and walked to catch the train what was to depart at eight. That train would take us from Castlebar to Kingsbridge Station in

Dublin. And from there we would get the bus to Amiens Street for the train to the mail boat in Dun Laoghaire – that train goes right up to the side of the boat, y'know. And then…"

O'Reilly is writing in his notebook. "You're going too fast for me, Ambie. So you and Charlie and Liam went to Dublin, and thence to Dun Laoghaire to get the mail boat to Holyhead, and that would get you a train to London. Is that right?"

"No, Guard O'Reilly. I'm comin' to that part. Meself and Charlie did all that. We were in London by six on the following morning. But Liam did not board the train in Castlebar."

"Back up there, Ambie. It's Liam I'm interested in. Tell me about Liam. When did you last see Liam?"

"That was in the Railway Bar. Meself and Charlie downed a few pints to while away the hours. Charlie went to find a comfortable chair where he could grab some sleep. But, Liam, now. Well, he sat up at the bar on one of those high stools."

"So, in the Railway Bar, you and Charlie sat in comfortable chairs while Liam drank at the bar. Is that so?"

"No. Meself and Charlie drank in comfortable chairs while Liam sat at the bar. **We** were drinking; Liam was talking to the barman. I don't think he took a single drink the whole night. Anyways, they shut the bar at eleven, but since we were stayin' there, they let us drink a bit longer. It was after midnight when Charlie says that he was going to sleep. So, the two of us – meself and Charlie – went out to the backroom."

"Ambie, this is important. When you left the barroom, who all was in it?"

"We were the last to leave the bar. Except for Liam who stayed there talking to the barman."

"Think carefully, Ambie, describe to me exactly the last time you saw Liam Tunnery."

"It's like I said. After midnight, we left the bar, meself and Charlie. Liam was still in there talking to the barman."

"And on the next morning, did you look for him?"

"We walked, meself and Charlie, to the train station. It took us ten minutes. We bought our tickets to Dublin and we waited on the platform. The train was already there, stopped at the platform. There was stuff being loaded onto the goods wagons. We looked up and down but there was no sign of Liam. He was nowhere to be seen."

"Were you not concerned that he was 'nowhere to be seen'?"

"No. Liam is old enough to look after himself. And anyways, he might have arrived at the station before us and already on the train sitting idle there waiting for the eight o'clock departure. We were not going to walk back to the Railway Bar to look for him. We didn't have a half-hour to spare, going there and back again, and for searching around. If we had done all that, sure we would have missed the train. And Charlie says that if Liam overslept and misses the train, he could get the one o'clock train. He could still get to the mail boat before nine. But I had another thought, Guard O'Reilly. Maybe, Liam changed his mind and was heading back to Tubberbawn. Anyways, wherever he got to, we never seen him again."

"Let me get this straight. The last time you saw Liam Tunnery was on the night of…"

"…early morning of…"

"…was in the early hours of Tuesday 27 April 1943, at the counter of the Railway Bar in Spencer Street, Castlebar?"

"That's the height of it."

"…talking with the barman?"

"That's what I told you, and that's how it was."

"Ambie, is there any chance that you know the barman's name?"

"Indeed I do. Sure didn't he greet everyone what came into the pub that night with his 'Good evening, my name is Fergal, I'll be right with you!' over and over about ten times that night."

"What else do you remember about him? His full name perhaps?"

"He only used the one name – 'Fergal' – and he would have been in his late twenties, and he had fair hair, and he wore a fancy waistcoat, and… well, that's all I remember."

"Thank you, Ambie. That's all I need to know. This information is very helpful."

"Helpful for what? Lord, the fuss you're making over Liam Tunnery's absence, you'd think that he was one of them dead bodies what you found in Famine Field." Ambie rushes out. He knows that his father expects a full day's work from him. Now he is obliged to work extra hard and a half-hour longer to make up for the lost time.

Garda O'Reilly places his notebook back into the breast pocket of his tunic. The three women look at him in silence. He rises from the table and walks to the doorway. "Good-day to you all, and thank you, Mrs Gorman, for your kind hospitality."

As he steps onto the front yard, O'Reilly hears Mary Anne question him from within the cottage, "So who **did** you dig up in the Famine Field, Guard O'Reilly?" O'Reilly pretends not to hear. He hurries away on his bicycle, not bothering to fasten his clips until he is out of sight around the bend of the laneway.

At 2:00pm. Garda O'Reilly is back at the Garda station in Killbawn. He is pleased with his progress. He hopes that his contribution to the inquiry will help the case and impress Murf and Fox.

CHAPTER NINETEEN

THE LATE BOBBY FEGAN

County Mayo, Ireland
Saturday afternoon 31 August 1946

Sarah Fegan, known locally as Mrs Fegan, is sitting on a high-backed dining-room chair outside the main doors in the portico of Scott Manor. Today she is dressed in a dusty-pink sleeveless sundress with matching high-heeled sling-back shoes. Her dress is low-waisted and falls flowingly to mid-calf. Her clothes are clearly expensive and meticulously tailored, albeit that they are from the 1920s, a time when her attire would have been considered the height of fashion. She is reading a book while awaiting the arrival of Casey, the proprietor of Casey's General Store.

At 12:10pm, a car arrives and parks in front. A man exits the car. This is not Casey. Sarah inserts a bookmark into the book on her lap and places the book on the window ledge behind her chair. The man approaches. He is dressed in a dark-blue coarse gabardine jacket over light-grey flannel trousers. His shirt is light-blue with black pin-stripes. The shirt style requires a detachable collar if worn correctly. This man has neglected to attach one. Hence, he is not wearing a tie. His trousers are tucked into his socks – woollen white socks with blue dots. And his footwear is dull scuffed boots. She considers this a strange manner in which to dress. He appears neither working-class nor professional, or he could be a hybrid of both. She surmises that it must be a well-to-do farmer dressed down for his farming tasks. What farmer would be here to pay her a visit, she wonders? She addresses him questioningly, "Mr Fitzpatrick, I believe?"

The man responds. "Mr Fitzpatrick? No, I'm afraid not.

My name is Inspector John Patrick Murphy. And do I have
the pleasure of addressing Mrs Sarah Fegan?" Murf studies
the slim attractive woman sitting in the portico of the
building, shaded from the midday sun. She could be 45, but
not much older. Murf has seen Mrs Fegan before, but not up
close. Coming nearer, he observes that her hair was once dark
brown. It is currently streaked with grey and is pulled back
neatly into a French roll. Her face has a sad mien, detracting
from her otherwise striking appearance. Murf sees his own
reflection in the window behind her. He sees now how his
own appearance might be considered a little too common for
a visit to the Scott Manor.

"An inspector? Oh, dear. I mistook you for Mr
Fitzpatrick of the neighbouring farm. And yes, I am Mrs
Fegan. But surely you have come here in error. If you are a
farm inspector, you should be talking to Mr Fitzpatrick. He is
the owner of all these lands around here now – everything
except the manor itself and its gardens."

"Pardon me, Mrs Fegan. I am Inspector Murphy of An
Garda Síochána, the police in Killbawn."

"An inspector with the local constabulary? Indeed. You
don't have the appearance of a police officer."

"This is 'plainclothes' for a rural community."

"I see. And if you are a police officer, then you should
be seated and partake of some tea." Murf notices an ornately-
carved backless teak chair beside Sarah Fegan. Murf sits on
it. The chair is impressive to behold, but it is uncomfortable
to sit upon. Sarah Fegan stretches down to the ground beneath
her chair. She locates a small brass hand-bell. She rings the
bell loudly. A servant promptly appears from around the back
of the manor. Murf recognises Nora Buckley, the wife of Tom
Buckley.

"You rang, Ma'am?"

"Yes, Nora. Inspector Murphy and I will have tea

served. Please ensure that you use the primrose-coloured bone china. It is such a lovely colour for this time of year." Nora hesitates and is unsure of whether to move or remain. "Is something the matter, Nora?"

"Ma'am, we finished the last of the tea this morning."

"Oh dear, then we must do without. But do not fret, Nora. Mr Casey is due to arrive for a visit this afternoon; actually, he is overdue. I'm sure he will bring tea." Nora returns to her servants' quarters in the rear of the building.

Murf brings up the purpose of his visit. "Mrs Fegan, I am going to show you something, and I shall impart to you some significant information. Now, this is important, and it may come as a shock to you. So please brace yourself in preparation."

Sarah Fegan looks at Murf incredulously. Her life is trying. It is unlikely that whatever Murf has to say, or show to her, can bring her any more hardship than she currently endures. Murf rises and goes to his car. He opens the boot and removes the heavy-duty corrugated evidence box. He returns to the uncomfortable seat that depicts a hunting scene of some kind. But before he is able to continue, Sarah Fegan interrupts. "Inspector, whatever you have to show me must wait. I see a car approaching. Now, **this** must be Mr Casey whom I am expecting."

Casey, from Casey's General Store, arrives and parks his car alongside Murf's. Casey is canny. He sees Murf and he is eager to ascertain why the detective is here. Casey knows, as does the entire parish and half the county, that Murf is investigating a triple-murder case. Casey wonders what connection this might have to Mrs Fegan. He exits the car and walks to the portico. "Good-day to ye, Mrs Fegan. Good-day, Guard Murphy."

"Good afternoon, Mr Casey," Sarah Fegan responds, and turns to Murf. "I'm sorry, Inspector, but you are sitting on

Mr Casey's chair."

Murf is apologetic. "Forgive me, Mrs Fegan. I did not realise that Mr Casey requires to sit here."

"No, Inspector, Mr Casey does not desire to sit on the chair. That's his chair."

It becomes clear to Murf as he observes the discourse between Mrs Fegan and Casey that a sales transaction is taking place. Casey removes a wad of banknotes from his pocket. He peels off a five-pound note and hands it to Sarah Fegan. Murf coughs loudly and looks at Casey. Casey makes eye contact for a brief moment. Then he peels off two further one-pound notes. Casey hands the additional money to Sarah Fegan and says, "There ye go, Mrs Fegan. Seven pounds in all. That's two pounds more than we agreed on for the teak chair. Never let it be said that Casey doesn't treat his customers rightly."

"You are most kind, Mr Casey. Now, did you remember to bring me some tea?"

"To be sure, Mrs Fegan. I have it right here in me pocket and all."

"And is it the 'gold leaf' tea. You know that I only consume the best, Mr Casey."

"Isn't that the truth, Mrs Fegan? It's 'gold leaf' all right, fit for a lady of your discerning taste."

"Yes. The tips of the leaves, and only the tips, are meticulously selected for 'gold leaf'. The tips of tea leaves have no veins, so the tea will not get bitter as it draws. Don't you agree, Inspector Murphy?"

Murf nods in agreement. He is impatient for Casey to conclude his visit and leave.

Casey, on the other hand, is in no hurry; he dallies in order to pick up some gossip. "Mrs Fegan, why don't I take back the five pounds and put it to your credit? I will have Peter Meehan come by later, and every day except Sunday, to replenish your larder until your credit is exhausted. Now, what would you like? Nice lean rashers of back-bacon? Eggs? Strawberry jam?"

"Peter Meehan your delivery man with that delightful donkey, Maeve? That is an excellent suggestion, Mr Casey."

Murf smiles to himself. Peter Meehan is Casey's delivery service but, more importantly in this instance, Peter Meehan is the parish's foremost rural gossip collector, on a par with the posh quidnunc Bertha Fitzpatrick.

Sarah returns the five-pound note to Casey. "Mr Casey, take the five pounds and do as you suggest. Now do me a favour. Go back and speak with Nora and determine what is required in the larder. Oh, and tell her to make the tea now."

Murf is eager to get back on track to the purpose of his visit. He refrains from proceeding while Casey is still nosing around. A few minutes later, Nora returns with a folded card table which she flips into an upright position beside Sarah. Then she brings a tray of tea and places it carefully on the card table.

Nora speaks. "Ma'am, I had to borrow a cup of sugar from Willie's beyond."

"Well, Nora, we will be able to repay William Buckley when Peter Meehan arrives later this evening with the provisions."

"I know, Ma'am. But that's three cups we owe him now."

"Very well, Nora. Now would you please bring out a second chair so that Inspector Murphy may be seated?" Nora enters the house through the front doors and reappears seconds later with a dining-room chair akin to the one occupied by Sarah Fegan. Murf is thankful that this chair is comfortable.

Minutes elapse. Sarah and Murf sip tea. Casey is still inspecting the larder, doubtless, with his ears alert. Murf becomes exhausted from making small-talk. After an arduous ten minutes, Casey thankfully departs. Then, at last, Murf is free to state precisely the purpose of his visit to Sarah Fegan. "Mrs Fegan, I would like to ask you about your son, Bobby Fegan."

"Bobby? Bobby is no longer with me. He was taken away. Did you not know that, Inspector?"

Murf is taken aback. Is Sarah Fegan admitting that she knows, or has reason to believe, that Bobby is dead?

Sarah continues. "Bobby was taken from me, with no prior warning, in the autumn of 1930, two weeks shy of his tenth birthday."

"He was **taken** from you?"

"Not in the sense of abduction, Inspector. Bobby had been enrolled in Portora as a boarder… by Captain Robert Scott, I understand. The actual transfer to Portora was handled by Vincent Kelly the solicitor. That is the same Vincent Kelly who escorted me to Uganda when I first commenced service with Captain Scott. I consented to Bobby's enrollment at boarding school at the time. I mean, it is an excellent school and Bobby was entitled to a good education. But, sadly, school life changed him. He quickly grew distant from me. In that sense, Bobby was taken from me. Notwithstanding, he excelled at school, by all accounts."

"But surely he must have returned to Ballycorry during school holidays."

"Of course he did. But after his enrollment in Portora, he was no longer 'my little boy'. He became increasingly distant. By the time he went to Trinity, he had become a very entertaining, and a very welcome, visitor. But, something had severed in our relationship and the bond was broken. I often wonder if I am to blame."

"Did school have that much influence on his development?"

"He was thrust into a new world. While in Trinity, he joined 'The Wilde Club'. That's 'W-I-L-D-E' club. It is a theatrical circle of friends with a strong affinity for the works of Oscar Wilde. The Wilde Club became his new family. And I became…" Murf waits. But Sarah Fegan fails to finish the sentence. Sarah Fegan sips from her teacup. She resumes her account. "The last time Bobby was here was in the summer of 1941. He was full of ideas for the future – what he might do, and where he might go. And then, he was gone."

"Mrs Fegan, I require your attention to an important matter. You see, we recovered a body from the Famine Field – that is a field located on the other side of Killbawn, about three miles outside the town. The body had been buried there for a number of years. We located personal items with the body, items which may determine the identity of the body."

"Inspector, I am unaware of events that take place in and around Killbawn. They don't pertain to me, so I have no interest in them. So why, pray, do you think I should concern myself with your 'important matter'?"

Murf is momentarily taken aback by Sarah Fegan's apparent disinterest. "Mrs Fegan,' he enunciates softly and slowly for emphasis, "these are the items we recovered." Murf removes the lid from the evidence box. "Brace yourself, Mrs Fegan, for what I am about to show you. Do you recognise any of these items?"

Sarah Fegan leans forward in her chair and glances inside the box. "Why, these are Bobby's things," she immediately exclaims.

"I'm sorry to break such sad news to you suddenly in this way – news pertaining to your son, Bobby."

Sarah continues to peer into the box, but she does not venture any closer. "These are Bobby's 'Cary Grant' glasses. He had recently acquired them that year – in 1941, just after St Patrick's Day. And those are the buttons from his blazer.

He liked nautical brass buttons with anchors on them." With that, Sarah leans back in her chair and resumes sipping her 'gold leaf' tea.

Murf is surprised at how calmly Sarah Fegan refers to Bobby's personal effects. He wonders if she understands the import of what she beholds. She sits calmly in her chair, delicately sipping her tea. She speaks softly as if to herself. "So Bobby is truly gone."

"Mrs Fegan, we are treating Bobby's death as a homicide." Murf hesitates. There is no reaction from Sarah Fegan. She sips her tea and looks at Murf. He continues. "In order to apprehend the person or persons responsible, and to bring them to justice, we are conducting a thorough investigation."

"And so you have questions?"

"Yes. If we can establish Bobby's last-known movements – where he intended to go, whom he was to meet – it could ultimately lead to a satisfactory conclusion in the case."

"There could be a 'satisfactory conclusion'?" Sarah Fegan poses this question to herself – a statement rendered in the form of a question. Then she addresses Murf. "Inspector, I have not seen or heard from Bobby since that summer in 1941. I have no knowledge of his movements since then."

"Mrs Fegan, the summer of 1941 is probably the time of his unfortunate demise…"

"Am I to understand that you are investigating a murder from 1941? That's five years ago."

"Yes. We have established that Bobby was buried in the Famine field, very likely in 1941. This came to light just four days ago. His body was discovered when the county council was excavating for a road-widening project at the hillside near the two-mile stone."

"And you want me to remember what Bobby was doing

back then – in the summer of 1941?" She continues to sip her tea as calmly as if she were discussing garden flowers.

"Yes, Mrs Fegan. What is your last recollection of him? Did he say anything that might indicate what he was about? Or do you have knowledge pertaining to those with whom he socialised at that time?"

Sarah Fegan places her cup and saucer on the card table. She frowns in concentration. "Inspector, Bobby was last here in the summer of 1941. I do not remember the date of his departure. I believe it was sometime in August, definitely before September. As to friends – of course, he had friends. But none ever came around here. You see, the rural Irish were not of his ilk – not like the members of 'The Wilde Club'. Once or twice he mentioned Sligo and Castlebar, but in what context I am unable to recall. You realise, Inspector, that in 1941, Bobby was twenty-one. He was no longer beholden to me – actually, in practice, he had been independent of me for a number of years. Bobby would come and go without any forewarning or advice to me. He suddenly appeared in the summer of 1941 and he just as suddenly disappeared again. That was completely in character for him. I was disappointed, of course, that he neglected to communicate with me subsequently, but I believed him to be off seeking his fortune somewhere and that he had put Ballycorry out of his head. And now, Inspector Murphy, you tell me that Bobby has been here all this time not more than ten miles distance? Here, but gone nonetheless?"

"I'm afraid so, Mrs Fegan. But, if I may, permit me to continue. Is it permissible that I access Bobby's effects? I wish to examine them. If Bobby has belongings stored in the manor, they might reveal a clue as to what interests he was involved in or with whom he was acquainted. And I would very much like to have a photograph of Bobby to assist us in making our inquiries."

Sarah Fegan rings her little brass bell. "Inspector, I understand. Of course, you have my permission." Nora arrives at the beckoning of the bell. "Nora, please re-fill the teapot with boiling water." And turning back to Murf, she asks, "More tea, Inspector?"

"Mrs Fegan, Bobby's effects, if I may?"

"Inspector, the front door is unlocked. Pray enter. It is not so large a house that you, a detective, would be unable to locate Bobby's room. I don't believe anyone has entered that room since Bobby himself was last there."

Murf rises from his chair. He retrieves his box of evidence and places the box back in the boot of the car. Next, he enters the manor through the massive doorway, passing from sunlight into the gloomy interior. He glances back at Sarah Fegan sipping tea. He is surprised at the lack of emotion displayed by her. She may be experiencing shock at the news of Bobby's death and the reality of the situation would hit her later. She cannot be as cold as she appears. Perhaps she is a stoic, conditioned to hiding her feelings. Or perhaps she has become desensitised to grief because of her circumstances. Murf shuts the heavy oak door and turns his attention to the great hallway looming before him in the interior of the manor.

It is dim inside the spacious house. A beam of light enters through the circular window above the front doorway and projects an oval of light to the foot of the staircase. Apart from this, the interior is in shadow. Murf is unable to see the full extent of the hallway. Regardless of what Sarah Fegan says, it is a large house. Locating Bobby's room might take some time. But the invitation to enter the manor affords Murf an opportunity to snoop around. Electricity is not installed in the manor, so he knows that it is pointless to search for a light switch. Murf waits for a few seconds to elapse in order to permit his eyes to adjust to the dim light. He sees a small ornate hall table close at hand. There is a candle in a candlestick on the table. The candlestick is formed of very plain tin, white with blue edges. Doubtless, this is the standard lighting for the servants' quarters. Once his eyes have adjusted, Murf proceeds farther into the interior of the large house. Bobby's room is likely on the upper level at the top of the wide ornate stairway facing him. Instead, Murf turns away from the staircase and walks the length of the massive hallway. He proceeds slowly, glancing into the numerous ground-floor rooms.

The hallway is wide, and the walls are bare. It is devoid of the usual pictures one would expect to see in a manor. The most peculiar feature in the hallway is the number of huge crates and packed furniture stacked along the walls. The first room he enters is the dining room. This room contains two smaller crates. Each crate is made of wood and is firmly nailed together. As an added security, these two crates are wrapped with steel bands. Murf is impressed by how fast these crates are secured. It would be a trying task, employing appropriate tools, to open either of these two crates. Otherwise, the room is devoid of furniture, pictures or curtains – except for one item.

The dining-room table stands alone, a solitary article of furniture in a large room. It must have been unpacked and extracted from one of the furniture stacks in the hallway. A folded tablecloth is laid out at the head of the table. A small portion of the cloth is unfolded, enough to cover one place-setting at the table. And the place is actually set for a meal. Murf examines the silverware. It is not actually silver. This is cutlery from the servants' quarters. A candlestick with a tallow candle stands on the bare table close to the tablecloth, a companion to the candlestick he observed in the hallway upon entering. There are no chairs at the table or anywhere else in the room. Murf remembers that there are two dining-room chairs outside in the portico, the chair occupied by Sarah Fegan and the one he himself sat in. Murf walks the length of the spacious dining room. His rubber-soled boots squeak on the bare floorboards. He speculates on what could have covered the oak floor previously – area rugs perhaps? He notes that there is a stack of fire-logs at the fireplace. The manor property is surrounded by many trees, so an ample supply of firewood is fitting. He walks back towards the doorway. He notes that each crate is marked with black letters – NO 10 and NO 11. Back in the hallway, he notes that all the crates are marked with similar unique numbers.

Murf continues to walk farther along the hallway. Shortly, he comes to the final crate. Thereafter, he encounters large items of furniture, items too large to be crated. These are tables and sideboards which are labelled and covered with protective canvas cloth. Whereas they are mostly stacked neatly along one wall, Murf sees that some articles have been disturbed from their original storage position. He deduces that items have been removed. That would explain the presence of the dining-room table in the dining room. Mrs Fegan, he presumes, has removed some items of furniture from storage – some for her own use, and perhaps more to trade with Casey. Walking past the large items of furniture, Murf observes that the hallway is totally bare beyond this point. Moreover, each and every room he subsequently enters is completely empty. Judging from the amount of dust he encounters, and the smell of mould and dampness, Murf concludes that this wing of the Scott Manor has not experienced human intrusion for many years.

Murf walks slowly back towards the main staircase. He mounts the stairway and ascends to the halfway point where the stairway splits to the left and to the right before continuing up to the first-floor level. He glances back at the entrance through which he had entered some ten minutes prior. Murf detects something that was imperceptible to him at ground level. There is a clipboard, heavily encrusted with dust, lying on top of the first crate. Neither the clipboard nor the crate displays any evidence of disturbance since they were first placed there. Murf wonders when that might have been.

Murf resumes his ascent and reaches the upper level, whereupon he enters the first room he encounters. At a glance, Murf determines that this is Sarah Fegan's bedroom and private quarters. The room contains exotic furnishings, probably Sarah's personal belongings brought back from Uganda. The walk-in wardrobe contains a generous supply of dresses and shoes from the flapper era of the twenties, but nothing from a subsequent era. The adjoining bathroom provides no surprises – both the hot and cold taps pour water when Murf turns them on. So, the water supply is not cut off. That means that the rates are being paid to the county. Murf's visit to the interior of Sarah Fegan's private rooms is short. Sarah Fegan is not the focus of his investigation and to linger unnecessarily in her private chambers is an intrusion. He decides that he has seen enough. He returns to the corridor.

The next room he enters is vacant and bare; and so too is the following room, and the one next to it. Murf walks the entire length of the corridor and encounters a series of empty rooms. He wonders if Bobby's room is located here at all. Perhaps it is close to the stairway but in the opposite wing of the house. Murf opens the last door in the corridor. Instantly, he recognises what could only be a boy's room. This room, the last room in the long corridor, is small. It is also the farthest room from Sarah Fegan's private room. Bobby, it appears, sought some distance from his mother.

The room is somewhat neat, certainly not in disorder. The bed is made. And surprisingly the room is dust-free. Could it be that Bobby's room is still being maintained in expectation of his possible return? If so, then Sarah Fegan's acceptance of Bobby's departure may not be as uncaring as she expressed to Murf earlier.

The neatness of the room presents a drawback for Murf. Items of value to the inquiry may have been removed. This appears to be the case. There are no books, no diaries, no notes, no address book; not in the bedside table or on the chest-of-drawers. The drawers are empty. Bobby's clothes are not here either. The wardrobe is likewise empty. But there are pictures on the walls and on stands on the chest-of-drawers. The picture on the bedside table interests Murf. It is a portrait photograph – one that an actor would use for publicity purposes. The writing on the back identifies the subject:

The Importance of Being Earnest
Robert Scott Fegan as Jack Worthing
The Gate Theatre
14 April 1941 (Easter Monday)

Murf notices the use of the name 'Scott' inserted as a middle name. Bobby must have had some knowledge, or strong suspicion, of his parentage to use the name 'Robert Scott Fegan'. Perhaps Bobby received some advantage in being associated with the landed gentry. Murf removes the photograph from its frame. He could not expect to obtain a better photograph than this to assist in his enquiries.

Murf views the other pictures in the room. One particular photograph hanging on the wall catches his attention. A newspaper cutting is attached. It is a picture of two men. In it, a young man dressed in a school blazer is being presented with an award medal. The newspaper cutting describes the recipient as Bobby Fegan who broke the Portora half-mile record in 1938. Presenting the award is a past pupil of the college and previous record-holder, Barry Glen Dennagher, a priest serving in the Catholic Church in

Salisbury, England. Murf is momentarily transfixed. This information is unexpected. It is also of significant importance to the case. It links Bobby to Glen Dennagher. Murf contemplates the importance of this link – Glen Dennagher is linked directly to two of the bodies, and he shares a common link with the third. Murf needs to get back to his office and to his notes. He is anxious to link, cross-link and interconnect common elements in the three murders. He wonders what all connects to what in this case. A lot more than what was apparent at first.

Murf takes the two pictures and the newspaper cutting. He scans the room one more time. Is there anything else of significance? Satisfied, he departs the room with the items of importance. He hurries down the corridor and descends the stairs.

He hesitates at the bottom. He remembers something. He searches for the clipboard he had previously observed. He locates it, as expected, atop the crate next to the stairway. He blows the dust off and discovers a number of papers clipped together. It is an inventory of items packed in preparation for export to Uganda in 1919 – apparently an export that was never executed. The items are cross-referred to specific numbers allocated to the packing orders and crates. Murf quickly scans the list. He searches for… There it is – a description of contents. Crate NO 10 contains silver. Even from a cursory glance, Murf determines that Crate NO 10 contains a fortune in silver – candlesticks, silverware etc. And Crate NO 11 contains a fortune in artworks. Murf is taken aback. The inhabitants of Scott Manor are living in poverty in the midst of enormous wealth – wealth that appears to have been forgotten and overlooked for twenty-seven years.

Murf places the clipboard back in its place and exits the manor. As he hurriedly descends the front steps, Sarah glances up from the book she has resumed reading. She inquires of Murf, "Inspector, were you able to find your way around inside?"

"Yes, thank you, Mrs Fegan," Murf answers without stopping.

"And did you find anything of interest?"

Murf halts upon reaching the pebbled weed-choked driveway. He turns to face Sarah and holds up the two photographs from Bobby's room. "I would like to avail of these pictures of Bobby. Do I have your permission to take them?"

"Very well, if you think they'll help."

"Thank you, Mrs Fegan."

Sarah points invitingly to the vacant chair beside her. "Another cup of tea, Inspector, before you depart?"

"Thanks, but no thanks. I bid you good-day." And with that, Murf enters his car and drives off. Sarah turns her attention back to her book and takes another sip of tea. Murf is impatient to return to his office to place this newly-acquired information into perspective. The dots are spilling rapidly in Murf's mind and he discerns a clear picture emerging. Barry Glen Dennagher features prominently front and centre.

Driving back to Killbawn, Murf's train of thought is disrupted by the lingering impression of Sarah Fegan. Sarah Fegan is not central to the investigation. Doubtless, she is an important element; she is a contributor of information. But she is peripheral to the core of the enquiry, the focus of which is the party (or parties) responsible for the murders of, and disposal of, the three bodies. So why is Murf disturbed by this needling distraction?

Saturday afternoon on the last Saturday in August is a busy market day in Killbawn. At 1:30pm, Murf manoeuvres cautiously through the pedestrians and hawkers in the square. His eyes light upon the window of a solicitor's office – John

Vincent Kelly, Solicitor. Murf knows Vinny Kelly quite well, having encountered him numerous times in the course of his work. The window is like a sign beckoning him. According to Sarah Fegan, Vincent Kelly is Robert Scott's solicitor, or one of his numerous lawyers, at any rate. Murf decides to pay Vincent Kelly a surprise visit. He parks his car at the rear of the garda station and walks back to the Market Square.

Murf enters Kelly's office. The receptionist asks if he has an appointment. "Police business. I think Vinny will see me." The receptionist invites him to be seated. Murf remains standing to indicate that he is not agreeable to waiting.

The receptionist is made to feel uncomfortable. "Is this urgent business, Inspector Murphy?"

"All police business is urgent."

The receptionist disappears into an inner office. Vincent Kelly appears immediately. The receptionist returns to her desk and hammers loudly on her typewriter. Vincent Kelly addresses Murf. "Inspector Murphy, you are working on a murder case? Is that so? Is your visit here connected to your inquiry in some way?"

Murf adopts an affable tone with Kelly. "No. Only in a remote way. Vinny, a private talk, if I may?"

Kelly notices Murf's switch in tone and responds informally in like manner. "Of course, Murf. Come right in."

Inside Vincent Kelly's office, Murf comes straight to the point. He informs Vincent Kelly that one of the bodies excavated from the Famine Field is positively identified as Bobby Fegan – the Bobby Fegan of Scott Manor; the same Bobby Fegan that he, Vincent Kelly himself, brought to Portora Royal School. And so, the police inquiry extends to those associated with the Scott Manor and with Bobby Fegan.

"You are not seriously considering me as a suspect, Murf?"

"Of course not, Vinny. But you may be privy to

valuable information that could lead to the perpetrator, or perpetrators, of the crime."

"Murf, I don't know how much information I can provide. I know very little. And much of what I know is subject to solicitor/client confidentiality. But I'll help you in so far as I am able."

Vincent Kelly has just confirmed to Murf that he has a client relationship with the Scott entity. "Is that a fact, Vinny? So you act for Robert Scott?"

"Only in certain matters. But, yes, I have a professional relationship with Robert Scott."

"And with Sarah Fegan and with the other residents of Scott Manor?"

"No. My relationship is with Robert Scott exclusively, and with his interests."

Murf manoeuvres Vincent into a discourse on the state of Scott Manor and on the poor conditions of employment for Sarah Fegan and Tom Buckley. Murf suggests that there could be labour code infractions which 'in the interests of Robert Fegan' should be addressed. Vinny is silent on this but is all ears. He wonders where Murf is going with this. Murf notes Kelly's attentiveness and continues. "I was there a short time ago – at Scott Manor. Sarah Fegan sold an ugly, but ornate, chair to Casey for £7. At that time of my visit, there was no food in the house." Murf looks hard at Vinny to elicit a response.

"You are telling me that Sarah Fegan sold a chair in order to obtain money to buy food? That may be strange, and even tragic. But Sarah Fegan has a right to do so. According to her contract of service, the housekeeper is mandated, in the discharge of her duties, to dispose of and to obtain household items deemed necessary and proper. To dispose of a chair in order to provide for the manor kitchen is perfectly in order. That is in keeping with the conditions of the contract – I know; I drew up the contract, and I am fully acquainted of the conditions."

"Hold it there, Vinny. You are telling me that Sarah Fegan can sell anything in the house that meets her fancy?"

"No, Murf. She may sell surplus items in order to obtain appropriate articles for the house. She is not permitted to sell items for personal gain. Monetary funds received must be lodged into the Scott Manor Housekeeping Account at the bank, and withdrawn as required. The Housekeeping Account is for the provision of the house and for maintenance repairs."

"Well, judging from the condition of the house, the Housekeeping Account has not provided for the manor for many years. Who has signing authority on this account, Vinny? Do you know?"

"Robert Fegan is the signing officer, but Sarah Fegan has per pro signing authority while employed as the Scott Manor housekeeper."

"And if Sarah Fegan is living in poverty, then one must conclude that the funds have been exhausted for many years." Vincent Kelly is deep in thought. He refrains from answering. Murf continues. "Vinny, Sarah Fegan and Tom Buckley (and his family) are living in poverty in the midst of great wealth."

"Murf, I do not monitor the bank account. The bank account is outside the terms of my engagement with Robert Scott. As I understand, the bank manager communicates with Robert Scott in the maintenance of the account. An allowance is paid into it regularly. At least, that is how the account was set up. From what you tell me, payments into the account have lapsed. I was not aware of that."

"Well, perhaps you should inform Robert Scott – 'in his interests'."

"I have not had a response to any of my communications with Robert Scott since Bobby was placed in Portora Royal. I continue to receive my retainer annually, paid by standing order from Barclays Bank into my account in Killbawn. But there is never any communication from Robert Scott. Whatever arrangements were made subsequently regarding Bobby were conducted without my involvement. I don't hold out much hope for a response pertaining to this current matter of concern. But, Murf, what 'wealth' are you referring to? Most of the land was sold off to Fitzpatrick years ago. The only asset is the manor building itself. And Sarah Fegan is not empowered to sell that."

"No, Vinny. I refer to the crates – crates containing silver and art and antiques and the myriad of valuable items. I just read through the inventory a few hours ago."

"What 'crates' are you referring to, Murf? There are no crates anywhere."

"I am referring to the furniture and packed crates from 1919 that are sitting in the hallway of Scott Manor."

Vincent Kelly rises from his chair and raises his voice in surprise. "The 1919 crates are still in Scott Manor? Good Lord. I was given to understand that the household effects of Scott Manor were exported to the plantation house soon after Mrs Elizabeth Scott's arrival there. And you are telling me that they are still in the house in Ballycorry?"

"Good Lord, Vinny, didn't you see them when you went to the manor – the hallway stacked to the ceiling with packed furniture and crates? The silverware and artwork are in crates in the dining room."

"Murf, in all my life, I have never entered into, nor seen inside, the Scott Manor. Whenever I met with Robert Scott, it was right here in my office. The first time I went to the manor was when I followed up on the estate's post-sale conditions, at which time I inquired about the newborn, Bobby. At that visit, I spoke with Mrs Fegan outside in the portico of the house. The next time I went to the manor was to bring Bobby to Portora. Then, Tom Buckley fetched the boy and his belongings from the house. I waited outside at the car.”

“Well, here is a challenge for you. Robert Fegan ‘in his interests’ needs to decide what to do with the wealth in Scott Manor. Someday, Sarah Fegan will likely unpack some of that wealth to repair the house and to provide for herself and for the residents within. Robert Scott may want someone other than Casey determining the value of the silverware.” Murf does not enlighten Vincent Kelly, that having learned the legitimate status of Sarah Fegan within the Scott Manor, Murf himself may drop a helpful hint to Sarah Fegan as to what appropriate steps she may take for the ‘benefit of the manor’.

“I take your advice, Murf. I will send a telegram forthwith to Robert Scott. I will inform him about Bobby’s death and of the situation in the Scott Manor and I will request his instructions regarding the remedy.”

Ten minutes later, Murf concludes his meeting with Vincent Kelly. He feels relieved that he has set the ball in motion regarding the appalling state of Scott Manor and its impoverished residents. As to the triple-murder case, Vincent Kelly is unable to provide any helpful information.

At 2:20pm, Murf steps out of Vincent Kelly’s office and enters the Market Square. Seeing Cannon’s pub, Murf realises that he is hungry. He nips in for a quick bite. He hurriedly sits at the bar and realises, too late, that he is seated next to Danny the Divil. Being in a hurry, Murf orders a beef sandwich and tea from Mick Cannon. The Divil swivels around on his barstool to face Murf. Murf shuts his eyes to avoid acknowledging the Divil’s presence. But the Divil is not easy to shake off.

“Guard Murphy, and have you solved your case yet?”

“Ah no, Danny. But it is progressing well.” Mick Cannon places a plate of food on the counter in front of Murf.

Murf concentrates on his sandwich and prays that the Divil leaves him alone.

"Y'know, Guard Murphy, them three was kilt for wearing strange clothes. It's not normal – clothes like that. That's why they got kilt."

"In that case, Danny, how come **you** are not killed?"

Danny turns to face the bar and addresses his own reflection in the wall mirror. "Hah! D'ya hear th'on? If anyone deserves to be kilt for their clothes it's this guard right here." Danny turns back to address Murf. He slips off his barstool and approaches him while keeping his elbows on the counter. He is cradling a glass of whiskey in both hands and he is fearful that he may spill a drop. He succeeds in reaching Murf without tipping the glass. Thereupon he ventures another sip, but he fails to coordinate his swallowing with his talking. He dribbles a mouthful of whiskey down his chin as he speaks. "It's the clothes, I tell you. Clothes make the man; and what man dresses like th'on three what was found out in the Famine Field? Hah?"

Murf's elbow catches some of the Divil's dribbled drink. He shakes his arm in annoyance. The Divil blinks. Murf leans away from him and responds. "So they were killed by someone who hates them for how they dressed? Is that right, Danny?"

"Hates them, you say?" The Divil breathes into Murf's face. "No, Guard Murphy. That's only half right. Love and hate are two sides of the same coin. Deep down, there's no differ. Love or hate – there's no differ 'atween the two."

Murf does not respond. He consumes his sandwich and swallows his tea. The Divil waves his hand dismissively at Murf and returns to his barstool. The Divil focuses his attention back to his whiskey. But Murf is disturbed by the drunkard's comments. Mentally, Murf poses a question to himself – what uncanny insight does the Divil possess, even in his semi-drunken state? Up to this point, Murf had been considering the various possible varieties of hate that could have motivated the murders. Consequently, these are significant factors in determining how he connects his dots. But the Divil has him thinking. Hatred, Murf understands, is an emotion of dislike or ill will against an individual or entity. When intense, it can provoke hostility. He considers whether hatred can be expressed against a loved one. He concludes that, in a perverse way, this is indeed possible. Familicide is a gruesome albeit extreme example. So, in the case of the three murders, what if hate was not the motive but love? Abruptly, the connections become much more complex.

2:35pm. Back in his office, Murf notices the picture of Liam Tunnery and friends on his desk. So, he concludes that Garda O'Reilly has been to Castlebar and has returned. "O'Reilly!" he shouts, hoping that O'Reilly is somewhere in the station within earshot. Murf arranges the articles on his desk. He lifts his notepad and inserts a checkmark against the third and final name:

#1, Edmund Ludwig, the Leper √
#2, Liam Tunnery, the Dandy √
#3, Bobby Fegan, the Dazzler √

The identities of all three cadavers are confirmed. Progress. He replaces the notepad on the corner of the desk and lifts the photograph of Tunnery. Murf studies the picture and glances from it to the investigation wall, and back again. Murf determines that an essential connection needs to be established at this juncture. He concentrates on finding the one peculiar link that is pressing foremost on his mind. Murf is irritated by what he sees, or more correctly, by what is **missing** from what he sees. He considers the relevance of the picture of Liam Tunnery, Liam Tunnery with five of his friends, coupled with the Divil's drunken logic.

Murf refers to missing data as 'white dots', blank spots that nevertheless form a solid part of the picture. Sometimes, it is in looking at what is **not** there that you really see what **is** there.

Murf lifts his desk phone. "Where is O'Reilly?" The front desk informs him that Garda O'Reilly is on a break and is eating a sandwich in the back room. "Tell O'Reilly that he can eat in the car. He is coming with me to Castlebar."

CHAPTER TWENTY

AN CHÙILFHIONN PRIVATE CLUB
(An Coolin Private Club)

County Mayo, Ireland
Saturday afternoon 31 August 1946

It is 2:50pm, and Murf is driving south on the R315. Garda O'Reilly, between bites of his ham sandwich, relates to him the result of his inquiries on Liam Tunnery. Murf turns off the R315 and continues driving on the Windy Gap. O'Reilly finishes his discourse – and his sandwich – and he looks at Murf for a reaction to the revelation that the last known person to have encountered Liam Tunnery is Fergal, the barman at the Railway Bar on Spencer Street in Castlebar.

Murf acknowledges O'Reilly's progress. "The early hours of Tuesday 27 April 1943, at the counter of the Railway Bar in Spencer Street you say? That's good work, O'Reilly. But the 'last **known** person' is not necessarily the 'last person' to have interacted with Liam Tunnery prior to his death. Nevertheless, it is an important step closer."

Murf proceeds to Pontoon Road and enters Castlebar. Saturday afternoon is a busy time in Castlebar. It is 4:10pm as Murf drives along Ellison Street. Garda O'Reilly expects Murf to turn left upon reaching The Mall. Murf surprises O'Reilly by failing to turn left. Instead, he continues straight ahead.

"Murf, you missed the turn for Spencer Street. This is Mountain View. This takes us to Westport Road and out of Castlebar."

"I know."

"If you're heading for the Railway Bar, you'll have to turn around."

316

"We're not going to… Oh, I was intending to go somewhere else first. But considering that we are so close to Spencer Street, let's go to the Railway Bar at this time. I suspect the traffic on Spencer Street could be dense at this time on a Saturday. If parking on the street is a problem, we can proceed to the rear of the garda station to park. It's just a short walk back along The Mall from there to the bar." Murf drives along Westport Road and onto Lannagh Road. He swings left on Humber Way and arrives at Spencer Street at 4:20pm. He encounters good luck and manages to find a kerbside parking spot outside the Railway Bar.

Murf instructs O'Reilly to question the patrons inside the barroom and to show them the photographs in the hope that someone may recognise one or more of the three victims, or even recognise some of Liam Tunnery's companions. They enter the Railway Bar together. Murf's focus is to engage the barman. He walks directly to the bar and leans on the counter next to the pumps. Without any preamble, he asks the barman if he is 'Fergal'. The barman is helpful. He informs Murf that his name is 'Paul'. Murf learns from the barman that Fergal has not worked here at the Railway Bar for two years. The barman summons Jim Cassidy, the owner. He believes that Jim would know more about the previous barman.

Jim Cassidy enters the saloon from an adjacent room. Murf introduces himself and Jim invites him to enter a snug where they may speak in private. Seated in the snug, Murf learns from Jim Cassidy that Fergal McKenna has been tending bars in Castlebar for over ten years. He is popular and efficient. For many years, he worked part-time in a number of pubs around the town. Back in 1943, he was engaged part-time at the Railway Bar. In order to relieve the full-time barman, Fergal worked two nights a week, but never on weekends. Weekends provided the greatest tips, and the regular barman ensured that he himself worked the most lucrative nights. Then, about two years ago, Fergal informed Jim that he had been offered the position of manager at another establishment. And so, in order to avail of the more lucrative full-time position, Fergal McKenna resigned from the Railway Bar. Jim Cassidy was sorry to lose him. "But who can blame him?" he says. "And lucky the man what got him."

"So, tell me, Jim, where is Fergal McKenna working now?"

"I don't rightly know. He never said. He was quiet about that, so he was. But, I'll tell you this, Inspector, he's not tending bars in any of the pubs that I know of here in Castlebar. But he can't be all that far away either. He still lives alone in a one-story semi-detached on the Newport Road across from the hat factory." Murf thanks him for the information. And seeing that O'Reilly has concluded questioning the patrons, they both leave the establishment.

Back in the car, Murf and O'Reilly compare their experiences in the Railway Bar. O'Reilly gained nothing of significance. Of the patrons present, not one recognised Liam Tunnery or any of his friends in the photograph. But Murf has the name and address of the barman, the last known person to have seen Liam Tunnery. O'Reilly asks, "So I take it that we are off to Newport Road to speak with Fergal McKenna?"

"No, O'Reilly. Not yet. Saturday evening is a busy time for a barman. Fergal McKenna will not be at home at this time of day. He is probably at work now."

"Where?"

"I have a hunch." Murf starts the car and drives back to the Westport Road.

"Murf, where are you going now?"

"To the place I originally set out for upon leaving Killbawn. We are going to Islandeady, O'Reilly."

"Islandeady? Sure there's nothing at Islandeady, except

an old graveyard. Why are we going to Islandeady at all?"

"O'Reilly, I have a lot of papers stuck to my investigation wall back at the station. And it struck me today, while looking at them, that there is a pattern of white dots – missing data like the invisible force that points a compass needle. It points to 'An Chúilfhionn'. 'An Chúilfhionn' is at Islandeady. It is a private club."

"We are going to a private club on a Saturday evening? And it's called 'An Chúilfhionn'? I've heard of that place, Murf. And that's where 'An Chúilfhionn' is located? At Islandeady?"

"That's right. At Islandeady Lough. And that is where we are going."

"You know what 'An Chúilfhionn' means?"

"Yes."

"It refers to fair hair."

"I know that."

"But it could also refer to the back of the head – if it is a fair-haired person."

"O'Reilly, I am aware of what 'An Chúilfhionn' means, and of the various connotations of the term."

"So you are taking me to a Nancy-boy club?"

"O'Reilly, if you are referring to homosexual males, use the term 'gay' or just 'homosexual'. But yes, we are going to a club frequented by homosexuals."

"Surely, you are not going there to arrest someone for 'gross indecency', are you? I thought you were focused on the murder investigation."

"O'Reilly, listen to me. Our visit to the private club is solely in connection with our current murder investigation. I need your help to get me in without a fuss."

"Why do you think I can get you in? I'm not a member of the club, or of any other gay club."

Murf continues to explain his reasons for visiting the

club. "The three murder victims may have been members of the club, or perhaps associated with members of the club. I have reason to believe that there is a connection between the club and the murders."

"By God, I think you are right there, Murf. All three victims were gay? And gays congregate with gays. So, they may have some association with this club. Is that what you are thinking, Murf?"

"It is a line of inquiry that must be explored."

"And how do you expect me to get you admittance into the club? Can you not just demand entry? Sure they can't stop the guards."

"To stomp in there uninvited would be improper. To enter legally, we need permission, or have 'probable cause'. This is not a raid or a witch-hunt against the gay community. No, O'Reilly, I prefer to enter lawfully with their permission."

"So what do you want me to do that will get you admitted?"

"Just walk up to the front door calmly, and knock on the door politely."

"That's it? So why don't **you** knock politely on the front door, if it's that easy?"

"Ah, O'Reilly, what did they teach you at Garda College, at all, at all?"

Murf reduces speed on Westport Road to identify his location. He turns right onto Cloggermagh Way. Cloggermagh Way is not identified, but O'Reilly remembers that this is the way to Islandeady Graveyard. The road reveals tyre tracks, an indication that it is frequently used. Before they reach the graveyard, Murf turns right again. This boreen is unfamiliar to O'Reilly. O'Reilly observes recent tyre tracks in the boreen. He concludes that there is regular light vehicular-traffic in the boreen. Fifty yards farther, Murf fords a small brook and brings the car to a halt.

Murf turns to O'Reilly and says, "O'Reilly, I stopped the car here for your benefit. I see how intently you are observing your surroundings."

"Like a detective. Right, Murf?"

"Tell me what you see."

"We are on an unmarked road in a remote location, yet it is frequently travelled by cars – cars rather than big farm tractors and the like."

"And in front? What is of significance ahead of us?"

"This is a frequently-used road giving access to a great house or to a manor house. I see a stone wall that can only be the perimeter of an estate, within which the ground is populated with mature trees – a forested area not employed in agriculture. And you are stopped in the roadway right at a gate into the property. The gate blocks the entrance, but it is clearly unlocked. It is a swing-to gate, commonly used to deter cattle from entering, rather than to bar access to human-vehicular traffic. Yes, Murf, this is the entrance to a great house."

"And you are sure of that, O'Reilly?"

"Yes, I am. Now is that good observation?"

"What do you **not** see? Picture the scene of your description, and from your conclusion tell me what is missing."

"Murf, if this is the way to the Nancy-boy club, just go there and stop with the detective lessons."

Murf's car remains stationary with the engine running. Murf is not yet ready to give up. He asks, "Detective O'Reilly, where is the gate-house?"

"Damn it, Murf, there is no gate-house. A manor always has a gate-house or land-steward's cottage at the entrance to the property. But there is no gate-house here."

"Correct. Now hop out and open the gate."

O'Reilly does as bidden and opens the gate. Murf drives though, and O'Reilly permits the gate to swing back into its closed position. He hears the click of the latch as it falls into place. Satisfied that the property is duly protected from wandering livestock, O'Reilly re-enters the car. Yet again, Murf maintains the car in a motionless state.

O'Reilly, seated in the front passenger seat, stares ahead and asks, "**Now** what is it? Why aren't you moving, instead of remaining here motionless?"

"Detective O'Reilly, tell me what you observe here."

"Lord, Murf, you have me demented. We are sitting still, when we should be going somewhere, on a gravel-surfaced lane. No, it's too big to be a lane, and it's too narrow to be a road."

"An avenue?"

"Yes. We are on an avenue to a great house, a great house that may not be all that great. The avenue is well-maintained – there are no pot-holes, no ruts and the edges of the roadway are trimmed to form nice straight lines against the grass verges on both sides. Oh, and the grass is mowed and the whole area is free of weeds. There are flowers growing in the grass verges, but they have passed blooming and only the green leaves remain. And beyond that, you see slender trees running parallel to the avenue on each side."

"English poplars."

"And beyond those, the English poplars, there are mature deciduous trees of different varieties. **Now** can we go, Murf?"

"You missed something."

"Nothing of importance. It is a nice neat road – avenue – but nothing really unusual about it."

"Where is the drainage sheugh?"

"You are right, Murf. Where is the sheugh? Sure every road requires drainage, otherwise there is a mess when it rains and, by God, that's often enough." O'Reilly peers more intently at the roadway and to the grass verges at the sides. The gravel surface, to be in such a neat condition, must have drainage. The lie of the road becomes clear to him. The roadway is not level like a plane; it is slightly sloped from the centre point to beyond the poplars. "I see them now. That's great engineering. The sheughs are over there past the poplars. They are not readily apparent. Sure a galloping horse would not see them."

"The avenue is designed so that unpleasant sights are hidden from the eye. O'Reilly, if you are to assist me, you need to develop the skills of seeing what is before your eyes, and, more importantly, seeing what is hidden. Now, we are off to our destination."

The avenue curves gently to the left. O'Reilly, heedful of Murf's instructions, is more observant than before. Of course, he sees the road curving to the left, but he is cognizant of the importance of deducing what is hidden from view – hidden but nevertheless inferred by that which is visibly evident. He gauges that this is a long gentle curve, much longer than what is perceptible in a single glance. Whereas he previously would have accepted that a road can be generally straight, notwithstanding multiple curves left and right, he is aware that this is not the case here. They have changed direction and are travelling north rather than east. They are headed for the lough.

Murf stops the car once more. Having journeyed 150 yards from the swing-to gate, they are at the end of the tree-lined avenue. Murf pulls the car to the side and parks in the shade of a rhododendron tree. The house, their destination, is visible in the clearing ahead. The avenue approaches the house from the gable end. O'Reilly had expected the avenue to terminate facing the front of the house. O'Reilly exclaims, "You are correct, Murf. This is not a manor. It is a rich farmer's farmhouse – or it once was."

"O'Reilly, there are no other buildings close by – no barn, no dairy, no byre, no shed. This house, grand as it is, stands alone. I don't believe it ever served as a farmhouse, rich or otherwise. No, O'Reilly, this is – was – a rectory."

"A clergyman's house?"

"It is an early nineteenth-century rectory-manor and this property may have been a glebe at one time. Notice that the avenue approaches the building from the side so as not to interfere with the view of the lough as observed from the house. Buildings like these were provided to ministers as accommodation befitting their social status. Later, parish priests also took a fancy to them. Today, clergymen are more attentive to convenience and prefer to live close to their respective churches, except for a few old-fashioned clerics who relish their elevated status. Rectories, like this one here, are frequently unoccupied now. Some are valued by city dwellers as country retreats."

"Or as private clubs." O'Reilly is still honing his craft of observation. He studies all that his eyes and ears behold. He is captivated by the delightful setting. A well-tended lawn spreads out from the front of the house down to the shore of the lough. The house is orientated to have a clear view of the lough, uninterrupted by the presence of the avenue or by trees. O'Reilly rolls down the car window to view the scene more clearly. He hears the water lapping gently against the pebbly shore.

Murf brings him back to the purpose of their visit. "O'Reilly, I hear the sound of an approaching car. I'll park at the rear of the building." He shifts the idling car into first gear and manoeuvres it gently into the parking area. He passes two parked cars and stops alongside a Ford Prefect. "No one will notice a Ford Prefect parked next to a Ford Prefect."

"Unless he is a detective."

"Come on, O'Reilly. Let's stand behind the rhododendrons over at the side and observe."

A Ford Prefect appears, driving up the avenue. It enters the parking area and stops next to Murf's car. Three Ford Prefects in a row. A man exits the car. He is dressed in a dark-blue gabardine raincoat and is wearing a fedora hat. Murf and O'Reilly observe the man walk confidently to the front of the building. He knocks on the front door – three raps, followed by two, and then by another three. The door is not immediately opened. Since they are watching from the side, Murf and O'Reilly study 'fedora man' in profile. They see his mouth move. He is talking, but his voice is low and they are unable to distinguish what he is saying. The door opens and the man enters the building. Neither Murf nor O'Reilly gets a clear view of his face, so the identity of 'fedora man' remains hidden.

"Murf, do you want me to snoop about in his car?"

"No, O'Reilly. I don't want to get side-tracked. We will forego the search of his car unless we subsequently learn that it may contain relevant information. Now pay attention. This is what I want you to do, O'Reilly. Count up to 30 slowly – one-thousand-and-one, one-thousand-and-two, and so on. Then go up to the front door, calmly and confidently, in the same manner as 'fedora-man'. Knock at the door with the code you observed and announce yourself when challenged."

"What should I say?"

"Tell them that you are Garda Seamus O'Reilly, and that you are conducting an investigation into a serious matter, and that you would greatly appreciate the assistance and cooperation of the occupants of the house."

Murf walks away. O'Reilly begins to count. Murf's plan is to wait at the back door, the door he observed accepting deliveries at his previous visit. He reaches the rear door. He stands with one arm raised and leans against the door-jam so as to block the exit area of the doorway. Some seconds later, the door opens. Two men, expecting to exit the house unobserved, are surprised to see Murf standing in the doorway. "Good evening, gentlemen. My name is Inspector…" The two men make a sudden U-turn and disappear back into the house. "…Murphy. I am conducting an inquiry into a series of events that could have serious implications for you." The barman is left standing alone at the open door. His instinct is to be accommodating to Murf, whom he remembers from his previous visit. But this is countered by his desire to protect the privacy of the patrons. He hesitates for a second. The need for privacy wins out.

He addresses Murf. "You again. I was wondering when you would show up a second time. Well, I'm sorry, Inspector. This club is for members only…" He slowly closes the door as he speaks.

Murf, on the other hand, continues to talk throughout the barman's retort. 'We have reason to believe that members of this club are being targeted by a serial killer…"

"…and admittance is by invitation…" The door swings to within two inches of shutting. Then it stops. The barman ceases speaking.

Murf strikes home his advantage. "…and their lives, or the lives of some of them, may very well be in danger. Now, Fergal, listen to what I tell you…"

The door suddenly swings fully open. "I'm sorry, Inspector. Did I hear you correctly? Members of this club are being targeted by a serial killer? And how did you learn my name?"

"Fergal McKenna, I have important information to impart, and I need your assistance. In the interests of your own safety and protection, it is important that we apprehend a possible serial killer before he strikes again." The barman is taken aback by Murf's addressing him by his full name. Murf has hooked Fergal McKenna's attention but, so far, Murf has not gained admittance. Now to reel him in gently. "Is it possible to speak inside, Fergal?"

"Well, if you step into the storeroom, that is fine by me." Thereupon Murf enters the building by invitation. Inside, in the storeroom, Murf quickly conveys to Fergal that he is investigating the murder of three victims and that it may have possible links to the club, either to the club itself or to members of the club. He convinces Fergal of the importance of conducting an investigation here in 'An Chúilfhionn Private Club'. Fergal is clearly shaken by the import of Murf's revelation. He reluctantly agrees to cooperate. Murf persuades him to consult with the patrons present in the lounge in the hope of enlisting their assistance too. "Inspector, if you don't mind waiting here for a few minutes, I'll go next door and talk to the members. Or if you prefer, you may wait in the kitchen with my two cousins, 'Big Maggie' and 'Maggeen'.

Murf enters the kitchen. The two Maggies step back from the doorway from where they had witnessed the exchange between Murf and Fergal. The kitchen is large. It is brightly lit due to a large window on the exterior wall. It is a well-equipped kitchen – sinks and tables and cupboards, and doorways leading into a pantry and a larder. The big black range radiates heat, and it is laden with a collection of cooking-pots all whistling and steaming. There is a pleasant odour of meat being grilled and of stew simmering. Murf has entered from the storeroom, and he notices another entrance door in the kitchen, one with direct access to the interior of the house and to the lounge he presumes.

Big Maggie is of average height, but she is broad and muscular. Her short pudding-bowl brown hair and the butcher-style apron add to her formidable appearance. The meat-knife in her right hand is dripping blood. Murf estimates that she must be in her mid-thirties. By contrast, Maggeen (little Maggie) is slender and petite. Her fair hair is fringed and is pulled back into a plait that falls to her shoulder-blades. She is dressed in a floral-patterned apron, and she is holding a mixing bowl in the crook of her left arm. She looks to be about twenty.

Big Maggie is not as intimidating as she looks, and neither is Maggeen as shy as appears. They quickly direct Murf to a chair and offer him tea to drink. Murf accepts the offer, not because he desires tea, but in order to engage them in conversation so as to obtain information. He learns that the two Maggies and Fergal maintain the house and the grounds. As to the identity of the owner, Big Maggie is unclear. All the members of the club have some share in the ownership – like a cooperative. The three McKennas manage the property and they are paid generously by 'the Board' for their dedicated work.

Before Murf is able to gather any more information, he is interrupted by Fergal re-entering the kitchen. "Inspector, the members, those that are here at the moment, are agreeable to your presence here in the execution of a criminal investigation. They will cooperate and assist. There is a condition, however. They insist on keeping their identity hidden from you. And there is a second condition, that you will not use this visit as leverage to conduct any future police-action against the club or its members."

Murf indicates his acceptance of the conditions. Murf is comfortable with condition number two. He has no desire to engage in any witch-hunt against the homosexual community. The first condition is not totally acceptable to Murf. But neither is it a surprise. He understands the delicate nature of the club members' situation. By agreeing, he is a step forward. Willing cooperation is more valuable than information extracted reluctantly. In the course of his investigation, he hopes to gain the trust of the club members.

Fergal communicates Murf's acceptance to the members. Then, the dedicated barman sets about arranging the lounge to accommodate an interview in keeping with the members' privacy requirements. He draws the blinds on the windows, and he lights the Tilley lamps hanging above the bar. When he is finished, the lounge is in darkness except for the bright area at the bar. Thereupon he leads Murf from the kitchen into the storeroom and thence into the back of the bar. Murf finds himself standing behind the counter of the brightly-lit bar. The occupants of the room sit well back. They are discernible only as dim forms in the semi-darkness. Murf requests that they permit his assistant, Garda O'Reilly to be present also 'before he raps the skin off his knuckles out at the front door'. Fergal goes to the front door and peers outside. Garda O'Reilly is standing there and is looking around in bewilderment. Fergal opens the door and invites Garda O'Reilly inside to join them.

Moments later, Murf and O'Reilly stand side by side behind the bar, in the space usually occupied by the barman. Fergal attends to the lamps. He pumps more air into the Tilley Lamps and opens the valves fully in order to produce maximum light. When finished, he stands next to the counter. The two Maggies are discernible from their stature. They stand inside the lounge next to the kitchen door. The remaining company, all seated at small round tables, appear as dim shadows shifting to and fro, left to right, due to the play of light from the still-swinging lamps suspended over the bar.

Murf addresses the room. "Gentlemen," and in deference to the two Maggies, he adds, "and ladies, rest assured that this is in no way a garda raid, nor is it a trick to entrap any of you. My focus, my **only** focus, is to concentrate solely on solving a murder case. The purpose is two-fold. The perpetrator (or perpetrators) must be caught and brought to justice. And secondly, and this should be of intense concern to you, the perpetrator must be caught before he (or she, or they) has the opportunity to commit another offence of dire consequences. We have uncovered three victims, killed two years apart from each other over the past five years. All three victims have been identified. We have reason to believe that all three may have had some connection with this club and/or its members. We cannot ignore the connection. We must take into consideration the very strong probability that members of the gay community are being targeted by a serial killer, or by an entity that seeks to do you serious injury." Murf hesitates. He hears the scraping of feet and low mutterings from the unsettled (albeit indiscernible) audience.

A stage-whisper emanates from one shadowy figure, a figure wearing a fedora. "And the guards have only recently come to this conclusion?" The figure continues. "We have been subjected to insults and threats for as long as I remember." There are murmurs of agreement from the company present. "Drunken louts assault us, empowered by the licence that they perceive is afforded to them from the rhetoric of our moral leaders – from the Church, the judiciary, police, and from society at large. We are fair game for ridicule and contempt. And to whom can we turn for protection and redress?" The invisible assembly grumbles in agreement. Murf is cognisant that 'fedora man' speaks in flawless west-Mayo country accent, yet his vocabulary and syntax betray his education. This is no rude rustic.

"Everything you say is true. And I do not have an answer. My focus is purely on the case under investigation. Surely, in this one thing, we can see our way to inter-cooperation to our mutual benefit." Murf hears sighs of assent – or sighs of resignation. It is already common knowledge that corpses have been unearthed in the Famine Field near

Killbawn. Murf delivers an informative summary of the case, starting with the discovery of the bodies in the Famine Field and ending with disclosing the names and identities of the victims. Murf chooses his words judiciously. He ensures that the information he thus imparts is sufficient to give due caution to the assembled members, yet he is careful to withhold details of the inquiry itself. Other than revealing the names of the three victims, he withholds details on their condition and is mute on matters pertaining to evidence.

Murf speaks for an hour hoping to elicit cooperation and glean some pertinent information. Fergal twice pumps the lamps to maximum brightness. Murf concludes, "Garda O'Reilly and I will withdraw to the kitchen. I leave you three photographs for your perusal. Fergal will pass them around to you. Look at them. If you choose to handle any of them, ensure that you do not place your fingers on the surface. Hold the photographs by the edges balanced between thumb and fingers, like this," he demonstrates, "and I will retrieve them from you afterwards. These pictures display the faces of the three victims – one picture of each. Bobby Fegan is alone in this one; Edmund Ludwig is photographed with a young girl; and one photograph depicts a cluster of six men, the victim Liam Tunnery surrounded by a group of friends. That picture, you will observe, is a photograph taken in the car park of this club, hence the obvious connection. I'll point this out to Fergal here, so that he may indicate to you which one of the group is the victim. It is important that we trace the last known movements of the three victims. Anything you are able to tell me, anything at all, could prove to be of significant importance in leading to an arrest. Now, one last thing. I realise that you may be reluctant to meet with me face-to-face. So please phone me at 'Killbawn two' – you can phone from any post office to maintain privacy – and I will arrange to communicate with you anonymously."

'Fedora man' asks in his contrived accent, "Can you guarantee that, Inspector? To safeguard anonymity?"

"Alas, no. I cannot guarantee the anonymity of…, let's say, a material witness who may be required to give evidence at a trial. And similarly, anonymity cannot be extended to a suspect – either with regards to the perpetrator himself or one who aided or abetted him. I will make every effort to protect your privacy but be advised – the thrust of the investigation is to solve the case. The protection of your identities is of secondary importance."

Murf and O'Reilly withdraw to the kitchen. They hear more members arrive at the club. The hum of voices rises and falls as the members discuss the matter and render opinions among themselves. Eventually, Fergal McKenna enters the kitchen. He walks over to Murf, who is standing next to one of the kitchen side-tables. He passes to Murf the stiff envelope containing the photographs. Murf examines the pictures. He is satisfied that they are free of fingerprints. Murf spreads the three photographs on the table.

"So, Fergal, did any of the members comment on the people in the photographs?"

"I can't really say, Inspector."

"Then how about yourself, Fergal? Let's look at them one at a time." Murf indicates to the photograph of Bobby Fegan. "Do you recognise this person?"

"Yes. But I did not know his name until tonight."

"Where did you see him?"

"Here at the club. He was a guest, not a member."

"Was he a frequent visitor?"

"I saw him here twice. That was back when I worked part-time four evenings per week."

"So, he could have visited the club on other occasions?"

"Yes, mid-week or early in the day."

"Do you remember when that was?"

"No. But at the time, England was two years into the war. There was speculative talk going around about the blitz and if it had finally stopped."

Murf nods. The blitz ended in May 1941. "You say that Bobby Fegan was a visitor. So, he must have been admitted as the guest of a member. Is that how he was granted admission? Who was he with on those occasions?"

"Inspector, you must understand, a requirement of my job is to **not** recognise people and **not** remember faces here. I am conditioned to blank that information from my awareness and erase it from my memory. I'm sorry."

Murf nods in understanding. He knows that he could press Fergal to divulge names. But there is a caveat to this. Fergal could mislead him. No, it is better to entrap him into making a disclosure. Murf requires a trivial distraction to talk around him. "Fergal, my throat is dry from all the talking. Could I have another cup of tea, please? With milk and sugar, if you don't mind?" Murf continues to talk to Fergal, while Fergal fulfils Murf's request – not an unusual task for an experienced barman.

Murf shows the Liam Tunnery picture to Fergal. "How about this one, Fergal?" This time, Murf knows that Fergal spoke with Liam Tunnery at the Railway Bar in Castlebar on the day of his departure from home.

Fergal acknowledges the picture hesitantly. "That's Liam Tunnery. I can tell you something about him. It may be of help. You see, three years ago, Liam Tunnery was on his way to England. He was to overnight in the Railway Bar in Castlebar and he intended to catch the morning train to Dublin on the following morning. I was tending bar that night – it was the evening of Easter Monday that year – 1943. Liam – I did not know his name other than 'Liam' – poured his heart out to me at the bar that night. He had no desire to work in England. He yearned to meet people he could relate to. He thought that by going to England he could start a new life and things would work out. But, deep down, he did not want to leave Mayo. I suggested to him that I could introduce him to young men of his own age here in Mayo – young men who felt the same way as he did.”

“And did you?”

“Yes. On Tuesday, the following morning, Liam chose to miss the train to Dublin. Later that day, I brought Liam to Islandeady as I was working here at the club that Tuesday. I admitted Liam into the club as a guest and I introduced him to… no, that’s not quite correct. I was **about** to introduce him to a young man when he, the other man, recognised Liam. It turns out that a month earlier, he and another member brought four guests here to the club. The policy is for one guest per member. And because it was a party of six, two members plus four guests, we were unable to accommodate them at that time. But one of the members from back then was present here on the night I admitted Liam. Now here is Liam again, and this time he is a guest in the club.”

“A party of six? Could this be a photograph of that party?”

“Hmm. It could be. I don’t know for sure. Only two of them are members…” Fergal stops mid-sentence.

“This photograph contains two members of An Chúilfhionn Private Club, plus Liam Tunnery? Is that so?”

“No. What I mean is, it **might** be.” Fergal realises that he slipped up.

Murf pretends not to notice. He attends to his cup of tea on the kitchen table, pouring milk and spooning sugar. He stirs his tea and acts as if nothing of significance has occurred. “Fergal, don’t let your tea get cold.”

Fergal takes advantage of the interruption to drink from his cup. The activity of consuming tea restore his self-confidence. He continues his discourse. "Well, after that night, I did not see Liam again."

"So was this 'member' with Liam, the last time you saw him?"

"Not so. That member introduced Liam to some others. Then he left soon afterwards – the member, that is. Liam, on the other hand, stayed until much later, enjoying his new-found friends."

"Was that the only time you saw Liam Tunnery?"

"Liam Tunnery was here in the club just that one time. He never returned for a second visit. I never saw him again."

"Now, Fergal, this is important. Who was with Liam when you last saw him?"

"Inspector, truly, I don't know. He was there, and later on, he was not there. I was busy that night and I did not notice him leave, nor did I notice who he was with prior to leaving."

Murf nods. He considers how accurate, or inaccurate, this information might be. Is Fergal concealing the identity of a member, or even protecting someone? Murf asks Fergal to replenish his teacup. There is a card he wishes to play. First, he needs to manipulate Fergal into dropping his guard. Then, when he has garnered an advantage, Murf will ask penetrating questions, the questions that may produce answers of significant substance.

Murf indicates to the third picture on the table, the photograph of Edmund Ludwig and Annie. "Fergal, do you recognise this man?"

"Edmund Ludwig. Yes. But I have never seen the girl."

"They worked together for a while. But, tell me about Edmund Ludwig."

"Before your visit here today, I never heard the name 'Edmund Ludwig'. But I remember seeing him once in the club. It was about a year ago."

"He was not a member. So whose guest was he?"

Murf notices that Fergal avoids naming the member. Fergal continues, "He was dressed in an unusual manner. Mind you, I am oblivious to flamboyant apparel here in the club. He was wearing tight white pants – tight pants are not unusual apparel here – and a black jacket that was too large for him. Tight white pants and a loose black jacket are an unusual combination – **that** is what was strange."

"Tight white pants are not surprising?"

"Not really."

"And an oversize jacket?"

"That is common. But not in combination with tight white pants. Clearly, this Edmund had not planned to dress like this. But then, I realised that he was merely wearing his friend's jacket – that's all. So, it didn't appear so out of place after all."

"What makes you say that it was 'his friend's jacket'?"

"I recognised the jacket from before."

"His friend, the person he was with, was that the member whose guest he was?"

"Yes."

"And he was wearing that member's jacket?"

"Yes. So what? This is not uncommon."

Murf signals to O'Reilly to join them. O'Reilly is drinking tea and is eating a 'Mikado' biscuit that Maggeen has slipped to him. Nevertheless, he is attentive to the detective's technique of questioning and he sees where the shrewd Murf is going. He places his cup by the sink and licks his fingers. Murf hands his car keys to O'Reilly and instructs him to fetch an 'item of interest' from the boot of his car. Murf turns back to Fergal. "Fergal, do you mind topping up my tea? It got cold during the talking." Fergal takes the teapot from the corner of the range and pours hot tea into Murf's cup and into his own. Murf adds more sugar to his cup and he slowly stirs his tea. He resumes speaking to Fergal. "Now, Fergal, you say that Edmund Ludwig was admitted into the club as the guest of a member. So, did he remain in the company of that member for the duration of his visit?"

"I believe so. He didn't speak English very well, so he didn't socialise."

"They arrived together – the member and Edmund Ludwig. Did they also leave together?"

"I suppose so. I did not see either of them leave, but the Ludwig person was not with anyone else all night. When I noticed that he had left, well, they were both gone. Yes, I believe they entered together and they left together."

Murf hears O'Reilly return, but he pretends not to notice him. Murf ceases stirring his tea. He removes the spoon from the cup and watches it drip. He appears to be concentrating on his dripping spoon. He resumes speaking to Fergal. "Now, Fergal, think back. This jacket that Edmund Ludwig was wearing the night – the one that belonged to the member he was with – did it look like this one?" Perfectly on cue, O'Reilly unfurls the garment he is carrying and holds it aloft. Murf shifts his attention from the dripping spoon to Fergal. Fergal's face registers surprise at O'Reilly's actions and he loses control of his cup. His fingers maintain a grip on the cup handle, but the cup tilts to the side and Fergal spills tea onto his feet. Murf calmly sips tea as if nothing unusual has occurred. He resumes speaking to Fergal. "I can see how you recognised the jacket on Edmund Ludwig last year. It is a unique jacket. Is it not?" Fergal opens and closes his mouth, unsure of what to say. Murf takes another sip of tea. The two Maggies freeze in the execution of their tasks as if stricken with immobility – one standing at the sink and the other standing at the range – ears cocked and listening.

Murf places his cup on the table and stands facing Fergal. "Fergal, from what you tell me, the last known person to be seen with Edmund Ludwig before his death was the member who escorted him to the club and who subsequently escorted him out from the club. And that member was the owner of a unique jacket, like the one that Garda O'Reilly is holding. Now, Fergal, I am certain as to the identity of the owner of the jacket, and I believe that you are equally certain…"

Fergal, who has been standing shock-still and speechless, suddenly becomes animated and vocal. "Ho no! You are not going there – suggesting that Father Barry Glen Dennagher had anything to do with it." Fergal has just admitted to Murf that Father Barry Glen Dennagher is a member of the club and that he was in the company of Edmund Ludwig when they were together on the one occasion that Edmund Ludwig was present in the club. Fergal does not hesitate in his talking. "Of all the people in the world, Father Barry Glen Dennagher is the best friend a gay could have. He speaks to everyone here; he counsels all those in need – particularly the young ones that are struggling with their sexual identity. If Father Barry Glen Dennagher was seen talking with Edmund Ludwig, that is not strange at all. He makes a point of speaking with **everyone**. And let me tell you, Inspector, there are many men, here in Mayo today, that are alive and well thanks to Father Barry Glen Dennagher. He saved them from self-destruction when they were fighting rejection from the 'good people' of the county. He infuses them with a sense of self-worth. And he shows them how to live fulfilling lives within a hostile society. Now, if you are looking for the saviour of the gays, Glen Dennagher is your man. But if you are looking for someone who would harm a gay, then it certainly is **not** Father Barry Glen Dennagher." Fergal has exhausted his voice. He attempts to drink from his cup, only to realise that it is empty. He pours water into his cup from the tap at the sink. He swallows a mouthful of water and continues to speak. "So why don't you guards concentrate on those who wish to harm us rather than on those who protect us?"

"Father Glen Dennagher speaks to **everyone** here? Did that include Liam Tunnery and Bobby Fegan."

"Yes, it did. Now you know; now you can leave."

Murf nods to O'Reilly. They both walk out through the kitchen doorway to the storeroom. The two Maggies resume their tasks. Fergal sits down at the kitchen table and rubs the heels of his hands on his forehead. Murf and O'Reilly exit the building. Murf checks the envelope he is carrying to ensure that he has retrieved the photographs. Satisfied, he places the envelope into the evidence box in the boot, and he folds and places the tweed jacket alongside. Inside his head, he hears the voice of Danny the Divil echoing ominously – 'Love and hate are two sides of the same coin. Deep down, there's no differ. Love or hate – there's no differ 'atween the two.' Murf considers 'love' and 'hate'. And the strongest emotion is love when it has soured.

They drive back to Killbawn in silence, each pondering on the significance of what they learned at An Chúilfhionn Private Club at Islandeady Lough.

CHAPTER TWENTY-ONE

THE MISSING MOTIVE

County Mayo, Ireland
Saturday night 31 August 1946

It is 8:50pm when Murf reaches the Killbawn Garda Station. Garda O'Reilly has fallen asleep in the passenger seat. When the car lurches and slows from the change in gears, O'Reilly wakens. Perceiving that he is home – almost home – he readies himself to leave. "Murf, it has been a tiring day. So, will I see you tomorrow when we pick up the case again?"

"Tomorrow? O'Reilly, on tomorrow morning, get Gildea to assist with the ushering at St Bawn's – to fill in for me."

"What? You are so tired that you are going to skip Mass tomorrow morning? Lord, Murf, you've no stamina…"

"Don't be cheeky, O'Reilly. I'm working the case. I'm working on it for a few more hours tonight, and I will be up and about early tomorrow. I need to concentrate on the case and see where it leads me – even if it leads me out of Killbawn." Murf brings the car to a complete halt. "Now, get out, O'Reilly. I will see you sometime tomorrow."

"So, you're working late? That means you won't be driving me home."

"O'Reilly, you're an athlete. I'm sure you can make it across town on shank's mare."

Moments later, Murf enters the station. Garda Eddie Caldwell is the officer on duty that night. Caldwell is surprised to see him. "Inspector Murphy? And what is it you'll be doing here at this hour?"

"Hello, Caldwell. I need to sort out my notes from

today's information. I'll be here for a couple of hours." Murf proceeds up the stairs and into his office. To a casual observer, Murf's office looks like a mess – lopsided pages are stuck to one wall; files and papers are piled upon the chairs; the desk has a clear area in the centre but is otherwise cluttered, and there are a few random pages on the floor. To Murf, this is in perfect order according to priority and relevance. He places the stiff envelope containing the three evidence photographs on the clear area of his desk. Then, while standing, Murf reads the documents on his desk. At intervals, he makes notations in pencil on the investigation wall. According to relevance, he writes in black, blue or red pencil. When he is satisfied with each phase of his work, he lightly scores each paper diagonally using a soft HB pencil. Then he carefully places the papers into appropriate folders. As he works through his papers in this manner, he clears a larger area on his desk, and he even manages to free his chair of clutter. With his chair thus clear, he sits on it and continues to work at his desk. He reads every document and paper in his office. He frequently interrupts his reading to make additional notes in his desk blotter and to make notations on the wall.

At 11:00pm Murf has rearranged the order of his papers – those on his desk, in his files and on his investigation wall. He makes one final adjustment to the strings on the wall and he stands back to view the picture. He sits on the edge of his desk with his feet firmly placed on the ground and twirls his pencils through his fingers. He is satisfied that a clear picture is emerging. But the clarity of the picture also reveals that an important element is missing – motive. If Murf is unable to establish motive, he does not have a solid case against anyone. Means and opportunity sans motive present an inconclusive and weak case. He speculates on all possible circumstances. If the three murders are **not** related, and if he were to approach them as three unrelated cases, he would be able to finger Marvin as a possible suspect in the Ludwig murder. Murf curses inwardly. The common factors shared by all three murders cannot be coincidental – Murf does not believe in coincidences. Therefore, the three murders **are** related, and Marvin could not possibly have any connection to two of them. That leaves no one person with sufficient motive to murder all three victims. Yet, the strongest connection common to all murders is Father Barry Glen Dennagher. Either Glen Dennagher has a motive that Murf has not yet discovered, or – he sighs – he must widen his investigation to other possible suspects. Fatigued, Murf walks to the other side of the desk and sits heavily in his chair. He leans on the desk and plays the information forward and backwards as if the investigation wall were a moving picture. Fatigued, he falls to sleep.

The phone rings. At first, Murf is unsure of where he is. Then, within a second or two, he is fully alert. He lifts his phone. Caldwell speaks to him from the front desk. "Inspector Murphy, there is a telephone call for you. Do you wish to take it?"

"What time is it, Eddie?"

"It's a quarter to twelve."

"Did the caller identify himself/herself?"

"No, Inspector. He says that you told him that he could contact you anonymously."

Someone is trying to contact Murf at this hour? It must be someone from An Chúilfhionn Private club; if so, Murf is eager to take the call. "Very well, Eddie. Put the call through." Murf hears the click of the call connecting. "This is Inspector Murphy. To whom am I speaking?"

"J." A soft male voice.

"Jay? So, Jay, why are you calling?"

"Not 'Jay' – just the letter 'J'. Do you know the photograph with Liam Tunnery and five others? You passed it around in the club today. On the back – you must have noticed the writing – J, L, P, N, T, B.? Well, I'm 'J'."

Murf is now on high alert. The desire to sleep is banished. "J, what have you to tell me? Is it relevant to Liam Tunnery?"

"Yes. I don't know if it will be of any help or not. But, Liam Tunnery was a nice lad – a good lad. If I am able to do something that will help you find the… find the…"

Murf waits. J stops speaking. But Murf hears him breathing. "Is it possible that we could we meet, J?"

"Yes."

"It is almost twelve midnight. Where are you now?"

"I am an hour and a half away from Killbawn. I could meet you tomorrow."

"Tomorrow is Sunday."

"I know. I'm free on Sundays."

"What time would suit you to come here? Or would you prefer to meet somewhere other than at the garda station?"

"Eight o'clock tomorrow morning, at the Famine Field by the two-mile stone. I'll park the car off the road, well out of sight. 'Click'. The line disconnects before Murf is able to respond.

Sunday 01 September 1946. Murf awakens at 6:00am. Or, more correctly, Murf checks the time on his bedroom clock and sees that it is 6:00am. He did not sleep much during the night. He tossed and turned the entire five hours. He decides that, since he is fully awake, he may as well arise for the day. Murf lives in a semi-detached cottage in Drumharriff, just outside the town of Killbawn. 'Just outside' means that the town water system stops short of his cottage… by fifty yards. Murf has been negligent in maintaining his household supply of water. He realises that there is no water in the enamelled bucket in his kitchen. He lifts a metal basin from the sink and takes it out to the rain barrel and obtains soft water for washing. The water is cold and, not having lit a fire, Murf accepts the water as is. He conducts a standing-up sponge-bath ritual. Later, having shaved, he is undecided whether he should don his 'Sunday clothes' or his usual 'plainclothes'. He opts for a compromise – his usual clothes, except for an added tie with his shirt and a navy-blue blazer instead of his rough gabardine jacket. He dresses. Then he walks to the pump, fifty yards away, and fills two enamelled buckets with drinking water. The early-morning air is damp with mist. Perhaps the sun will come out later and evaporate it. Murf returns to the cottage and, since he is not observing the ritual fast for Communion, he intends to prepare breakfast. In his kitchen, Murf discovers that he has no food in the larder. Even the tea caddy is empty and the milk in the jug has turned thick and sour. It is 7:00am. It is too early to knock and wake up Suey McBride next door and avail of her larder. And it is Sunday, a day when shops are closed. Murf sighs in resignation. He must forego breakfast. Later, he will go to Quinn's on Water Street and obtain some essential groceries – Quinn, being a newsagent, operates the only shop permitted to open for a half-day on a Sunday in Killbawn.

Murf sets off to meet J at the Famine Field. As he drives through Killbawn, Murf remembers the comforting teapot in the garda station. He detours to the station, within which he avails of Fox's supply of tea and brews a potful of the welcoming liquid. Ten minutes later, Murf resumes his journey to the Famine Field, his mug of hot tea lodged precariously between his thighs. He checks his watch. It is 7:25am, much too early to expect J to be at the location. He rounds the corner at the two-mile stone, taking care not to upset the steaming mug of tea. He proceeds into Delahunty's farmyard. Ever since the county council started surveying the

Famine Field, Delahunty is quite familiar with the presence of cars in his yard. Furthermore, his yard is so immense that cars parked closest to the Famine Field are unobservable from his farmhouse. Murf parks his car, turns off the engine, and sips his hot tea. His windows fog up very quickly so he opens the side window. The dank morning air of the estuary drifts lazily into the car. The smell of wet seaweed is an unwelcome accompaniment to tea, so Murf shuts the window.

8:00am. Murf steps out of his car. There is no sign of any other car, or of any other person within his range of vision. Perhaps J changed his mind and did not arrive. Murf walks over the spine of the dolmen hill in the direction of the bend at the two-mile stone. The fog is thick on the coastal side of the hill, so heavy that it beads on Murf's clothes and trickles down to drip onto the ground. He continues walking through the field, past the grazing cattle and down the slippery hillside. The wet grass saturates his trousers up to his knees. Truly, these conditions would discourage a person from visiting the Famine Field. So is J here? Or is he likely to arrive at all? Then Murf sees a motionless figure standing next to the excavated pit. He approaches silently in order to observe him undetected. The figure is facing the road and has his back to Murf. This must be J. He is dressed in a perfectly-fitted light-tan trench coat. It is fully fastened and he has the collar turned up against the penetrating damp fog. He sports a fashionable, and expensive, dark-tan Bankside Elite Fedora on his head. The tilt of the hat conveys self-confidence. Protruding from beneath the bottom of the trench coat, Murf perceives his trousers. The trouser legs are pressed to a razor-sharp crease and the turn-ups rest gently, without wrinkling, against the upper-facings of his shoes. The trouser material is a fine weave of worsted wool of the same colour and tone as the fedora. The shoes are light-tan leather brogues, highly polished except for the area now coated in wet mud from the dolmen moraine. From the absence of moisture on his lower legs, Murf determines that J could not have walked through the moist grass of the hillside meadow. And considering the neat crease on the trousers, Murf deduces that the material is water-repellant, or, at the very least, Mayo-fog-resistant. Murf reasons that J must have accessed the Famine Field directly from the road thus avoiding the water-laden grass. Murf cannot help but admire the well-tailored person standing motionless at the edge of the excavated trench. He has never seen a man this well-dressed in Killbawn, except in magazines. One could imagine that this is a model thrust down here for a fashion shoot – except that the shoes are uncharacteristically muddied.

J speaks but otherwise remains still. "Good morning, Inspector. You realise that your boots squelch on the moist earth." J's astuteness surprises Murf. Murf tries to identify the accent of the voice. Before Murf is able to respond, J continues to speak. "Do you mind if I smoke, Inspector?" Murf is again surprised – J actually asks permission to smoke.

This time Murf speaks. "Good morning, J. And of course you may smoke." Murf approaches closer and stands facing J's profile. J continues to look straight ahead but, doubtless, he is observing Murf in his peripheral vision. J slides his right hand inside the closed breast flap of his coat and withdraws a silver cigarette case from the breast pocket within. He snaps open the case and tilts it in Murf's direction – an invitation to him of avail of one of the cigarettes lining the interior of the case. There are two rows of cigarettes – one on each side of the opened case. Murf perceives that one row is 'Sweet Afton'; the other row is 'Helmar Turkish'. Murf declines the offer.

J's free hand hovers over a Helmar and then selects a Sweet Afton. "Sweet Afton." J utters the name apologetically. "It is Irish, and it is stronger than Helmar. Helmar is still difficult to obtain. Anyways, Helmar is more fitting for after dinner." Murf is still unable to place the accent. J speaks delicately and precisely. The 's' and 'r' are rendered with a faint lisp. J snaps shut the cigarette case and he replaces it within his inner pocket. In the same movement, he withdraws a silver lighter and applies a flame to the Sweet Afton. He replaces the lighter back into the inner pocket and blows a stream of smoke against the drift of moist fog that is invading his face. This action does nothing to deter the fog's stubborn approach. It continues to drift unrelentingly from the estuary to the dolmen and it coats the two men in its moist malodorous breath. So far, J has not altered his gaze. Again, he speaks. "I was present at 'An Chúilfhionn' yesterday afternoon, you know. You circulated pictures of the three victims. It got me to thinking and…" He hesitates, unsure of how to finish his remark. He draws on his cigarette and exhales slowly, watching the smoke combine with the fog until fog and smoke are indistinguishable from each other. He resumes speaking. "So, this is where you found Liam Tunnery?"

"Yes. And two others."

"Would it be possible to see him – Liam Tunnery, I mean?"

"Liam's body will be delivered to the family tomorrow for a Requiem Mass in St Bawn's Church and burial thereafter in Killbawn Abbey. The coffin is closed, J. Sadly, there are no recognisable features to his body. When we recovered it, there were only skeletal remains. We identified Liam by the articles of clothing that were intact and present with the remains – belt, buttons, shoes…"

"Ah, yes, Liam's shoes. He was referred to as 'the Dandy'. Did you know that?"

They are silent for a moment. Murf asks, "J, are you from around here?"

"From Killbawn? No. From Mayo? Yes." Murf is still unable to place the accent. Surely this is not a Mayo manner of speech. Neither is J's attire from a Mayo wardrobe. J continues to smoke. He holds the cigarette delicately by the tips of his fingers, and he holds it aloft to view the glowing tip, rotating it slowly before his face. He speaks again. "I'm from… well, you would not recognise the name of the townland. Many would regard it as a 'bog hole'," a drag on the cigarette. And while holding his cigarette close to his lips, he turns his head towards Murf. Murf is taken by his unusual mannerism. The cigarette is still poised where J's mouth had been before turning his head; it is now poised at his cheek. J continues, "and some refer to it rather coarsely as an 'arse hole' – with pointed emphasis."

Murf bites his lip to stifle a smile. J has rendered the word 'arse' so delicately that it could be taken as an encomium. The 'a' is rendered as 'aw' rather than as 'ah', and the 'r' is almost imperceptible. Murf asks, "And do you work locally in Mayo?"

"Sometimes. I am a representative. I travel."

"I see." Actually, Murf does not 'see'. He remains puzzled by J. "So tell me about Liam Tunnery, J."

"I first met Liam in September 1942. I was in Irwin's menswear shop in Castlebar at the time. Liam came in and enquired about clothing that would fully reflect his personality. He had a magazine in his hand and he pointed to some film actors depicted in the fashion section. They were all dressed in some tasteless and hideous Hollywood overkill. I looked at this young man, some two to three years younger than I. He was dressed in rough clothes, clearly not tailored. But nevertheless, he displayed a bohemian flair in the manner in which he carried his apparel. I was mindful of how I must have looked three years earlier. I approached Liam; I took the magazine from his hands and I ripped the pages into shreds. I told him that his personality is uniquely his and that he deserves better than American muck. I then referred him to a tailor in Cleary's of Sligo – someone who understands the quintessence of exuberant youth and how best to express it with appropriate apparel. I gave Liam my card, on which I wrote the name of the recommended tailor in Cleary's. Liam went off happily with this information."

"To Cleary's in Sligo?"

"Yes. I later learned that he went through with the visit to the tailor. The tailor is 'B' in the photograph."

"So 'B' is from Sligo?"

"No. 'B' is from west Mayo. He works in Sligo. He frequently returns home – it is only about an hour's drive."

"And after that? Did you have any subsequent association with Liam Tunnery?"

"Yes. About a month later, Liam telephoned me – I had given him my business card when I first encountered him in Castlebar – to thank me for steering him to 'B' at Cleary's."

J continues to relate his account to Murf. At intervals, he turns his face to access his cigarette while maintaining his raised hand immobile. Thus, he continues to smoke – moving his head to access the cigarette in preference to bringing the cigarette to his mouth. "I did not hear from Liam or gain further knowledge of him until St Patrick's Day 1943. 'B' was home for the holiday and he arranged to gather together a few friends for a celebration. We met at 'The Hovel' in Westport. Liam arrived with one of the lads – 'N' – and we – all six of us – sat at a table. We ordered drinks and settled into a relaxed mood to enjoy the céili music and the fiddlers. Liam was upset due to his father having smacked him on the head earlier that day – 'to knock that nonsense about England' out of his head. I had 'B' obtain a Jameson's Crested Ten for Liam. Liam drank the whiskey – a bit too swiftly, I would say – and he mellowed. After that, Liam turned his attention to the music, tapping his toe to the rhythm. All went well until the room got overly crowded. That is when some drunken louts objected to the group of 'freezing fags' taking up space – space that would be better occupied by 'real men'." J pauses to face his smouldering cigarette. He turns his wrist so that the burning tip faces him. He blows off the ash and he slowly rotates the cigarette as if concentrating on the progress of the smouldering spark. "Inspector, you understand that the drunken louts did not use the word 'freezing' but an odious synonym, aptly appropriate to the delivery of their thinly-veiled threat." J considers the progress of the smouldering spark and determines that it is time to discard the cigarette. He flicks it in the air, and both men watch it arc over the fence and land in a puddle on the roadway.

Murf waits for J to continue his narrative. J places both his hands behind his back, standing at ease. He resumes speaking. "Rather than cause a scene – gays are **always** the 'cause' of a disturbance that involves them – I suggested that we leave 'The Hovel' and go elsewhere, to where we would not be rejected. So, I drove us – all six of us – to 'An Chúilfhionn'."

"I see. All six in one car?"

"I travel in a big car." J says this soberly as if one would expect him to travel in nothing else.

"So, all six of you went to 'An Chúilfhionn' on the evening of St Patrick's Day. And you are members of the private club?

"Not quite, Inspector. Of the six, only 'B' and I are members."

"And the policy is to admit members only, plus one guest per member?"

"Precisely."

"So how did you expect to gain admittance? Surely, you were aware of the rule?"

"I had hoped to enlist the assistance of Father Barry Glen Dennagher. He and a fellow member could be enlisted to gain us admittance – four members for four guests. At the club, I enquired if he were present inside. Unfortunately, Father Glen Dennagher was not present in the club that night, so we aborted our plan to gain entry and left. We returned to Westport where we located our parked cars. It was late by then and the following day was a work-day so we dispersed back to our respective abodes."

"J, you expected Father Barry Glen Dennagher at the club that night?"

"Yes. Father Glen Dennagher is a member and a frequent visitor at the club. I did not really 'expect' him to be there that night. I did not expect him to be absent. There is a difference."

"I see. And what else of Liam Tunnery?"

"I did not hear from Liam Tunnery, or even hear any news about Liam Tunnery, until he surprised me by arriving unexpectedly at the club six weeks later in the company of Fergal the barman, now the club manager."

"So what transpired on that occasion?"

"Fergal was busily engaged with his tasks, so I introduced Liam to Father Glen Dennagher – Father Glen Dennagher was there **that** evening. I informed Father Glen Dennagher of the conflict between Liam and his father. And I surmised from Liam's demeanour that the conflict remained unresolved. As it turned out, I was correct. The relationship had become so strained that Liam was considering drastic steps. At that point, I left Liam in the capable hands of Father Glen Dennagher, a gifted and experienced counsellor in matters such as this."

"And then?"

"And then nothing. That was all. It was Tuesday night of Easter Week. I had appointments early on the next day, so I called it a night and departed the club."

"I see. But what about Liam Tunnery?"

"The last I saw of Liam Tunnery, he was sitting with Father Glen Dennagher at a quiet corner table. They appeared to be in intense, but hushed, conversation. But that is not unusual. Father Glen Dennagher is devoted to helping troubled youths – young men like Liam Tunnery who are confused about their sexuality and their gender identity. What is worthy of note, Inspector, is the confrontation which occurred earlier in Westport. I am of the opinion that those who threatened us at 'The Hovel' on St Patrick's Day are the most likely offenders responsible for Liam's demise. The proprietor of 'The Hovel' should be able to identify the belligerent louts. They made quite a scene that night."

"I understand, J."

"I hope this discourse has been of some help to you, Inspector. And if there is nothing further…"

"That's all for now, J. But I may need to contact you later."

"Indeed. I'm confident that you, a proficient detective, will have no difficulty in locating me. If there is a pressing need, you could pin a note to the message-board at the club. Many members exchange personal messages at the club in this manner. Communication is prompt and confidentiality is assured."

"Fine. Oh, J, I don't see your car…"

"It is hidden from view close by, near the old workhouse. Good-day, Inspector."

Murf leaves. Before he disappears from sight over the spine of the ridge, Murf glances back. He sees J still standing in the moist fog at the edge of the excavated pit in the Famine Field.

Back in his car, Murf writes an account into his notebook. J's information is valuable, and Murf ensures that he records it accurately while it is still fresh in his mind. He resolves to follow up on 'the drunken louts' in Westport. Rowdy behaviour in a pub is not unusual. In itself, it has no bearing on the case. Nevertheless, it requires investigation as it may introduce a new element in the case. To be thorough, anyone who had an adverse interaction with Liam Tunnery warrants investigation. Murf shuts his notebook and places it back in his pocket. He decides on his next course of inquiry. He starts the engine and drives back to Killbawn. He is now more anxious than ever to get an understanding of Barry Glen Dennagher. And so his next stop is a visit to St Bawn's Church.

9:15am. Murf arrives at St Bawn's. Today is Sunday. Murf's attention is so fixed on the information he obtained from J that it had slipped his mind. Nine o'clock Mass is in progress. A few cars are parked kerbside and a number of bicycles are secured to the bicycle rack at the gable-end. Murf ascends the steps to the church. Danny the Divil is standing in the doorway of the porch, venturing no further than the threshold of the narthex. The Divil turns around at the sound of approaching footsteps.

"Guard Murphy? You are late for the nine o'clock Mass. Or are you early for the eleven o'clock one? Sure isn't that the one you go to anyways?"

"Hello, Danny." Murf is circumspect about the purpose of his visit to the church at an unusual time. But the Divil is inquisitive.

The Divil descends the step of the threshold so as to stand face-to-face with Murf. "Lord, Guard Murphy, you're not going into St Bawn's looking like that."

Murf looks at the Divil. The Divil is dressed in his usual suit and tie – a suit that is shiny and oily from wear and abuse, and a tie that has not been unknotted in years. On this occasion, the Divil is more properly dressed than Murf. Murf glances down at his own clothes. His trousers are still soaked from walking through the wet grass of the dolmen ridge and his boots have accumulated a thick ring of moraine mud.

The Divil attempts to pry information from Murf. "I see you've been to the Famine Field. So you're working the case, are you? And it takes you to St Bawn's. Well, that's interesting."

Murf is reluctant to enter the building. He strains to hear the Mass in an attempt to identify the celebrant.

The Divil smiles at Murf. "Guard Murphy, if you are cocking your ear to hear who's saying Mass, well, it's the canon. And if you're here to see the canon, you'll have to wait 'til Mass is done." The Divil sits down on the top step and fishes a small bottle of whiskey out of his pocket. He takes a quick swig and looks up at Murf. "Working the case on a Sunday, and waiting to speak with the canon? That's very interesting."

Murf knows that it is difficult to shake off the Divil when he is burning with curiosity. Being averse to entering the church with muddy boots, and choosing to deflect the Divil's curiosity, Murf changes the subject. He attempts to distract the Divil onto a different subject. "So, Danny, you are a churchgoer I see."

"Oh, I am, to be sure. But I only **hear** Mass; I never **see** Mass. I always stay out here by the door. I don't suppose I'd bother to come at all if it weren't for having to drive the doctor here." He takes another swig of whiskey. "She insists on being dropped off at the kerb there and picked up again. I mean, she only has to walk a short distance, but she is big on appearances and all that sort of thing."

Murf smiles. The doctor is 'big on appearances' yet she engages the town inebriate as her trusted driver. Now that the Divil is off the subject of the police investigation, Murf sits down on the lower step and assembles his thoughts.

Thereupon he realises that the step is damp, but what is a bit more moisture on his already-damp clothes? A minute later, the Divil, still sitting on the upper step, appears to have fallen asleep, lulled by the rising and falling tones of the Latin Mass emanating from the nave interior of the church. Murf looks over at him and sees him sitting with his chin resting on his chest. Murf removes the stiff envelope from his inside pocket. He checks that the contents remained dry. He is satisfied that they have suffered no ill-effects from the morning's visit to the Famine Field. He peers at the photograph of Liam Tunnery and his five companions. He looks more intently at the face of J, trying to determine if he has ever seen him previously.

"What do you have there, Guard Murphy. A photy, is it? And who is it a photy of at all, at all?" The Divil has awoken and his curiosity is re-ignited.

Murf is about to place the photograph back into its protective envelope to conceal it from the Divil's prying eyes, but he hesitates. There is nothing to lose by showing it to the Divil. "It has to do with the investigation. Do you know any of these men in the picture, Danny?"

The Divil shifts his position from the upper step to the lower step and sits close to Murf. Murf leans away from the mixture of smells – whiskey and car-grease, and… God only knows what. The Divil peers at the photograph and comments. "That's the 'Dandy-boy' there, so it is. Young Tunnery, you know. The one what was dug out of the Famine Field. And that one on the end is… I can't mind his name. But the doctor should know. I seen him come to the dispensary once." The Divil indicates to J and then scans the others "They're not from around here, that lot. So who are they all, Guard Murphy?"

"Companions of the deceased Liam Tunnery, that's who they are."

After a few more minutes of idle banter in which Murf continues to deflect the Divil's probing questions, Murf hears the sounds of people moving. Mass is over. He stands well out of the way as the congregation departs the church until he spots Doctor McBratt. He engages the doctor long enough to show her the picture of Liam Tunnery and companions. Sure enough, she identifies Jonathon Kirby, a commercial traveller who represents Blascor, a pharmaceutical manufacturer and supplier of medical equipment. Jonathon's territory is all Ireland. "He is highly respected, particularly by the veterinarian profession and by the horse-breeding community of the Golden Vale. This picture," she points out, "must be from a few years ago. Jonathon has matured since then and he no longer sports a boyish hairstyle. But, that is a picture of Jonathon Kirby without a doubt." She scans the photograph closely. "One other in the photograph bears a family resemblance to the Tunnery family in Tubberbawn." She points to Liam Tunnery's picture. "Isn't this the picture of the deceased Tunnery boy that you received from Mrs Tunnery on Friday; the very photograph you were so reticent to discuss with me back then when I asked you about it? Hmm, the others in the photograph are all strangers to me." Murf thanks her for the information. Now he knows the identity of 'J'. And he knows how and where to contact him, if necessary.

Murf turns next to the pressing reason he is at St Bawn's. He walks around to the parochial house beside the church. He is familiar with the house, so he walks to the back door and knocks to gain admittance. Mrs Friel, the housekeeper, opens the door. She recognises Murf and admits him. She orders him to remove his muddy boots so as not to soil her clean floor. She rolls her eyes and directs him into the kitchen to stand by the range to dry out. She is busy. And Canon MacMorrow has another Mass to celebrate at

11:00am. Mrs Friel insists that Murf remains in the kitchen until he has dried out. Consequently, Murf is obliged to wait until the conclusion of 11:00am Mass in order to meet with the canon. He is annoyed and exhausted after a sleepless night followed by a wet encounter in the Famine Field. He is disappointed that Mrs Friel has not provided him with as much as a cup of hot tea.

At 12:15pm, Canon MacMorrow has concluded the 11:00am Mass in St Bawn's, and Father MacNamara has returned from celebrating Masses at the two chapels-of-ease. Both clerics observe the fasting rule – no food or drink, including water, from midnight until the conclusion of Mass. Mrs Friel's primary task at this point is to serve breakfast to the two hungry clerics in the dining room.

Murf is still drying out in the kitchen. He attempts to state the purpose of his visit. He speaks to Mrs Friel as she appears and disappears between the kitchen and the dining room. "Mrs Friel, I'm here to speak with the canon! Mrs Friel!" he shouts after her, "Tell Canon MacMorrow that I wish to speak with him."

Mrs Friel re-enters the kitchen. "Are you dry yet, Guard Murphy? Lord Almighty, what have you been up to, comin' in all wet and muddy like this. Sit ye down at the table. The canon knows you're here." While she is thus speaking, Mrs Friel places a plate in front of Murf and piles a load of fried sausages and rashers of bacon onto it. "And eat up! You look like something the cat dragged in. And you have big black rings under your eyes. And one of your socks is inside-out. Lord Almighty, are you not able to look after yourself?" She slaps him on the back of his head, disturbing his hair. Murf realises that he has not eaten since Saturday afternoon; the aroma of the food arouses his appetite and he attacks the food with gusto. Mrs Friel is accurate in her assessment of Murf. He has not slept properly in two nights and he has not eaten a square meal in two days.

Murf is finishing his fried bread, liberally saturated with ample bacon fat, when he is aware that Canon MacMorrow is standing at the kitchen door observing him. Canon MacMorrow declines to enter the kitchen – years of conditioning to respect Mrs Friel's domain. He addresses Murf. "Murf, you want to see me? Come into the dining room when you are finished here. I'll be in there, having a cup of tea and a biscuit."

Some minutes later, Murf is sitting at the dining-room table with Canon MacMorrow. Father MacNamara withdraws to the sitting room to listen to the GAA football game on the radio. Murf comes straight to the point. "Canon, what all do you know about Father Barry Glen Dennagher?"

"Murf, are you trying to weasel priests' gossip out of me? Or is this part of your murder investigation?"

"I am attempting to put into context whatever relationship Father Glen Dennagher may have had with the three murder victims. It could shed light on the victims' lives and on their acquaintances and thus widen the field of potential witnesses. So, tell me, what exactly does Glen Dennagher do? And why would he have had any relationship with any of the victims? Who exactly is Father Barry Glen Dennagher?"

Canon MacMorrow frowns in concentration. "I don't know much about him. He comes from Sligo, as far as I know. Do you know who would be able to fill you in on Father Glen Dennagher? Bishop Byrne, that's who." Canon MacMorrow reads the expression on Murf's face. This is not the answer Murf was hoping for. The canon continues. "Ah, you have met Bishop Byrne already. And you do not expect old 'Burn-in-hell' to be of any help. But if you want to know what Father Glen Dennagher is about – or, rather, what he is commissioned to do – I'm afraid Bishop Byrne is the only one who can fill you in. Or, why don't you just ask Father Glen Dennagher himself?"

"Oh, be assured, I will be talking to the bishop **and** to Father Glen Dennagher shortly. But first, I need to build a profile of the man – to get sound background knowledge of him."

"'Sound background knowledge', you say? Tell you what – Father Alan Larkin may be able to fill you in."

"Father Alan Larkin? I never heard of him. Is he stationed around here?"

"He is currently in the parish of Kilgefin in Ballagh, in the diocese of Elphin."

"You are referring to Balla in County Mayo?"

"No, I'm referring to the townland of Ballagh, outside Ballyleague in County Roscommon."

"Ballyleague? The Ballyleague at the Shannon? That's over two hours from here."

"So it is. But Father Larkin and Father Glen Dennagher worked together on a book, a historical dissertation on the devastation wrought by the Great Famine. They wrote an account of a forgotten and neglected consequence of the Famine – the bankruptcy of landowners in the Diocese of Elphin. We all know that the poor suffered greatly in the Famine and that many of them died as a result. But the rich land-owners did not come out of the Famine unscathed either. Some of them are still paying interest on the debts they incurred a hundred years ago. And they are forced to… ah, but I am going off on a tangent. Larkin and Glen Dennagher know each other from way back, and they both fancy themselves as historians. If anyone knows Glen Dennagher, it's Larkin."

"Thanks, Canon. Then I'll be off to Ballagh, to the parish of Kilgefin outside Ballyleague."

"Now, hold on there, Murf. This interest you have in

Glen Dennagher. He's not a suspect in your investigation, now is he?"

"He is 'a person of interest'…"

"Boloney of interest. You're investigating Glen Dennagher. Well, boys-a-boys."

"No! No! Canon. He is 'a person of interest'. When I fully investigate the circumstances surrounding the case, Father Glen Dennagher **may** be treated as a suspect. Or, maybe I will discover that he was a manipulated enabler. Or, perhaps I find that he was an unwitting facilitator. Or, and this is a real concern, maybe he is a potential victim who up to now has fortuitously evaded the same dire misfortune as the three deceased."

"Ah, I see your dilemma. His association with the three deceased could place him in either polarised position. Or, perhaps neither."

"Exactly. Hence, I need to pursue the inquiry thoroughly and to consider **all** angles. And don't jump to conclusions, Canon."

"You'll want this wee talk kept confidential, no doubt. But that's all right. So, be off with you, Murf. You have your work cut out."

1:40pm. Murf enters the garda station. He checks for messages. Garda Caldwell tells him that Garda O'Reilly is upstairs. Murf locates O'Reilly viewing the investigation wall in Murf's own office. O'Reilly is in civilian clothes – his 'Sunday best'. Murf addresses him. "O'Reilly, and what are you doing in here today?"

"Sure you said to me yesterday – 'Now, get out, O'Reilly. I will see you sometime tomorrow'. You didn't say when or where, so I popped into your office today on my way home from Mass just to check, you know. So here I am. And Murf, I was reading all the stuff stuck up on your wall. Does that all make sense to you?"

"All my stuff makes sense when viewed in perspective. And since you're here, O'Reilly, you're coming with me to Ballagh in County Roscommon."

"You mean 'Balla in County Mayo'. Balla is in County Mayo, Murf; it's nowhere near Roscommon."

"Not the town of Balla – the townland of Ballagh outside Ballyleague."

"And where is Ballyleague? I can't rightly place it."

"It's across the Shannon from Lanesborough."

"Lanesborough is in County Longford,"

"I know that."

"…beside Lough Ree."

"I know that, too."

"It's halfway across the country."

"No, it's not, O'Reilly. Ballagh is a two-hour drive from here. We leave in half an hour. I'm going home to change into clean clothes. You are going to grab a bite to eat – try Mrs Cannon in the pub around the corner. Now listen to me, O'Reilly, I need to put my thoughts down on paper. So you'll be driving us to Ballagh while I write my notes beside you in the car. I'll see you in half an hour." Murf leaves the station.

O'Reilly punches the air in excitement. He is to drive a Ford 10-HP Prefect, and in plainclothes just like a detective.

Back in his office a short time later, Murf places a telephone call to Ballagh Church. He speaks briefly with Father Larkin to confirm a meeting. And he makes a note of the directions to the location.

2:00pm. Garda O'Reilly, in plainclothes (not approved by the district officer), is driving out of Killbawn. Murf has an open briefcase on his lap. He is already writing and sorting his notes. "O'Reilly," he says, "stop in Ballina to fill up with petrol. I'll tell you the way from there." On the way to Ballagh, they take the N26 from Ballina to Swinford; and the

N5 from Swinford to the fork in the road at the N61; the N61 to Roscommon; then the N63 in the direction of Lanesborough. So far, the signposts have been accurate and they clearly mark their journey. At the small village of Clonadra, Murf tells O'Reilly to turn left. Lough Ree is visible to their right. Murf is attentive to the road from this point on. He spots the first turn left that is not an entrance to a farm. Here, they turn left and there ahead of them is Ballagh National School and Ballagh Church fornenst. The parochial house is beside the church. Except for two farmhouses visible in the distance, they are entirely surrounded by grassy fields.

"O'Reilly, this is Ballagh, County Roscommon."

O'Reilly stops the car and looks around. It is 4:00pm on a Sunday afternoon. The church is quiet; the school is closed. There is no one about, not even a cow is present in any of the fields. "**This** is Ballagh? You must have made a mistake, Murf. There is nothing here – not even a beast."

"No mistake, O'Reilly. Now drive up by the side of the church and park close to the parochial house. We are visiting Father Alan Larkin."

Murf and O'Reilly approach the front door of the house. They are within ten feet when the door is thrust wide open. A jovial priest, standing in the doorway, greets them pleasantly. He is dressed in a typical black suit with a clerical collar, except that his jacket is unbuttoned and reveals a black cardigan worn in place of a waistcoat. This can only be Father Alan Larkin. He shouts down to the two plain-clothed gardaí, "Inspector Murphy, is it? I see that you made it here in good time. I trust my directions were clear for you."

Murf reaches the door. He shakes Father Larkin's outstretched hand. "Father Larkin, I am Inspector Murphy, as you are expecting. And yes, your directions were spot-on. With me is Garda O'Reilly."

Father Larkin eagerly invites them into his parlour.

"Two detectives are visiting me here today? Boys-a-boys. You know that the parishioners here – God bless them – are shy about talking to me. Sure what would we talk about anyways – the weather, the crops, the price of store cattle? And all three are bad news at any time, it would seem. And now two detectives come visiting. This is exciting. You must be working on a very serious case. And you want to ask me something, is it? Well, fire away."

Murf does not enlighten him on the nature of, or seriousness of, his investigation. And Father Larkin expresses no interest. Instead, he is delighted at having someone to talk to about matters other than agriculture. He has no hesitation in speaking about Father Glen Dennagher. He does not inquire as to why Glen Dennagher would be of any interest to a police inquiry. He just keeps talking and talking. Murf steers him to keep focused on Glen Dennagher as he occasionally drifts into statistics about the Famine. It appears that Larkin and Glen Dennagher have known each other since school-days. Their common passion is local history. Throughout the lengthy narrative, O'Reilly attempts to keep pace in notating all that is spoken. After two hours, Father Larkin concludes his lengthy, and sometimes rambling, narrative.

"Father Larkin, I am impressed with your store of knowledge."

"Oh, storing and retrieving data is one of my talents." Father Larkin launches into more statistics on the Famine.

Murf interrupts him. "I see that you know Father Glen Dennagher quite well and for some time…"

"Yes, for twenty-five years or more."

"Impressive. You have known him for twenty-five years?"

"Actually, that's not quite true. I lost touch with him for a few years when he was in England. That was in the thirties.

That was not a happy time for Barry."

"Why is that?"

"Oh, there was a bit of scandal. Well, no. There was **no** scandal. It turned out to be a false accusation and the charges were dropped. That was in Coventry – in 1934, I believe."

"You say that 'charges were dropped'? What kind of scandal was it?"

"Barry never talks about it. All I know is that there was an accusation against him for making advances – sexual advances – to a man. The police determined that the accusation was groundless, so all charges were dropped. The man who made the accusation was later charged with gross indecency – but that did not involve Barry in any way. The whole situation was very disconcerting to Barry. After that, he became a Catholic – a **Roman** Catholic – and returned to Ireland."

"What do you mean – 'he became a Roman Catholic'? Was he not a Catholic priest while in Coventry?"

"Oh, did you not know? Barry was brought up in the Church of Ireland. He entered Holy Orders as a priest in the Anglo-Catholic Church in England. You realise that 'Catholic' in England is not the same as 'Catholic' in Ireland, hence the preferred use of the descriptive qualifier 'Roman' for us Catholics. But with regard to Barry Glen Dennagher, he converted from 'Anglo' to 'Roman'. And he is not the only Anglo-Catholic priest to convert, you know." O'Reilly scribbles frantically to fully record this information.

It is 7:00pm when Murf and O'Reilly commence the journey back to Killbawn. Murf directs O'Reilly to drive so that he can review the interview and place relevance on the newly-acquired information. O'Reilly twice attempts to speak to Murf. "It's Glen Dennagher. You must know that, Murf."

Murf is busy concentrating on reading O'Reilly's notes

and appears to be lost in thought. He makes no response to O'Reilly. They drive in silence and arrive at Killbawn Garda Station at 9:00pm. Murf exits the car mutely without a 'good-night' to O'Reilly. O'Reilly parks the car and rushes after Murf to return the car keys to him. Upon entering the garda station, O'Reilly sees Murf ahead ascending the stairs, so he gives the keys to the night-time duty officer at the front desk. O'Reilly is keen to cease work for the day. He makes no attempt to re-connect with the non-communicative Inspector Murphy. He leaves the station and goes home. Murf, on the other hand, hurries to his office where he immediately lengthens one of the strings on the investigation wall.

CHAPTER TWENTY-TWO

AE FOND KISS AND THEN WE SEVER

Killbawn, County Mayo, Ireland
Monday 02 September 1946

Murf decides to walk to work today. It is a twenty-minute walk from Drumharriff to Killbawn Garda Station. A half-hour has elapsed and Murf has not yet arrived at his destination. He is standing on the pathway that runs along the bank of the river. He reaches down and scoops up a handful of pebbles from the path. He places the pebbles on the river wall. The river is named 'An Abhainn Mhór' or 'The Blackwater'. Either name is appropriate. It is a wide and deep river, and the water is black from the presence of peat. Murf places the pebbles in a row as in an abacus. He mentally checks off points in his mind. When he is satisfied that his thoughts are in order, he casts one of the pebbles into the black swirling water. And so he proceeds with a second pebble. The turbulent water instantly swallows the pebble into its dark depths. After performing this ritual with the fifth pebble, Murf flings the remaining pebbles high in the air. They arc and fall into the black water – plop, plop, plop. Murf slaps his hands together to dislodge the dirt and he walks with hurried purpose to the station. He has reached a decision and he is intent on executing his next move.

He enters the station at 8:40am. A very young garda is at the front counter. "O'Flaherty is it? Sean O'Flaherty?"

"Yes, Inspector, I'm Garda Sean O'Flaherty."

"Find O'Reilly and send him up to my office." Murf proceeds up the stairs before the young garda has formed his reply. In his office, Murf lifts the receiver of his phone and spins the handle. The front desk picks up. "O'Flaherty, put a call through to Coventry City Police. I wish to speak to the head of their Crime Unit – the Assistant Chief Constable Crime or the senior inspector on duty. Put the call through to me when you have connected." Murf turns his attention to the data on the wall. He leans towards the doorway and shouts, "O'Reilly!" A timid Garda O'Flaherty enters his office.

"Inspector Murphy, I tried to tell you that Garda O'Reilly starts at nine o'clock. It's just gone a quarter to nine…"

"All right, then send him up as soon as he arrives – and that means before he puts the kettle on."

"And the morning post came in. Superintendent Fox says that this is for you." O'Flaherty hands him a brown envelope. Murf sees that it is from 'An Roinn Iompar'. The envelope is unsealed. Superintendent Fox would have already opened it and read what is inside. Murf whips out the contents and scrutinises the single sheet. With a quick glance, he sees that it confirms the vehicle tax on car registration number EI 4493. The registered owner is the 'Diocese of Killala'. Father Barry Glen Dennagher's car is actually owned by the diocese. Bishop Byrne, it appears, extends a lot of privilege to his vicar forane.

8:55am. Murf is connected to Coventry City Police. He speaks with Chief Inspector Masterson. Murf requests information on a closed/dropped case – Gross Indecency involving Barry Glen Dennagher circa 1934 – give or take a year. Murf gives the reason – a triple murder here in Mayo in which all the victims were homosexual and all had a connection with Barry Glen Dennagher. Masterson promises to look into the matter and phone back.

9:01am. O'Reilly enters Murf's office. Murf is making adjustments to his wall notes. He addresses O'Reilly while continuing to attend to his task. "O'Reilly, today you go to Castlebar to fetch the photographs from the crime lab."

"Right you be, Inspector. And how do I get to Castlebar?"

"You're a big boy, O'Reilly. Work it out."

"And that's it? Go to Castlebar?"

"Not all, O'Reilly. You want to play detective, right? So, look at the desk there behind me. You see the photograph on it?"

"Yes. I see the one with Liam Tunnery and his mates? What of it?"

"Each subject is identified by a single letter written on the back of the photograph."

O'Reilly lifts the photograph and checks the back. "I know that, Murf. I've seen you examine it."

"O'Reilly, I want you to conduct a background check on 'J' and on 'B'. 'J' is Jonathon Kirby from some 'bog hole' place in Mayo – probably west or north Mayo. He is a commercial traveller representative for Blascor, a pharmaceutical manufacturer and supplier of medical equipment. Any chemist specialising in veterinary supplies would know him. As a local son of Mayo, some of them would know from whence he hails. 'B' is an employee of Cleary's of Sligo, working in menswear."

O'Reilly is scribbling in his pocket diary. "Is this my assignment for the week?"

"O'Reilly, this is your assignment for **today**. If you want to be a detective you'll figure out how to assemble information fast. Use the phone and contact other garda stations for help. You'll be amazed at how well a garda knows his local community – like the way you know the Puckany Johnsons."

At the mention of the 'Puckany Johnsons', O'Reilly breaks the tip of his pencil. Lest Murf notices his surprise, O'Reilly pretends to continue writing. "Righty-oh, Murf. Is that all?"

"One more thing, I need you to contact the Diocese of Killala… No, I'll look after that end, myself. So, O'Reilly, go and get yourself a desk and a phone and hop to it."

O'Reilly leaves the office intent on carrying out his detective duties. Murf calls after him, "O'Reilly!" O'Reilly spins around and re-enters Murf's office. Murf lowers his voice. "Seamus, I'm giving you forewarning. There is a chance that we may make an arrest tomorrow. I am putting the last bits of information on the wall. With what we learn today, this might turn out to be the final dots in my picture. We will meet back here later today, regardless of how late is, and settle on the following day's course of action."

"O'Reilly whispers back, "An arrest? Wow! It's the priest, isn't it? So, you have enough evidence to bring him to justice?"

"Not yet, O'Reilly."

O'Reilly ponders on this for a moment. "You have a plan?"

"A technique. Now let's put together the final pieces." O'Reilly, still puzzled, nods in agreement and departs to execute his tasks.

At 9:50am, Murf receives a telephone call from Inspector Waring of the Coventry City Police. Inspector Waring is the officer who worked the Glen Dennagher case in 1934. Waring relates to Murf a summary of the case:

Barry Glen Dennagher, a newly-ordained priest in the Anglo-Catholic Church was accused by Wilber Brown, a fellow cleric, of having made improper advances of a sexual nature. Glen Dennagher was arrested and charged. Brown subsequently withdrew his complaint. Without Brown's testimony, the case could not be proven, so the Crown had no alternative but to withdraw the charges against Glen Dennagher and release him.

Murf waits a moment. He realises that Inspector

Waring has concluded his account. "That's it? Inspector Waring, is there nothing more?"

"It really was a non-case from the beginning. These cases typically are. There may have been substance to it but, without a participant's testimony, there is usually no other evidence to fall back on. And the complainant, if he is a fellow participant, runs the risk of incurring the same charge, and then both participants are equally charged. Actually, I was pleased that the case was dropped."

"So tell me, the case was dropped, but you were of the opinion that the original complaint had substance? So, off the record, what was your gut feeling about the case?"

"Off the record? It was a lovers' spat. Two homos had a relationship, one broke it off, and the jilted one wanted to strike back. Later, he relented, either because he hoped to reconcile, or he feared that a scandal would drag them down – both of them."

"To your knowledge, did they eventually reconcile – Brown and Glen Dennagher?"

"I really don't know. After his release, Glen Dennagher left Coventry. And that's it, I'm afraid." Murf and Inspector Waring terminate the conversation and hang up.

Murf next contacts Westport Garda Station. He speaks with the station sergeant and relates the account of the incident at 'The Hovel' as described by J (Jonathon Kirby). The sergeant is able to pinpoint the episode in the station's incident book. March 17, St Patrick's Day 1943, is a notable date. On that night, four trouble-makers were picked up and put into lockup for the night. No charges were laid. The same four trouble-makers are known to the gardaí, and the incident of St Patrick's Day 1943 was not out of character for them. A fight erupted in 'The Hovel' between the supporters of the local football team and the visiting Castlebar team. These same ruffians had earlier attempted to engage in a fight with another group that evening, but that group of six youths left before fists started to fly. Murf speaks with the sergeant for some minutes. From the information rendered by the sergeant, Murf concludes that the four ruffians had no particular interest in the six youths, Liam Tunnery and friends, other than to initiate a barroom brawl. Murf eliminates the four ruffians as possible suspects.

Murf focuses his attention on Glen Dennagher. It appears that when Glen Dennagher was in England, he had been in a homosexual relationship and he terminated it. He severed the relationship in keeping with his choice homiletic theme based on Mark 9:43-48 – *'If your hand causes you to stumble, cut it off.'* Murf poses the obvious question. Is this how Father Glen Dennagher deals with his sin – he severs the offending element?

Murf has some more thinking to do. He walks back to the river and he stares at the black eddies swirling in the current. It is past 10:00am. The pubs are open. Murf hears a street-singer plying his skills in Market Square. Murf turns around and leans his back against the river wall and he tilts his ear to catch the melodic sounds. Robbie Burns speaks to him – *'Ae fond kiss, and then we sever. Ae fareweel and then forever!'* Thus, he garners an unexpected clarity.

Murf returns to his office and begins to write with urgent undertaking. He heads the page – 'Ae Fond Kiss, And Then We Sever'. His focus is concentrated on his prime suspect. He compiles a comprehensive profile on Barry Glen Dennagher, drawing upon Father Larkin's account, on Inspector Waring's account, and on the information he himself has acquired.

Bartholomew Philip Glen Dennagher was born on 05 July 1910, in Sligo. Father – John James Dennagher; Mother – Margaret Elizabeth née Glen. Both the Dennagher family and the Glen family objected strongly to the union of J.J. Dennagher to Liz Glen. The Dennagher family business engages in the importation and distribution of fuel, mostly coal. At the time of J.J.'s marriage to Liz, the Dennaghers were a Catholic family of 'comfortable' wealth. The Glen family, on the other hand, had been a small, but prosperous, Protestant land-owning family in County Sligo. During the Great Famine, the Glen family went into debt in attempting to alleviate the suffering of their tenants. Thereafter, the family was obliged to sell off most of their land holdings to pay off their bank loan. In 1910, the Glen family was regarded with respectful esteem notwithstanding their reduced financial status. At the time of the Dennagher-Glen marriage, Liz's father was the dean of the Cathedral of St Mary the Virgin and St John the Baptist (Church of Ireland) in Sligo. Liz's marriage to a Catholic Dennagher was the source of acute embarrassment for Dean Glen.

The pressure of a 'mixed marriage' was very trying on Liz. She bore three children, all boys, the last of which was Barry. When Liz's mother passed away unexpectedly, she attempted to reconcile with her widowed father. She had two siblings – Howard, who disappeared during the Great War while flying his Alcock A.1., and Thomas, who was too young to enlist, and who joined the Irish Guards in 1918. Thomas remained with the Irish Guards and is still in their service to this day. Liz separated from J.J. Dennagher, and she and Barry moved in with Dean Glen. Liz was warmly accepted back into the Glen household and the dean was greatly taken by his grandson, Barry. Previously, the dean had hoped that Howard would follow him into holy orders, now he pinned his hopes on Barry. Thus the path of Barry's young life was directed to this one goal. And Barry fulfilled the Dean's dreams at every turn. He was enrolled in Portora Royal School in Enniskillen where he excelled in academic endeavours and in sports. He later finished his ecclesiastical training in Oxford and he was ordained a priest in the Anglican Church. He was a strong adherent to the ancient traditions of the Church. He gravitated immediately to High Anglicanism and embraced the tradition of 'Anglo-Catholicism', which sought to renew 'catholic' thought and practice within the Church of England.

In Coventry, Dennagher had his first homosexual relationship. Wracked by subsequent guilt, he severed the relationship. Barry Glen Dennagher's 'kiss-and-sever' episode did not go well for him. It drew attention that almost ruined his career. And for as long as he remained in Coventry the risk of discovery was ever present. The homosexual scandal of 1934 shook him severely. He longed to return to Ireland.

At that time, a number of Anglo-Catholics were converting to Roman Catholicism as influenced by the 'Oxford Movement', a group with which Barry was closely associated. In 1938, Barry Glen Dennagher was accepted into the Roman Catholic Church. The Bishop of Killala accepted him as a vicar forane in the diocese. At that time, the bishop was concerned that Catholics were being influenced by foreign anti-Christian life-styles – fascism, communism and immoral practices. The bishop relied on Father Barry's education and experience to steer lapsed Catholics back into the fold – Catholics who had embraced atheistic and hedonistic principles. And there was the added bonus – the trophy of having a priest snatched away from the Anglicans.

Barry Glen Dennagher admires young athletic men and he finds them sexually attractive. And he clearly recognises his own homosexuality. Since returning to Ireland, Barry currently engages in physical activity as a means of strengthening his character and resolve. Mindful of Leviticus chapter 18 verse 22, he disciplines himself to practice the 'three pillars of good health'. He goes to great pains to suppress his sexual desires, and he foregoes any physical expression of the 'sinful abomination'.

From 1938 to 1945, Barry Glen Dennagher experiences three significant breaches in his principled determination. He succumbs to three more 'kiss-and-sever' episodes in his life. Of the many young men he encounters and admires, he connects with three who are amorously receptive to his admiration. The temptations presented by these opportunities break his stoical resolve, and so he engages in homosexual acts of intimacy. As before, he experiences guilt. So as not to repeat the serious error he made in Coventry, Barry ensures that each of these three encounters is quickly and quietly severed and that each is rendered final and untraceable. He severs, and casts away, all which 'causes him to sin'. He slays his lovers and buries them securely in the Famine Field where they lie hidden and forgotten – for a time.

Then in 1946, the Mayo County Council unexpectedly decides to cut a new road through the Famine Field. With the excavation of the site, Barry Glen Dennagher's dead lovers return to exact reparation and justice.

Murf puts down his pencil. This is speculation and conjecture. It is a perfect fit to his sometimes-confusing picture – the dots finally connect. He pins the summary sheet – the one entitled 'Ae Fond Kiss, And Then We Sever' – to the wall next to the sheet entitled 'Barry Glen Dennagher'. This time, he connects all three coloured strings – means, opportunity and motive – linking 'Barry Glen Dennagher' to 'Famine Field Triple-Murder Victims'. He steps back and sits against the edge of his desk. He studies the investigation wall. Murf is satisfied that the picture is finally complete. But completing the picture is a far cry from having sufficient proof to substantiate his case. Notwithstanding the credibility of his speculative summary, he is faced with the formidable task of acquiring and assembling the necessary proof to present a strong case – a case strong enough to make a charge and ultimately render a conviction. And he still needs to confirm two more things – that Glen Dennagher acted alone without an accomplice or enabler and, secondly, he needs to be certain that his net of inquiry is spread sufficiently wide to account for **all** possible suspects. He cautions himself against the mistake of focusing so intently on one suspect that he overlooks other viable suspects. Garda O'Reilly's investigative inquiries should provide the final information. Murf lifts the receiver of his phone and spins the handle. "O'Flaherty, connect me to the Diocese of Killala… actually, to the office of the dean of the cathedral."

At 6:00pm, O'Reilly reports to Murf. He delivers the sets of photographs from Divers. Divers astutely has included extra copies of the requested pictures, plus three copies of the photograph of the six comrades. O'Reilly then renders his reports on 'J' and 'B'.

Jonathon Kirby is from the Lough Greney Bog, about five miles outside Westport. He attended Brackloon National School. He succeeded in achieving a County Council Scholarship that provided him with free secondary-school education. He eventually matriculated for entry into university but, due to limited family funds, he was obliged to take up employment. The gardaí in Westport speak favourably of him. Other than being a bit too 'posh' for west Mayo since becoming employed by Blascor, he is regarded as an exemplary citizen.

'B' is Benedict McCusker. He hails from Pontoon, from a middle-class family. Like his friend Jonathon, Benedict is also regarded as an exemplary citizen, albeit a bit 'artsy-fartsy' for Pontoon – being west of Lough Cullin it is considered 'west Mayo'. He is well suited to his position in men's fashion in Cleary's of Sligo.

Murf examines the quality of the photographs as he listens to O'Reilly's report. He is satisfied with the results – both O'Reilly's information, and the quality of the pictures. He pins one portrait picture of each murder victim on his respective profile sheet on the wall. He says to O'Reilly, "The picture is complete."

"And now we make an arrest and charge Barry Glen Dennagher?"

"Not so fast, O'Reilly. We make an arrest on suspicion of murder. But what you see before you is still insufficient to charge him."

"Why not? You have the complete picture – you just said so."

"We do not have proof. All the evidence we have is circumstantial. Based on this alone, we do not have a strong case – actually, we do not have sufficient evidence to go to trial."

"You've lost me, Murf. If we are unable to obtain the necessary proof, what is the point of making an arrest? Sure will we not have to release him shortly after placing him in custody?"

"O'Reilly, Glen Dennagher does not know the extent of the evidence we have against him. If he believes that we have overwhelming evidence we can disarm his defences. The suspect's Achilles heel is his guilt. It was guilt that drove him to commit the murders, and it is guilt that will ensnare him and deliver him to us."

"Murf, if we bring in Glen Dennagher and he sits mute, he will walk after twelve hours. Are you certain that he will confess?"

"O'Reilly, Father Barry Glen Dennagher is scheduled to celebrate Mass at 8:00am in the cathedral tomorrow. You and I will be in attendance. We leave the station here at 7:15 tomorrow morning. Dress well in uniform; I will be in my 'Sunday best'. And, O'Reilly, brush up on the correct procedure for executing an arrest. Good-night, O'Reilly."

Tuesday 03 September 1946. Inspector Murphy drives his black Ford Prefect 10HP car into the parking area beside St Muredach's Cathedral in Ballina. He brings his car to a halt, at an angle, a few inches from a similar-looking parked car – EI 4493. He and Garda O'Reilly enter the cathedral at 7:55am. They sit in the rear pew close to the main entrance.

The interior of the cathedral is spacious and dark. It is constructed in the traditional cross-shaped form of narthex-nave-transept-apse. Their attention is drawn to the two Mass candles burning on the altar in the sanctuary. The stone floor is cold, even for an early morning in autumn, and there is the ever-present lingering smell of smoke, the scent of burning wax candles, hanging in the still air. Footsteps, even quiet footsteps, echo throughout the spacious interior. Even though there are fifty people in attendance, the large nave appears to be sparsely occupied. The regular attendees sit in their familiar places. The quiet sombre environment is punctuated by a suppressed cough. The echo resounds and fades away.

Father Glen Dennagher, carrying the veiled chalice, enters from the transept side. He approaches the altar steps accompanied by an altar server. The congregation rises. Glen Dennagher frequently celebrates Mass on a Tuesday morning in the cathedral. As is his custom, he scans the interior of the nave and, in one quick glance, he recognises all the familiar faces ensconced in their accustomed places. But this morning, he is surprised to see two additional people in attendance. He distinguishes Murf, with whom he had a recent unpleasant encounter on Thursday 22 August. And standing alongside Murf is a garda in uniform. This does not bode well for him.

Father Glen Dennagher genuflects in front of the altar. He then places the chalice in the centre of the altar. He steps back and removes his black biretta and stands at the foot of the altar. *"In nomine Patris, et Filii, et Spíritus Sancti. Amen."* Thus facing the altar, he has his back to the congregation and he experiences discomfort. He feels two pairs of eyes fixed upon him. He knows that the garda inspector and the uniformed garda are not here for the celebration of Mass. *"Introibo ad altáre Dei."* He compels himself to concentrate on the sacred prayers. He continues. He bows down in penitence and commences *"Confiteor..."* At *"mea culpa"* he beats his breast loudly, followed by a second *"mea culpa"*. He hesitates, and continues after a brief pause, *"mea máxima culpa"*.

Murf nudges O'Reilly and whispers "Guilt."

O'Reilly whispers back "Or fear."

After the Gospel, Father Glen Dennagher gives a short sermon – a sermon is not usually delivered at a low Mass on a Tuesday morning. He recites Mark 9:43-48 – *"If your hand causes you to stumble, cut it off; it is better for you to enter life maimed than to have two hands and to go to hell, to the unquenchable fire. And if your foot causes you to stumble, cut it off; it is better for you to enter life lame than to have two feet and to be thrown into hell. And if your eye causes you to stumble, tear it out; it is better for you to enter the kingdom of God with one eye than to have two eyes and to be thrown into hell, where their worm never dies, and the fire is never quenched."*

O'Reilly whispers a second time to Murf. "Who is this sermon directed at?"

At the conclusion of Mass, O'Reilly inquires of Murf, "So when do we arrest him? Do we follow him into the sacristy?"

"He knows that we are here. He also must suspect the

reason. Remain seated."

"And what if he nips out a back door and skedaddles?"

"And where will he go? If he flits, in an attempt to evade us, that will indicate guilt, and so it will strengthen our case. Anyways, did you notice that I parked my car up against the bumper of EI 4493?"

"That is **his** car? I thought you just parked badly because you were impatient and that you would be moving the car directly after Mass."

"Quiet. Here he comes now."

Father Barry Glen Dennagher, dressed in a black cassock and black biretta, walks slowly up the centre aisle. The altar server extinguishes the candles and hurries off. The young lad would have school classes at nine o'clock. Glen Dennagher reaches the last pew. The cathedral is now empty except for the three men. He addresses Murf and O'Reilly. "Are you gentlemen here for a reason, perhaps to see me?"

Murf responds by alluding to the sermon. "One thing that puzzles me about Mark chapter nine – are we to follow the instructions literally? If so, what if it is your heart that causes you to stumble? What then?" He looks hard at Glen Dennagher.

"Are you implying that my heart…? Are you accusing me of some offence?"

Murf and O'Reilly stand up and exit the pew. They stand in the aisle next to Glen Dennagher. Murf addresses Glen Dennagher. "Is there some place where we may speak – somewhere other than here?"

Glen Dennagher indicates back towards the sanctuary. "Perhaps in the sacristy."

In the sacristy, Glen Dennagher stands facing the two policemen. His face betrays his feeling of trepidation. Murf nods to O'Reilly. O'Reilly understands that Murf requires him to make the arrest. He clears his throat and addresses

Glen Dennagher. "Barry Glen Dennagher, I am arresting you on suspicion of the murder of Liam Tunnery, and on suspicion of the murder of Robert Fegan, and on suspicion of the murder of Edmund Ludwig. You are not obliged to say anything unless you wish to do so, but whatever you say will be taken down in writing and may be given in evidence. You have the right to consult a solicitor; you have the right to notify another person that you are in custody. You will now accompany us to the garda station in Killbawn where you will be presented with a paper detailing the offences in writing; you will be cautioned once more and you will be given the opportunity to exercise your rights."

Glen Dennagher hangs his head but remains standing in silence. After a few moments of quiet immobility, Murf asks him, "Do you understand?"

Glen Dennagher raises his head. "Yes. I understand."

Murf nods to O'Reilly to complete the arrest by placing his hand on the shoulder of the suspect. Glen Dennagher feels the weight of the arresting hand and shuts his eyes in acceptance. O'Reilly advises the suspect, "Consider yourself under arrest. You will now accompany us to the garda station."

Murf looks at the priest and considers his clerical garb inappropriate for custodial attire. "You may wish to change out of your cassock and biretta."

Glen Dennagher looks at his reflection in the full-length mirror in the sacristy. "Yes, I should change. In my office in the pastoral centre…"

Moments later, the trio exit Glen Dennagher's office. Glen Dennagher is now dressed in clerical street-clothes and is characteristically wearing his distinctive brier-proof black-and-white herring-bone tweed jacket. As they leave the pastoral centre, Father McGill inquires of him, "Father Glen

Dennagher, are you leaving?"

He responds in a monosyllable. "Yes."

Father McGill deduces that Glen Dennagher is being taken into custody. He asks, "What about your appointments? And what will I tell people if they inquire?"

"I don't know. I…"

"And what will I tell his lordship?"

"I'll contact the bishop as soon as I am able."

They leave the building – Murf and O'Reilly with Glen Dennagher in custody. Father McGill proceeds to the door and watches them depart in Murf's car. He rushes back inside to report the news to the bishop.

At 9:50am, Barry Glen Dennagher is seated in the interview room of the Killbawn Garda Station. The correct procedures are fulfilled. The suspect has been fingerprinted. He is presented with a detailed written statement of the offence. District Officer Fox introduces himself to the suspect, informing him that he is the garda 'member in charge'; he reminds the suspect of his rights and elicits an acknowledgement of his understanding. The 'member in charge' is to ensure that all procedures and laws regarding the detainee's care and rights are adhered to. Glen Dennagher expresses his desire to remain silent until he speaks with a solicitor. He exercises his right to contact a solicitor and a family friend. Satisfied that all parties are cognisant of the detainee's rights, Fox exits the interview room. Inspector Murphy and Garda O'Reilly are left alone with Glen Dennagher. All three are seated at a table with the suspect facing Murf and O'Reilly.

Murf looks at Glen Dennagher. The suspect appears uncertain. Murf addresses him. "Barry Glen Dennagher, you have indicated that you wish to contact a solicitor and a family friend. Please follow me. You may use the phone in my office."

In Murf's office, Glen Dennagher chooses to speak with the bishop of Killala and have him contact the solicitor. Murf requests the duty officer to place the call. While waiting for the call to go through, Glen Dennagher looks at the assortment of papers pinned to one wall. He distinguishes his own name prominently displayed, and he notices the portrait photographs of the three murder victims. He is puzzled by the apparent haphazard disorder on the wall and the random pencil notes in various colours. And he wonders what purpose is served by coloured strings. Then he puts it into perspective – the wall contains information displayed in sections encircling the centre point. It is like a giant spider-web. By way of explanation, Murf says, "This is our investigation wall. It contains all the evidence relevant to the case. As you can see, it is quite extensive. And it all points to the centre." And at the centre is the sheet entitled 'Ae Fond Kiss and Then We Sever', the sheet that first grabbed the suspect's attention, the sheet that prominently bears the name of Barry Glen Dennagher in large block lettering. Murf steps in front of the wall, blocking the suspect's view.

This episode is part of Murf's strategy. Murf wants to give the suspect plenty to think about. The suspect does not know how much evidence has been accumulated against him. But if this investigation wall is any indication, he fears that there must be a large volume of incriminating evidence.

Murf is playing on the suspect's guilt. Murf is undermining the suspect's hope and he is taxing his conscience and his sense of shame. Already he notices the effect on Glen Dennagher – the moist eyes, slumping shoulders, and head hung down to avoid making eye contact. Murf understands that a suspect's perception of the strength of police evidence is one of the most important factors influencing his decision to confess.

The phone rings. Murf picks it up and checks with the front desk. He hands the receiver to Glen Dennagher. "You are connected to the Diocese of Killala Pastoral Office."

Glen Dennagher requests to speak with the bishop. Almost immediately, he hangs up. He turns to Murf and says, "His Lordship is already on his way here. He left twenty minutes ago. He is coming with Jacob Feeney of Feeney & Feeney."

"Very well. Let's return to the interview room. We have a few minutes before the bishop and the solicitor arrive. We'll get you a cup of tea while we wait." Murf grabs a bulky folder off his desk and they troop back to the interview room.

Back in the interview room, Murf and O'Reilly and the suspect resume their seats. Murf speaks. "While we wait, I'll just sort my files into order." Murf 'sorts' his files. He takes out the photograph of Liam Tunnery and friends. He turns it over and reads the back. He then 'files it in order' within the folder. Glen Dennagher observes Murf's 'sorting'. He is getting more anxious and he is filled with foreboding. Glen Dennagher begins tapping his heel on the ground, he jerks his head a few times left and right and he resumes a downward gaze with his chin on his chest. His upper lip is beginning to perspire. This bothers him; he repeatedly rubs his forefinger across his upper lip. Murf continues to quietly 'sort' his papers. Garda Sean O'Flaherty enters the room. He places a full water jug on the table along with four glasses. He leaves and re-enters with a tray of tea – a steaming-hot teapot, four cups and milk and sugar. Murf notices that the tea set is not comprised of the usual bulky ceramic mugs, but that O'Flaherty has presented them with delicate china cups and saucers and silver spoons. This can only be Fox's touch. And it fits in perfectly with Murf's strategy – everything is orderly and civilised. The only thing out of place is the aberration of the offence. It is 10:22am.

At 10:28am the bishop of Killala, Patrick Byrne, and Jacob Feeney of Feeney & Feeney are admitted into the interview room. The bishop immediately asks, "So what's this all about? Can somebody tell me, eh?"

O'Reilly surrenders his chair to the bishop. The bishop ignores him and remains standing. Murf, who has remained seated, looks up at the bishop and says, "I understand that you are a friend of the suspect and that your presence here is at his request and approval." He looks over at Glen Dennagher, who gives a nod of assent. Murf continues, "And this is the solicitor requested by the suspect?" Again, Glen Dennagher gives a nod of agreement.

The solicitor introduces himself. My name is Jacob Feeney. I am here as the solicitor for the accused."

Murf corrects him. "Barry Glen Dennagher is a suspect; he has not been charged in a crime." Murf continues for the benefit of the visitors. "I direct your attention to the sheet of paper on the table. It details the offences for which Barry Glen Dennagher has been arrested – specifically, arrested on suspicion of three murders. And it has been duly read by the suspect who has acknowledged that he understands the contents and the reason for his arrest. At this point, the visitor and the solicitor may have five minutes in private with the suspect. After that, the visitor – that is you, my Lord Bishop – is obliged to vacate this room. You may observe the interview from the adjoining room. The solicitor may remain in the interview room during the interview and subsequent questioning and, should it be required, the interrogation. Let it be understood, the solicitor has no right to be present. This courtesy is afforded in order to ensure that the rights and comfort of the suspect are respected. The suspect may request a break in the meeting in order to consult privately with the solicitor. I will conduct the meeting, during which I will question the suspect and present evidence in support of the case. Garda O'Reilly will assist me, but he will not ask questions directly of the suspect. He may, of course, communicate with me with respect to the questions addressed to the suspect, and he may help me in presenting evidence. He will record, in writing, the proceedings, and he may question me to clarify a statement or a response from the suspect. Whereas Garda O'Reilly and I may inter-communicate, this privilege is not extended to the suspect and his solicitor. During this meeting, the solicitor is prohibited from communicating with the suspect – by word, or gesture or by expression. Any attempt by the solicitor to prompt the suspect on how to answer a question, or to signal him to **not** answer a question, will result in his immediate removal and reprimand. The solicitor is free to make notes to record the meeting, and he is entitled to challenge improper questioning. The meeting will be supplied with adequate drinking water at all times; there will be a five-minute break every hour; a hot beverage will be provided upon request; after four hours we will break for forty-five minutes and provide a light meal; and at no time will the number of gardaí in the room exceed four. Is this understood by all?" Murf looks at the bishop, at the solicitor and at Glen Dennagher. All three acknowledge their acceptance. "Good. It is now past 10:35. Garda O'Reilly and I will depart the room at this time. The interview will resume at 10:45am."

At 10:45am, Murf begins to question Barry Glen Dennagher. The suspect has the right to remain silent, so Murf starts with non-incriminating questions in order to establish a comfort zone. Glen Dennagher falls for it. The questions are posed in order to confirm Glen Dennagher's identity. He answers questions pertaining to his name – Yes, 'Barry' is short for 'Bartholomew'; 'Glen' is not part of his surname, 'Glen' is actually his middle name but it became attached to his surname through usage when he moved in with his grandfather, Dean Stewart Glen. After a few minutes of easy questions and easy answers, Murf determines that it is time to move on.

Murf extracts three photographs from his bulky folder and slides them on the table towards the suspect like a croupier dealing a hand. But these pictures are not of a knave, a queen and a king; these are pictures of the three murder victims. Murf looks at Glen Dennagher's face to read his reaction. The suspect registers a slight recoiling motion. Murf speaks to him. "Look at these pictures. Do you recognise anyone?"

"Yes."

"Who do you recognise?"

Glen Dennagher points to each in turn. "This one, this one and this one."

"You recognise all three?"

"Yes."

"Are you able to put a name to each one?"

Glen Dennagher is reluctant to utter their names. Murf is uncertain as to whether Glen Dennagher is refusing to answer, or if he is too ashamed to speak their names. Murf points to the picture of Bobby Fegan. "What is the first letter of his surname?"

"F"

Murf writes on a sheet of paper – 'F'. He then asks Glen Dennagher for the second letter, and so on. When he has written the name in full – FEGAN – he holds up the sheet paper and presents it to Glen Dennagher. "So tell me, what is written here?"

"Fegan."

"And does Fegan have a first name."

"Bobby. His name is Bobby Fegan."

Murf points to a second picture. "What is **his** name?"

"Liam Tunnery."

"And the third picture, who is this?"

"Edmund Ludwig."

"Thank you. You have correctly identified the three murder victims from their photographs. Now tell me, how well did you know each of them?"

"I did not really know them. I just saw them around at, at… I just saw them in some places."

Murf notes that the suspect glanced evasively to the right before answering. "I will ask the question again. But before you answer, be advised that lying to the police in an inquiry is a criminal offence. And we have eye-witness accounts of you in the company of each of them. I should tell you that members of 'An Chúilfhionn' are very tight-lipped and steadfast about keeping secrets. But their adherence to confidentiality does not extend to murder. Now, I ask you again, how well did you know Liam Tunnery, Bobby Fegan and Edmund Ludwig?"

Glen Dennagher could answer by stating 'no comment'. Refusing to answer is within his rights, but to render misleading answers and/or deceptive statements is not a viable option. These are punishable offences in themselves. Glen Dennagher composes himself, coughs, and admits to knowing all three murder victims. He continues, and he proceeds to speak more easily. He gives an account of how he knew all three victims and in what capacity he engaged with them in the context of his outreach ministry. Murf permits Glen Dennagher to speak freely. The more he talks, the more likely he will trip up if he later contradicts himself. In his narrative, Glen Dennagher is admitting that he had a close relationship with each of the three victims, albeit for a brief time.

At 11:40am, Murf grants a five-minute break. At 11:45am the meeting resumes. At this point, Murf conducts the next stage of the meeting – the interrogation. On this occasion, Murf has the sample brier-proof jacket on the table, the jacket that he previously showed to Barry Glen Dennagher. He addresses the suspect. "Mr Glen Dennagher, on Thursday 22 August, I questioned you about your jacket, the one similar to this one here and similar to the one you are wearing. At that time you told me that you lost your original jacket. Do you remember?"

"Yes."

"And do you remember what you told me?"

"That I lost it at the circus."

"And did you ever find it? Or did you have it subsequent to your visit to the circus on Sunday 19 August 1945?"

"I did not have that jacket after that day."

"That is not what I asked. Did you have your jacket, or did you know the whereabouts of your jacket, after you left the circus?"

"I do not remember ever seeing that jacket after my visit to the circus."

"Do you remember what I said to you at the conclusion of our meeting on 22 August?"

"You said that I have nothing to worry about." The suspect is drumming his fingers lightly on the table in tempo to his tapping heel. This behaviour is apt while listening to a céili band, but there is no music within earshot of the interview room. It is not a dance tune that is playing in Glen Dennagher's mind.

The suspect's fidgeting is noted by Murf. "I said to you that if your explanation checks out, you have nothing to worry about. Well, we checked, and you have some things to worry about. This file here," Murf thumps the bulky file on the desk, "contains a lot of information on the case – indisputable evidence. What you are telling me now is at variance with the facts. Let me refer to one witness account." Murf removes a page from the file and peruses it. He resumes speaking. "On the evening of Sunday 19 August 1945, after the last performance of the circus, you were observed in a private club in the company of Edmund Ludwig. And, at that time, Edmund Ludwig was wearing your jacket. You departed from the club together. On the next day, you purchased a new jacket to replace your lost jacket. Only your jacket was not lost. It was still on Edmund Ludwig. And Edmund Ludwig, at the time, was dead and buried, hidden to avoid discovery." Murf pauses to observe the effect this information has on Glen Dennagher. The suspect is totally taken aback and is rendered speechless. Murf continues. He thumps his bulky folder once more. "The facts are that three young men were killed callously, causing pain and anguish to them and to their loved ones."

Glen Dennagher's resolve collapses. He utters a feeble rebuttal to Murf's statement. "There was no pain or anguish. They did not experience any suffering."

"And why is that?"

"They were asleep."

CHAPTER TWENTY-THREE

FATHER GLEN DENNAGHER AT CONFESSION

Killbawn Garda Station, County Mayo, Ireland
Tuesday 03 September 1946

Murf glances at his watch. It is 11:57am. The interrogation of Barry Glen Dennagher is progressing swiftly and favourably. It took a mere ten minutes for the suspect to acknowledge that he has intimate knowledge of circumstances of the deaths of the three murder victims. But 'sleep' does not necessarily denote 'death'. Murf continues at a steady pace in order to draw a clear and precise confession from the crestfallen cleric. "So you buried them while they were asleep?"

"No. That's monstrous. I bled them first."

"What did you do to 'bleed them'?"

"I opened the carotid arteries in the neck."

"While they were asleep? And they did not awaken and resist?"

"It was because of the sleeping pills."

"You killed them by administering a sleeping-pill overdose and opening an artery? Is that what you are saying?"

"Yes. But I had to. And I went to great lengths to ensure that they did not experience any pain or suffering. They died happily. They were not happy when alive. However, they died blissfully and I buried them with dignity."

"And it was necessary to end their lives in this manner? Why do you say you **had** to? Why is that?"

"They caused me to fall into sin. I had to cut off and cast away the source of my sin."

"Bobby Fegan and Liam Tunnery and Edmund Ludwig

caused you to sin, so you killed them?"

"No. That sounds barbaric. I had a brief intimate encounter with each of them – they led me into doing it. Afterwards, separation was necessary, a separation in which I put them to sleep gently, and then I sent them to eternal rest."

And there it is. Murf has a confession. But he must guard against a false confession. To be credible, a confession must be supported by the evidence in the case. Murf needs to be certain that there are no contradictions that could undermine the integrity of the confession. He looks at O'Reilly and at Feeney. Both men are writing vigorously in an attempt to accurately record what is being said. Murf leans forward and speaks gently to Glen Dennagher. "Barry, start at the beginning. Tell me how you put Bobby Fegan and Liam Tunnery and Edmund Ludwig to sleep and how you sent them to their eternal rest."

Barry Glen Dennagher is slumped in his chair. He no longer looks like a fit and vigorous athlete. He is a defeated man weighed down by guilt. Murf deduces that Glen Dennagher has reached an acceptance of his own guilt – the cause of his sin lies not in the three young men who befriended him but in his own heart. This realisation did not come suddenly to Glen Dennagher. The guilt was present from the moment of his first murderous deed, eating at him day after day, growing until it now weighs heavily upon him. At this point, he wishes to unburden his soul of this unbearable load.

12:15pm. Murf's interrogation of Barry Glen Dennagher is at a critical juncture. The suspect has admitted to having killed all three victims in the 'Famine Field' case. In his attempt to purge his soul of the unbearable load of guilt, he relates an account on each of the three murders. The solicitor Jacob Feeney and Garda Seamus O'Reilly write vigorously to keep pace with the narrative. The suspect tenders a lengthy statement. He delivers it at his own pace, without prompting, in the third person and in the present tense. It is a running witness account as if Glen Dennagher is reliving the events and describing them as a detached observer.

Bobby Fegan:
On Friday, 22 August 1941, Bobby Fegan is admitted to 'An Chúilfhionn' private club at Islandeady Lough. Although not a member, this privilege is afforded him due to a reciprocal arrangement with similar clubs in Ireland. In this instance, Bobby Fegan, a member in good standing in 'the Wilde Club', is permitted entry by one of the board members of 'An Chúilfhionn'. This is not Bobby's first visit to the club. He has availed of this courtesy three times in the summer of 1941.

On this occasion, Bobby encounters Barry Glen Dennagher in the club. They instantly recognise each other and immediately reminisce on Portora and on their respective academic and athletic achievements while attending the elite school. The conversation progresses to their current occupations and interests. Their tête-à-tête quickly reveals a shared interest – the works of Oscar Wilde. Glen Dennagher offers to show Bobby his library, which includes the complete works of Oscar Wilde. Bobby responds by offering to read to him from the said works. They agree to leave the club and go to the cleric's remote house situated by the sea in County Sligo. They depart from the private club and Glen Dennagher drives home to the townland of Lacken, an hour's journey away. Thereafter, they indulge in a night of 'Oscar Wilde' and resolve to repeat and relive the experience in the near future.

On the following morning, Glen Dennagher goes jogging at dawn. The sea air clears his head. The intimate experience of the previous night weighs heavily on his conscience and fills him with guilt. He regrets having agreed to subsequent meetings with the youth. He wonders how best to avoid the potential development of a relationship. Later, at 7:30am, he sets off for his duties in the diocese. Bobbie remains behind in the house. At the pastoral centre, Glen Dennagher proffers an excuse in order to absent himself from his duties. He returns to Lacken. He needs to devise a plan to sever his association with Bobby before a relationship develops. At this point, the priest is not considering murder as a viable option. He plans to put Bobby on a train to Dublin so that he can reconnect with his friends at 'the Wilde Club'. And this is his only plan.

However, Bobby is not at the house when Glen Dennagher returns home. The cleric is worried and begins to fret. Sometime later, Bobby Fegan returns. He had borrowed the priest's track-suit and had gone jogging along the coastal path by the sea. This is very disconcerting for Glen Dennagher. Bobby could easily have been spotted on the treeless coastline. To make matters worse, Bobby expresses his desire to form a relationship. He states that he can divide his time between Dublin and Sligo. He knows other people in the literary community who balance city life with country life quite successfully. Glen Dennagher strives to talk him out of it, but to no avail. The apprehensive priest is then faced with the predicament of repeating the same blunder he made in Oxford. He undertakes immediate and drastic measures to thwart the relationship before it begins.

Glen Dennagher drives back to Ballina and obtains a prescription of sleeping pills. Later, he shares a cup of hot cocoa with Bobby. Bobby's cocoa is liberally laced with sleeping pills. Glen Dennagher has come to a drastic decision to kill Bobby, but he is undecided as to where he should dispose of the remains. He considers throwing the body into the sea, but the tide could wash him back to land. He considers burial. The soil in the nearby fields is dense and would require much labour with a pick and shovel, and there is the almost-certain risk of discovery. He considers a sandy beach, but no, all the beaches are too public. Finally, He settles on an ideal location, the Famine Field near Killbawn.

By now, Bobby has succumbed to the effects of the sleeping pills and is sound asleep on the couch. The crafty cleric plans his subsequent steps with care and forethought. He selects a large book from his library – from the lavish section on health and fitness. His choice of book is a medical encyclopaedia. As an aficionado of the human body, the athletic priest frequently refers to this informative tome. He quickly turns to a full-colour fold-out page depicting the entire human body. The book contains four pictures in succession – the human body as perceived by the eye, the body depicted according to its muscle distribution, the body's circulatory system, and the skeletal assembly of the bones. Glen Dennagher focuses his attention on the depiction of the body's blood circulation. He unfurls the folded page to its full size and identifies the carotid arteries in the human neck. Next, he carries the open book to the couch and places it alongside the sleeping youth. Using the book as a reference, he locates Bobby's arteries and feels the pulse with the fingers of his right hand. Thereupon the priest goes to his writing desk and dips the forefinger of his left hand into the inkwell. He returns to the couch and to the sleeping youth, whereupon he re-checks the location of the arteries with his right hand. Satisfied that he has located the pulse in the neck, between the jaw and the ear, he smears his inked finger to mark the spot. Thus, he marks the left side of the neck and repeats his action with a similar mark on the right side.

Glen Dennagher proceeds to the next step. He walks out of the house and enters the garden shed. He selects a snub-nosed spade from the assemblage of tools and keep-fit equipment. He places the spade in the boot of his car and, to prevent it from shifting, he places it inside the large gym bag in the boot. Next, he returns to the shed. He extracts a penknife from his pocket and slides open the blade. He lifts a whetting stone from a shelf and brushes it against the blade in even strokes until the knife is razor-sharp.

He returns to the house. Glen Dennagher is ready to remove the sleeping youth from the house and transport him to the Famine Field. He lifts the limp body and is surprised at the weight. And it is not just the weight. With concentrated effort, the athletic cleric is sufficiently strong to lift the body and carry it, but the sleeping body is droopy and cumbersome. Carrying a body in this manner is inefficient and fatiguing. He places the sleeping youth back onto the couch. He considers wrapping him, perhaps in a blanket. The astute priest decides on a solution. He returns to the shed and selects a folded canvas square from a shelf; these squares serve as his athletic mats during his physical exercise. An array of skipping ropes is hanging on hooks beside the shelves. This is fortuitous. He selects a stout rope and returns once more to the house. Utilising the canvas sheet and the skipping rope, Glen Dennagher deftly slides the sleeping youth from the couch to the car, stopping briefly to lift the body clear of the doorstep. He places Bobby in the back seat of the car. This is executed awkwardly. First, he pushes the youth through the back door of the car and then he enters from the opposite side in order to drag the body into a secure prone position. He closes both doors and goes to the boot of the car. Inside the boot, he gropes in the side pocket of the gym bag and extracts a towel. He mops his perspiring face and studies his progress. He mentally enumerates each step of his plan and, satisfied, he drives to the Famine Field.

It is night-time when he arrives at the Famine Field. He remembers that there is a break in the hedge. It serves as access to the pilgrims and penitents that visit the Famine Filed annually on the morning of All Souls' Day to gain indulgences for the release of souls from Purgatory. The access is narrow, too narrow to permit a heifer to pass through, but wide enough for a person to squeeze his way into the field. This is the night of the new moon. The sky is unusually cloudless for north Mayo and the Milky Way provides a ghostly dim light for Glen Dennagher's nocturnal visit. He lifts the sleeping Bobby from the back seat of his car and carries him through the bushy hedge. (In 1941, the wire fence had not yet been erected.) He slides the body along the grass and he conceals it under a hazel scrub. He quickly fetches his gym bag and lays it alongside the sedated youth.

Next, Glen Dennagher drives to the derelict workhouse and parks his car out of sight. He jogs back to the Famine Field. He chooses a suitable spot behind the hazel, close to the road. He takes the spade out of his gym bag and, wielding it with skilful ease, he carefully removes the surface sod and proceeds to dig a grave. The digging is easy, but he is careful not to overexert himself. He paces the progress of his labour in order to conserve his strength. After four hours he is satisfied with the depth. Then he gently positions the sleeping Bobby Fegan in the bed of the pit. Standing astride the peaceful body, he straightens Bobby's clothing and crosses his limp hands across his chest. Thus, Bobby is lying in a comfortable posture of tranquil repose. After a thoughtful moment, Barry Glen Dennagher removes his pen-knife from his pocket. He levers the blade to its open position and, with serious consideration, he deftly lances the carotid arteries in the neck of the sleeping youth. The body stirs but Bobby does not awaken. To watch the life drain out of Bobby Fegan is unsettling for Barry Glen Dennagher. He is not prepared for the rush of blood. It gushes out in spurts, frothing and steaming. The startled cleric promptly vaults out of the grave.

The scattering blood gurgles and slows, and the flow abates. Glen Dennagher averts his eyes. Not being familiar with exsanguination, he is unable to calculate how quickly death occurs from arterial bleeding – seconds or minutes. Furthermore, he is unable to bear the sight of the body losing its lifeblood. Instead, he listens until the body is silent – no sounds of breathing, no audible trickle of blood. Unable to look directly at the body, Glen Dennagher declines to check if Bobby is actually dead – he assumes that a quiet unmoving body is dead. He sprinkles a handful of dirt onto the body, uncertain if this is an appropriate ritual in the circumstances. Thereupon he quickly pushes the mound of recently-dug sandy moraine soil into the pit. The soil spills noisily onto the body causing it to move. Glen Dennagher shudders and averts his eyes. He hurriedly shovels the remaining soil into the trench and thus the body is buried and hidden from his eyes. He carefully replaces the surface sods on top and scatters the residue of sandy soil beneath the hawthorns. The slight mound of the grave is unnoticeable in the uneven surface of the dolmen slope, and it is well hidden from view from the road. Glen Dennagher rubs a shaking hand across his forehead and inadvertently smears it with mud. The resulting stain is in the shape of a cross. He exhales a sigh. It is done.

Liam Tunnery:

On the day he missed his train to Dublin, Liam Tunnery is permitted to enter 'An Chúilfhionn' private club at Islandeady Lough. He is afforded guest privilege by the barman of that day, Fergal McKenna. The day is the Tuesday after Easter 1943 (27 April). The barman, being busy, introduces Liam to Glen Dennagher, who is present in the club that day. The cleric is greatly taken by the young man who relates to him how he is constantly at odds with his father. After some heart-to-heart conversation, the priest deduces that the young Liam Tunnery is a homosexual not fully in tune with his sexual identity. Consequently, he offers to enlighten him and provide guidance to him. They agree to leave the club and go to Glen Dennagher's remote house situated by the sea in Lacken, County Sligo. They wait until nightfall. Then they depart from the club.

Later that night, Liam is exuberant about his new-found identity and the satisfying experience it affords him. Glen Dennagher, on the other hand, is undergoing feelings of regret at yet another lapse in conduct. He is anxious for Liam to leave. And, having learned from his previous experience, he is not going to risk having any future visitors visible at his house during daylight hours. His neighbours are curious by nature. A nosy farmer could spot a stranger by chance. Glen Dennagher decides to put Liam on an early-morning train to Dublin so that he can avail of passage to England as he had previously intended. Alas, Liam has lost all interest in going to England. He is greatly taken by the sophisticated older man who appears knowledgeable on matters of the human condition, especially in his understanding of Liam's atypical 'condition'. Thus, the working-class youth looks to the refined man as his life-mentor. Liam resolves to remain in Mayo and expresses his desire to continue in a relationship with Glen Dennagher. The priest strives to talk him out of it but to no avail. It is after midnight when Glen Dennagher realises that he has made another serious blunder with inescapable adverse repercussions.

Like the previous time, Glen Dennagher performs the same mode of execution as he did with Bobby Fegan. After engaging in forbidden intimacy, he administers sleeping pills, concealed in hot cocoa, to Liam Tunnery. This time, Glen Dennagher is better prepared. He has sleeping pills on hand. Later, with Liam sound asleep, he drives to the Famine Field, intent on performing his gruesome task before the new day dawns. He thus ensures that there will be no chance of anyone sighting a visitor at his house when day breaks.

The night of 27 April 1943 contains a half-moon. At the Famine Field, a gentle night-breeze is blowing across the estuary. Scattered clouds drift high aloft to repeatedly veil the face of the half-moon. In 1943, there are fewer shrubs growing at the roadside of the Famine Field compared to 1941. The hazel scrub is gone and the hawthorn is slashed down close to the ground in order to provide visibility to traffic rounding the bend at the two-mile stone. This time, Barry Glen Dennagher is obliged to transport the body of Liam Tunnery a bit farther in order to locate a suitable burial site – to the hidden area behind the sloe bushes. It is 3:00am when he commences digging. A short time later, the grave is excavated to a suitable depth. As in the previous occasion, he carefully carries the sleeping body and places him gently in the bed of the excavated grave. He straightens Liam's clothes; he places his arms across the chest with hands folded; he adjusts his 'Cary Grant' glasses to their correct position. Satisfied, he views the sleeping Liam Tunnery. Having learned from his previous deed, Glen Dennagher climbs out of the grave before applying the sharp blade of his pen-knife to the exposed neck of the victim. He lies face down at the edge of the grave and reaches down to execute the bloody deed. The cleric stifles a cry of alarm and drops the knife – Liam Tunnery is staring at him. Frozen in fear, Glen Dennagher stares back. Two immobile bodies stare at each other, fixed in their respective places like stone statues. Suddenly, Liam's stare disappears. The frightened cleric continues to peer at the reposed body in the grave. He listens for signs of movement. The body remains still. He gazes intently at the eyes in an effort to detect movement. He sees, reflected in Liam's glasses, a cloud drift over the face of the moon. The cloud passes and, as the moon shines again upon the inert body, two miniature moons stare up at the frightened executioner from the glasses below. The cleric blinks in understanding and exhales loudly in relief. He retrieves his knife. But he is too unnerved to commit the final deed. Glen Dennagher goes to his carry-all gym bag and takes a cotton towel from the side pocket. He drapes the towel over Liam's face, cloaking him from head to waist. With Liam's eyes thus covered, the priest proceeds to the final act of execution. The victim's neck is no longer visible, but the cleric is sure of the correct location where to apply the quick incisions. He executes two rapid and decisive strokes and the deed is done. Thus, he proceeds as before, just as he did on the night of 22 August 1941.

It is already light when Glen Dennagher finishes his task. The sloe bushes conceal him from the road, but he is visible in the field to anyone approaching from the spine of the drumlin. Some cattle, grazing on the slope of the hill, approach to gaze in lazy curiosity. Luckily for Glen Dennagher, these cattle are bullocks and no drover arrives to herd them. Dairy cows, on the other hand, would have been rounded up for the morning milking. He succeeds in completing his task and vacates the site undetected. Glen Dennagher cautions himself on this serious miscalculation – he should have organised his operation at the Famine Field to conclude forty-five minutes before dawn.

Edmund Ludwig:
The encounter with Edmund Ludwig in 1945 takes an unexpected turn. On Sunday 19 August 1945, Barry Glen Dennagher drives away from The John Edge Travelling Show at 10:05pm. Edmund Ludwig is sitting in the front passenger seat, still dressed in his unitard but wearing Glen Dennagher's tweed jacket. The jacket is two sizes too large for him, so he wears it like a cloak. The well-organised cleric expects this

tryst to proceed similarly to the two previous encounters – the one with Bobby Fegan and the one with Liam Tunnery. This time, it takes a decidedly different course. Glen Dennagher takes Edmund to 'An Chúilfhionn' private club at Islandeady Lough. In the club, Edmund is uncomfortable dressed in his performance garb. He attempts to envelop himself within Glen Dennagher's spacious jacket. He has not yet mastered the English language. He is unable to follow conversations and he is confused by the anecdotes that are bandied about. After only a few minutes – a few minutes too long for Edmund Ludwig – Glen Dennagher senses his discomfort and they leave the club at 11:15pm. On the journey to Lacken, Edmund is restless. He fidgets with pieces of string, tying them into various knots and stuffing the knotted twine into the pockets of the tweed jacket. They arrive at Glen Dennagher's house before midnight.

Edmund is agitated with his disappointing situation in life – the war that wiped out his family, the rebuff at the travelling show, and his uncertain future. They engage in intimacy, but the experience is inadequate for both of them. The mood is wrong and they are left feeling unfulfilled. Edmund promises that tomorrow will be better when he recovers fully from the rejection he suffered earlier at the hands of the Marvellous Magyars. Glen Dennagher suddenly realises that Edmund, having left the travelling show, has nowhere else to go. He has no home and no friends. Hence, he is talking about 'tomorrow' as if he now considers this as his current abode. The apprehensive cleric finds himself in another predicament and, to resolve it, he needs to employ drastic measures.

Glen Dennagher prepares hot cocoa. Edmund dislikes cocoa and declines to drink it. He requests some food. Glen Dennagher prepares a ham sandwich into which he sprinkles finely-ground sleeping pills smeared with salad cream. He gives the sandwich to Edmund. Edmund detects the unwelcome taste of the sleeping pills. After a few bites, he complains that the ham must be off. He ceases eating. He has consumed less than half the sandwich.

To put him at ease, Glen Dennagher invites Edmund to avail of his collection of gramophone records and to choose some music for his listening pleasure. Glen Dennagher indicates to his gramophone situated in a corner of the room. Edmund perks up at the offer. He is familiar with the operation of a wind-up gramophone. He goes to the device and opens the cabinet underneath. There, he locates Glen Dennagher's collection of records. He flips through the 78s and selects a recording of Mozart's 'Eine Kleine Nachtmusik'. He flips open the upper lid of the cabinet to access the turntable. He secures the hinge to remain rigid and locks the lid open. Thereupon he gently places the record on the turntable and checks the quality of the needle. Dissatisfied with the needle, he removes it from the arm and picks another from the tray. He carefully examines the selected needle, peering intently at the point. Content with his choice, he secures the needle in the play-arm and turns the windup handle. He checks the tension of the spring – too low and the record will rotate at less than 78 RPM rendering the music flat, too tight and the spring could be strained and thus would malfunction. He toggles the release button and the 78 begins to spin. Whereupon he lifts the arm and places the needle in the appropriate position at the edge of the now-spinning record. He adjusts the volume and the music wafts out to fill the room. As he listens to the music, he resumes flipping through the collection of records. He stops at 'Lili Marleen' sung by Marlene Dietrich. He removes the record and views the other side – 'Das Mädchen unter der Laterne'. He then removes Mozart from the turntable in preference to Marlene Dietrich. With Marlene singing in her soothing low tones,

Edmund sits in a wingchair close by and sings along – 'Wie einst Lili Marleen'.

Edmund is at ease and relaxed. He is so relaxed that he neglects to turn the windup handle to maintain a constant speed of 78 RPM. The spring winds down, the record slows, Marleen's low alto voice drops even lower, and Edmund drops to sleep in the chair.

At 1:40am, Edmund Ludwig, still cloaked in the oversize tweed jacket, is sound asleep. Once again, Glen Dennagher drives to the Famine Field. Edmund is asleep in the back seat, still blanketed in the priest's tweed jacket and wrapped within a canvas sheet. They reach the location at 2:20am. The night is dark. It is the time of the waxing gibbous moon, but it is only faintly discernible through the rainclouds. A fine drizzle is blowing in from the sea. Glen Dennagher lifts Edmund from the rear seat of the car. Edmund stirs when he is exposed to the drifting fog and the odour of marsh gas. He awakens but is groggy. Glen Dennagher waits for a few moments. Edmund settles back to sleep again. Glen Dennagher resumes his task and carries Edmund gently into the field. In this visit, Glen Dennagher is confronted by a wire fence and brambles where the hawthorn once grew. The hawthorn has been totally removed since his previous visit. Edmund, by this time, is weighing heavily in his arms. He places him prone on the grass verge. The cleric succeeds in pressing down on the sagging wire sufficiently to step over it, but the briers snag his trousers. He tugs himself free. Next, he drags the sleeping youth through the fence, ensuring that there is sufficient clearance under the wire. Thus accomplished, he proceeds as before to the rear of the sloe bushes. He then delicately positions the sleeping Edmund Ludwig on the lush grass of the soft ground. The shock of the wet grass wakens Edmund. He groans and rolls over onto his side. He raises himself on one arm and inquires as to what is happening. He is confused by the unfamiliar setting and by the inclemency of the weather. He manages to get to his feet. He is alarmed by the inhospitable surroundings and he takes fright. He staggers drunkenly towards the road. Due to the darkness, he fails to see the wire fence. He stumbles against it. The strands of wire halt his progress and he is propelled backwards. He falls, landing in a sitting position with his back to Glen Dennagher. The priest approaches the confused youth from behind and crooks one arm around Edmund's head, tilting it back to expose his neck. And with one swift cutting stroke, Glen Dennagher draws his pocketknife across the exposed skin, slashing both carotid arteries. In less than five seconds, Edmund Ludwig is unconscious. Glen Dennagher drags him hurriedly from the exposed area at the fence, back to the cover of the sloe bushes. There is a trail of blood marking the spot, all the way from the fence to the bushes. In twenty seconds, Edmund Ludwig is dead.

Glen Dennagher is fearful of being observed. He jumps over the fence and fetches his gym bag (containing the spade) from the boot of his car. He hurls it over the bushes and into the field. During this troublesome incident, Glen Dennagher's car has remained stationary on the narrow roadway blocking any possible traffic. Should anyone approach along the road, the homicidal incident would be discovered. He quickly drives away and conceals the car as before at the old workhouse building, a short distance from the Famine Field.

Upon returning to the concealed area behind the sloe bushes Glen Dennagher considers retrieving his tweed jacket from the inert corpse but, seeing that it is saturated in blood, he leaves it on the dead body of Edmund Ludwig. This decision would later turn out to be a serious mistake on his part.

As before, Glen Dennagher digs a pit in the sandy soil.

A short time later, when he has completed the burial and has concluded the task to his satisfaction, he views his surroundings. There are noticeable deposits of blood on the ground. He waits in the rain until daylight. He sees that blood has seeped onto the roadway and is mixing with the rainwater. It runs in rivulets and flows into the sheugh. Eventually, the rain obliterates all traces of blood, either forcing it into the porous soil or washing it into the roadside drainage ditch.

A wet and bedraggled Barry Glen Dennagher walks to his car. He thrusts the gym bag and spade back inside the boot. He drives home. This incident with Edmund Ludwig has shaken him greatly. He swears an oath that he will never again permit himself to be drawn into a similar situation.

At 12:50pm, Barry Glen Dennagher has concluded his account to Murf, in the presence of Garda O'Reilly and Solicitor Jack Feeney. He is exhausted. Murf fills a glass with water and offers it him. Glen Dennagher takes it and holds it with trembling hands. He drinks clumsily and dribbles some water onto his chest. Meanwhile, O'Reilly compares his notes with Feeney. The solicitor is satisfied that O'Reilly's written account of the confession is accurate. It is now 1:05pm. Murf calls for a 45-minute break in the interrogation.

They reconvene at 1:50pm. O'Reilly tenders a typed copy of the confession to Murf. Murf reads it. He then passes it to Feeney, who also reads it. Lastly, he hands it to Barry Glen Dennagher. He instructs him to read it, and to question any inaccuracies or omissions. Glen Dennagher glances at it and hands it back. Murf thrusts it back at him and instructs him to read it carefully aloud in its entirety. Murf, O'Reilly and Feeney sit in sombre silence as Glen Dennagher recites the entire confession. O'Reilly is visibly disturbed by the confession. He looks to Murf for understanding, but Murf stoically maintains a neutral expression. The suspect, having concluded his account, places the typed confession on the table and looks at Murf questioningly. Murf instructs him on the procedure required to show that the confession is freely given and that it is a true and accurate account. Glen Dennagher acknowledges his understanding and signs the document according to the authorised procedure. The solicitor notes that it is duly executed. Glen Dennagher states that he wishes to add an addendum at the bottom. He is still holding the pen. He writes the concluding section in legible longhand. Unlike the foregoing confession, the addendum is written in the first person singular. It is a passage from scripture.

Romans 7:8-20
But sin, seizing an opportunity in the commandment, produced in me all kinds of covetousness. I was once alive, but sin revived and I died. For sin, seizing an opportunity, deceived me and killed me.

For we know that the law is spiritual: but I am of the flesh, sold into slavery under sin. I do not understand my own actions. For I do not do what I want, but I do the very thing I hate. Now if I do what I do not want, I agree that the law is good. But in fact, it is no longer I that do it, but sin that dwells within me. For I know that nothing good dwells within me, that is, in my flesh. I can will what is right, but I cannot do it. For I do not do the good I want, but the evil I do not want is what I do. Now if I do what I do not want, it is no longer I that do it, but sin that dwells within me.

Barry Glen Dennagher adds his signature to the

addendum.

It is now 2:15pm. Murf advises the suspect that the charge sheet will be prepared immediately. This should take an hour. But, as of now, the suspect must remove all belongings from his person and surrender them to the arresting officer. In recognition of his right to meet with his 'selected friend', he may elect to turn over some or all of his belongings to Bishop Byrne. This is the suspect's right and he elects to do so. The arresting officer has the right to take possession of any item that may have a bearing on the case. Bishop Byrne is directed to enter the interview room. Glen Dennagher empties his pockets and places the contents on the table – fountain pen, keys, coins, a wallet and a pen-knife. Murf scrutinizes the items as they are revealed and O'Reilly records the inventory in his notebook. Murf checks the contents of the wallet and he notes that the penknife is a commemorative souvenir and a recent acquisition. He is satisfied that none of the objects are relevant as items of evidence. The bishop looks at the bits and pieces on the table. Murf speaks to him, "Bishop Byrne, you are permitted to take possession of the items the suspect has placed before you."

The bishop gathers all the items and puts them in his pockets one at a time. With each item, the bishop considers how non-personal some of these objects really are to Glen Dennagher – a pen from the diocesan office, a key to a diocesan car, a key to a diocesan house. The prelate declines to open the wallet, choosing not to know its contents. Of all the items, only the pen-knife truly belongs to Glen Dennagher. The bishop hesitates, wondering if this knife could be the instrument of execution mentioned in the confession statement. He is relieved to see that the pen-knife is a souvenir of Knock and is dated 1946.

The bishop questions Murf. "Inspector, why remove all

his possessions at this time?"

"Once the prisoner is formally charged, everything will be removed from him, even his clothing. This will be explained fully when the formal charge is tendered."

"I see."

Murf continues. "It is 2:25pm. We will reconvene at 3:15pm. This is to give an opportunity to eat lunch. And during this time the charge sheet will be completed. At 3:15pm, when we reconvene, Barry Glen Dennagher will be formally charged for the willful and premeditated murders of Bobby Fegan, Liam Tunnery and Edmund Ludwig. Once charged, Barry Glen Dennagher will no longer be 'the suspect', he will be remanded in custody as 'the accused'. Any questions at this time?"

Glen Dennagher, dejected, looks up at Murf and speaks quietly. "I request a private consultation with my solicitor." This is his right and the request is granted.

Five minutes later, at 2:30pm, the solicitor speaks with the garda member in charge, which in this case is District Officer Superintendent David Fox. Barry Glen Dennagher, through his solicitor, requests that he be permitted to visit St Bawn's Church – with appropriate escort – to avail of Confession. Shortly, Glen Dennagher will be formally charged, whereupon he will be escorted to the Garda Divisional Office to be held in custody until he appears before the District Court. Superintendent Fox considers the suspect's request. A Bishop and a priest are present in the garda station. Fox suggests that the prisoner should consult with either of them here in the station. Solicitor Feeney reminds Fox that this is the last time Barry Glen Dennagher will ever be permitted to visit a church, other than a prison chapel. He points out that Glen Dennagher is agreeable to be handcuffed to a garda while visiting the church. Fox considers that the request may be granted subject to prudent precautions. He decides that Glen Dennagher be allowed to visit St Bawn's – it is less than a hundred yards away – but he will be escorted by two garda officers and his solicitor, and he will be handcuffed to one of the officers. Thus, he will remain in garda custody.

At 2:45pm they walk from the garda station to the church via the river pathway so as to avoid attracting undue attention. A light drizzle is falling – not unusual for Killbawn. No one takes any notice of two gardaí, two priests and a man in a suit, walking along the riverbank to the church. Barry Glen Dennagher is still dressed in his priest's rural casual clothes – all black except for the brier-proof tweed jacket – the black jacket with the white flecks that give it a charcoal-grey hue. He is flanked by Garda O'Reilly and Garda Caldwell, both in uniform. Jacob Feeney, the solicitor, and Father Tommy Martin, the bishop's assistant, follow close behind. Garda O'Reilly's left wrist is handcuffed to Glen Dennagher's right wrist. And thus they enter St Bawn's Church.

St Bawn's Church is quiet inside. There is the still-lingering odour of the smoke from the wax candles that burned during the morning Mass. And a faint smell of furniture polish emanates from the wooden pews. The only light in the spacious nave is the daylight from the dull Mayo day struggling to penetrate through the stained-glass windows. Inside the church, Glen Dennagher indicates to the confessional box in the west aisle – the aisle that leads to the side altar of the Sacred Heart of Jesus. He looks at Father Tommy Martin. Father Martin understands and enters the confessor's compartment through the middle door of the confessional box. Glen Dennagher stands at the penitent's door. He holds his wrist aloft to indicate to Garda O'Reilly that he desires to be released from his handcuff during the sacramental rite. O'Reilly nods to Garda Caldwell and points to the church door with his eyes. Caldwell understands. He is to stand at the church door to guard against any attempt by the suspect to flee the building. O'Reilly unlocks the handcuff and Glen Dennagher enters the confessional box on the side reserved for the penitent. O'Reilly remains standing outside the box, one ring of the handcuff still securely fastened on his left wrist, and the other ring, unclasped, hanging free.

Ten minutes elapse. Glen Dennagher and Father Martin are still inside the confessional box. O'Reilly is apprehensive – he is concerned for the security of the accused who may attempt to flee, and he is worried about the safety of the confessor. He leans his head close to the confessional box. He discerns two distinct voices speaking low. Satisfied that there is no reason for alarm, O'Reilly sits in the nearest pew. He accepts that Glen Dennagher, having confessed his crimes to the police, would need as much time, or maybe more time, to confess his sins to God.

At 3:05pm, Glen Dennagher emerges from the confessional box. O'Reilly approaches him. He holds aloft the handcuffs to indicate that he intends to secure the prisoner. Glen Dennagher points to the main altar and he walks slowly towards it. Before O'Reilly intercepts him, Glen Dennagher kneels at the altar rail at the entrance to the sanctuary. O'Reilly is familiar with the rite of Confession. Glen Dennagher is reciting the prayers of penance. O'Reilly sighs and sits in a nearby pew. He wonders how long this is going to take. Some minutes pass. O'Reilly resolves to interrupt the prayers of penance if they protrude past 3:10pm. Beyond that, Glen Dennagher will be required to conclude his prayers in a holding cell back at the garda station where he is scheduled to be formally charged at 3:15pm.

Eventually, Glen Dennagher stands up. He ascends the altar steps and circumambulates the altar, bowing at intervals. O'Reilly rises from the pew but remains standing. He is annoyed. Glen Dennagher, he determines, is taking advantage of his short period of unfettered freedom to stretch it out for as long as possible. Glen Dennagher walks, and bows, and walks through the doorway connecting the sanctuary to the sacristy. This is too much for O'Reilly. Glen Dennagher, he decides, is taking advantage of the concession afforded him to visit the church. O'Reilly marches up the altar steps and thence into the sacristy with the intent of promptly slapping the handcuff on Glen Dennagher's wrist without further delay. The sacristy is windowless and is dim inside. O'Reilly's attention is drawn to the one bright light in the room – the daylight shining in through the crack of the partly-open door standing ajar at the rear of the room – the sacristy exit to the outside. O'Reilly immediately comprehends the situation. He shouts back to the nave of the church, "He has bolted. The prisoner has bolted."

O'Reilly darts out through the open doorway. Rain is falling. He glimpses the suspect running away in the direction of the river. Glen Dennagher is athletic and he is fit. He runs fast and confidently. O'Reilly is younger, lankier, and is on the county football team. O'Reilly is also fit. O'Reilly runs after the fleeing prisoner. After a few strides, it is clear that O'Reilly is the superior runner. He will quickly overtake and get hold of the escapee. Glen Dennagher has chosen to run along the riverside pathway, back the way that they had come. Previously, on their walk to the church, the group of five men did not merit any attention. Now it is different. This unusual sight attracts quite a lot of attention – a priest running vigorously alongside the river wall, followed by a uniformed garda running faster, followed by a second garda not quite as fast, followed in turn by a second priest somewhat clumsily, and coming up the rear, a man in a suit struggling to rise to a slow jog and attempting to dodge the rain puddles on the pathway. Two fishermen at the river wall turn around and laugh at the comical sight. Four dogs, playing in the riverside parkland, join in the chase, barking in merriment and, in their exuberance, endanger the runners by running through their legs. Three more strides and O'Reilly is confident that he will grab hold of Glen Dennagher. The fleeing priest runs up the slope of the grassy embankment to access the upper-surface road. O'Reilly's boots lose traction on the moist grass and he loses space. The lanky garda succeeds in reaching the sidewalk of Blackwater Road leading to Market Square. He increases his speed and he regains his lost space. He is prepared, once again, to lay hold of Glen Dennagher. But Glen Dennagher unexpectedly turns sharp left and runs along Blackwater Road in the direction of the bridge. Pedestrians, hurrying across the bridge in the rain, stand back to avoid colliding with the running men – except for Danny the Divil. The Divil is leaning on the bridge wall, staring down at the swirling dark waters just as Murf is frequently apt to do. He appears to be oblivious to the rain and to the commotion.

O'Reilly has finally caught up with Glen Dennagher. On the next stride, he will grab hold of him. But the fugitive eludes him once more. Just as O'Reilly's hand is in position to make a secure catch, the athletic priest vaults up and over the bridge wall. O'Reilly's hand makes contact with Glen Dennagher's jacket but fails to get a grip. Surprisingly, the Divil strikes his arm out in a lightening-speed reaction and grabs hold of the falling cleric by the scruff of the neck. The Divil has managed to grab hold of the rear collar of Glen Dennagher's tweed jacket, and the surprised priest is swinging helplessly over the turbulent Blackwater. The Divil's action is an instinctive reaction. It is also imprudent. Glen Dennagher's weight and the momentum of his fall pull the Divil off the ground. The Divil is lodged on the bridge wall, half hanging over the river and half hanging over the roadway. O'Reilly manages to hold fast to the Divil to prevent his falling into the river – to prevent two men from plunging into the black water below. O'Reilly shouts for assistance. He is holding onto the Divil, who is holding onto Glen Dennagher. Garda Caldwell arrives at the scene. Together, O'Reilly and Caldwell haul the Divil back from falling into the river. Suddenly, the Divil becomes significantly lighter, and Caldwell and O'Reilly tumble backwards onto the sidewalk. The Divil falls on top of them. From the other side of the bridge wall they hear a voice shout, "Domine, salvum me fac!" followed by a distinctly loud splash. The Divil is lying on his back with his arm raised skyward clutching a brier-proof tweed jacket – now an empty tweed jacket. All three rise to their feet and peer over the bridge wall. They are joined by Father Tommy Martin and by Jacob Feeney. They look intently at the swirling black river below, attempting to gaze into the peaty water. It is futile. No stare, no matter how concentrated, can penetrate these deep dark turbulent waters. There is no trace of Barry Glen Dennagher.

The five men look at each other, unsure of what next to do. The Divil is the first to speak. "So what was that what he said when he slipped out of his coat?"

Father Martin responds, "'Domine, salvum me fac.' St Peter cried out to Our Lord in this manner when he was sinking in the Sea of Galilee – 'Lord, save me.'"

It is 3:50pm in Killbawn Garda Station. Garda O'Reilly has concluded his verbal report of how he lost a prisoner in his custody. Garda Caldwell corroborates O'Reilly's account and he confirms that they ran along the riverbank in the hope that the suspect might resurface further downstream. After ten minutes of futile searching, they concluded that Glen Dennagher sank into the tumultuous water and never reappeared. This account is also confirmed by Father Tommy

Martin and by Jacob Feeney. Superintendent Fox listens in silence. Also present during the report are Murf and Bishop Byrne. After a moment's uncomfortable silence, Fox exclaims, "This is a tragedy. This is the worst outcome."

The bishop is smarting from his fair-haired boy's fall from grace. This will reflect badly on him. But if Glen Dennagher is dead and gone, the bishop will avoid the publicity of a scandalous trial. Bishop Byrnes remarks, perhaps to himself, perhaps to no one at all, "This is a tragedy, yes, but not necessarily the **worst** outcome."

Fox continues, "We lost a prisoner, and he had not been formally charged. I have no idea how to proceed with the required protocol in this situation. Do I refer to Glen Dennagher as 'the suspect' or 'the accused' or 'the prisoner' or what? And we need to search for the body. It is probably on its way to the Atlantic as we speak. In another hour or so it will be lost forever in the depth of the sea. Lord, what a mess. I must get in touch with O'Neill in Divisional Headquarters. He'll know what procedure is appropriate. And I expect there will be hell to pay."

The Divil walks into the station. He is still clutching Glen Dennagher's jacket in his hand. "So what do I do with this jacket here? It's a right good jacket. And if nobody claims it, can I have it?"

CHAPTER TWENTY-FOUR

DEAD END AT THE TWO-MILE STONE

Killbawn, County Mayo, Ireland
Monday 09 September 1946

9:30am. Murf is driving on the Blackwater Road. It is a pleasant day – sunny periods between brief showers. Yesterday the weather was different – brief showers between sunny periods. He passes the familiar caution signs posted on the roadside – 'GO MALL' and a short distance farther, 'NÍOS MOILLE'. He is approaching the dangerous bend at the two-mile stone. And then, Murf's ride to the two-mile stone is blocked by a diversion sign – 'Road Closed'. A county council worker is diverting traffic. The worker recognises Murf.

"Ah, Guard Murphy, is it? Well, as you can see, the road is closed. It is a dead-end at the Devil's Bend now."

"The 'Devil's Bend'? Oh yes, you are referring to the new road construction – the curve that will bypass the dangerous bend at the two-mile stone."

"That's right, Guard Murphy. The new section of road is called 'the Devil's Bend'. We just started work on the project this morning. Now, if you're lookin' to go out to the Coast Road, you'll hafta go up round about the old derelict workhouse, and from there to Delahunty's farmyard, and that will bring you out to the road again. But I should warn you, Guard Murphy, that bit of laneway that connects the workhouse to Delahunty's is fierce mucky. It'll make a right mess of your car. Sure it's only fit for tractors and the like. I'm just sayin', you know."

Murf thanks the worker for his advice. He drives a short distance along the detour and parks his car beside the workhouse wall. The workhouse is actually on Delahunty's land ever since his family acquired the property. The farmer utilizes the spacious stone building to store his tractor, his plough, his harrower, his reaper and other farm equipment. Murf takes a quick look at the detour laneway. The access lane to Delahunty's farmyard is much worse than the worker described. There is no drainage sheugh at the side of the laneway and rainwater is lying in deep pools on the surface. Murf fears that the muddy water may conceal large potholes. It is not prudent to drive a car through this detour route. He ambles away from his parked almost-clean 10HP Ford Prefect and walks the short distance to the two-mile stone.

Murf is relieved at the outcome of his recent case. The 'Famine Field' case is solved. Not quite closed yet, not until the police succeed in recovering the drowned body of Barry Glen Dennagher. Murf mentally re-runs the events of the past few weeks. His inquiry started in the Famine Field at the two-mile stone on 19 August. Today, he desires to view the Famine Field one last time before the roadworks obliterate the site where the murder victims were discovered. It would be ironic if the same site were to feature in the final closure of the case.

The roadway from the 'Road Closed' sign to the two-mile stone is lined with workers' bicycles, digging equipment and tools. Upon reaching the site, Murf recognises the ganger, Big Bill Tunnery. Big Bill greets him. There are twenty men working on the site. Already, the field has undergone some changes – the wire fence and the shrubs have been cut down and removed. The workers are busy removing the sod and the topsoil. The topsoil will be relocated later in the new configuration of the field. The pits where the bodies were discovered are no longer discernible. Big Bill made sure to obliterate all traces of them as quickly as possible. Murf understands. There is nothing more of interest to Murf at the site. He walks back to his car and drives to the garda station.

Later, sitting at his desk, Murf flips through the contents of the case file and notes the things that have met closure:

The perpetrator of the crimes was caught and, in a perverse way, met with justice – albeit at his own hands.

The remains of the three victims were claimed by their respective families and they received dignified funerals. Edmund Ludwig, not having any known family, was claimed by a charitable organisation dedicated to providing funerals for unclaimed dead German servicemen. He was buried with compatriots, many of whom are identified simply as "Ein Seeman', in the 'German Cemetery' in Glencree, County Wicklow.

Bobby Fegan was buried, with proper funeral rites, in Killbawn Abbey's Protestant graveyard. Captain Robert Scott arrived from Uganda and was present at the funeral. His presence took everyone by surprise. Robert Scott had not set foot in Killbawn since July 1919. Back in 1919, travel from Uganda to Ireland would have taken three to four weeks. Today, in 1946, the same trip from Kabujogera Plantation to Scott Manor takes three days, thanks chiefly to BOAC's commitment to 'connect the Empire by air'. Murf learned from Vincent Kelly that Robert Scott reacted to the telegram he sent, in which the solicitor made reference to the death of Bobby Fegan and to the sorry state of Scott Manor. So, Captain Scott arrived in time for Bobby Fegan's funeral and is currently staying in the Scott Manor, his childhood family home. He is already considering restoring the manor house to its former grandeur. This is a welcome relief to Sarah Fegan and Tom Buckley. Their services – that of housekeeper and house steward – are to be resurrected and reinstated to a status befitting a grand house. The captain's opinion of 'Irish

Hooligans' running the country has softened since he left
Ireland in 1919. He is surprised that the country has not fallen
into ruin as he once predicted. Furthermore, all Europe is
currently undergoing reconstruction and recovery from the
war, and Captain Scott sees economic potential here.
Conversely, the general strike in Uganda in January 1945
revealed an undercurrent of discontent that continues to
simmer and will likely erupt with dire consequences for the
colony in the near future. Uganda's economic prospects are
on a downward slide, whereas Ireland's future is on the rise.
Captain Scott is already devising plans to divide his time
between Ireland and Uganda.

Liam Tunnery had a requiem Mass celebrated at St
Bawn's Church, and he is interred in Killbawn Abbey
graveyard not far from Bobby Fegan's resting place – albeit
in the Catholic section.

Garda Chief Superintendent Ultan O'Neill, Divisional
HQ Castlebar, regards the demise of the prisoner Barry Glen
Dennagher as fortuitous. A public trial of a priest of the
Diocese of Killala would have exposed a number of
unwelcome scandals, all of which are better kept out of sight
and out of mind. The official explanation of Barry Glen
Dennagher's death is 'accidental death at his own hands
while attempting to escape garda custody'. The Diocese of
Killala concurs with this explanation.

After the prisoner Glen Dennagher disappeared into the
Blackwater River, the waters were dredged. It was a period of
heavy rainfall in the Glen Corry Mountains and the river was
in flood at the time of his disappearance and for many days
thereafter. The search was called off after two days. The body
was not found.

Murf closes the file folder. He looks up at his now-
blank investigation wall. It bears some scars of his earlier

notes. Bits of torn cellotape are still on the wall, stuck here and there in random disorder, and some of the paint is missing from where the tape was roughly removed. His room is emptier now. The evidence boxes are gone. At present, O'Reilly is transporting them to Castlebar where they will be catalogued and stored at HQ. Murf is restless. He rises from his chair. He departs from the garda station and walks to the Blackwater. At the river wall, he scoops up a handful of pebbles and commences flinging them into the dark water one at a time. As each pebble disappears, he wonders where the current carries the sinking stones.

At 2:00pm, the quiet of the Killbawn Garda Station is disturbed by the blustering entrance of Danny the Divil. Garda Seamus O'Reilly and Garda Eddie Caldwell are jolted from their mundane tasks of updating and clearing the notice board. They cease what they are doing and look at Danny the Divil in amazement. It is two in the afternoon and Danny the Divil is still sober? Something is truly wrong.

The Divil announces loudly, "I've just come from the two-mile stone…"

O'Reilly interrupts him. "What? Another car is stuck in the ditch, Danny?"

"Car, me arse. There's no car at the two-mile stone at all. Sure it's a dead end now, what with the new road being put through and all."

"So, what is it that has you all in a fluster?"

"They found a body out there."

"Good God, not another body in the Famine Field is it?"

"There's no body in the Famine Field. At least not in the part what is called 'The Divil's Bend' now."

"Then, what 'body' are you talking about?"

"The floating body, that's what I'm talking about. Big

Bill and his crew are chopping down the hedges and digging out the sheugh where the new road is going to cut through the shoreline. That's when they seen it – a body floating face down in the glar. There's a full moon and the tides are high, you know. That's what done it, you see – the high tide pushin' up agin' the river where it meets the sea."

O'Reilly whispers to himself as he realises the import of the Divil's information, "Glen Dennagher." Then he shouts, so loud that he is heard throughout the station. "Glen Dennagher's body! It was carried downstream and is lying in the sea inlet at the two-mile stone."

O'Reilly sprints up the stairs two at a time and runs into the office of Superintendent Fox. Unlike the previous visit, when he entered smartly and saluted, this time O'Reilly bursts unceremoniously into the district officer's sanctum. The excited garda's loud voice had preceded him from the hallway. Superintendent Fox requires no prompting. He immediately dispatches O'Reilly and Caldwell to the location of the reported corpse to secure the integrity of the scene. And not on bicycles either. O'Reilly is entrusted with the use of the garda patrol car and is instructed to report back by radio from the site.

At 3:00pm, Murf and Divers from the forensics unit are present at the site. Finbar Dorrian, the county medical examiner, is dressed in waders and is conducting his onsite preliminary examination in the mucky glar. Even though the body is bloated and exhibits a pink hue, Murf is in no doubt as to its identity. When Finbar is finished with the preliminary examination, Divers directs his team to lift the body clear of the quagmire. He looks at Murf quizzically and asks, "So, Detective-in-Charge, are you not going to check the deceased's clothing for clues to his identity?"

Murf remains immobile with his hands in his pockets.

He responds with certainty. "No need to. I know the identity of the deceased. And as you can see, he is not wearing a jacket and his trousers pockets are empty. The only easily-removable belongings left on him are his clerical collar, his belt and his shoelaces."

Divers is annoyed at Murf. He directs his team to examine the deceased's clothing. They confirm Murf's statement. Divers is taken aback. He asks, "Lord, Murf, and how did you know that?"

"I'm a detective, Divers. That's how."

Divers snorts, unable to express a comeback.

Within an hour, the dead body is removed and transported to Castlebar to undergo a pathological examination and a forensic autopsy. (Later, the body would be positively identified as Barry Glen Dennagher, with drowning as the confirmed cause of death, consistent with the details in the police report.)

Murf watches the forensic team drive away from the two-mile stone, transporting the remains of Barry Glen Dennagher to Castlebar. Murf has no need to wait for confirmation from the medical examiner other than to complete official formalities – the paperwork, the signatures and the stamps.

It is 4:25pm. The work crew departs. They have completed their day's work and there is nothing more at the two-mile-stone to feed their curiosity. Murf remains alone at the Famine Field. Well, almost. The Divil has become a familiar presence and Murf regards him as part of the scenery. Big Bill has removed the Divil's plank, his preferred seating accommodation. As a result, the Divil lingers in his new preferred place at the hawthorn bush just outside the current work area. The Divil moves quietly. His newly-acquired dark brier-proof jacket blends in with the shadow of the bush, rendering him indistinguishable from his surroundings. He disengages himself from the shelter of the scrub and walks slowly towards Murf. Murf acknowledges his presence with a nod of his head. The two men stand shoulder to shoulder in silence.

The ancient milestone is visible at the roadside, albeit partially submerged in the bank of the ditch – 'Killbawn 2 miles'. It serves no purpose now. The air in the estuary is still. The seacoast is uncharacteristically calm. From the distance, ghostly cries emanate from the curlews in the marsh and penetrate the silence of the Famine Field. An unusual phenomenon occurs when the sea is thus calm – a cloudbank cloaks the land in shadow while the distant sea glitters in sunlight. The two silent men view this strange sight. Light beams eerily from the distant horizon in a vain attempt to dispel the gloom of the Famine Field. It shines on the black glar of the estuary causing it to blink sparks of light through the rising fog of marsh gas. The quagmire appears to be smoking like a slumbering coal. The marsh gurgles, breathing its subterranean life to the surface. It senses the stillness of the luckless site and stretches its malodorous tentacles slowly inland to lay claim to the deserted road. Wisps of fetid fog creep landward and encircle the solitary milestone like white spectral fingers. The ancient milestone casts a forlorn shadow back onto the road surface in the shape of a gravestone.

At the two-mile stone, it is a dead end.

ACKNOWLEDGEMENTS

Allied technological cooperation during World War II – Wikipedia

An Garda Síochána – www.garda.ie

Archaeological tools – www.uiparchaeology.com

County Mayo – mayo-ireland.ie

Criminal Investigation: Processes, Practices and Thinking – pressbooks.bccampus.ca

Dental Fillings – www.123dentist.com

Driving distances – Google Maps

Drumlin – Wikipedia

Exsanguination (bleeding from an arterial source) – www.wikipedia.com

Factors Affecting Human Decomposition – Hanna, J-A, & Moyce, A. (2008), Queen's University Belfast

Fashion History – Women's Clothing – Bellatory

Forensic autopsy – www.science.howstuffworks.com

Guide to the Criminal Justice System – www.dppireland.ie

Hierarchy of Domestic Servants in a Manor – www.waynesthisandthat.com

JCT Legal – www.jctlegal.com

Labouchere Amendment (Criminal Law Amendment Act 1885) – a law used to prosecute homosexuals

Making Documents More Legible – Smithsonian Institute Archives

Translations – Google Translate

U-boats and Kriegsmarine – www.uboataces.com

Uganda, Geography of, and East Africa Airways – Wikipedia

ABOUT THE AUTHOR

Fergus Patrick Egan was born in 1945 in Donegal in the northwest of Ireland. His childhood home was a small village at the Donegal / Fermanagh border between the Irish Free State (later the Republic of Ireland) and Northern Ireland. He spent summers with his paternal grandparents in Mayo. While employed as a banker he lived in ten different areas, where he observed and absorbed the cultural peculiarities of urban and rural communities in the Republic of Ireland and in Northern Ireland. He currently resides in Ontario, Canada.

Books Written by Fergus P Egan:

Black Donnelly, Rats and Pigs
The Coin and the Key
The Famine Field
Dorinda Trapper of Red Rapids
Field of Endeavour and Death
Lanta: Song of the Sea